PILGRIM
OF THE
SUBLIME

Geoffrey Carpenter

PILGRIM
OF THE
SUBLIME

GEOFFREY PAUL CARPENTER

Cover and title page image:
Cotopaxi, 1862
Frederic Edwin Church
Founders Society Purchase, Robert H. Tannahill Foundation Fund, Gibbs-Williams
Fund, Dexter M. Ferry, Jr., Fund, Merrill Fund, Beatrice W. Rogers Funde, and
Richard A. Manoogian Fund Photograph © 1985 The Detroit Institute of the Arts
"Nothing Gold Can Stay." *The Poetry of Robert Frost: The Collected Poems, Complete
and Unabridged.* Edited by Edward Connery Lathem. New York: Henry Holt and
Co., 1969. ISBN: 0-8050-0502-1.

Library of Congress Number: 2003090615
ISBN :   Hardcover   1-4010-9434-1
                Softcover   1-4010-9433-3

This is a work of fiction. Names, characters, places and incidents either are the
product of the author's imagination or are used fictitiously, and any resemblance to
any actual persons, living or dead, events, or locales is entirely coincidental.

This book was printed in the United States of America.

To order additional copies of this book, contact:
Xlibris Corporation
1-888-795-4274
www.Xlibris.com
Orders@Xlibris.com
17902

Dedication

To Jennifer

. . . and to all that is beautiful

ACKNOWLEDGMENTS

For her constant support and for her enriching illustrations, I would like to thank Jennifer Gadsden-Carpenter. My deepest appreciation goes to the many kind people who opened their homes and hearts to me and Jennifer during our travels. I would also like to thank Francisco Florencio de Assis, Ana Luiza de Assis, Jack Brown and Mark McFarland for assistance with editing, verifying geographical details and for translations. Finally, I am immensely grateful to my family and to the Gadsdens for the unwavering faith they have expressed in my art.

WINTER

When the winter solstice sun filters down from the hard blue sky to warm the frozen stones, the simultaneous expression of vital heat and bitter cold serves as disquieting testimony that paradox, not certainty, is the defining characteristic of existence. Pleasure and pain, life and death, beauty and ugliness do not have their own seasons, but coexist at all times—one giving rise to the other. Out of fear we shut our eyes to the truth that no particular instant is fated for ice or for blossoms in order that we may live with the comfortable illusion that life is predictable and that everything has its time. We seek guaranties that Beauty is ordained by the universe and that nature abhors suffering. In reality, as the winter sun shows, creation, destruction, and renewal occupy every moment, and thus no experience of joy is ever free of the twinge of longing, nor will the soul suffer torment without some reason for hope. But paradox is not to be lamented. Uncertainty and indeterminacy are winter's gifts, since the knowledge that the sun may at any moment be blotted out by the clouds makes one pause to feel the gentle yellow fingers settle soft upon closed lids. The wonder of life is that nothing—not even purple crocus tips pushing up through the snow—can be taken for granted.

DECEMBER

As the very last seconds of December 8, 1999 ebbed away and a new night-born dawn flowed in upon time's unalterable currents, Taylor Moreland stood on the shore of Copacabana beach in Rio de Janeiro amid a thousand twinkling candlelit offerings to the sea goddess *Iemanjá,* watching worshippers of *Candomblé* appear out of the darkness like blossoming clusters of exotic, nocturnal flowers. All along the strand, men and women dressed in ceremonial white linens set up impromptu altars in celebration of the *Festa de Nossa Senhora da Conceição,* a day dedicated to the Catholic saint but—after centuries of cultural permutations—dominated by demonstrations of fidelity to the *orixas,* ancient African gods and goddesses. Up and down the beach for as far as Taylor could see, dozens of improvised temples glowed over the soft, gold sand. At a makeshift shrine nearest to the young man, a Baihian priestess, her head tied in a traditional white wrap, laid out fresh grapes, a bowl of dried meat, a pack of cigarettes, and a bottle of *cachaça* before a palm-sized print of *Exú*, the messenger. With the help of a small gathering of followers, she planted over a hundred little candles on a terrace which she had neatly sculpted out of sand. As the woman lit the last votive taper, her intimate congregation joined hands in a tight square around the altar, their expectant faces glowing from the shimmer of that radiant spectacle and from the dreams newly kindled in their hearts for the upcoming year. While the faithful prayed and chanted, Taylor purchased a rod of pearl-white gladiolas from a flower girl and carried it down to the ocean to make his own offering. At the water's edge a few bathers dove into the Atlantic, still dressed in their ceremonial linens. In the dark lapping waters, the white clothing pillowed out around the swimmers and they bobbed about on the waves like phosphorescent jellyfish. Others, their faces hovering at wave level, appeared to be smiling otters bedded on translucent kelp.

Taylor waded into the bay up to his middle past floating flowers and little rafts of candles to cast his prayers out on the water. Holding his bright, white gladiolas above his head, he meditated inwardly on what he wanted in the coming year but had trouble formulating exactly what it was he expected. He was about to begin a journey up the Amazon River and into the heart of the equatorial Andes on a personal search for something as of yet undefined, but approaching Beauty. He thought about the artists he had come to admire so much and about his own faltering efforts to paint and gradually the notion came over him to dedicate himself to learning how to live an aesthetic life. And so, holding his shining flowers above the gently undulating waves he said aloud: "to all that is beautiful." With that, he flung the bright white and green stalk out upon the water and watched a gentle but steady tide pull the row of blossoms into the bay until he could see it no longer. He didn't know to what god or what force he was addressing his prayer, he only felt a compelling need to justify or to explain—or maybe even apologize for—his presence in South America at a time when he should have been at his family's farm, Rockwater Ranch, as he had been for every other Christmas break for the past four years.

When he planned the year-long leave from Boston College of Fine Arts, he had intended to make a pilgrimage through some of the most sublime landscapes in the world on the chance that the experience would give him insights into what it meant to be an artist. That evening, bathed in a glow of hope that seemed to hover all about him like a palpable essence, he felt a sense of beginning and of closure. The world of the farm and his obligations to his family were a continent away and it seemed that at this precise moment his life had broken out of its orbit and was floating on a tangential trajectory, entirely free of gravity. For the previous four years, he labored at his graduate studies with the fear that it was only a matter of time before he would lose his outward momentum and come spiraling back to the inescapable mass of Rockwater, adding the accumulated matter of his existence to the layered lives of his father, his father's father, and his and his and his before him.

In the previous semester, Taylor made a profoundly moving discovery of an artist who captured in color, light, and form in an aesthetic relationship to the world which he had been trying unconsciously to create in his own life from the moment he left home. Quite by accident, he came across the landscapes of the American Romantic Frederic Edwin Church while doing research on allegorical paintings for an art history course. Church was a traveler, diarist, and painter in the tradition of the Hudson River School, popular in nineteenth century New England. At first he was impressed by the monumental scope of his paintings, with their epic proportions, shimmering energy and luminous colors. But as he delved into the artist's journals, he realized that the artwork reflected Church's implicit philosophy of life, where there were no discernible boundaries between one's being and one's creative expression. It was an approach to life that Taylor could not imitate, since he had become accustomed to seeing his art as a distraction—something with which to amuse himself, but which had no bearing on the practical world. This skepticism about the value of his work had stymied his creativity and, as a result, he had not completed a painting for several years. He realized that if he were ever going to paint again, he needed to leave behind everything which had made him see the pursuit of beauty as merely an idle game.

Here in Rio de Janeiro, Taylor began the first leg of a pilgrimage to see the vistas of the towering peaks that inspired what he considered to be Frederic Church's grandest work, "The Heart of the Andes," a massive five foot by ten foot oil painting completed in 1859. He had a three-day layover in Rio before flying to Manaus, where he would continue the journey by boat up the Amazon and its tributaries as far as Misahualli, Ecuador. From there he would make the last stage up the slopes of the Andes on foot, joining Church's route in Cotopaxi National Park. At journey's end, he planned on camping at the base of the towering snow-capped Cotopaxi, the highest active volcano in the world, to do a series of studies in charcoal and watercolor which he could use back home as drafts for full scale oils.

The circuitous route to Church's beloved Andes mirrored the indirect path his life had taken lately. He wished sometimes that he was more like his father who always seemed to have a single-minded approach to life, focusing on only one concrete goal at a time and pursuing it by marching in a straight line. For Taylor, indecision and self-doubt had worked to pull the course of his intentions into a serpentine tangle of meandering and back-tracking. His initial idea was to follow the artist's route up Rio Magdellena which wound its way up through central Colombia. But when he mentioned the plan to his parents and explained to them why he wouldn't be home for the holidays, his mother could not comprehend his rationale. His father expressed his displeasure by refusing to acknowledge the trip, and when they talked on the phone on Taylor's birthday he spoke only of the upcoming lambing season and football games. Beth was more explicit in her disapproval. A toughened farm wife, her interactions with those she loved were marked by a hard compassion which, although often critical, was born of good intentions. When she realized her son was serious about his plans, she tried to convince him to abandon the trip, focusing on the danger involved in such an expedition.

"You're lost in your imaginings again," she would argue. "Haven't you paid attention to all the reports of kidnappings and killings in Colombia? They don't like gringos, not after all we've done to interrupt the drug trade."

He listened to her concerns and tried to counter with unsubstantiated reassurances that tensions had eased a bit. He knew that as an American on his own, travel through the rural highland areas where he was headed was a foolhardy proposition, but he was working hard to circumvent any impediment that threatened to keep him from going. Having just turned twenty-eight, he felt that he had arrived at a pivotal moment in his life. He had to determine once and for all whether he was going to finish his degree or return home for good to live on the farm.

"The risks to travelers are lower now," lied Taylor unconvincingly. "Besides, if harassed I'll say I'm Canadian," he joked. But his levity only made Beth grow more frustrated.

"Have you fully thought this through?" she sighed. "It doesn't seem to me that you have a realistic sense of what a trip like this involves."

"Don't worry about me, Mom. I may have to be careful, but this is something I've been planning for months. I want to do this for my studies. Think of it as research."

"What kind of research is it that you, an art student, have to do in the jungles of South America?" she asked dubiously, sensing there was much more left unsaid. "What is it you're doing that you just can't do from the library?"

Taylor was quiet for a minute, drained at the exertion of constantly swimming against the tide of his family's wishes. He felt himself relenting to the pull of what seemed to be destiny's current; how easy it would be, he thought, to stop this resistance and slip quietly into the channel already carved out for him. But this surrender gave rise to the thought of another holiday on the farm, of the probing questions about when he was coming home for good, and of the cords of guilt that wound themselves around his throat and chest with every reminder of his filial duty. Gathering his resolve, he tried again to explain to his mother that he had an obligation to himself that was as of yet unfulfilled.

"I want to see the mountain landscapes and volcanoes around Quito as Church saw them. I want to try to understand why I can't seem to finish anything in my life—"

"Oh, come on Taylor. You done enough—"

"No, Mom. No I haven't" he asserted firmly. He suddenly felt cornered by his own lies. He had always worked to give the impression that he was doing well in school to keep up the pretense that his absence from home was justified. But with his scheduled graduation date just six months off and no more excuses at hand for his expectant family, he knew he could not deflect the questions forever. Abandoning his usual tactics of evasion and half-truths, he decided to try honesty. With great effort he made a shameful confession. "Mom, I haven't done a painting in years. If I don't show some progress towards the studio component of the degree, the department is going to recommend that I not be allowed to register next semester." He expected to feel horrible for revealing his failures, but as he dropped this facade he felt a wave of relief. His voice began to tremble with excitement as he finally spoke openly to his mother about his desire to become an artist. "I want to know how to live a beautiful life," he said, the thought taking shape as he found the words. "But right now, I don't know how to do that. Too often I do things because I am supposed to do them. Nothing I have done for the past few years feels sincere or original. But I know there is a way to live . . . authentically, where what I do is indistinguishable from who I am. I'm going on this trip so I can stand in the footsteps of Church in the hopes that I will see a little of what he saw. I may even learn what it means to live as an artist."

Having emptied himself, he slumped into a chair and held the phone close to his ear, almost expecting to hear his level-headed mother sigh out of pity for such a pathetically romantic conception of life. He was prepared for her to take the painful revelation about his failures and turn it into ammunition in her arsenal of arguments for his return to Rockwater. Instead, there was a long pause on the other side of the phone and when she spoke again it was with a tone of grudging support, but with an edge of frustration that suggested she was determined to compel him to apply a bit of common sense.

"So what you really want to see are the mountains around Quito?" she asked.

"Yes."

"And if you saw those landscapes he painted, you would accomplish what you need to do?" she, said, reflecting back to him what he had shared with her.

"Yes," replied Taylor, curious now about where she was taking this line of questioning. "If I spend time in the areas he painted, I think I can get some research done on both his subject matter and technique that may spark something in my own art, maybe even save my candidacy at school."

"Well in that case why not go straight to Quito and start there?" she concluded as if the safer and easier solution were obvious.

Taylor brightened a bit at the sign that she was willing to negotiate. He mulled it over in his mind, reinvigorated at the idea that he might get his mother's approval. But something would be missing if he did not make the journey himself. He felt that to land on top of a mountain for a quick look was not the same as making the trek from the lowland jungles to stand at the base of a twenty-thousand-foot peak. The building intensity of that dramatic contrast would be lost. He would also forfeit the particular spiritual affinity one feels for the landscape as a consequence of intimate contact, of living in and not merely moving through a place.

"It's not the same Mom," he said, disheartened again. "Church traveled from the sea to the middle of the continent aboard a river steamer. Then he went on foot through valleys and the foothills before arriving at the base of the Andes. When you look at his views of Cotopaxi, you experience the thrill of breaking through the brush after days of walking and being suddenly confronted with the spectacle of those soaring mountains. His excitement at that discovery gets mixed up in his paint. Everything glows! I just want to look at the world and feel that feeling, just once in my life."

"I don't know anything about this Church guy or what you expect you're going to find, but I understand that the trip means a lot to you. But does it have to be a river in *Colombia?*" she replied, a little annoyed that he wasn't helping her find a compromise.

"Not necessarily," thought Taylor out loud. "I suppose I could come at the range from the other side, up from the Brazilian Amazon."

"That plan would have its own hazards, but it sounds better than your other route," she said with encouragement. "You will have to send us maps, the names of the places you are going to stay, and a list of names and phone numbers of people who will know how to contact you."

Slowly it began to occur to him that his mother had given him her blessing to make his journey, but under conditions which would allow her to feel she was still sheltering him from the uncertainties and dangers of a hostile world. The trip would not be exactly what he had anticipated, but it was a concession he was willing to make if it meant that he could go make his pilgrimage without lugging around his family's disapproval like a stone in his gut.

"Promise me you won't go through Columbia, and I'll explain the advantages of this new route to your dad," she said, opening a new door for him, coaxing him to step through. Taylor considered for a minute.

"I promise," he said, grateful for her help. When he hung up, he reflected on the sacrifices she must be making and felt that he had done her an injustice by believing that she was an impediment to his happiness. Instead, she surprised him by lending her assistance and he actually thought that he detected an edge of excitement in her voice once she had accepted that he was determined to make the journey.

In keeping with their agreement, Taylor scrambled to revise his plans. He changed his airline tickets from Barranquilla to Rio de Janeiro. In the weeks leading up to his trip, he purchased some essential camping gear and a travel-size pad and pallet for doing sketches and studies. He found guide books about the flora and fauna of South America and took a few introductory lessons in Portuguese from a Brazilian student who lived in his apartment building. Of all the resources he had on Church, he selected a thin copy of his diaries and some representative black and white reproductions and color plates of the artist's South American scenes. When school let out in early December, he withdrew all his remaining money, loaded all his gear in a light backpack, and flew to Rio.

Aside from breaking the news of his trip to his family, the most difficult thing for Taylor to do was to say good-bye to his fiancé, Quinn Yarbrough. She was a theology student at Harvard Divinity School who, with the patience of an archeologist, was unearthing the fossilized remains of God within the philosophical musings of Emerson, the riddles of the Upanishads, the novels of James Joyce, or any other sacred text she could excavate. More interested in spirituality as an abstract concept than in being swept up by religious fervor, she sporadically attended her Unitarian church and adhered only to those doctrines which did not offend her own liberal blend of deism and rationalism. She possessed boundless optimism in the potential of the human spirit, and this gift of hopefulness infused all she did with a brimming, yellow intensity. In her presence, Taylor often had the sensation that he was a leaf inclining towards her sun. She thrived on conversation, and he came to admire her confident expression of intelligence and wit. It was this complex blend of probing intellectualism and buoyant charm that Taylor found so compelling.

She was lovely to look at, with a soft arch in her back that lifted her shoulders and gave her the appearance of being taller than she really was. Slim with fine features, Quinn always looked light and ephemeral, as if all her time spent in the realm of ideas had prevented her body from taking full material form in this world. She had the fingers of a pianist and her brown eyes were clear and bright. Never greatly concerned about her appearance,

Quinn dressed simply, wore wire rim glasses, and pulled her straight dark hair into a glossy pony-tail. Taylor loved her with an intensity that amazed him, and at times he wondered if he was worthy of her faith.

When he explained why he wanted to go to South America, she was understanding, but she asked him to consider the implications that such an undertaking would have on his career and on their relationship. More than anyone, Quinn had come to know Taylor's heart, and there were times when she possessed greater insight into his motives and emotions than even he.

"If you find what you are looking for, you won't need me as much," she explained to him as they waited for his plane in the airport. "And if you don't find it, I don't know if I'll be able to bear you up under the weight of your disappointment."

"This won't affect our relationship," he reassured her.

"Oh yes it will," said Quinn prophetically. "If this trip didn't have the power to change you and your life you wouldn't be going." When he reviewed his motives, he knew that part of what she had said was true and he did not want to hear it. At its best his trip was a voyage of self-discovery, but at its worst it was an act of escape. They held each other before he left, but the embrace felt like the false and trite reassurances people give one another at a funeral— the soothing lie that after a great loss life will return to normal and those left behind will forgive the departed.

On the morning he was scheduled to fly from Rio de Janeiro to Manaus, Taylor wanted to call Quinn and ask her to wait for him. He wanted to share with her the breath-taking spectacle that he had witnessed on the beach the night before and to call her by the secret names he used in their most tender moments. He tried unsuccessfully from his hotel, from a kiosk at the beach, and finally from a payphone at the airport. As the airlines announced the boarding call for his flight, he gave up on speaking to her in person and settled for talking into Quinn's answering machine. He left an awkward message, saying that he hoped she was on her way to see her family for the holidays and that he loved her. For the duration of his flight, he sat looking out the window, wondering if he had missed some compromise where he could have both stayed with her and renewed his stagnating creative life. By the time the plane touched ground in the heart of the Amazon, he felt as if he had condemned himself to an indeterminate period of solitude.

In Manaus, he hoped to line up a guide and a few more supplies before setting off for the Andes. He had no idea how long the trip would take him or how much it might cost, but he went with the faith that with a bit of luck and careful management of his modest budget he could make the entire trek in three month's time. He arrived at mid-day when the heat was the most oppressive. He changed some dollars for *reais* in the small airport lobby and caught a clunky city bus for the waterfront neighborhoods where he had hoped to find a cheap hotel. At first he shared the bus with a few tourists—a young couple speaking German and a slim, blond haired man with a tattered backpack. But all of them seemed to understand that they had come all the way to the Amazon the get away from other gringos so they pretended not to see one another. At every stop locals piled on and the bus was soon standing room only. The majority of the people had Indian features—black straight hair, high cheekbones, and brown skin. One older woman with two long black and silver braids made her way down the crowded aisle to where Taylor was seated and, pointing to his chair, said something in Portuguese that Taylor understood as a request for his spot. He politely relinquished his seat and stood in the aisle for the next fifteen minutes as the bus lurched and bounced its way towards the river. At one stop a fruit vendor got on with a box of mangos. Lacking change, he paid the driver with three of the fragrant, red-green fruits.

At the Cathedral at Praca da Matriz, Taylor got off and started canvassing the neighborhood for a hotel. The streets were bustling and dirty, and vendors hawked their wares from stalls and carts set up impromptu on the sidewalks. Taylor passed a produce stall which displayed an odd assortment of fruits and vegetables—half of which he couldn't identify. There were small smooth-skinned yellow fruits labeled *maracujá*; bulbous, prickly breadfruit that looked more like weapons than food; and knobby *fruta de conde* which, with its fleshy lobes, had the appearance of an exposed brain. Stopping by one stall, he picked up a round, green nut that fit in the palm of his hand. The old man in a faded linen shirt smiled and said "*muito bom!*" Taylor bought three and the old man peeled off the hard outer rind, revealing an orange layer covering a large hard seed. The orange meat tasted like a mixture between an unripe avocado and mild cheese, and it made a good snack as he wandered through the alleys.

In a residential district, Taylor found a modestly priced hotel called the Rio Negro where he stayed for two nights while he made preparations for his trip. The accommodations were simple— a stiff bed, a chair, an end table stained with water rings, and a mildewed bathroom. It was tolerable for a few nights' rest and at R$20 a day it was within his budget. On his first full day in Manaus, he locked his gear in the hotel's storage locker and went down to the Mercado Municipal to line up some provisions. The huge hangar-like structure was constructed with wrought iron trimmings to look Parisian-bourgeois, but the pervasive layer of rust combined with the grit and sweat of Manaus gave it a spirit that was unmistakably proletariat. In one section there were barrels and bags of dried goods, fresh fruits and vegetables, and shoddily made Indian souvenirs. Taylor saw burlap sacks filled to overflowing with ground spices, fist-sized plugs of sweet cured tobacco, and stacks of dried salted cod, called *bacalhau*. In another partition, fish mongers had spread their catch over stainless steel tables and challenged passers-by to haggling matches. A stout woman with a bloody apron followed him around the market trying to sell him a stringer of grinning piranha and, when that failed, a three-foot eel. The sights, sounds, and smells were overwhelming and Taylor found himself reeling from the kaleidoscopic sensory impressions that vied for his attention. He picked his way through the maze of stalls to a cramped store that sold dried goods. Here he purchased toasted oats, raisins, rice, and some crunchy banana flakes—enough to make granola to last a week or so.

Tucking his provisions in a plastic sack, he made his way towards the waterfront for his first look at the Amazon. For all the lush images he had created in his mind of the exotic and wild river, his view from the wharf did not fit his expectations. The river was brown, turgid, and crowded with all sizes and dimensions of water craft. Sliver-thin water taxis zigged and zagged across the river, dodging the wakes of huge rusty freighters. On the near shore, stork-like construction cranes stood on spindly legs at the water's edge, swinging their sagging loads to feed the nascent buildings that sprouted skyward. The far bank was so distant that it was but a dirty green fringe on the horizon. On the dock nearest him, a double-decker cattle truck was backing on to a waiting barge. A lean man ran a hose over the panting animals to keep them from dying in the heat. The cows on the lower deck were so desperately thirsty that they lapped at the brown drizzle of water and manure that puddled at their feet. In the distance, a tired, red-smudge sun slipped quietly into a brown haze that could have been either river or sky. Taylor looked for signs of the green and vital river he had seen in photographs, but, finding none, turned his steps towards the hotel, disappointed and apprehensive that his whole trip may be a series of unsatisfied expectations.

On the way, he passed the Manaus Opera House and decided to step in for a look. It was a grand place for a rough and muddy frontier town, with parquet hard wood floors, marble balustrades, and painted ceilings. The place had the feeling of faded opulence, with its tired chairs and musty air. But it was spacious and dignified, a testament to its creators' yearning for art and culture.

Sitting before the stage, he looked around him with great interest at the images depicting Indians and maidens, but his enjoyment was diminished by his longing to be with Quinn. He briefly considered calling off his trip, searching his memory for why he had felt compelled to leave her in the first place. She was elemental to his happiness. Falling in love with her had been accompanied by so many unexpected delights. While she was serious about her studies, she possessed a whimsical sense of humor which found expression in an unselfconscious and sometimes mischievous playfulness. Looking around the theater, Taylor was reminded of a time when they had worked together at a playhouse. Quinn had found a way for them to volunteer at a Cambridge repertory theater in exchange for tickets. They worked as ushers and, after the audience was seated, they were allowed to occupy the empty seats. The problem was finding each other in a darkened theater. Using their flashlights, they worked out a code for indicating seat and row number so they could direct each other to an open pair. During a particularly crowded showing of *Hamlet*, Quinn signaled to Taylor to meet her in an aisle seat down front. Picking his way stealthily in the dark, he approached the row and eased into the chair. He could see a form in the seat next to him and, fumbling to take Quinn's hand, found himself trying to interlace fingers with an elderly man.

"What's this?" the man hurrumphed, jerking his hand away with a start. Immediately, Taylor heard a stifled laugh from behind the back row where Quinn had placed herself to watch her joke unfold. He hastily excused himself and left the theater. He found her in the lobby pretending to fold programs and struggling to suppress an impish grin. Still red-faced, Taylor marched over to her sputtering indignantly out of sheer embarrassment. Unable to contain her amusement any longer, she burst out with a great, pent up laugh and soon both of them were laughing so much that they had to leave the playhouse.

Taylor would have preferred to have gone on with her in their happiness indefinitely. But it would not have lasted. He had, of late, begun to despise himself for his lack of direction. Sitting there before the empty stage, he realized that the time had come to act upon his dream. As much as he was in love with her, he was beginning to despise himself. He wanted Quinn in his life, but he would never be able to believe that she fully loved him for who he was until he could present himself to her feeling at peace with himself and unencumbered. Reconciling himself to his loneliness, he realized that he had to go on with the journey, even if it meant having his expectations dashed along the way. Taking one last look at the great hall, he gathered his resolve for the long voyage ahead and set off to purchase the remainder of his supplies.

The next day, he awoke early to the sounds of traffic and, with some helpful tips from the desk clerk, went out in search of a guide. He stopped in at a number of hotels frequented by tourists and by noon he had a handful of brochures advertising anything from a day trip to the meeting of the waters—where the leaf stained stream of the Rio Negro runs side by side with the milky-gray current of the Rio Solimoes—to two-week tours of the surrounding jungle. After several hours of gathering information, he stopped in at a little bar opposite the Manaus Opera House and evaluated his options. It didn't look promising. The day rates for most tours equaled his entire weekly budget and the services were all geared for armchair tourists—"comfortable cruises" with "gourmet local cuisine" on the way to "air-conditioned jungle lodges." Taylor ordered a beer and realized that his trip may end here if this was all he had to choose from. By his third drink he was cursing himself for not being more attentive to details. Nearby, a man playing dominos with a group of friends noticed his frustration and offered to help.

"*Precisa-se ajuda?*" he asked.

"*O que?*" replied Taylor, not used to the northern accent.

"Do you need help?" said the man in passable English.

"Uh, no. Well, yes, actually. I think I could use some help," said Taylor, realizing that it may be time to trust in a stranger. "I'm trying to find someone who will take me up the Amazon."

"So is just about every gringo around here," replied the man in deadpan. He was short and barrel-chested like the indigenous people Taylor had seen, but his complexion was light brown and his accent sounded British.

"I'm going to try to make it as far as the Rio Napo in Ecuador," replied Taylor, testing out the idea with the riverman. His reaction was not what Taylor had wanted to hear. He let out a few great belly laughs and turned to his friends to share the joke.

"*Ele quer viajar para Equador!*" The group of men looked at Taylor and laughed hard, raising their glasses and toasting him for his folly. The stout man turned to him and offered him an alternative. "I don't know if I can get you to Ecuador, but I'll take you a few days up river. But you'll need to help carry my gear and I can't feed you."

"O.K., *tudo bem,*" replied Taylor. "*Preciso de um transporte,* not a tour." The man appreciated Taylor's attempts at Portuguese and extended his hand.

"I'm Guilherme," he smiled. Over a few beers they solidified a deal where Taylor would agree to haul gear, set up and break down camp, and, if the temperamental outboard motor faltered, help paddle the longboat. In return, Guilherme would take him up the Rio Solimoes for about a week and line up a friend to carry him further into the jungle, perhaps even to the border of Peru where the river was known as the Maranon.

Taylor awoke the next day to the sound of rain. A slight drizzle gathered the airborne dust and smeared it on walls and sidewalks in streaky gray and red washes. Taylor put on a light rain coat and rain pants and pulled a pack-cover over his gear. He met Guilherme at the waterfront where barges and water taxis crowded up to the muddy embankment. When Guilherme saw Taylor in his hiking boots and rain gear he laughed his belly laugh again and, pointing to the gray sky, said "you're gonna have to get used to getting wet here." Taylor looked around and saw all the boatmen wore light T-shirts, cotton shorts, and rubber sandals, perfect for the wet-and-dry cycle of the changeable Amazon weather. He laughed a little at himself and stripped down to similar attire and immediately felt cooler and more comfortable. Together they loaded provisions on the fourteen foot motorized canoe and Guilherme did a quick tune up on the outboard. Soon they were pulling away from the chaos of boats near the bank and into the wide channel of the river.

Once on the water, Taylor could appreciate the immense dimensions of the Amazon. It was over a mile wide and in the deeper channels the water boiled up from below in brown billows with frightening force. Every once in a while a partially submerged tree swept past them and the waters were dotted with islets of floating grass which had been torn loose from their anchorage in the shallows. Guilherme piloted his small boat over the waves and chop with attentive care that instilled confidence in Taylor for his new guide. They first headed downstream on the more northerly fork of the Amazon, the Rio Negro, to where it merged with Rio Solimoes at the *Econtro das Aguas.* There they would run upstream on the more southerly tributary. Near the meeting of the two mighty currents they passed a huge freighter which plowed up a four foot wake which threatened to swamp the little canoe. But Guilherme pointed the prow of the craft into the fast moving wave and they slammed into it with a force that nearly knocked Taylor out of the boat. A spray of warm brown water hit him full in the face and left him sputtering and clinging to the gunwale. "Hang on!" laughed Guilherme, "if you don't want to become piranha food!"

Over the course of a few days on the river, Taylor learned that Guilherme Mendosa was a third generation prospector of sorts. His grandfather was a British adventurer who came to Brazil in search of gems and gold but died a premature death as a result of repeated exposure to the lethal mercury he used to extract scant traces of precious metals from the soil. While in the jungles, he fathered a daughter, Guilherme's mother, with a Yanomani Indian from the state of Roraima. He never married her but came to think of her as his wife and decided to remain in Brazil, even when it became obvious that he would not strike it rich in that leafy paradise. When his grandson was born, the old Brit communicated only in English with the boy, calling the foreign tongue their "special code." He knew he was dying and, in a last act of nostalgia for his distant homeland, he wanted to pass on some aspect of himself to the quick-witted child. Guilherme's father, also of Yanomani descent, had hoped to make a decent living tapping rubber, but he too failed to get anything more than mere sustenance from the grudging forest. Guilherme had sworn to accomplish what neither father nor grandfather could do by harvesting tropical hardwoods. Scouting out ebony, mahogany, and teak in the jungles around his family's small farm, he would fell the giants and, over the course of several months, transport the trunk segments to a distant mill. For all his efforts he only managed to find and cut about two trees a year, earning only slightly more than his father had. But, unlike his forbearers, he had come to accept the limitations of the jungle and had shed any illusions of finding an El Dorado.

An hour outside of Manaus on the Rio Solimoes, the rain abated and Taylor started to dry out with the help of a light breeze. Signs of the bustling frontier town had all but fallen away, and it was difficult to imagine it could ever have gained a foothold in the dense jungle that now lined the river banks. The land in every direction was flat and clothed in a thick layer of green. A tangle of trees and vines crowded up to the river's edge and spread their leafy canopy to the sky to be washed by sun and rain. The height of the treetops was almost uniform wherever one looked, but every once in a while as the small canoe rounded a bend Taylor would see an enormous *Samauma* tree thrusting its umbrella fan of limbs and leaves above the heads of all its neighbors. In some places there were signs of human life—a banana boat passing in the opposite direction, a slash and burn clearing for manioc and squash, and houses on stilts with corrugated tin roofs. But most of the river was hemmed by unbroken forests. Around mid-day when the sun was beginning to be unbearable, Guilherme pulled into a floating house to make a delivery of necessities. "I promised to get this family some supplies while I was in town," explained Guilherme. "They don't have an outboard so they don't go far from home." Set on floating foundation of logs, the little blue and white shack bobbed softly on the canoe's little wake and a woman's face appeared at a shuttered window. A weathered looking young man in a greasy baseball cap stood in the doorway and looked at the boat and gear with interest.

"*Oi!*" called Guilherme to the woman.

"*Oi Guilherme, Boa-tarde,*" she smiled, gesturing to him to tie up along side.

Taylor took the opportunity to stretch his legs and stepped out of the canoe onto the warped decking that formed an apron around the outside of the house. While Guilherme unloaded a few boxes filled with cigarettes, canned goods, and medicines, Taylor asked to use the toilet and a young boy showed him to a little room at the back of the house. Stepping past the man in the cap, Taylor was led through a low doorway and he was surprised to see a bare central room filled with people. The entire extended family lived in the cramped quarters. An old woman and two young girls sat at a table shaving the husks off Brazil nuts with sharp knives. A middle aged man slept soundly in a hammock strung along the wall while a teenage boy was busy over the broken innards of an ancient transistor radio. The family smiled faintly in welcome and went back to their tasks. The bathroom was at the back end of the house adjacent to a tiny kitchen and screened off sleeping quarters. As he passed the kitchen he peered in and saw a woman who appeared to be the grandmother stirring a large battered pot over a blue flame. Above her head were shelves lined with canisters of flour, bags of rice, and sacks of dried beans. It was crowded but functional in a way that reminded Taylor of galleys. The people had the necessities of life but little more. And yet they were generous and warm, and Taylor sensed a strong familial bond. "The people out here are just trying to make it," Guilherme had told him on the river. "They can be rough around the edges, but they're good people. We depend on each other for our lives."

When Taylor returned to the boat, the man with the greasy cap had taken his place in the front of the boat. Guilherme and the woman were discussing the man and assessing how to fit his gear in the small craft. He had a battered chain saw with an extended blade which he had sheathed in an old pant leg. It was obvious that Guilherme doubted whether or not the extra passenger and the saw could fit, but the stranger was maneuvering the blade around, insisting that it was possible. After a few minutes of negotiations, Guilherme agreed to take the man, named Bruno, to Manacapuru where he would join a logging crew. Bruno explained that he was from Manaus and he was looking for work in the interior. He had been catching rides up river before being marooned at the woman's house for two days. Taylor settled himself awkwardly in the middle of the boat and Guilherme kissed the woman on either cheek. She thanked Guilherme profusely for taking Bruno with him and by the expression of relief in her eyes Taylor understood that she was glad to be rid of the unwanted guest.

Back on the river, the sun beat down relentlessly on the three men in the boat. Taylor pulled off his shirt and splashed river water over his head and shoulders. Guilherme looked at Taylor's exposed white skin and waggled his finger in warning. Bruno said something under his breath in Portuguese that was intended as a private joke with Guilherme, but apparently it was a little too caustic even for Guilherme and the guide smiled uncomfortably while Bruno laughed at his own slur. Beginning to feel indignant about always appearing naive and ignorant in his new environment, Taylor decided to show the two Brazilians that he knew how to take care of himself by leaving his shirt off and slathering a layer of sunscreen over his body. Besides, he reasoned, the breeze would keep him cool and he didn't want to sweat up all his clean shirts. Five hours later when they pulled into Ilha Paciencia to make camp, Taylor's skin glowed with a red heat and stung with the tingle of a thousand tiny pins. Guilherme said nothing, but Bruno laughed at Taylor and threatened playfully to slap him on the shoulders. That night they shared a bottle of *caçacha*, a strong sugar cane whiskey, as they sat around the fire. Bruno and Guilherme drank most of the booze, and as the moon slipped below the tree line they sank deeper and deeper into the bottle. By the early morning hours, Bruno was shouting belligerently and Guilherme was laughing at his antics. Occasionally the drunken logger would lower his voice and converse in confidential tones with Guilherme; Taylor knew he was most certainly the subject of these conferences and, irritated at being the subject of speculation excused himself and went to sleep.

The next few days followed a regular pattern. Guilherme would rise before the sun and start a pot of coffee on a campfire. He then roused Taylor who had the job of breaking camp and loading the boat. They shared the coffee but ate whatever was convenient. Taylor usually munched on handfuls of granola and dried fruit while Guilherme had a more civilized breakfast of manioc flour pancakes spread with guava jelly and margarine. Bruno ate nothing and preferred to sleep to the last possible moment before rolling up his hammock and climbing into the waiting boat. During the day they would motor up the river through dense vegetation, occasionally passing rough-hewn settlements on stilts. Careful not to overstrain the motor, Guilherme would make between 80 to 100 kilometers a day. When light began to fade, they usually pulled into an island in the channel or a sheltered bend in the river and set up camp. Within their hammocks suspended in the trees, they slept like pupae cocooned in a gauzy veil of fine mosquito netting. When it rained, a plastic tarp served as a roof. Taylor was usually so tired that he could have slept through a hoard of biting insects and a downpour without stirring.

On the third day they pulled into Manacapuru, a shabby little city at a bend in the river. Guilherme tied off the boat at the dilapidated wharf and Bruno pulled his saw out and thanked Guilherme for the ride. Turning to Taylor he sneered "*Tchau Gringo!*" and tried to land a slap on his reddened shoulders. Taylor deftly caught him at the wrist and, pulling his arm down, turned the would-be slap into a handshake. Bruno jerked his hand away and glared in a way that was intended as a threat. Raising his chainsaw to Taylor's neck level he waved the blade side to side in the air before him. Taylor refused to flinch. "Rrrrrrrr!" laughed Bruno. Then, sneering contemptuously, he added one final insult: "Fawk you Gringo!" and turned and walked away. On impulse Taylor felt like pursuing Bruno and knocking him down but Guilherme stepped up and offered a diversion.

"Let's go into town for a cold beer and to restock a few food supplies," he suggested. Taylor watched Bruno disappear down an alley. Guilherme shook his head. "The son of a bitch didn't even offer to pay for gas," he grumbled.

The residential streets were crowded with flimsy tin-roof shacks that teetered a few feet above the ground upon straining stilts. The sewage drained into open runnels along the alleys. In a vacant lot, children played soccer barefoot in the mud while a mangy dog with teats sagging to the ground snuffed through trash piles for scraps. Dusty buses rumbled over muddy, pot-hole riddled roads. At the fringes of the town, a front of vegetation threatened to advance over the pitiful human structures and reclaim the territory for the green world. Guilherme led Taylor to the main square where they did their shopping at an outdoor *mercado*. Afterwards they had lunch at a *barzinho* that opened out onto one of the main avenues. While Guilherme drank and smoked with the owner, an old acquaintance, Taylor watched a steady flow of people and cars go by from his little plastic table on the sidewalk. When his food came, the chicken was cool and the salad tasted a little like bleach, but he was hungry and cleaned his plate.

That evening, Taylor began to have intestinal cramps and he wished that he had not been so careless about what he had put in his stomach. By the time they had set up camp, he was nauseous and could not eat. He had a sleepless night, alternately vomiting and going diarrhea about every thirty minutes. By morning he was tired, sweating, and a little delirious. The rest of the day was spent lying prone in the bottom of the boat. He wavered in and out of a fitful sleep, catching glimpses of the sky or clouds between naps. At times it rained on him and he felt grateful for the cooling drops. But then chills would set in and he would curl into a fetal position and shake uncontrollably until he was hit by another wave of fever. In the evening he staggered to his hammock and Guilherme fixed him an herbal tea that seemed to reduce his cramps. "You were supposed to take care of yourself!" Guilherme joked, but Taylor couldn't even muster a smile. "Sorry," he groaned.

By the second day, Taylor's condition remained unchanged and it was all he could do to keep down water. He began to hallucinate and he convinced himself that if he fell asleep he would die. To fight off sleep, he would talk to himself or rock back and forth methodically. He had the disturbing experience of hearing his own voice mumbling incoherent gibberish and yet he was powerless to control it. That night, as he lay in his hammock, he looked through the mesh of the mosquito netting and trembled to see huge threatening shadows lean over him. While he laid there paralyzed by fear, it appeared that long, dark banana leaves were reaching over either side of his hammock and knitting their broad rubbery fingers into a crushing grip. He wanted to brush the shadows from his face, but it seemed to him that muscular vines had snaked up the trunks of trees and down his hammock strings to curl around his wrists and ankles so he couldn't lift his heavy limbs, no matter how hard he struggled. Shadows flitted about in the night, and, as he peered through the chinks of his vegetable cage some sort of invisible demons were impaling him through the bowels with sword-like palmettos. In the darkest hour he was awakened by the sensation that something was hovering above him, and—cautiously opening his eyes—he was terrified to see the image of Bruno leaning over him. He heard himself yell out in fright and what followed seemed a jumble of footsteps and shouting, but Taylor was never sure where or when he was, since time and space had melted and curled into one another within the furnace of his overheated mind.

Maybe minutes had passed or perhaps an hour, but something dragged Taylor from his fitful sleep. The baking of his brain had left him parched and he wanted to wash the residue of his nightmares from his mind. Climbing unsteadily out of the hammock he began to search for his water bottle. He went to retrieve it from his pack and by the feeble glow of an early morning light he could see that the covering tarp had been pulled aside and his possessions were scattered. Every pocket had been opened and half his gear was missing. He turned to Guilherme's camp and noticed that the hammock was gone and so was his bag. Taylor felt weak from the fever and the impact of this shock was almost more than he could bear. Leaning against a tree he looked frantically for Guilherme, fearing that his guide had robbed him and left him in the jungle to die of fever or starvation. Anger clouded his brain.

"Guilherme! Guilherme!" Taylor shouted the name almost as a curse. There was no response. Then Taylor heard dry leaves rustling behind him. He spun around expecting to see Guilherme slinking away into the jungle and found instead that he was standing face to face with Bruno. The logger carried a heavy stick in one hand and Taylor's money belt in the other. Taylor started back in fright and, in his weakened state, fell sprawling on his back. Before he could regain his feet, Bruno straddled him and threatened him with the club, brandishing it as if he would smash Taylor's brains in.

"Wait! Wait!" gasped Taylor, his hands before his face. Bruno laughed to see him pinned and pleading. He waved the money belt in front of Taylor's face, back and forth, taunting him to snatch it. Taylor saw by Bruno's dull, brutish, half-lidded glare that he was drunk. He swayed above him and waved the stick unsteadily. With but a second to assess his situation, he decided that if he were going to be beaten like a dog, he'd rather get in one last bite. Lodged between Bruno's legs, there was little he could do, but if he could topple Bruno he might be able to make a run for the boat. Taylor threw a solid punch to Bruno's knee that sent his assailant howling. Still too weak from fever, he stumbled feebly as he tried to regain his feet. He started to stagger towards the river, but Bruno cut off his escape and lunged at him with the stick. Swinging the club like a baseball bat, Bruno struck his victim square in the ribcage. As Taylor doubled over and gasped for air, Bruno swung again and clipped him in the side of the head with a vicious blow. The club hit Taylor with a hot, white flash, felling him like a tree. He felt his body hit the ground and his vision began to go dark. He was sure that Bruno was standing over him, ready to crush his head, but when he forced himself to open his eyes he saw the world tilted on its side and Bruno running in the direction of the river. He watched helplessly as the bandit climbed into Guilherme's loaded boat and pushed it off into the stream. The guide was still nowhere to be seen. A second, smaller boat, also loaded with their gear, was tied to the stern. Then he saw nothing; a little trickle of red worked its way into his eye and he blacked out from the pain in his head. All he could think was that he had not talked to Quinn since that day he left Boston, and that if he were to die now she would only have an awkward recording on an answering machine to remember him by.

JANUARY

In the winters of his boyhood, Taylor herded his family's flock to the distant alfalfa fields where the animals could forage through the stubble for whatever resilient shoots had outlasted the biting frosts. A few months after turning twelve, his father decided that his son was old enough to begin assuming responsibility for the family's herd of sheep, leaving himself more time for managing the orchards, hay fields, and the cattle. Jim Moreland sat down with the lanky boy over a lunch of New Year's leftovers and outlined all the duties he would need to perform now that he was "a young man." As he explained how to manage the herd, Jim wrote down his instructions on the back of a feed sack label that Taylor was to post in the barn and follow step by step every day. The son was anxious at first, but in the space of a few weeks he had mastered the routine. Of all his chores, he liked watching over the grazing sheep the most. An active but solitary boy, he truly enjoyed the hours spent alone outdoors where his imagination ranged freely past the boundaries of the family property to the rolling Ahtanum hills and the white-capped North Cascades beyond.

And yet, while he was content during those private hours spent with the animals, he possessed what his father would later come to see as a debilitating defect of mind that would prevent him from embracing farming as a lifestyle. In that first winter of managing the herd, he was never fully attentive of his task. Once the sheep had moved down the long dirt road and through the gate, he would let them scatter over eighty acres of brown hay stubble while he would lie flat on his back on a rise in the field and look up at the dark hulls of fast-moving cloud ships as they floated over the surface of the gray sky. Often he would carry a matchbox car in his coat pocket and, upon finding a large mound of cool earth pushed up from a gopher, he would build roads and drive the car over stick bridges and through lanes of little rock houses. Between looking up to check the ever-more dispersed flock, he would construct entire towns and people them with an intermingling of his family members, eccentric characters from the neighboring farms, and an occasional storybook hero. Then, setting their world into motion, he would watch the threads of their lives warp and weave into intricate and beautiful tangles.

When he tired of this, he would simply sit and watch the meandering sheep or follow the play of shadows and light over the barren desert bluffs. He would pass the hours this way until it was time to gather the flock and herd them back towards the barns. Because of his inattentive shepherding, this was a difficult chore, but early on he decided that a few hours of vivid daydreaming followed by a spurt of intense work were preferable to the constant vigilance his father recommended for keeping the flock in check. So, as the sun began to set, he would run a wide arc around the straying animals, whooping and flailing his arms, until the sheep were sauntering down the dirt road for the corral.

Watching over the grazing animals was but one of his many chores. He had to work before and after school, like many of the other farm kids in the Yakima Valley. His daily ritual was to rise at 5:30 in the morning and, with wicker basket in hand, go gather the eggs from the chicken coop. Returning with his find, he would turn them over to his mother who would begin breakfast. Then he would go back outside to feed the two pigs behind the tool shed with cracked corn and table scraps. Finally, he would help his father spread fresh hay in the troughs throughout the various stalls and pens. After school there were more chores. In the winter months, the animals spent much more time in the protective out-buildings and barns to avoid the bitter temperatures. This meant that he and his father had to devote about an hour or more each evening to cleaning out the manure and damp straw and to spread dry bedding in the pens. While many of his friends were shooting baskets or watching television, Taylor was pushing hulking wheelbarrow loads of manure or lugging heavy bales of hay and sacks of grain to the feeding troughs. All these chores he performed with the same distracted disconnectedness that he applied to tending the sheep. Watching his son dally through his work, Jim suspected that the boy was, for the most part, only physically present for his chores, but he assumed that he would grow into a more active role in running the farm as he matured.

While it was true that his son's friends from neighboring farms did not do as much hard labor as Taylor, Jim continued stubbornly in the tradition of his own father in refusing to hire outsiders to work his land unless absolutely necessary. Most of the farms the size of Rockwater Ranch and larger regularly hired cheap immigrant laborers from Mexico and Central America to do an increasingly significant portion of the most difficult and unpleasant chores. Jim would only hire seasonal help to get the apples off during picking time, but as for the rest of the year he virulently rejected the idea of having "a bunch of idle strangers loafing around just waitin' on me to tell them what to do and how to do it." Beth feared the long hours would take a toll on her son and when a major project came along such as shearing the sheep or baling hay she would press Jim to reconsider. Invariably he would make a stand on the assumption that nobody could be entrusted with the care of his land. "I'd rather we do it and sweat a little," was always his reply, "'cause at least *we've* got our hearts in it."

Rockwater Ranch was a three hundred sixty-five acre diversified farm on the banks of the Yakima River in central Washington's prime apple growing region. Like many farmers around him, the Morelands raised red delicious apples, but he also had eighty acres of alfalfa, twelve acres of pears, and one hundred seventy acres of range land for livestock. The remainder was in a tangle of scrub brush and willow thickets and cottonwood trees which formed a wild fringe along the river's edge. The barnyard looked like a cross between a traditional family farm and a petting zoo, reflecting the different interests of husband and wife. Jim was captivated by the idea of self-sufficiency and insisted on raising dairy cows and beef cattle, Rambolette sheep for their wool and Suffolk for the mutton, and both laying hens and fryers—even though they could never use all the meat and produce from the animals. Beth, who was always a little ashamed about her lack of education and her rural lifestyle, tried to set herself apart from the other farm wives by distinguishing Rockwater as an enchanted garden amid a desert of mono-cultured crops and pre-fab tin sheds. This little extravagancy ran counter to her more utilitarian instincts, but it was the one whim she allowed herself. She bought a pair of peacocks to strut around the yards and kept a hutch of angora rabbits. She had Jim dredge out the irrigation pond and stocked it with trout and brightly colored wood ducks. And while the women at her Grange had given into the convenience of buying the more unusual ingredients at the supermarket, Beth planted her garden with rhubarb and blueberries, endive and arugula. Instead of using cow's milk for her cheeses, she kept a few goats around so she could experiment with making chèvre.

Jim's determination to work the entire place without the benefit of hired labor meant there was always more to do around Rockwater than could possibly get done and, as a result, the Morelands did not take vacations. With livestock, even Thanksgiving and Christmas were working days since—as Jim observed when Taylor complained about having to get out of bed to do chores one Christmas morning—"It may be Jesus' birthday, but the animals don't take a holiday from eating." From time to time Jim did take a break from chores on the occasion of an important football Sunday. But because of his almost monastic devotion to the farm, he had not left the property for more than a day trip since he and Beth had returned from their honeymoon.

In the early years of their marriage, Beth respected Jim's work ethic because she shared his passion for productivity. A slim woman with bright, blue eyes, her narrow frame contained a dynamic force that propelled her into perpetual motion. She would go humming through her day with an industrious fervor for cleaning her kitchen and weeding the garden. For years that was enough. But as the children got older, she found that they needed a change of scenery from time to time and she began taking them away for a week or two while Jim stayed home to tend the farm. After ten years had passed this way, Beth began to realize that the children needed to relate to their father as a parent and not merely as someone who assigned chores. In addition, she sensed that she and her husband had neglected their relationship, and that going through life as help-mates would eventually leave them more co-workers than lovers and friends. But by then Jim was fully entrenched in his routines and would not leave the farm unless she forced the issue. She suggested that he take time off to go on a family holiday, but this only elicited grumbling explanations from Jim about how things would fall apart should he leave the farm. Not wanting to forego another family vacation, she decided to be blunt and explained to him over their morning coffee that it was no longer about the kids, that "their marriage needed it." Sensing in her voice a frustration he had never heard before, Jim responded with promises that he would take her out to dinner more often, thinking that would be the end of it. Throwing up her hands in anger, Beth stung him with a reminder of the loneliness his own father had brought upon himself: "Do you want to end up like J.P.?" That was all she needed to say. Confronted with an image of his own potential embittered solitude, Jim broke with Moreland tradition and hired the teenage son of a neighbor to watch the animals for a few days while he joined the family for a vacation to Depoe Bay on the Oregon coast—about as distant a destination as he would allow himself.

Compared to central Washington where temperatures hovered around freezing in January, the Oregon coast was a relatively balmy 40 to 50 degrees for much of the winter. Because the holiday season was over, Beth found an affordable hotel near the ocean, negotiating four nights for the price of three. One week before the trip, she announced at the dinner table that the entire family was going on vacation—including Grandpa, Uncle Ed *and* Dad. When Taylor heard this, he looked at his father for confirmation. Jim felt all eyes upon him and without looking up grumbled an insincere "should be fun," over his soup and went back to eating. His young daughter Sara clapped her hands with delight and starting singing "vacation, vacaaashun, we're goin' on vacaaaashun!"

The days leading up to the trip were a torturous wait for Taylor. The farthest he had ever been from home was when he had gone to Richmond for a school outing to a theme park with dilapidated water slides. By comparison, the upcoming trip to another state made him feel as if he were going away to some exotic land, and he tried to envision the forests he had heard about with tree-trunks as big around as grain silos. After chores every night, he would look over the map of the state of Oregon and trace the route they would take through the Columbia River valley and down along the coast. With the atlas spread out on the kitchen table, he looked at the names of so many unfamiliar-sounding towns and the unknown topography of broad rivers and green mountains. He studied the maps as if he were an explorer picking a trail through unknown territory, committing to memory the words which seemed to hold a sacred music—Umatilla, Multnomah, Clackamas, Tillamook, Yaquina—so that he might feel a certain mastery over their ancient magic. He would run his finger along the roads and then, where the green ran out on the map and there was only blue, he would pause and try to imagine what the crashing waves would sound like when he finally stood upon shore and gazed upon the expansive Pacific with his own eyes.

On the morning of their departure, the family piled into the big, boxy Wagoneer which Beth usually reserved for going to town or for calling on friends. In the back seat, Taylor fought off Sara for a spot by the window, forcing her to sit in the middle next to Uncle Ed. Sara wrestled with Taylor to trade places and, when that failed, appealed to her mother and grandfather in the front seat: "Taylor's being a bully and Uncle Ed always pokes at me!" whined Sara.

Beth, intolerant of any squeamishness around her retarded brother, shot an icy glare at her daughter that quieted the girl instantly. Then turning to Ed, who was smiling impishly and waving a threatening index finger at Sara's exposed neck, she gently pleaded with him to stay on his side of the seat. "Eddy, Sara has a favor to ask you. It's going to be a long ride and we all need to get along." Encouraging a reconciliation, she looked at her daughter, who wore a heavy frown.

Sara let out a resigned "humph" and turned to Ed to set things straight. "Uncle Ed, please don't poke me because it bugs me," she said matter-of-factly, as an adult might reason with a toddler.

At this point, Jim's father cut in and threatened to undo the fragile treaty Beth had brokered in the back seat. "If he pokes you jab him right back!" the old man said combatively.

Taylor caught a flash of irritation in his mother's eyes and slunk down in his seat, hoping this wouldn't break out into one of the strained "discussions" his parents had with his grandfather from time to time. But his mother seemed in no mood for a fight on the first day of their vacation so she said nothing and, instead, got out of the car under the pretense of finding her husband.

Jim had spent most of the morning going over the chores with Ben Feldmen, the neighbor's youngest son. He walked Ben through the barns, writing down lists of instructions, labeling keys, and offering a number of contingency plans at every turn. Ben trailed behind, knit hat slouched down over his ears and hands in his pockets, listening politely. But Jim nurtured a suspicion that he was more interested in getting the lesson over with so he could return to the warmth of the house. After checking everything off his list, Jim reluctantly turned the keys over to the teen and shuffled grudgingly towards the waiting car. To Taylor, his father looked incredibly awkward without his work boots and dusty jean jacket. He wore his tan slacks (Taylor never knew he owned pants that were not denim) and tennis shoes. It was obvious that Jim did not like wearing clothes that he had to worry about getting dirty. He moved cautiously along the driveway, straddling puddles and stepping on tip-toe from one dry island to another. As they drove away Jim grumbled to Beth for almost half an hour about how he was sure that Ben was "soft in the head" and wouldn't take his work seriously. Taylor feared that at any moment his father would turn the car around and head back to the farm, wrestle the keys from the neighbor boy and send him home. It wasn't until they were an hour underway that Taylor started to feel comfortable that the trip was actually going to happen.

When they passed out of Yakima County, the landscape looked more ancient and mysterious than Taylor could have imagined. Running the length of central Washington is an arid basalt plateau formed eons earlier when the earth cracked open and a lake of lava fanned out over hundreds of square miles. After millions of years of erosion, the volcanic crust was transformed into the rich soil which made the region bountiful, but remnants of the flow were still found in the form of shipwrecked basalt bluffs and statuesque black pillars scattered throughout the region. Farmers and ranchers claimed the low-lying valleys and the high flat tops for cultivation, working around the untamable cliffs and monoliths. The result was a strange contrast of pastoral farmland juxtaposed with barren stone outcroppings dotted with sage and scrub pine. The southern border to the flow is drawn in dramatic fashion by plunging canyons with sheer rock walls. When the car approached the rim of The Gorge, a deep cut carved in the earth by the wild Columbia River, Beth had Jim pull over at a scenic turnout so she could take a picture.

Taylor hopped out of the car and stood looking out over the jagged tear in the land. On either side, towering vertical cliffs of black and rust-red basalt cliffs formed terrace after terrace of exposed rock. From where Taylor stood, the canyon was over a mile wide, and it was another thousand feet or more down to the broad brown river below. In the distance, a red-tailed hawk cut figure eights and spirals on the powerful updrafts billowing out of The Gorge. The boy looked at a bend in the wide river and saw white water carving away relentlessly at the wetted stone. Taylor had never seen such a violent and yet compelling manifestation of nature's forces. He felt grateful towards his parents for having exposed him to such a wonder and, simultaneously, he felt a twinge of resentment for having been deprived of the experience for so long.

Jim waited impatiently in the car for Beth to take a few snapshots and then he tapped the horn to signal his readiness to get back on the road. She took a few hurried photos, pulled her wide-eyed son away from the outlook, and soon they were on their way. Despite the fact that it was January, Oregon was still a muted green. Taylor looked out the window and saw pine covered hills, pastures dotted with Holstein cows, wet red barns and clear running streams. As they neared Newport, the air suddenly took on the scent of brine and juniper. As if on cue, everyone seated at a window started rolling the cranks to let the air flood in. The smell of the ocean, borne upon a clinging gray mist, washed over Taylor and filled him with the thrill of discovery. He took great deep breaths through his nose and held them in his lungs to contain within him that strange elemental freshness of the sea. Even the adults were infected by the anticipation of reaching the shore. Uncle Ed started to moan with delight—a low and steady "aaaahhhaaa, aaaaahhhaaa."

"Who's going to see the ocean first?" asked Beth.

"Me!" shouted the whole back seat in unison.

It was in fact Ed who glimpsed the water first. Sara and Taylor became embroiled in an undeclared war for the prize and, jostling each other for window position, became disoriented and craned their necks eastward. Uncle Ed, happy simply to look out the window, caught sight of the vast, stony slate of the wintering Pacific and gasped in astonishment. Everyone turned to take in the view. Heavy charcoal blue clouds hung on the horizon and the swells were dark and moody. Here and there the wind touched down and licked up wakes of foam on the tips of the rollers. Where the waves broke on the shore, a tumult of froth and churning sand blurred the line between land and sea.

Taylor's first glimpse of the ocean was a thrilling yet unsettling experience. He was expecting to see waves, but he had never anticipated how huge and relentless they could be. In his mind he had imagined a few discrete breakers splashing against a rock or washing up on a patch of sand. He did not realize that the entire ocean was in the constant flux of undulations. As far as he could see up and down the coastline and as far as he could see out towards the horizon, the waves rose and fell, rose and fell without ceasing. Furthermore, he had never seen a body of water so expansive that he couldn't make out what lie on the other side. The immense ocean before him faded into the very curvature of the earth and at its furthest vanishing point became indistinguishable from the sky. Looking out over the rolling swells, he had the sensation that he had come into contact with an immeasurable and enigmatic force; before him was an emblem of a world so vast in its proportions that he strained to understand it. He watched the ocean through the window in silent reverie, rehearsing every color, every line, and every shift in quality of light so that he could encapsulate the experience in a timeless moment that he could then return to at will in any place, at any time, forever. The reverberations of the emotion resounded faintly and steadily in his heart, compelling him to seek out the thing that would strike the chord again. It was a sense of awe that he would not experience again for sixteen years, when he would travel up the Amazon River and ascend the equatorial Andes for a glimpse of the massive Cotopaxi.

When the Morelands finally pulled into Depot Bay, it was late afternoon and a light mist had begun to fall. Following the directions she had received over the phone, Beth pointed Jim to a little single-story blue and white hotel not far from the town center. The Whale Inn sat on a rocky rise near the Depot Bay Bridge. Sandwiched between the more pricey hotels on the ocean side and the coastal highway on the other, the hotel lacked a good view, and

Sara, not wanting to lose sight of the water complained about this unjust inconvenience. "Why can't we move to that big white hotel in front of us," she whined, gesturing to the three-story Hamilton Inn. With the selfish honesty typical of a nine year old, Sara had voiced a frustration that her older brother shared but knew not to express. While Taylor realized that his family was not exactly poor, he knew that living off the land was a precarious existence and every killing frost and scorching drought that visited Rockwater carried with it the unmistakable scent of hardship. Only a few years earlier, Mount Saint Helens had nearly sealed their fate within the sediments of time's cruel misfortunes, but the family had saved the farm by scratching and scrabbling for every dollar they could coax from the ash-burdened soil. Still, like Sara, he resented the fact that he had come all this way to be introduced to the epic Pacific only to be teased with the rumbling of unseen waves.

"They should only be allowed to build shorter hotels near the water," he mumbled to Sara. "It's not fair that some people hog all the views."

"Don't be so lazy," said Jim, overhearing his son's complaint. "If you want to see the ocean, just walk down the lane a bit and there it is." Signaling the discussion was over, he went to unloading the car and Taylor and Sara wandered off in the direction of the rocky shore to satiate their curiosity. Jim put his father and Ed together in one room and he and Beth rented another room with two double beds that they would share with the kids. He knew J.P. would protest having to room with Ed, and he tried to gather his resolve for the inevitable confrontation with his father.

"Aw Christ!," griped the old man to Jim when Beth and her brother were out of earshot. "What did I do to get the retard? Was that Beth's idea? I know she doesn't like me, but sonuvabitch! a week with slobbering Ed?!"

"Look Dad, it's four nights, not a week, and you know that Beth likes you just fine. It's just your temper she doesn't like." Jim hoisted his father's bag on his shoulder and started for the hotel room, undeterred by the old man's complaints.

"Give me the goddam bag. I'll carry my own gear," said J.P.

reaching for the strap.

"Take it easy Dad. You're on vacation. Besides, if you go and put your back out on day one you'll be laid up in bed the whole time."

"If it would give me a private room in a hospital away from that idiot I'll take it," growled J.P.

But the older man let his son carry the luggage to the room, since his gesture to take the heavy bag was just for the effect. He couldn't carry much more than a light cane anymore. Jim placed his father's bag in a simple but clean double room adjacent to where he and the kids were staying. Then the two of them watched as Ed dragged his duffel bag across the parking lot and into the hotel room by a broken strap. Once inside the room, he promptly dumped its contents all over the larger of the two beds, effectively claiming it as his own. He looked over at Jim and J.P. standing by the doorway and smiled. "I'm gonna sleep here!"

"Aw Jeazzuuuss Christ," J.P. muttered to himself.

Folding his arms resolutely, Jim tried to contain his exasperation. "Try, Dad. Just try. He keeps to himself and it's not like we're asking you to baby-sit him. Beth will do that. Enjoy yourself while we're here."

"I would if I didn't have to feel beholden to anyone. I'd do my own damn thing," retorted J.P. with accusation.

"You're beholden to no one but yourself," replied Jim, trying not to get pulled into another rehash of how J.P. would work if he could and how his dependence on others made him, as he put it, "no better than a brat in diapers." The more the family did for J.P., the more contemptuous he seemed of their charity. Not wanting his father's bile to poison the vacation, Jim began a campaign of trying to ignore his antagonistic jabs and, by doing so, perhaps disarm their power to unnerve him. "We'll stop by here on our way to dinner. Let Ed watch TV. He'll be fine." Jim closed the door behind him and left the two to draw out their own boundaries.

In the adjoining room, Beth was unpacking into a rickety set of drawers. She saw by his expression that he was irritated.

"How did it go?" she asked tentatively.

"Great."

"Sure," she said, unzipping her luggage. "Did he say the word 'retard' in front of him?"

"Not loud enough to be heard; he knows better than that after your last confrontation. He'll be all right. He just needs to get some rest after the drive."

"I wish it were only that," said Beth sitting down on the edge of the bed. "He hasn't had a vacation in as many years as us, maybe even longer. You'd think he would be happy."

Jim sat on the bed opposite and stroked his chin thoughtfully. "You know," he said, talking as much to himself as to Beth, "I don't know if Dad ever took a vacation."

"So that's where you get it," said Beth, half teasing, half serious. "Aren't you glad now that you got off the farm?"

Jim grunted a neutral "mmm" and tried to retreat from the question. He was reminded again that he resembled his father in some undesirable ways. He began to review his father's history, trying to revive a memory or even a fragment of a family story about J.P. taking time away from Rockwater. He could find none. The farm was, for most of his father's life, an earthen appendage of himself. His blood coursed through the soil and the soil infiltrated his veins and lodged in the tissues of his heart, giving the old man a greater affinity with rock and sage brush than with people. For J.P., his desire to master the land became more compelling than his feelings for those who should have been closest to him, and thus he tended the livestock, orchards, and fields with greater passion than he could give to his family.

James Patrick Moreland Senior.—he preferred to go by J.P.— started off with a small plot he had purchased from a Yakima Indian named John Round Belly in 1946. The land was bought at a bargain because it was situated in the Yakima River flood plain. Typical of bottom land, it was a bed of stones covered with a fine layer of silt, topped with wiry grass and thickets of willow brush. But J.P. had an intense greed for land, and when presented with a parcel of twenty-seven acres (which to him looked like a small kingdom), he snatched up the deed as quickly as possible. He had just returned from the horrors of World War II and liked the idea of isolating himself from humanity with a protective ring of private property. His young wife, Ida, and several friends tried persistently to talk him out of it, but he was able to justify the reckless move to himself by asserting that he could, through the force of his own will, make the near worthless land yield a living and more. J.P. possessed a fierce pride in the powers of his own two leathery hands. He lived by a personal creed that there was nothing in the physical world which, when the right amount of labor was applied, could not be transformed by sweat and ingenuity to meet human ends. "Look at the railroads!" he would say vaguely to doubters. "Look at the Erie Canal! There ain't nothing a person can't do if he sets his mind to it." To J.P., the universe abided by a simple, common sense law of work: the level of one's success was directly proportional to the grit and stamina of one's efforts. (It never occurred to him that one's efforts could be misdirected). Therefore, he had acquired an unshakable faith that he could move any obstacle in life if he simply put his shoulder into it and pushed and grunted long enough. He interpreted his detractors' advice as an insult to his person, as if they had identified some defect in his character or a deficiency in his strength and industry. To his wife's pleas that he start with a smaller and more fertile patch and work up, he reacted bitterly, as if he had been betrayed. "So you don't think I can do it? You think I'm too lazy and ignornt to make a decent living for us and should give up before I've even started!" When confronted by such defiant obstinacy, Ida decided to say nothing on the matter.

Beginning on the day after his marriage, J.P. started five years of straight labors. Aside from Christmas and Easter, he worked every day, ten to twelve hours a day. He put his shoulder to the immovable object, thrust the weight of his wiry, sun-browned, toughened body against it, and it budged. He removed loads and loads of rocks from the fields with a team of mules and a flatbed wagon. He cut acres of spindly willow stands and thorny rose hips, and burned many more acres of worthless, dry cheat grass and stabbing thistles. Using the scattered pines, aspen and birch on the property, he cut fence posts and strung a sturdy barbed wire fence around the perimeter. Purchasing one or two skinny or sickly calves at a time, he nursed and fattened them until he turned the lot into a healthy herd of more than a hundred. At every opportunity he bought up the surrounding fields, increasing the size of his little kingdom from twenty-seven to three hundred and sixty-five acres by the time he was thirty. The farm, which he named Rockwater for its two dominant features, eventually yielded enough hay and grain to feed over three hundred head of cattle. On higher ground he had planted the pear trees and apple trees—both good cash crops. Through years of hard work driven by stubborn pride, he had turned the barren river-bottom into a relatively productive farm that could comfortably support his wife and three growing boys.

J.P. named his eldest son Jim because, as he told Ida, he "wanted to make sure he wouldn't forget where he came from." Jim, born in his parents' bedroom in the heat of July, 1948, was the eldest and most responsible of the three boys. He worked long hours like his father and, as a result, never finished high school. While he was bright enough, he missed too many days of classes due to the demands of working the farm with his father. In the fall he was busy putting up hay for the winter; in the winter he was busy managing the feed lots; the spring was calving season and seeding time; and in the summer he irrigated and mowed the alfalfa and the pastures. While he knew that the lessons he missed in school were of some importance to the wider world, he saw little application of much of the information dispensed by his teachers and, early on, paid careful attention to just the bits he figured he could make use of. When he quit school at seventeen, he could read enough to comprehend the complicated instructions on pesticide jugs or in equipment manuals. Out of necessity, he became quite proficient at basic math skills and took a special pride in calculating the count of bales in a multi-tiered stack or the irrigation capacity of a pump without the aid of pencil and paper.

Jim had two younger brothers who, after leaving home, became virtual strangers to him. Steve and Frank, born a year apart, could not keep up with the frenetic pace of work their father demanded of them and joined the army and the navy, respectively, as soon as they turned eighteen. All the boys suffered under the rigorous discipline of J.P. He expected his sons to act like men as soon as they were physically able to do a day's labor. He tolerated no disrespect and was quick to beat the boys with a willow switch or whatever was handy if they "back-talked" him or "dragged their asses." He put a great premium on upholding the family name, and—when it didn't interfere with their responsibilities on the farm—he grudgingly allowed the boys to participate in sports for as long as they kept winning. As a result, Steve and Frank saw sports as an escape from the bone-wearing work of the farm and turned their desperation upon their opponents with the ferocity of condemned prisoners on furlough. In high school, Steve was a star wrestler while Frank was brutally successful in the boxing ring. Following every championship, the boys would dutifully hand their medals over to their father who would display them on nails tacked along the living room wall.

After they joined the service, they never communicated with their father again. When J.P. realized they were not coming home, he forbid their names to be mentioned in his presence, reserving that right to himself alone. When he dropped a hammer on his foot, when he raked his knuckles turning a bolt, or when a cow died while calving he could always find a way to incorporate their names in a string of curses which damned them and their lineage to hell for their lack of loyalty to family. From time to time he felt that his last remaining son had yearnings to see the world beyond the valley. He tried to ensure that Jim would remain on the farm by explaining that he only had one true son to inherit the land. The others he had permanently and irrevocably disowned.

Jim's mother was a moderating influence in his life. Ida was serious, resourceful, and unemotional. When J.P. would come in from the fields raving at the weather and declaring war on God for all the money he would lose as a result of this flood or that drought, Ida would calmly set the table and matter-of-factly tell her husband "you might be the king of your cows but you can't go around shouting orders at the weather or God." She took his curses as a regular event of nature and reacted to his tantrums of yelling and throwing things as one might react if the breeze were to flap the curtains or the rain were to dampen the grass.

But in the summer of his forty-eighth year, J.P. fell off the barn and broke his back, bringing to an end his on-going battle to dominate the land. He spent a year in a wheelchair and another on crutches. During this period, his tirades became more frequent and more vitriolic. Whereas before his storms passed through the house and left when he returned to the fields, now he spent his entire day in Ida's kitchen barking orders at her and hurling insults at the way she washed the glasses. All the energy he used to exert on the hard stones and tough weeds of Rockwater turned caustic and now poured out in a bitter stream of resentment, fermented in the frustration of being an invalid with nothing more in life to live for. Ida stayed with him until the day that he set aside his crutches and took his first independent step since the accident. Then she announced with a resolve born of two years of misery that she was leaving him for good and that there were ten frozen dinners in the freezer. J.P. stood speechless as she took a small suitcase, $500, and a set of cast iron pans and drove off down the dusty lane in their dilapidated Ford Falcon.

Lost in memories, Jim sat on the edge of the hotel bed for a while and let the ghosts of his mother swirl around, settle and disperse. Beth had gone outside to check on the children and the sound of their voices brought him back to the moment. He sat quietly for a minute thinking of the unsmiling, angular woman and he felt a residual sadness from the apparitions of her suffering. From the moment she left, Jim had taken on the burden of caring for his father while trying to accomplish the old man's unfulfilled plans for the farm. Now, as the children were growing older, he knew that he should devote more time to participating in their lives. And yet—because of his sense of pride and duty—he could not see a way out of his commitments to the land. As a result, the family's demands on his time only made him feel pressured and guilty.

Outside, Taylor and Sara were talking excitedly about the huge waves and the scooped-out bowls of black rock filled with little crabs. Jim stepped out of the hotel room to find that both children were wet up to their knees and shivering. "Aww Taylor. Look at you," scolded Jim. "Those are your only shoes. And you should have kept a better eye on your sister," he grumbled, pointing at her soaked jeans. The boy looked at his sodden feet and Sara's dripping pants and started to defend himself:

"We were standing on some rocks near the water and a big wave came up real fast and splashed us and I—" But the words were addressed to the open air as Jim walked off by himself in the direction of the ocean. Beth watched him go and felt a twinge of guilt, wondering if the parallels she had drawn between her husband and the hardened man who was his father were too real and too painful for him to look at.

"Go in and wash up kids," she said. "Put your wet clothes over the back of a chair to dry and we'll go out for something to eat soon."

After Sara and Taylor bathed and changed into dry clothes, the family walked a short distance into town in search of an affordable seafood restaurant. Beth took Ed's hand and kept him from getting into traffic while J.P. and Jim walked along debating the merits of banding the lambs' tails as opposed to cutting them with a hot iron. Taylor and Sara, their shoes still squishing with sea water, ran ahead to peer into the windows of the Candy Works with its electric taffy puller stretching thick cords of pink and green. The Morelands walked up and down the quaint main street for almost an hour, window shopping and comparing menus among the few family style restaurants. While the kids wanted to gorge themselves on taffy, fudge, chocolate, and peanut brittle, Jim steered them back to a waterfront restaurant adjacent the Depoe Bay Bridge. The interior was simple but spacious and all six were seated together at a picnic table near a large window overlooking the marina.

From his seat, Taylor could watch all the comings and goings of water traffic in the harbor. Charter boats returned from the open waters with their cargo of pale, green tourists and plastic crates filled with sea bass and ling cod. The restaurant was perched right above the docks, so Taylor was able to watch the fishermen clean and process their catch. Ruddy men dressed in yellow hip-waders worked quickly, moving sharp knives between the skin and flesh of the fish, separating the silvery outer sheath from the slabs of muscles in a matter of seconds. The skins with heads attached were tossed off the deck and furled and flashed in a slow-motion dead swim towards the bottom. To Taylor's amazement, dark forms like flying torpedoes shot up from the depths to swallow the scraps.

"Look! Look at that!" he cried excitedly, pointing at a flurry of shadows now swirling around the boat.

"They're seals," explained his mother, "They're here for a seafood dinner, too."

Sara crowded up to the window for a look: "Let me see. Let me see!" she cried. Taylor followed the graceful seals with his eyes, enthralled by their fluid, gliding acrobatics. For a long time he sat entranced with the scene, watching them appear and disappear in the murky tide. He imagined himself clinging to their backs as they cut through the sea on their watery flights, turning and tacking with the ease of swallows knifing the air.

From time to time he looked up to share his amazement in the seals' antics with his family, but the adults were soon engrossed in talk of farming and Sara had lost interest and was coloring away in a book. Uncle Ed was perforating his napkin with a fork. The loudest person at the table was his grandfather. He appeared to be in his lecturing mode, and despite Taylor's best efforts to tune out the din, he was distracted from his meditation.

"I don't know why you're going to change things now," said J.P. to Jim. "Cutting off the tails has always worked for us."

"But banding is quick and easy, and Taylor can even do it himself," replied Jim. "It is almost painless and it doesn't take two people to hold the lamb down."

"I still say you're gonna stunt their growth and run the risk of infection. They may kick and scream, but it's better to get it over with quick. Make a clean cut and cauterize it."

"Could we change the topic?" asked Beth, conscious that the patrons next to them—their plates loaded with red salmon filets—appeared to have lost their appetites.

"We're just trying to figure out whether or not to invest in the bands and the applicator before lambing season," explained Jim. Around his father, Jim constantly felt he needed to justify every decision he made about Rockwater, and he did not want to let the discussion end with J.P. having the last word. Beth saw a contest of wills developing and decided to remind the men that the outcome of their wrangling would ultimately affect her son.

"Why don't you ask Taylor, since he will be managing the flock from now on," Beth suggested. The idea obviously struck the Moreland men as novel and they both looked at each other blankly and then back at Taylor to see if he really had an opinion on the matter. Taylor, still looking out his window, sensed the lull in the conversation and realized that he was being scrutinized.

"What?" he said vaguely, turning away from the flying seals.

"Weren't you listening?" asked Jim with slight irritation. "We may switch to banding the tails instead of cutting them off this year. What do you think? I think it's worth looking into, but your Grandpa says stick with cutting."

Taylor began to realize the implications of his promotion to the world of adult responsibilities. From the time he was eight years old he had known that his father intended to will the farm to him. Behind everything he did, that expectation loomed over him like a cloud of judgment. With his recent assignment to the herd, he would be making decisions with weighty consequences. He tried to address himself to his father's question. He thought of the hot docking knife and the struggling, bleating lambs. He remembered the smell of burning flesh and singed wool and the piles of tiny severed tails and his stomach knotted involuntarily. "I think we should give the bands a try this year and see how they work," he said diplomatically, looking between his father and grandfather. "Then if they don't, we can always go back to cutting them next year."

"Humph," grunted J.P. dismissively. Changing the topic, he

turned to Jim and engaged him in their running disagreement over how to prune the apple trees. This concern occupied them through the course of the meal and well into dessert.

Beth spent most of the meal cleaning soup from Ed's chin or cutting his fish into fork-sized bites. After the plates were cleared, Taylor and Sara occupied a vacant table nearby and did drawings of fish, seals, boats, waves, and lighthouses on their napkins. Sara loved to busy herself with crafts and, in particular, anything mechanical or repetitive. She would spend hours meticulously filling in paint-by-the-numbers sheets and, even at nine years old, she was quite competent at embroidery. Despite an element of rivalry that always pervaded their relationship, brother and sister were close companions. They depended on each other to make the isolation of the farm more bearable. There was an unspoken agreement between them that they had to indulge in each other's games, no matter how much they may diverge from one's individual tastes. Thus, Taylor would play hours of tether ball with Sara and she would tag along with her older brother when he needed someone to help him track his GI Joes on their perilous rafting adventures down the irrigation ditches. It was an arrangement that established a strong bond of sympathy between them, and they had a pact of allegiance to support each other when they were subjected to their parents' punishments, Uncle Ed's annoyances, or their grandfather's tirades. Conspiring together over their drawings, they discussed in lowered voices how they could get their parents to drive them to the beach the next day for some treasure hunting.

Fortunately for the children, the next morning broke with a brilliance uncharacteristic of Oregon in January. With the sun announcing its arrival through the hotel window, Beth and Jim formulated a plan for a drive to nearby Agate Beach and the whole family was soon loaded in the Wagoneer. The drive took them along a scenic coastal road that followed the curving and rocky coastline to where the contours mellowed and the road dipped down to long flat stretches of dunes and sand. Here they found a secluded turnout where they pulled over to park the car. No sooner had the tires stopped moving and the children and Ed were out and running for the beach, buckets in hand, car doors left ajar. They followed a narrow, deeply rutted lane from the road down to the beach, winding through toughened wisps of sea grass and chest-high scotch broom. Jim and Beth left the car at the trailhead and strolled hand in hand towards the sea, J.P. straggling behind.

On the beach, Taylor and Sara walked along in the sand, heads bent, eyes focused intently on the space a few feet in front of them. In their hands they carried plastic pails for holding their findings. Ed plopped himself down on the beach the moment he hit the shore and methodically ran his hands through the fine grains. Beth found him deeply engrossed in a game of stirring circles in the sand so she left him with Jim and J.P. while she caught up with her children. Together they walked a short way down the beach and in a matter of minutes Beth collected two very different agates. Beth called Taylor and Sara to her and held the stones up to the sun so they could see how to recognize an agate among the ordinary rocks. One of her stones was blocky and opaque and the children were quick to dismiss it.

"Look at it carefully," encouraged Beth. "The rough outside hides all sorts of rare qualities."

Taylor rubbed some water on the dusky surface and, to his amazement, as he lifted it to the sun it glowed cool like a drop of molten blue sky that had been scooped out of the air by a curling wave and then congealed in the cold sea before washing up on the shore. The other was a nearly oval orange stone with fine yellow veins streaking through it. Taylor noticed that the agate held the light and it seemed to shine with a contained yellow heat.

The young boy gazed thoughtfully at the hard, fiery stone and, as he considered its improbable and incongruent properties, he began to associate it with his mother. She seemed to radiate an intense and vibrant energy and yet, under the harsh, unrelenting pressures of life, she had become hard and durable. She possessed a keen mind and a playful imagination, but she only gave expression to those creative energies within the confines of what she could justify as practical. She would spend hours trimming her prolific roses, but only after she had tended to her vegetable garden. To her lady friends at the Grange, she justified the few peacocks she raised by noting that they earned their keep by yowling out an ear-splitting warning whenever a stranger drove up the driveway. From time to time she would toy with some fanciful idea like cultivating orchids or raising llamas. Most recently, she had talked to Taylor about piano lessons, but when Jim asked him to take a greater role in working the farm, she reluctantly relinquished her son to her husband's world of work. Taylor loved to see his mother try to knit sweaters from rabbit hair or make goat cheese, but he recognized that her flights of fancy would always be contained within her own prescribed boundaries of what was safe. Finding no sensible reason for pursuing her more whimsical interests—she invariably sacrificed those dreams to the immediate concerns of surviving in a world where, in her mind, hunger and suffering lurked just around the corner

Approaching her son on the beach, she peered over his shoulder and into his bucket, hoping that his find may give her some insights into his agile imagination.

"What are you looking for?" she asked him. Taylor paused over the question. He had not been conscious of his own method, so he gazed into the pail himself to see what had attracted him. He saw gnarled bits of driftwood twisted into contorted grimaces; he saw jet black stones worn smooth and round as eggs; he saw salt-bleached clam shells and purple scallops shining in a veneer of sea water.

"I'm looking for treasures," he replied simply.

"Can I help you?" she ventured. Taylor gave it a moment's thought and politely rejected the idea.

"It would be too hard for me to explain. And I need to do it myself," he said, smiling with anticipation at his quest.

"O.K.," said his mother. "I'll see if Sara needs any help." She joined her daughter and all three continued scanning the sand.

At first they walked near the water's edge like a triad of sandpipers, trotting away before the advancing apron of water and then chasing the retreating wavelet down the sheen of wet sand on its glassy slide back into the surf. But eventually, each person became lost in his or her own world and they drifted apart, dotting the trackless sand with three erratic and meandering trails.

Taylor soon became absorbed by his search. He had a very liberal conception of what constituted a good find, and soon his pail was heavy with a growing collection of stones and shells. While the others contented themselves with what could be found in a sheltered cove near the trailhead, Taylor preferred the wide open beach and set his sights on walking until he could go no further. Near the far end of the beach, a tumble of rocks came down from the green hillside to meet the sea. A natural breakwater of wet, black stones jutted out into the water, and mussel-encrusted boulders lay strewn about the sand. Those rocks closest to the sea had succumbed to the infinite abrasive powers of the waves and were worn flat across the top, forming natural pools that were constantly being filled, purged and replenished by the tide. Alone now, Taylor walked over to the largest stone near the water's edge and, between the intermittent waves, hopped up to the highest outcropping. He found a small tide pool there which supported a world of its own.

Enjoying the solitude, he listened to the rolling wash of the waves and the cries of the whirling gulls. He took in the unfamiliar salt air and stared at the frighteningly endless line of swells on the horizon. It seemed to him that he was the only person in the world to see this scene. He felt a sudden longing—a desire to hold everything before him and to see all that he hadn't seen—and at that precise moment a huge void opened up in his heart. He understood in a wordless instant with the metaphorical reasoning possessed only of children that he was a grain of sand. Before this, all he knew and all he had experienced had filled the corners of his imagination; now all he *didn't* know created a nagging feeling of emptiness and a yearning that would stay with him for many years. He had been drawn towards the far horizon in search of beauty and solitude and he had found both, but in the process his naive, childish conceptions of himself and of his world had been obliterated. Ten minutes earlier, Rockwater had been his insular universe where, with a stretch his fingers and toes, he could trace its boundaries in every direction. Now a cold wave from the outside world had rushed upon him and swept him out to a boundless ocean of uncertainty, leaving him gasping and terrified, yet liberated.

Transfixed by his revelation, Taylor sat motionless by the edge of the tide pool for a long while, staring out at the expanse of ocean before him, barely breathing. He made an effort to focus on the immediate present and looked around to re-examine his world as a grain of sand would look at the sea. At his feet, life in the tide pool went about its usual business, unaware of the vast ocean that enveloped the little rock and extended out beyond the limits of time and imagination. A green anemone fixed to the side of the pool clung blindly to a piece of stone it mistook for a meal; a little yellow star fish wedged itself tightly in a crevice; a hermit crab with an under-sized shell on its back scampered along the sandy bottom, futilely picking through shards of whelks in search of better housing. Taylor watched the crab move about the small pool on its errand until, finding no suitable shell to inhabit, it hunkered down in a corner, motionless and mindless. Seeing that the tide was on its way out, he reached into the pool and grasped the unseeing crab by its shell, lifting it out of the water. The little hermit crab did its best to slink into the recesses of the spiral coil, but even fully retracted, its legs and its eyes still protruded awkwardly out of its restrictive house. With crab in hand, Taylor stepped off the rock and waded through ankle-deep wavelets to a long finger of black rock that extended into the sea like a ramp. Finding a deep, well-flushed depression at the base of the stone, he moved to place the now squirming crab into this appendage of the sea. But as he held the creature over the water something unexpected happened. The crab abandoned its house, leaping into the water below, leaving Taylor holding the empty, outgrown shell. The little crab, looking pink and exposed, scrambled along the bottom of the pool towards the sanctuary of a rock wall. Before he could determine the fate of his little transplant, a wave washed in from the ocean, flooding the pool with an influx of cool, swirling water. When the rippling surface settled, the crab was gone. He could not be sure whether he had just saved the hermit or condemned it to a certain death; but when he looked at the tiny shell grasped between his thumb and fingers, he decided he had done the little captive a good turn. Pocketing the shell, he left the tide pools and began making his way towards the other end of the cove where his family would surely be waiting. But only part of him would return to them that day; another part of him had been swept away and was now floating free upon the irresistible ebb of life's tide.

He met his sister when he was half-way down the beach. "Where have you been?" she asked scoldingly. "Mom sent me to look for you. She thought you'd fell in." Sara noticed Taylor's sopping wet shoes. "Uh-oh!" she gasped with drama. "You got wet again!" She taunted him with predictions that he would be in big trouble, dancing a little circle around him as they returned to the car. "I stayed with Mom and Dad and my shoes are all dried out. They're gonna be mad when they see you went off and got soaked."

When they met up with their mother, Beth was sifting through Ed's over-laden bucket of rocks and detritus.

"Didn't we tell you not to get wet again, Taylor?" his mother complained as he approached. "Can't you consider the rest of us? Now you're going to get the car all wet and sandy. You're going to have to ride in the back on some newspapers." She turned back to sorting Ed's treasures and shook her head to express her disappointment in her son's irresponsibility, hoping he would register some guilt.

"That's O.K.," conceded Taylor, happy to pay just about any price for his experience. Beth heard something unusual in the tone of his voice that made her look up from Ed's stones for a moment. When she saw his face, she couldn't interpret the emotion expressed in his eyes, but it unsettled her in the way that a door left open to the wind might do. She tried to pinpoint her feeling, but Ed tugged hard on her arm when he sensed that he had lost his sister's attention for a moment.

"Where's Dad and Grandpa?" asked Taylor.

"They're over there working on the car." She gestured towards the sandy lane that linked the road to the shore. "They tried to bring it down here on the beach but it got stuck in the sand," she explained.

Taylor could tell by the way she refused to look up from her sorting that it was a mess that she did not want to deal with. "Why don't you go try to help. Your father wants you to learn to be more mechanical."

Taylor left the little group there by the shore and walked up the access road in the direction of the highway. The lane was little more than two deep ruts cut into the soft sand, and it wound its way through tall grass and scotch broom. As he neared the highway he could hear the revving of the Wagoneer's engine. He rounded a bend in the lane and saw the heavy vehicle sunk up to its axle in sand. J.P. was at the wheel trying to rock the car back and forth out of the rut. His father was running frantically around the back end trying to shove anything solid—limbs, rocks, clumps of brush—under the spinning wheels. The air was full of curses.

"Wait until I'm rolling *forward* goddamit! forward! Before you stick that shit in," shouted J.P., his head poking out of the cab.

"What?!" shouted Jim, barely concealing his irritation with his father.

"Wait!" barked the old man. The car rolled back into the trough.

"Shit!" shouted Jim, throwing a stone at the half-sunken tire, but by the way he threw it Taylor could not help thinking it was meant for his grandfather's face. There was a lull in the storm of swearing and J.P. noticed Taylor standing in the lane.

"Taylor!" called J.P. "Come here and do this driving so I can push!"

"Jesus Christ Dad, you *can't* push," said Jim, throwing his hands up in the air.

"Don't you jesuschrist me boy! I can do a damn bit better'n that twelve-year-old," he said pointing to Taylor. With that he climbed out of the car and slammed the door.

"Taylor, get in there and put it in first when I tell ya," commanded J.P.

"Dad, he doesn't know how to drive," explained Jim with a wearied voice.

"Bullshit. He drives tractors don't he? Same principle. A clutch, gears, gas, and breaks," the old man retorted obstinately. "Taylor. Climb up in there." The boy obediently started for the driver's seat.

"Hold on Taylor," said Jim firmly, walking around to the driver's side door and barring the way. "Dad, he can't drive this rig. We put him in this seat and he's likely to lurch out of here and kill himself running into that tree or he'll hop backwards out of the rut and smash both of us in the process." At being contradicted, J.P.'s face turned red and he puffed himself up in indignation.

"Now you listen to me," he began, almost trembling with rage. "There are a few things you don't know, and one of them appears to be how to go about raising *men*. You coddle and cover for that boy and he'll never grow up. He *should* know how to drive this rig, and by God now's a good time to teach him."

Although J.P. was enfeebled by a fractured back, he was still a formidable man. His skin was toughened from decades of sun, sweat, and labor, and he leaned forward combatively whenever he spoke. His hands were broad and powerfully built, and he gripped his cane like a club. Jim pretended to concede nothing at first, standing before the door with his arms folded, but Taylor saw the defeat seep slowly into his posture. Under the bullying gaze, Jim slowly retreated from the role of father to resume his place as son and yielded to the old patriarch's will. His shoulders slumped a little, and he looked between his father and his son, trying to maintain the appearance that he was still in charge. But the truth was that he was now just a frightened boy standing before his father and, right or wrong, he felt compelled to obey the old man's edict. Perhaps to save face with Taylor, he played the ruse out a little further.

"If we're going to do this, we'll do it my way and Taylor uses only first gear," said Jim with hollow authority. The old man nodded in agreement and smiled almost imperceptibly at Taylor, communicating the notion that he had somehow just won a victory for the boy. Taylor climbed into the cab and, after a few minutes of instruction from his father about how to pop the clutch without killing the engine, the three Morelands tried to get the car unstuck. The scene was mostly a repeat of the former attempts, with the two men throwing props under the spinning wheels and cursing the Jeep Corporation, God, and each other. Between tries, Jim shouted at Taylor not to give the engine too much gas. Nervous, Taylor worked the clutch and gas as he was ordered, but in the final effort his feet confused the two pedals and he stomped on the accelerator long and hard, sending the back wheels into a whirlwind of digging which showered the men in grit and sucked the rig so deep into the sand that the drive shaft rested on the center ridge.

"Stop! Stop! Stop!" shouted Jim at his son. "Godammit stop!"

Taylor pulled both feet back and the Wagoneer cut out. He realized by the silence that the battle was over and stepped out of the car to observe the situation. Jim and J.P. stood on opposite sides and stared at the entrenched vehicle, both of them were smoldering at the defeat—each blaming the other for the predicament.

"What do we do now?" asked Taylor cautiously.

"We'll have to call for a tow," responded Jim resolutely. "That'll cost us," he said loud and clear for J.P. to hear.

"If you hadn't gotten stuck in the first place, we wouldn't be in this shithole right now," announced J.P. "If you had just rode the crest instead of driving in the tracks, none of this would have happened."

"How could I have known that?" said Jim defensively. "I've never driven in the sand. There aren't a hell of a lot of beaches at Rockwater." He paused, his face darkened by anger and humiliation. "I've had enough of this vacation," he snapped. "I think it's time we went home."

"Fine with me," snorted J.P.

Taylor tucked his chilled hands into his pockets and felt the crab's confining shell rub up against his fingertips. He watched as the two men walked up the lane towards the highway, dragging upon their shoulders their hulking little burdens. His chest suddenly felt compressed and heavy. Moved by a sudden impulse, he pulled the shell from his pocket and hurled it into the bushes as far as he could. As the two strode off, he could hear them making plans to return to Rockwater that evening. Turning away from the men, he walked back towards the ocean.

FEBRUARY

As the weak afternoon light slowly froze and stiffened in the bitter winter air, Quinn hurried along Mass. Ave. towards the Harvard Square T-station. It was February 14, 2000, her second winter in Boston, and she still hadn't gotten used to the sub-freezing temperatures mingled with a bone-chilling dampness. In the pedestrian square near the subway entrance, commuters bundled up in scarves and heavy coats walked briskly to and fro—their hard, cold heels echoing off brick and concrete. With her collar pulled high about her cheeks, Quinn crossed the plaza and descended the stairs into the red-tiled tunnels. A cluster of people shuffled impatiently on the outbound platform. From out of the dark and snaking tubes, a train approached, pushing a wave of cold, foul-smelling air before it. Car after car rolled by until the long, segmented body slowed and slid to a stop before her, opening its doors and disgorging its human cargo onto the platform. A tight pack of passengers jostled through the throng of waiting commuters. Caught up with the advancing crowd, Quinn pressed her way into the car. The doors thumped shut. The train exhaled a pent-up hiss and lurched forward. Few people spoke. The chill and the drab winter light had a way of extinguishing cheer. Arriving at Porter Square, Quinn filed out of the train and ascended several flights of stairs. At street level, the wind seemed to cut through her clothes and she pulled her coat tight about the waist and the neck to keep out the cold. She walked a few blocks to a Chinese take-out restaurant, bought some stir fry for dinner, and headed home in silence.

Along the way, she passed shops displaying heart-shaped boxes of chocolates and chubby cupids in the windows. Seeing a poster of smiling lovers, she felt a pang of isolation. It had been several weeks since she had received a message from Taylor, and she was beginning to wonder if he had been so caught up with the adventure of travel that he had relegated her to the periphery of his thoughts. When she arrived home, the apartment was dark and still. To ward off her loneliness, she put on some of Taylor's favorite jazz and switched on all the lights. She un-boxed her dinner and ate in front of the television. Afterwards, she tried to get some reading done, but she could not concentrate. She missed Taylor and a host of familiar things about living with him: the sound of the water running in the sink as he shaved, his canvasses piled against the couch, the sight of his shoes in the entryway telling her that he was home. She found herself questioning why she had not guarded her heart against the seemingly relentless series of agonies which came with being in love. And yet, this unfamiliar sentimental longing was a kind of sweet torment that she preferred to her life before Taylor which was, by comparison, unencumbered and empty.

She met him at the Boston Museum of Fine Arts in the fall of 1998. He was in his second year of his MFA—a unique program that combined studio art and theory, and she had recently started her first semester in the Divinity School. He was writing a journal article on allegorical portraits, and he went almost every day for a week to sit in front of Sargent's "The Daughters of Edward D. Boit." For hours he would make detailed observations about the artist's technique and the haunting loneliness of the four little girls in their identical white pinafores, each representing a stage of life from toddler to adolescence. Quinn was working part-time as a sales clerk at the gift store and had seen him several times while taking her breaks in the galleries. She was attracted by his quiet intensity. One day, unable to resist her curiosity, she asked about his work and they discovered their common interest in the American Romantics.

When things were slow at the store, she would stand over his shoulder and watch him sketch and he would entertain her with scandalous rumors surrounding the life of Sargent and other prominent artists and writers of nineteenth-century Boston. Long after Taylor finished his article, he continued to go to the museum in order to spend time with Quinn until her supervisor became irritated with her increasing distractedness and suggested to her— as the two chatted over the postcard rack—that she "not flirt with her boyfriend while she was at work." Quinn went red with embarrassment to think that she had been that obvious in showing her interest. But Taylor flashed a smile which revealed that he was flattered by the notion that they were together, confirming that the attraction was mutual. At the end of her shift he was waiting for her outside the museum.

"That was a pretty wild assumption by your boss," he said with exaggerated surprise.

"Was I flirting?" she asked in mock incredulity.

"Like a hussy!" he laughed.

That evening, they went to a bookstore cafe in Cambridge and talked until two in the morning about their dreams and insecurities, their families, and about their favorite poems. Taylor asked when he could see her again, and they ended up planning to get together three times before the week was out.

To Quinn, Taylor was at first an unexpected distraction from her studies.

She wanted him near her so that any time she could feel the

pressure of his arm around her shoulders or trace the lines on the back of his strong hands with her fingers, but she knew that in letting someone into her life she would need to sacrifice some of her academic goals. While her mind may have been focused on metaphysical matters, her heart had other priorities. One evening while she was at her studies, she found herself hovering mid-sentence over Emerson's enigmatic thoughts on "the Oversoul" and realized that she had been poised there for over half an hour, lost in an image of herself walking hand in hand with Taylor along the Charles River. Every time she tried to work her way into the abstract realm of transcendental philosophy, his bright eyes and warm smile kept pulling her back down to solid earth. Eventually she realized that she was diverting too much effort trying to devise ways of *not* thinking of him and had to reconcile herself to the fact that part of her life was now given over to nurturing these new affections.

Creating space in her life for Taylor was not merely a matter of balancing her classes and her personal life. Falling in love entailed re-evaluating entire constellations of goals, each made up with meticulously plotted points of light. She had planned out the course of her life from an early age and had faithfully traveled the path for years. In high school she was always at the top of her class, winning scholarships to a number of prestigious universities. She went on to the University of Virginia, taking a double major in Philosophy and English. She had visions of excelling at Harvard and earning a teaching post at a prominent college or seminary. Determined to pay for school herself, she worked part-time and took reduced course loads, hoping to finish all her requirements in three years. At every stage of her life, she fixed her gaze on a single goal, made the mark, and then set her sights a little higher, never giving herself time to rest on her accomplishments.

Her interest in theology could be traced back, through various lines of inspiration, to that romantic capacity for hope which is the prerogative of childhood. As a young girl, she would spend hours in her father's study looking for pictures of God. Judging by the vivid sermons her father gave every Sunday, she imagined Him to be a very magnificent and beautiful creature. Spreading an armload of books upon his desk, she would open them all to illustrations of the creation, the flood, the annunciation, and the resurrection. She expected to see a being vast in comparison to humans—maybe even so great that his proportions sprawled off the boundaries of the page—with an expression like a flame or the sun, beaming with light and goodness. What she found instead were depictions that reminded her of grumpy, old Mr. Taggart from her father's congregation who was always picking the black from under his nails and complaining that the chapel was "too unbearably hot" or "too unbearably cold." As she matured, the desire to look upon the face of God remained, but she began to feel that the answer to the riddle of her own existence might be discovered with the application of pure reason—a gift which had, after all, yielded great discoveries about the nature of the physical universe. Why not, therefore, the metaphysical? Common sense dictated that there were spiritual laws to be discovered and spiritual space to be mapped. Instead of preserving religion as an area of her life that was beyond question, she wanted to scrutinize faith so that, in the end, she would be compelled to say "This *must* be so. It is irrefutable!"

In part, she inherited her tireless curiosity from her parents. Her father was a Unitarian minister who had made it his life's work to document the correlations between Christianity and Eastern mysticism. Franklin Yarbrough had family from Charleston, South Carolina, and he could trace their heritage, through a variety of twists and turns on the genealogical tree, to Sir Walter Raleigh and the colonial aristocracy. By contrast, his wife was a Yankee journalist from Massachusetts with socialist sympathies and a fierce sense of justice. After they were married, Gail Northrup—she insisted on keeping her maiden name—relocated to Charleston and had been writing left-of-center articles for the local newspaper as part of a crusade for reform ever since. Franklin was more private about his passions. He kept copious notes primarily for his own pleasure and saw no incentive for ever making them public. Quinn's parents never imposed expectations upon their daughter, but, because she was raised in an environment of intellectual rigor, she came to associate her academic success with their approval.

Besides having reservations about how becoming involved with Taylor would impact her studies, Quinn was also wary of being inflamed by false fire. A few years earlier, she had been in a relationship founded upon a sense of compatibility, but their commonalties had only served to mask profound differences which, in the end, proved insurmountable. As a college junior, she met a student named John Viccars who was kind and handsome and who expressed an uncompromising conviction that there was a reason for everything in life, all working towards some greater good. In her naiveté, Quinn thought that these were the attributes she was looking for in a man, so she let herself believe that she loved him. But she gradually discovered that he had a myopic morality and a timid intellect. When compelled by his professors or peers to question his own convictions, John refused to hold them up for scrutiny for fear that he would have to revise his notion of himself or his definitions of truth. Their final falling out stemmed from an argument about Poseidon originally initiated in their mythology course. He had been repeatedly frustrated with the god's hostile treatment of Odysseus in *The Odyssey*. He could not reconcile the deity's pettiness, vindictiveness, and hypocrisy with his faith in a benevolent universe and thus, he reasoned, the myth's depiction of our world was deceptive and the moral lessons expressed within the stories were entirely invalid. "Gods *have to* follow higher rules," he would argue emphatically, "or they're not gods!" Quinn and others would point out the logical trap of placing human laws above the gods or in dismissing the value of an entire myth because of some perceived flaws within one part, but John would hear none of it. She could have accepted his intellectual inferiority, but she could not respect a man who jealously guarded his core beliefs like a house of cards in the wind. As a result, any warm feelings that had sprung up between them quickly cooled.

But in Taylor, Quinn immediately sensed a mind sharply attuned to all the possible expressions of life. He gave her the impression that he was constantly examining his world and himself;

this acuity, in turn, had enriched her life. One fall day while they were walking together through Boston Commons, Taylor stopped to show her a small praying mantis in a bush. It was camouflaged green, and it stood stick-still amid a network of twigs. It was a relatively rare find in the city, and how he picked it out amid the foliage and the distractions that cluttered the mind was a marvel to her. He was always pointing out things like that to her. With her time so heavily scheduled with academic obligations, she realized that she missed seeing the finer details of day to day existence. Taylor had given her new eyes with which to see the colors that adorned the clouds in the sky or the symmetry within the architecture of a leaf. He had a heightened sensitivity for every minute detail of his immediate world. And yet, at the same time, he seemed incapable sometimes of envisioning a plan for his future. He could not imagine what shape his life would take five or ten years into the future, and he often relied on her for advice about how to direct his efforts in his MFA program. In this way, they gradually came to depend on each other and to compensate for their respective weaknesses.

Sitting alone in the apartment on St. Valentine's Day, Quinn was certain that Taylor was thinking of her. A few students from her program had asked her to join them at a Cambridge pub, but she had declined in order to wait for his call. Surely, she thought, if he were anywhere near a phone, he would try to contact her.

While passing the time, her thoughts returned to the night when they had become lovers, exactly one year prior. As that first Valentine's Day approached, Quinn thought that it would be the perfect opportunity to recognize the distance they had covered and perhaps, if Taylor seemed receptive, to sketch out a more definitive map of where they were going. They had not talked of their love as a something that needed any sort of commitment; rather, they had just kept coming back to each other week after week, for the genuine pleasure they found in spending time together. But as Quinn's affections grew, she reached a point with Taylor where all the stimulating conversations, all the passionate embraces, and all the tender words no longer satisfied her desires. She wanted more from him, and she felt that no matter how ardently she expressed her feelings, nothing she said came close to communicating the depth and intensity of her caring. The word "love" seemed so insubstantial, so inadequate, and when she tried to use it, the sound fell dry and brittle from her lips.

Taylor also seemed to want some sort of consummation. He had not demanded more from her than she was ready to give, but Quinn noticed that he seemed anxious for assurances of her affections, often going to excess to please her. To mark Valentine's, he bought tickets for a concert at the Isabella Stuart Gardner Museum and made reservations at her favorite Thai restaurant. Accustomed to the sprawling metropolitan museum where she worked, Quinn was looking forward to seeing the private Gardner collection and its smaller, more intimate setting. When the evening arrived, he showed up at her apartment dressed in his one good suit and bearing an armload of freesias, roses, and baby's breath. Quinn met him at the door in an elegant, black dress, a fine lace shawl draped over her white shoulders. Her hair fell softly down her back, and the way Taylor lit up when he saw her made her feel pretty.

They took the T to the Huntington Avenue stop nearest to the restaurant and treated themselves to an array of exotic dishes. Then they walked a short distance to the museum where a prominent cellist was giving a recital in the Tapestry Room. As they made their way to the concert, Taylor's step quickened with the anticipation of showing her around the collection. The place was once the residence of the wealthy patrons of the arts, Isabella and Jack Gardner, and was normally closed to the public in the evenings. As it was within a few blocks of his campus, the museum had become a kind of sanctuary for Taylor, and he chattered away to Quinn about all his favorite paintings as if they were life-long friends. As the couple entered the foyer, they could see that the normally hushed environment had been transformed into a lively and bubbling reception. Dominating the three-story mansion was a glass-covered courtyard with gardens and fountains. Candles were placed all along the balconies overlooking the courtyard, and tuxedoed waiters circulated through the patrons with trays of champagne flutes. The spacious chambers that were once the opulent quarters of the Boston aristocrats were now crowded with art that the two had collected over their lifetimes. But the museum never lost the sense that it was a residence, and the classical paintings, the solid furniture, the gleaming silverware and crystal chandeliers were not presented as articles on display, but existed together as components in a larger aesthetic plan designed to create an atmosphere saturated in beauty.

Enchanted, Quinn laced her arm through Taylor's and they strolled through the lavish rooms. They walked around the colonnaded perimeter of the garden, sipping champagne from prism-faceted glasses, past ebullient plants and plashing fountains. After seeing the main chambers, the two wandered down a long, cool hallway and into a room called the Spanish Cloister, a gallery dominated by an imposing painting of a Spanish dancer. Sitting on a bench in front of John Singer Sargent's massive "El Jaleo," the couple took in the drama on the canvas. It was a swaying, pulsating scene of a woman dancing in a dimly lit salon while, in the background, black jacketed musicians strummed guitars to the rhythm in her step. With her right hand the young dancer had grabbed the folds of her skirt over her thigh and had lifted up her hem-line to free her dancing feet. She held her left arm straight out at shoulder level, her hand clutching at something—as if she were curling her fingers around the emotional substance of that music that hung in the air. The woman threw her shoulders back and thrust her chin up in an expression of uninhibited pleasure. It was a gesture of pure bliss. They looked for a long while before speaking.

"She's lost herself," said Taylor with wonder.

"Yes, but to what?" asked Quinn.

"To the moment. To a fleeting feeling maybe," replied Taylor, walking closer for a look. "It's as if she has been emptied out and in place of her self now there is nothing but the music. Looking at her eyes, it seems that, for her, nothing else exists in the world at that moment besides the music, of which she is a part. Everything she is and feels is concentrated into the dance. That's why I like it. It's those little spots in time of pure joy that make my life feel meaningful."

"Is that what you feel like when you're painting?" she asked. Taylor thought for a moment, searching for the words that could express the strange, unsettling passion.

"Sometimes I paint and paint, and what I see developing on the canvas is an image that always seems a shade out of alignment with my desires—close enough to keep me chasing the illusion yet never satisfying. And then, on rare occasions, when I stop thinking about what I want to achieve and have become totally caught up in the colors and the light, I . . . I disappear. And then there's just a scene unfolding in front of me, and there's no distinction between the image in my mind and the effect of the paint as I apply it to the canvas. But it's been a long time since I've been able to enter that space." He laughed a little at himself for his rough hewn explanation. "Does that make any sense?"

"It does when I put it in contexts I know," replied Quinn. "In a certain light, the dancer could be compared to a shaman or a monk or some sort of whirling dervish. There is a quality of rapture in her gaze."

"Have you ever experienced anything like that while at prayer?" asked Taylor.

"Me?" Quinn chuckled at the thought. "No. I prefer the type of quiet meditation that allows me to think clearly. Too often, I'm afraid, people who get swept up in religious fervor lose sight of religion entirely. In the worst cases it leads to evangelizing and self-righteous persecution." She considered again the ecstasy of the woman moving to the music. "But there is a time and place for that kind of fire in life. In the hands of an artist it seems to me that energy gets channeled into a vital, productive force."

They sat quietly looking at the painting for a while, each trying to view the work through the other's perspective, until a guard came up and told them that the recital was about to begin. Pulling themselves away from the flamenco rhythms of "El Jaleo," they made their way upstairs to the Tapestry Room for the classical performance.

The high-ceilinged hall was hung round with ancient tapestries, and the chandeliers cast a crystalline glow into the shadows. The patrons assumed their places in chairs set up before a raised platform. A tuxedoed soloist took the stage and a reverent hush settled over the room. He lifted the bow, poised it over the instrument until all was still, and began playing. The sound set the entire room vibrating and soon the lovers were transformed by the melodic strains of Bach. As the rich baritone voice of the cello reverberated through the great hall, they held hands and let the music wash away all thought and language until they were no longer hearing the notes, but resonating with emotion. Quinn sat with her eyes closed, experiencing the music as looming, lofty geometric forms—an architecture of sound being erected in emotional space. At one point in the arrangement it seemed that the notes had captured the tone of her relationship with Taylor. The structure was complex and unpredictable, but the melody was playfully sensual, climbing precipitously and then diving and spiraling back on itself before returning to the central motif. It created a vital tension that Quinn found disquieting yet inexplicably stimulating. At the climax, she looked over to gauge the effect of the composition on Taylor. He sat listening intensely, his eyes fixed on the musician, his brow furrowed with concentration. It was an expression that looked faintly familiar, but she could not place it. Then the notes ascended on a blue wave and she saw him catch his breath a little and it struck her: he bore an unmistakable resemblance to Sargent's dancer. It was a flicker of an instant, but in that moment she felt her heart bound to his forever.

After the performance, both Quinn and Taylor felt light and happy, but as they stepped out into the street and buttoned their coats for the walk to the T, Taylor became quiet and thoughtful.

"Didn't you enjoy yourself?" asked Quinn.

"I don't want to go home yet," he said with anxious resolve. "I never seem to be able to get enough time with you."

"What do you want to do?" asked Quinn. Taylor thought for a moment and then, almost as a whim, he invited her to his studio.

"Would you like to see some projects I'm working on?" he blurted out.

"That would be great! I've only seen bits and pieces so far."

"Well I'm afraid that's all there is," apologized Taylor. "I've got nothing but drafts to show for all my efforts. Maybe this is a bad idea," he back-pedaled.

"No! It's a great idea," she reassured him. "It would give me a window on that part of your world."

"Ok," said Taylor with a little reservation. She did not understand his lack of confidence, and it surprised her when he denigrated his own abilities. What she had seen revealed impressive talent, but of all the works he had shared with her, she had yet to see a completed painting. This troubled her, but she had always dismissed her concerns by speculating that the problem could be attributed to a lack of time or materials. She took his arm and, offering assurances that she was going as his invited guest and not an art critic, they set off for campus.

The studio facility for Taylor's program was housed in a converted three-story warehouse near the edge of campus. Studios for graduate students were housed on the top floor. Four to five students shared large, rough work spaces—their individual studios defined within the rooms by make-shift cubicles formed with folding walls. When the couple arrived, it was getting dark, and there were a few students and faculty lingering in the common areas and hallways. Taylor introduced her to a friend and then led her up a broad stairway. When he arrived before his door, he paused for a minute to apologize again for not having anything which he considered worthy of her time.

"It's mostly sketches and studies for a portfolio I'm working on," he stammered, working the key.

"Don't worry, Taylor," reiterated Quinn.

Swinging the door open, he switched on several banks of track lights, illuminating a cavernous room with exposed brick walls hung with all manner of works in progress. Heavy concrete pillars supported a high roof, crisscrossed by exposed ventilation ducts and electrical wiring. Tables and sinks ran the length of the walls, while the center was partitioned off into four semi-private work spaces. The air smelled of paint and turpentine, and there was an aura of contained madness about the place. On the far wall, someone had tacked up hundreds of decapitated dolls. In place of a head, each doll had been given either a plastic penis or a plastic nipple. On the central pillar, a plaster bust of Beethoven with eyeless sockets and ears stopped up with chewing gum presided over the room. A mobile of melted model air planes and toy soldiers smeared with blood hung suspended from a rafter. Along another wall leaned stacks of paintings in progress—all images of bicycles from various angles and in various color schemes.

"Which of these creations is yours?" asked Quinn, searching the images for something that would resonate with the man she knew.

"I tend to keep to myself," said Taylor, motioning her to one of the cubicles. He unlocked a flimsy door and showed her into a small, private work space. A broad work bench was set up with paints and thinners, charcoal and pallet knives, old rags and photographs. Everything looked well-used: tubes of paint crumpled under the pressure of a firm hand, a white pallet dotted with molten coils of color, scraps of paper covered with annotations and measurements. Taylor reached under the workbench and drew out a pile of his prefatory watercolors and sketches, all of them in various stages of development, but nothing completed.

"Want to see some samples?" he asked.

"That's what I'm here for," she smiled.

He fanned the stack of sheets out upon the floor before her, blanketing the area with his art. His sketches revealed a penchant for verisimilitude—seated figures draped in clinging robes, an old woman's hands with papery skin pressed together in prayer, a twisted male torso in muscular relief. Flipping through the paintings upon the floor, she saw pieces of landscapes with grand skies and sweeping vistas; still-lifes with incomplete bouquets and the shining orbs of half-finished fruits; bright rooms without walls. In the more developed sections, he took great care in creating the impression of accurate detail in form and proportion, and yet everything had a romantic sense of the Ideal, as if the images were in essence emotions or abstract concepts seeking expression through the forms. In the center of the pile was a large canvas half covered with a design of a mountain done in pencil.

"What place is this?" asked Quinn holding the canvas before her.

"I don't know," he replied, standing back to look at it.

"Why not?" she asked.

"It's not anyplace I've been," he answered.

"Well you must have gotten the idea from somewhere," she coaxed.

"From an artist named Church. He's one of those painters who seems to work on pure inspiration." Taylor examined his sketch with an air of melancholy dissatisfaction. She placed the sheet on an easel to admire it, but Taylor frowned at the piece and became absorbed in mental revisions.

"What inspires you?" asked Quinn, trying to re-direct his attention. He left off his brooding, brightening at her smile.

"You, of course," replied Taylor.

"Then why don't you paint me?" she asked, putting on an air of vanity.

"I've always wanted to do that," said Taylor with exaggerated resolve. Turning quickly to his workbench he picked up a brush and, before she had time to react, ran it playfully down the nape of her neck.

"That's not what I meant!" she cried, flinching away and laughing. She grabbed his hand as he curved it under her chin and saw that he was holding a new brush and was only toying with her. The touch had left a little trail of arcing pleasure in its wake and she let him make another pass on her cheek. The fine camel hair tip felt soft on her skin and sent an electric thrill along her nerves. She closed her eyes as he ran the silky brush behind her ear, over her closed eyelids, and into the little hollow where her neck sloped into her shoulder. He paused there for a moment to caress the skin with gentle strokes. When she opened her eyes she saw he was no longer teasing her. He was looking with great pleasure at the lines of her face and the light on her skin. During their game, some of her hair had fallen out of her hair clip and trailed across her eye. Taylor moved to place the strand back behind her ear but she arrested his hand and released her hair from the silver clasp, letting it fall forward along her cheeks, trailing lightly down her neck and chest. He tipped her chin up and they kissed, slowly and deliberately. It sent her heart racing, but the press of his lips could not satisfy the urgent desire she felt to be consumed completely in the pleasure that flamed within her heart. She wanted to lose herself in the strange, warm wave that now rushed over her. These physical sensations were so akin to those engendered by their emotional intimacy that making love was a natural progression of her affections. Her legs began to tremble and she felt that at any second she would collapse. Taking Taylor by the shoulders she pulled him gently down to the floor. Then, pledging love in a poetry of whispers, the pair undressed each other and lay down together upon the sheets of canvases strewn about the studio.

To Quinn, it seemed as if she were floating in a timeless space of pure impressions, bathed in a host of pleasurable images drawn from the paintings all about her. She saw a sky blue room with an open window, white gauzy curtains billowing sail-full upon a summer breeze. She thought she smelled the slightest hint of lilacs. She felt the sun alighting on her skin, warm and yellow. She arched her back and the earth seemed to rise up beneath her, solid yet yielding, strong and comforting. And then, as they caressed, the world melted away and she felt as if the boundaries between her self and this man she loved had been erased, had never even existed, and the two rose and fell together on an undulating sea of bliss, transformed into light and color, orange curving into blue, like dawn pressing into day, one consuming the other until everything burned away into a flare of blinding white.

As the evening of February 14, 2000 waned, so did Quinn's hopes for a call from Taylor. She waited up past the point of fatigue and then fell asleep on the couch, still in her clothes. When the morning dawned, the distance which separated her from Taylor had increased by the length of another day and she wondered if he had suffered some misfortune or, simply, if his heart had cooled towards her. Needing something to prevent herself from worrying endlessly about Taylor's well-being, Quinn tried unsuccessfully to throw herself back into her studies. For most of her life, Quinn had taken great pleasure in her intellectual pursuits and thus school had always been a comfortable refuge for her. But she had come to Harvard Divinity School with different expectations about what she was going to gain from the experience. What she hoped to get was a kind of cultural anthropology of religion. After her first semester, what she realized was that—while there were courses in world religions—two thirds of the classes were geared for scriptural interpretation and church history. Adding to her frustration, she felt alienated from many of her peers. While she made a few good friends, she discovered that the study of theology attracted a whole range of lost souls who, for a variety of causes, could not find solace in either faith or in reason. As a result, they went about their lives in an eternal state of inner conflict. In the worst cases, some saw school as a form of personal therapy. These needy few were continuously wrestling with the professors to turn class discussions into a forum for resolving an endless string of petty crises. For others, the impetus for studying theology was that it was perceived as the pursuit of the highest truths, a quest for nothing less than absolute knowledge of the nature of God, humanity, and existence. These students constituted the most pretentious set of individuals, as they took great satisfaction in being in possession of the rules and conditions of everyone else's salvation. In religion some found reassurances that the world was ordered in strict hierarchies and, by unraveling the riddles of the scriptures, they hoped to secure a place for themselves in the upper echelons.

Quinn's closest companion at Harvard was a soft-spoken young woman named Elsie who wanted to be the first female pastor to take a church in her home town in rural Texas. Fair skinned with pink-rimmed eye-lids, she was painfully shy and would go flush red when called upon in class. And yet, if pressed to speak, it was obvious that she was brimming with intensity and it was all she could do to keep her voice from quivering with nervous enthusiasm. Quinn sat next to her in their hermeneutics course, and, after they had compared their impressions of a few lectures, they realized that they shared a similar non-prescriptive approach to faith. Quinn liked that Elsie would alternate between referring to God as "She" and "He." Not contented with merely discussing an ethic if compassion, she was willing to expend great time and energy for others if she thought she could improve their lives. In addition to her courses at Harvard, Elsie took Spanish lessons "just in case," she told Quinn, "I'm successful at welcoming the migrant-worker population into my services." Her shyness, Quinn realized, belied a rich inner life and an unwavering strength in her convictions.

On the last Friday in February, Elsie and Quinn planned to meet for coffee after their afternoon classes. Elsie knew that Quinn had been worrying about Taylor and thought her friend could use a break from her ritual of waiting around her apartment in the evenings on the chance that he might call. Much of the social life for the theology students centered around casual gatherings at a college cafe called Our Place on Mass Ave. Located in a basement of a tenement building, Our Place was a funky, dimly lit coffee house with maroon naugahide couches, battered floor lamps, and tired Persian carpets. The walls were lined with teetering bookshelves, and beaded curtains partitioned off two smaller rooms from the main lounge area. A long bar ran the length of the back wall where the owner (his skin always a curious tanning-bed-orange) and his tattooed girlfriend served Turkish coffees, micro-brews, organic sodas, and a schizophrenic menu of Mediterranean appetizers and bar snacks. A few street-level windows admitted pale shafts of light into the room and the air was always filled with the aroma of roasted coffee and the sound of sitar music. In the afternoons, unsociable students staked out corner couches, spread their books on the low tables, and sipped coffee while pretending to read.

As Quinn arrived at Our Place, Elsie was already seated at a table with a few fellow students. The others, second-year students in the ministerial preparation program, were engaged in some engrossing topic while Elsie played the uncomfortable spectator. Her face lit up with relief when she saw Quinn, and she waved to her with an expression that said "Ah! An ally!" Quinn pulled up a chair and the group exchanged pleasantries before the two divinity students went back to their discussion.

"I just think that Professor Whitman has stretched the definition of religion too far, that's all," said Allen, a tall, bespectacled man with a long face.

"It's not his definition of religion that bothers me," complained a severe-looking woman named Dianne. "It's his assumption that a system of beliefs is valid simply because people believe in it." She took a mouthful of ice from her water glass and crunched some cubes between her molars. The furrow in her brow told everyone that she wasn't done talking yet, so the table waited for her to finish her crushing. "It's just kind of circular logic if you think about it," she concluded.

"Are you referring to the professor for The Ministry in Crisis Seminar?" asked Quinn.

"Yes," replied Elsie. "We're all taking his class this semester."

"His main point," explained Allen, "is that the heightened interest within pop culture in self-help books and in personal shrinks is, in fact, an expression of religiosity."

"But the evidence before our eyes is all to the contrary," said Dianne, her hands outstretched in an appeal to common sense. "Religious sentiment has all but faded in the modern world," she declared with a kind of perverse satisfaction. "When our generation of theology students is gone," she continued, "I doubt that there will be sufficient interest to fill the ranks again. Harvard Divinity is doomed to become a relic—a mere curiosity in the history books, like those institutions established for the study of phrenology or alchemy."

"I'm not so certain," said Elsie, who was growing impatient on the sidelines.

"Why not?" asked Allen.

"How would you account for the fact that, in this town alone, there is a church every ten blocks?" she asked, flushed with agitation. "It seems to me, that we're not unique in our interest in spirituality."

"Those chapels stand empty most of the time," he countered, shaking his head. "Churches have become convenient spaces for weddings and baptisms. That's their primary function today."

"Even if that were so," replied Elsie, "you can't pronounce religion dead just because people don't worship in a church."

"That's exactly what I would argue," said Allen, stabbing at his point with a raised coffee cup. "If you lose the institutions of religion—the traditions, the rituals, the rule of consensus—then religion itself ceases to exist. How can you share a common faith without a community of worshippers who adhere to a common set of doctrines?" he demanded with an undertone of rebuke. Elsie sat stiffly in her chair, red blotches dotting her throat

"Faith can be individual," suggested Quinn, coming to her friend's aid.

"That's right," Elsie agreed. "You don't need a formal institution to ask Who am I? and What am I?"

"I agree with that part—that anyone can be curious," conceded Allen. "But it's the Church that offers the answers to those questions. Left to their own devices, people can come to whatever conclusions seem convenient."

"Just think of the chaos that would ensue if everyone set up his or her own morality," Dianne argued. "Whitman is opening the door to a dangerous kind of moral relativism."

"But he's not asking us to adopt any of these alternative perspectives, only to see where they line up with Christianity," countered Elsie.

"That's fine," said Dianne. "But after familiarizing ourselves with those other views, we should be able to evaluate them and determine which approaches are more valid than the others. And when I've done that in the past, I always seem to re-affirm my faith in the Christian Church." She said it with a sense of confident determination that did not invite a response. The discussion closed, the four sipped down their coffees for a while, filling time with affected small talk until the group dispersed.

When Quinn and Elsie left the bar, it was early evening. As they walked towards the T station, Elsie, who was uncomfortable with confrontations, asked Quinn if she had come off too strident.

"Of course not," Quinn reassured her. "If anything, they were a bit aggressive. Why do those two find professor Whitman's ideas so distressing?"

"Well, . . ." thought Elsie, "I guess it's because his class is pushing them into uncharted territories."

"How so?"

"He sent us out to research some of these 'alternative expressions of spirituality.' Some people were assigned books that re-packaged Buddhism for western readers, others were asked to look into weekend courses that promise personal fulfillment within one's career, and Allen was asked to try meditation and yoga." The thought of Allen sitting cross-legged on his floor chanting "Om" made them both laugh.

"What did you get?" asked Quinn, genuinely interested.

"Something called Spirit Guides. It's a kind of a self-reflection game that borrows from Native American traditions of looking to nature for answers."

"I could use a few answers in my life," laughed Quinn.

"Want to play?" offered Elsie.

"Sure. Why not? Anything for the pursuit of knowledge!" she said cavalierly.

The two friends took the T to Somerville where Elsie shared an apartment with a friend. They had the place to themselves, so they cleared a low table in the living room, spread the Spirit Guide materials out on a white cloth, and opened a bottle of wine.

"So how does this work," asked Quinn, picking up a little

velvet bag filled with small objects.

"Take a look," encouraged Elsie. Quinn loosened the ties on the bag and poured the contents out upon the cloth. The Spirit Guides were small stone fetishes—intricately carved animals, birds, amphibians, reptiles and insects. "The basic idea is that each animal stands for certain inner qualities or spiritual messages."

"So, do I just pick an animal?" asked Quinn.

"Well, depending on what you want to know, you can choose between a few variations of readings. Each reading requires that you pick a set number of fetishes and lay them out in specific configurations. As you review the creatures you've selected and the order you've chosen them, the Spirit Guides are supposed to help you reflect upon some specific aspect of your life." Elsie produced a book which explained the various attributes that Native American tribes ascribed to each animal.

"You go first," said Quinn with a bit of an anxious laugh.

"Now how would that work?" asked Elsie. "You don't know how to interpret the fetishes."

"And you do?"

"I'm writing my research paper on these things," she assured her, "and I've done some homework. Come on," pleaded Elsie. "Be a good sport. You can help me with my paper. Because it won't be the same if I just do it on myself."

"OK," agreed Quinn.

"Great!" smiled Elsie, squeezing Quinn's hands. "I'm going to do the Past, Present, and Future reading for you."

"Don't I get to choose?" said Quinn, reminding her.

"No."

"Why not?"

"Because this is the only one I know how to do," she said apologetically. Placing the little carvings back in the bag, Elsie made sure that Quinn could not see inside and had her draw three at random, laying them out on the table left to right, corresponding to past, present and future.

"This little guy," she explained, pointing at an odd-shaped

carving to the left, "will give you insight into interpreting your past."

"I already know my past. That's no mystery," joked Quinn.

"But you may not appreciate the significance of certain elements of your past. So take a close look at it and let's see what your Spirit Guide has to say."

Quinn scrutinized the soapstone carving. "A mole?!" she cried. "That's amazing! How did the Spirit Guides know that when I was a kid I went around covered with dirt, squinting at the world through coke-bottle glasses?" Quinn screwed up her eyes, setting them both to laughing.

"No, that's not how they work" said her friend, returning to the game. She flipped through the pages of her book. "Ah. Here it is. When you draw this animal guide, it is trying to show you the defining characteristics of your life up to this moment. The mole is a near-sighted digger who tunnels around below the surface of things. This means that, in the past, your life has been defined by subterranean probing where you've looked at things up close."

"Doesn't sound very pleasant," grimaced Quinn.

"It can be," explained Elsie. "A mole moves about unseen, quiet, and safe. It accomplishes enormous feats of strength and endurance, and it finds hidden rewards where few others think to look."

"And now I'm fabulously wealthy, if you count roots as currency," said Quinn, lifting her glass of wine in a toast to herself.

"But . . ."

"Don't say that."

"But," continued Elsie. "The mole is sometimes too near-sighted and fails to see obstacles in its path and lacks the ability to gain a broader perspective on things."

"OK. I'm starting not to like this little pip-squeak; let's move on," said Quinn.

"That's a short-sighted, mole thing to say," said Elsie with wry humor.

"Next!" insisted Quinn good-naturedly. Elsie thumped her

finger before the center fetish. Quinn picked it up and turned it over in her hands—the image of a beaver on a dam of sticks.

"That's a good one!" said Elsie.

"How so?" asked Quinn.

"If this spirit guide appears in the present spot, it means that you are currently in a very productive period. You're building towards your goals with single-minded determination. I've seen how you work," said Elsie, "and there are few of us in the program who could hold down a job and pull off the grades that you earn."

"That kinda fits," said Quinn with hesitation, thinking of her disappointment in some aspects of her choice of studies. "But, isn't the beaver good at transforming an unfit environment into something more comfortable? I don't seem to be able to do that with the program here."

"Maybe the transformation could be internal rather than external," speculated Elsie. Quinn nodded thoughtfully, but made no reply. "Have you completely ruled out the ministry?" wondered Elsie.

"I just can't see myself pretending to be anyone else's guide," Quinn explained. "No offense intended guys," she said, patting the animals in front of her.

"But you have a solid foundation in religion and obviously benefited from going to church."

"Up to a point," agreed Quinn. "But I don't attend very regularly anymore."

"Why not?" asked Elsie, refilling their glasses.

"It just doesn't do anything for me," shrugged Quinn. "And I'm not going to go through the motions just to check off rituals on a list."

"So, when you get the degree you're going to teach for certain then?" concluded Elsie.

"That's what I have planned, but the spirit guides may say otherwise!"

"Shall we have a peak at your future?" asked Elsie.

"Ok," agreed Quinn. "Let's see where these wild animals will lead me." She picked up the carving on the right, a snake in an undulating S.

"Hmm," said her friend.

"Hmm?" repeated Quinn. "Is that bad?"

"It depends. The snake is a complex symbol, so I need to review how to interpret it." She turned to the page and read silently for a minute. Quinn tried to look unaffected, but she was enjoying the game and was anxious to know what the carving meant.

"The snake is very much dependent on its environment for its vital heat. Stay in a cave and you will be cold and listless. Move into the sun and you will soak up the energy."

"So, what do you think this means?" asked Quinn.

"I'm not sure," replied Elsie. "These things seem purposely vague sometimes. Like a horoscope. They have to be broad enough to apply to all kinds of people in all stages of life. But I guess that's not too different from the scriptures," she laughed.

"Is that all your book has to say?"

"Well, here's something interesting," replied Elsie sipping her drink. "As it grows, the snake is able to shed its skin, a sign of renewal. If you draw this Spirit Guide in the future position, it may suggest that you are entering a period of transformation."

"As if I don't have enough to worry about," lamented Quinn.

"It may be a teaching job waiting for you at the end of the degree," suggested Elsie optimistically.

"Now that would fit," agreed Quinn, "like shedding the role of apprentice to begin my life's work." But as she tried to envision herself in her profession, no images came to mind. They talked for a while about the dismal job prospects and demanding classes, eventually returning to the predictions of the fetishes.

"Do you believe this stuff works," asked Quinn, tipping the last of the wine into their glasses.

"I don't know," mused Elsie. "I think it's like anything that offers answers to life's questions. It's a tool. If nothing else, the comments about the animals and their qualities encourage you to reflect on your own life, on your hopes and fears. That's probably what I'll write in my essay."

"Do you want to go next?" asked Quinn.

"Some other time, maybe. It's getting late."

Quinn helped Elsie put the room back in order and said goodbye. In a short while she was back in her apartment. She checked the answering machine as she came in the door, but found no messages. As she brushed her teeth and prepared for bed, she wondered once again if Taylor was safe and happy. She wished that he were home so she could discuss the evening's events with him. The conversation in the bar had reminded her of the distance between herself and the majority of the other students. And while doing the reading with the Spirit Guides had been a fun diversion, it left her strangely unsettled. She took it as a game only, but she felt exposed, like someone accused of perpetrating a fraud, not on others but on oneself.

Climbing into bed, she felt emotionally exhausted. Pushing aside a host of nagging concerns, she comforted herself with the notion that her worries were born of fatigue and by morning she would awaken revived from a good night's rest. But after laying awake in the dark for a long while, she finally drifted off to a troubled sleep.

She dreamed that she was walking through a massive, deserted cathedral. At first it was very pleasant, with a wide nave and a soaring roof supported by towering columns. She walked on for a long time, enjoying the space and solitude. But as she made her way towards the altar, the roof began to slope downwards and the columns were spaced closer and closer together. Gradually, almost by imperceptible degrees, the room closed in upon her on all sides. The roof was now just above her head and the columns closed ranks to form a narrow aisle on either side. She began to doubt the wisdom of proceeding, but laughing at her own fears she pressed on, reassuring herself that there was a rationale for the design of the place and that she could be certain that there was a way out just ahead. Walking on, she was soon stooping over to avoid the low ceiling and she noticed the tightly spaced columns had become two solid walls at either elbow. The passage became increasingly dark and the air thin, and Quinn could feel herself becoming more and more anxious and claustrophobic. Her breath came hard and fast, and, at one point, she looked over her shoulder thinking she might re-trace her steps, only to find a dark hall closed off with a solid door. Her desperation increasing, she searched for a point of light or a draft of refreshing air that might confirm that she would soon be delivered from her trial. Thinking she could make out a faint glimmer ahead, she began running down the narrowing passage until, pressed into an awkward stoop, she was forced to get down on her knees and crawl. Fear overpowered her now, and she began scrabbling along as quickly as she could down what had become nothing more than a rough tunnel. Her knees were bleeding and her hands were raw, but she felt that if she did not escape her confinement she would soon suffocate or go mad. Then, after a long stretch where she had to hitch herself along on her elbows and belly, she suddenly found herself wedged at the hip between the stony walls of a tight tunnel. Frantic, she strained and pulled to get free, but only succeeded in wedging herself even tighter. Heart pounding and gasping for air, she cried out again and again and again as the last, dim traces of bleary light faded to total blackness.

Awakening with a start, Quinn opened her eyes to a darkened room. Her chest still pounding, she wiped a cold sweat from her brow and sat up in bed. From where she sat, she could see a few bright white stars out her window. She reviewed the frightening images in her mind, trying to exorcise their power over her. She did not understand the meaning of all the strange details, but she intuited that it was her own heart telling her that she was not satisfied. She had always achieved what she had set out to accomplish, but contentment escaped her. Sitting in the darkness, her nightmare still hovering about the room, she felt more alone than ever before. For the first time in her life, Quinn was adrift, floating upon a sea of ambivalence without a clear sense of purpose or direction.

SPRING

MARCH

When March comes to the Amazon, the boundaries which normally define land from water and river from sky become confused, and the world is transformed into one disorienting realm of flooded jungle. In the early hours of the morning, the rains crash down upon the trees and tributaries in sheets of stone-heavy drops that beat the leaves and churn the surface of the water into a spitting frenzy of river and air. Then, just when the air becomes as saturated as the river itself, the rains cease, as if some huge faucet in the sky had been hastily screwed shut by a gardener who discovered he had inadvertently flooded the world. By the middle of the day, the sun is beaming down upon the jungle and the eye can barely discern a trace of cloud in the sky. But as the evening approaches, the dark billows quickly coalesce in the hot, humid air and the drenching begins all over with a violent pounding that lasts for hours. The daily dousing raises all the channels of the

Amazon several meters during the rainy season, stranding animals and people alike on what few patches of jungle stand above the water level. On some days there is no respite from the rains at all, and the falling waters form rivers in the air that begin in the mountainous clouds and end at the sodden jungle floor before starting all over again as terrestrial rivers.

March 3, 2000 was one of those gray, liquid days. For a man named Antonio Coelho, the rising water lifted his spirits because he had an extra boat to sell. In a world where water is the dominant element, a good boat is essential to survival. He had bought it a week before from a rough-looking drifter named Bruno who was passing through the nearby river town of Coari. The stranger said he was on his way to a logging job. He said that he was in a hurry to sell it because he needed the money. So Antonio got it at a steal. Now he wanted to sell it himself and make a profit. He tied it to the rickety floating dock below his house and taped a sign to it: "*Vendo: R$400.*" That morning, a wet man paddled by in a tired dugout canoe. "Now there's a man in need of a boat!" Antonio thought to himself. "He's paddling in a sunken log with a notch carved in it." As the man in the boat got nearer, Antonio recognized him as a neighbor who lived downstream and so he called to him, motioning towards the tied up boat.

Hearing Antonio hail to him, the wet man paddled over through a persistent drizzle to have a look. He tied up along side the dock and scrambled out to examine the boat. He had a bad limp and a patch over one eye and—much to Antonio's surprise—from the look on his face and the trembling in his hands, he was seething inside.

"Still not feeling better Guilherme?" asked Antonio cautiously.

"Where did you get this boat?" snapped Guilherme, ignoring the question.

"I bought it from a guy just last week. He said he had two and—"

"That's my boat!" cried Guilherme, stepping in and looking over the entire craft, quickly trying to assess its condition. The spare paddle, a small tool box, and his fishing net were missing, and his sturdy outboard had been replaced by an oily relic of a motor. "Somehow my boat followed me home," he said incredulously.

"Now wait a minute," said Antonio, "do you mean to tell me this is the boat you told me about a month ago? When you got beat up? Are you sure? If the engine is different, it might be—"

"It's mine, all right! It's still got my numbers on it." Guilherme pointed to the registration numbers on the prow. "And look. Here is where my boy scratched his name on the bench." Antonio stepped forward and examined the clues. He suspected from the start that he was dealing in contraband, but never guessed it would be the property of his neighbor.

"Damn!" said Antonio, "That logger Bruno said—"

"Bruno?!" gasped Guilherme.

The shock of hearing that name again made Guilherme recoil involuntarily and he almost tipped over the boat. The assault had been particularly brutal, and he had barely escaped with his life. It had all happened so fast, but within the span of a few cruel minutes, he had been rendered partially blind and crippled for life. By coincidence, Bruno had been on the same stretch of river that day as he made his way up the Solimoes in a small canoe fitted with a cheap motor. He had come upon their camp in the early evening and decided to hide himself around a bend in the river downstream until nightfall. Under the cover of darkness, he paddled his boat into their cove intent on stealthily robbing them. But as the night went on and his brain became inflamed with alcohol, he felt a savage malice well up within him. He decided that to kill them and see their blood run would make him feel full and satiated, much in the way he felt after gorging himself on a large meal. And he would have realized his desire if Guilherme had not prevented him. In the dim morning light, Guilherme was roused by Taylor's delirious yelling. He awoke to see a man standing over Taylor's hammock. He was wielding a heavy club and the weapon was raised and ready for murder. Guilherme had to act immediately, so, intending to momentarily distract the would-be killer from his victim, he called out. Startled at being discovered, Bruno rushed at Guilherme, hacking away at him with the stick. Guilherme was unable to free himself from his hammock, making him an easy target for Bruno. The logger swung his club like he was chopping wood. To protect himself, Guilherme instinctively ducked into a ball. Bruno struck his legs and head again and again, laughing maniacally as the helpless man wriggled and lurched in the hammock. As the beating continued, Guilherme realized that his assailant wouldn't stop until he was dead, so he went limp. Bruno beat relentlessly at the passive body until he had all but exhausted himself. But before he walked away, he landed one last savage blow across his victim's brow, puncturing Guilherme's right eye. It was all the injured man could do not to scream out, but he remained motionless and silent.

Panting from the exertion of his brutality, Bruno leaned on his stick for a few minutes. He then poked the body in the hammock several times until satisfied that the man was dead before cutting him down, hammock and all. Drunk and not thinking clearly, Bruno did not bother to check for a pulse or signs of breathing. Instead, he grabbed the two ends of the hammock and dragged Guilherme down to the river with the idea of disposing of the body. Staggering and straining, he lugged the man to the water's edge and rolled him into the murky river. Guilherme allowed himself to be carried off a little on the current and pushed the air out of his lungs so he would sink below the surface. When he was sure he had drifted a ways downstream, he paddled painfully to the surface to fill his burning lungs with air. Latching on to a partially submerged root, he held himself there near the shore, concealed by some foliage that extended out into the muddy fringe at the river's edge. Through a chink in the leaves he watched, powerless to do anything, as Bruno trotted unsteadily back to Taylor's hammock. Then, through his one eye, he watched as Bruno beat Taylor, crushing him to the ground with a series of savage blows to the ribs and head. It was not until Bruno had motored away, both boats loaded with the evening's takings, that he dared to struggle to the bank. His right shin bone was shattered and he was bleeding from numerous cuts. During the last few moments of hiding in the river, the wounds had begun to attract piranhas. A few of the voracious fish had taken nips at his leg, but his pants had protected him from a thorough shredding and he came away with only a few bloody divots.

Guilherme realized that if he did not find help soon, he and his friend were in danger of dying anonymously on their nameless island. Gritting his teeth against the pain, he hopped back up to where Taylor lie. The younger man was still alive and a coagulated mat of blood encrusted leaves and dirt clung to his face. The pain in Guilherme's leg was now becoming unbearable, but he managed to limp back down to the river and prop himself up against a tree in clear view of the channel. His only hope now was that a boat would pass in range of his voice and he could hail some help. While the river was sparsely populated in the area, anyone who needed to travel did so by boat, so he knew there was a good chance of spotting someone before the day was through. By mid-morning Guilherme heard a motor approaching and struggled to his feet. Two fishermen in an aluminum canoe came into sight and Guilherme waved his arms and yelled with all his strength. It worked. As the men drew closer, they were shocked by the bloody scene they found. They carried the injured men to the boat and rushed them to a missionary an hour distant. Taylor and Guilherme were left in the care of a poor but generous family of Christian Evangelicals who salved their wounds with antibiotic ointments and improvised a splint for Guilherme's leg. A week later they made their way by hitching passage on passing boats to Guilherme's home off a tributary near Coari.

Even though the trauma was now months behind him, the pain and frustration of the ordeal was still fresh in the riverman's memory and, standing in his boat again, his heart raced with adrenaline.

"Steady! Steady," said Antonio, offering Guilherme his arm. Shaking a little on his bad leg, Guilherme stepped onto the warped decking and sat down, rubbing his shin.

"What did you pay for it?" he asked after composing himself.

"Two fifty."

"I'll give you one fifty."

"Come on now, Guilher—

"One hundred." Guilherme shoved two fifties at him. "And I won't bring the police into this." Antonio scowled but took the offered notes. Guilherme pointed to his own leaky dugout at the dock. "You want the rest of your money? Then sell *that!*" He stepped into his recovered boat and pull-started the battered motor, moving quickly downstream towards his house as the rains began again in force.

Taylor hunkered down against the watery assault on a roofed platform over the river and, for the hundredth time in the past few months, counted his losses. He was thin, lonely, and nearly broke, living off the charity of Guilherme's family near the tiny river town of Coari on the Solimoes. Because of the robbery, his entire trip had been suspended indefinitely, and he was beginning to doubt whether he would ever get out of the jungle at all, let alone resume his pilgrimage to Cotopaxi. It would be difficult now. He had lost almost all his money, his passport, and some of his most important gear. But Bruno had been hasty and indiscriminate in ransacking Taylor's pack, taking some things that appeared to be of value and leaving other useful articles strewn about the camp. For some reason, he thought to steal the cooking set, and the bed roll, but he didn't take Taylor's cold weather clothes, the pack, or the tent. He also neglected to steal his journals, a pocket knife, and an old pair of tennis shoes. For this Taylor was grateful, since he had hidden three one-hundred dollar bills under the insole of his shoes for just such an emergency. For the most part, these few supplies were all he had needed for the past few months and he was beginning to learn just how few possessions one really needed to get by.

His shaky health proved to be the most serious setback. The beating he had taken from Bruno had cracked a rib and had opened a wound on his right temple that became infected, sending him into another round of sweats and chills. He had spent the entire month of January and most of February trying to recover his strength and regain the weight he had lost. Guilherme's wife had tended to him with great generosity and had nursed him slowly back to health. But now with the rainy season in full force, the swollen rivers made navigating the channels slow and difficult. So many obstacles now loomed between him and Cotopaxi that he felt it was almost inevitable that he give up the journey and return home.

Ever since that night in December, Taylor had wondered if he could have done something different—yelled louder, dodged a blow, carried a weapon, slept somewhere else—to have prevented the assault. Yet he always ended up feeling like the event was unavoidable and that he was being punished by whatever hostile gods were in charge of his fate for trying to live out his romantic illusions.Like so many times before in his life, he had the sensation that he was struggling futilely against a universe that had intended him for other things, and, thus, he was damned to be beaten back every time he tried to run counter to the current which bore him relentlessly towards Rockwater. Taylor watched the water drip through a hole in the palm-frond roof and puddle on the warped wooden planking at his feet. It rained and rained and the river over-spilled its banks, just as nature had designed. And gravity tugged every drop inexorably towards the sea, just as nature had designed. And Taylor sat in a hut a half a continent from his goals, wretched and wet, his plans thwarted, wondering why suffering seemed to be part of his life's design. Most of all, he thought about Bruno, hating him with a smoldering anger.

Guilherme motored up to the house and tied off on one of the stilts. Climbing a few rickety steps, he joined Taylor on the deck, settling a three legged stool next to his friend who was lost in thought.

"Thinking about that *filho da puta* again?" asked Guilherme, breaking Taylor's morose meditation. The older man rung the water out of his hat onto the deck and watched it drip through the slats and into the water underneath the house. Where his right eye had been there was now only a puckered, pink socket.

"Yeah," said Taylor. "Is it that obvious?"

"You look like you want to kill someone," laughed Guilherme.

"Don't *you?*" asked Taylor. "Don't you wish you had another shot at that bastard? You came out of this worse than I did and you can still laugh. Between the two of us, Bruno detested me more. I should have been the one with a busted leg and a punctured eye. It doesn't make any sense." Guilherme didn't talk much about his injuries, and Taylor always wondered if he harbored any resentment, and if so, for whom? More than this, however, he wanted to know if Guilherme shared his suspicions that the world was, at the very least, indifferent to human strivings or, in the extreme, hostile to the wild aspirations of dreamers. Guilherme grew quiet for a minute and began to rub his right leg.

"It might make me feel good to meet up with Bruno one day and return the favor. Wouldn't change what's done," he replied. The leg was swollen and the bone in the calf had set wrong and crooked unnaturally, giving it the appearance of a stick in water.

"Your leg still hurt?" asked Taylor.

"Only when it rains." Taylor looked at Guilherme. He was wearing a wry smile. Taylor couldn't help himself and laughed out loud and Guilherme joined in.

"Oh, damn, my ribs!" laughed Taylor, holding his side. It was good medicine and by Guilherme's smile he understood that his friend did not hold him responsible for his misfortune. "What put you in such a good mood?"

"I got my boat back." He gestured to the canoe tied up to the stilts.

"How did you manage that?" asked Taylor, walking to the deck rail to see the old boat.

"Oh, it turned up at a neighbor's dock," said Guilherme. "That gives me a clue to explain how Bruno ended up on the same island as us. He was making his way up river too. Probably a day behind us, but traveling lighter. It was just random chance that he decided to pull into the same campsite."

"You think there's such a thing?" asked Taylor dubiously. "Chance, I mean. Where things just happen unexpectedly?" He looked at the drops working their way into the river and the current conforming noiselessly to the channels. "I'm beginning to think that Fate plots out a course for you, good or bad, and then, to ensure that you don't get off track, sends a storm your way or sucks the wind out of the sky whenever you try to veer from the plan. You may want to go left or right, but the sadistic old hag keeps pulling you along and you're powerless to direct your life." Guilherme nodded thoughtfully. He was not accustomed to talking philosophy. For him, thoughts on life were kept to oneself and were more appropriately expressed through one's mode of living. But he could see that Taylor wanted to get a hold on his ideas by dressing them up in words, so he obliged. He found a dangling palm frond in the thatching and began to repair the leak in the roof as he told Taylor a story that seemed to address the point.

"Remember my grandmother I told you about? The Yanomani Indian?" he began. "She used to have stories about all sorts of things. She used to say that life was a river. You can put your boat in and paddle upstream. You can rest your oars and float on the current downstream. You could paddle back and forth across the stream. All of this was within your control. But your course was always contained within the banks."

Taylor thought about it for a minute. It was a nice compromise—free will within the limits of some inevitable universal dictates. "If that's so," replied Taylor, thinking out loud, "it seems like everything that I am interested in lies on the other side of the channel that Fate has cut for me and I just seem to be hemmed in between the two banks."

"No river has just two banks," replied Guilherme, a little surprised by Taylor's lack of common sense. "There are a million forks and tributaries to follow. In my little boat, I can go north, south, east and west from here by choosing the right combinations of routes." He finished his work on the roof and went to the edge of the deck, pointing at the water that seemed to surround them. "Now in the rainy season, that's a different story. Look out there and tell me where the river begins and where it ends."

Taylor looked at the rising waters and the river spreading its fingers in every direction into the jungle. In a few weeks, it would be difficult to believe that the waters had ever been contained within any channel. He saw that the rains that he had once cursed because they seemed to hem him in could—if he knew how to take advantage of the opportunity they presented—afford him with great freedom and mobility. He reached up to a loose frond and tucked it into the thatch, thinking again about far off Cotopaxi and what it would take to hire a boat to get him to the Peruvian border.

"Know any qualified river guides?" he asked tentatively.

"Think about that after you've fattened up a little. Let's go eat. Ana Paula made *fiejoada!*"

The two men stepped inside the house. It was simple but functional, with a living area, kitchen, and two bedrooms, partitioned off with unfinished plywood walls. Guilherme had built the place himself, sinking the foundation stilts into the orange mud of an embankment overlooking a wide, slow moving tributary of the Solimoes. In the dry season, one had to use a small ladder to climb up to the deck, but when the floods came, the river sometimes lapped up under the floorboards. On the deck facing the main channel, Guilherme had strung a few hammocks and the children's toys were spread liberally about, as this was their yard for several months at a time. Guilherme had two girls, Nicola age three and Bettina age five, and an eight year old boy named Guilherme. Ana Paula, was petite and shy. Her skin was Brazilwood red and her black hair hung in a braid that reached almost to the back of her knees. Together they were as happy a family as Taylor had ever encountered. They lived in idyllic isolation and, in such intimate proximity, became each other's best friends. In all directions they were surrounded by dense jungle and the air was scented with the verdant exhalations of so many millions of plants.

Behind the house was a lush garden patch on a raised hillock. On the east side was an outbuilding—now partially underwater—that was used for everything from chicken plucking to small engine repair. A few half-hewn canoes were suspended above the water by hand-made twine harnesses lashed to the rafters. A dilapidated chicken coop lay further off with only the corrugated roof line above the water. "An easy way to clean the shit," Guilherme had joked. In the rainy season, the motley birds were relocated to the rise and given free range in the garden to keep the bug population down. But the family's pigs had to be penned to keep them from eating up all the produce. A small dog named Pepe had the run of the house and the boats, and he was nimble in a dugout as he was on dry land.

Between the rains, Taylor tried to help out around Guilherme's farm. In the sections of garden that were not submerged, the family had planted manioc and peppers, and there were always seasonal fruits and nuts to be gathered from the forest. Several times a week, Guilherme, Taylor, and Sergio—Guilherme's brother in law— would go fishing or hunting. They could generally count on some sort of game or fish every day which, when combined with the take from the farm and jungle, made the family self-sufficient. Because of Guilherme's bad leg, he could not do some of the heavy work around the place, so, when he was well enough, Taylor kept the weeds hoed and dug the manioc root. There were some Brazil nut trees within a few kilometers and, with Guilherme's son as guide, Taylor collected the softball-sized husks and cracked and peeled them—a difficult and time consuming task, but well worth it. Taylor found that fresh Brazil nuts tasted nothing like the hard, dried things he'd had in the States. When eaten immediately after being removed from the husk, they taste a little like creamy coconut and soon became one of Taylor's favorite foods. After a few months of eating fresh fish, starchy manioc, and fresh fruits and vegetables, Taylor had to regain his strength and stamina.

Near the middle of March, the rains abated temporarily and there were a few unseasonable days of sunshine. On the first day of blue skies, Guilherme decided that the break in weather was a prime opportunity for an overnight fishing trip. The catch had been poor lately and the family was running low on food stocks. The fish were no longer contained in the river channels but moved out into the jungle, swimming into the shallows around the submerged trunks of trees, finding food and cover in areas which, a few months before, were the scavenging grounds of wild pigs and *capivara*, a large hamster-like rodent. While the flood plain around the Rio Solimoes was under several feet of water, it was still possible to find a few well-defined channels on the smaller *igarapés* where fish tended to congregate. Sergio told Guilherme that he knew of streams that fed Lagoa Coari, a fattened artery of the Rio Solimoes, where good fishing could still be had. The work of hauling back a large catch would require two men, so Taylor was invited to join Sergio on the outing.

The following day, Sergio came by in his dugout canoe with a small outboard. The motor had an extended prop especially designed for the weedy waters of the *igarapés*, giving it the appearance of a motorized grass trimmer with three oval blades on the rotor. Sergio pulled up to Guilherme's house and held on to the stilts to steady the shallow canoe for Taylor. The ancient boat was hand carved from a single tree and was stained a dark brown with the accumulated oils of human sweat and fish blood. For gear, Sergio packed a tightly rolled fish net, a shotgun, a small harpoon with a detachable point, a machete, and a small duffel bag containing a few cooking utensils, some food, and dry clothing. Taylor carried two light hammocks and mosquito netting, his journal, a change of clothes and his knife. Stepping carefully off the deck, he climbed in at the front of the dugout and set his small day-pack in the center.

As the sun rose, the two men wound their way out past a few tree trunks and joined the larger tributary. Soon they were on the broad, milky brown waters of the Solimoes, headed for the Lagoa Coari a few hours distant. The morning was brilliantly blue and the sun sparked and glinted off the ripples pushed up by their little boat. Most of the world was covered with water. But occasionally a clump of trees on a rise formed an island and the leaves rattled with capuchin monkeys while silent white egrets sat sentinel on the highest limbs, watching them with their yellow eyes on swiveling heads. In spots along the central channel, scattered hillocks became grassy oases of higher ground protruding above the flood waters. Here *jacaré*, small caiman, lined up on the bank side by side like reptilian logs, bathing in the bright sunlight.

From time to time flocks of bright green parakeets would flit over and fill the air with their argumentative chatter.

Seated at the prow, Taylor looked at the blue and green world with wonder. At one point he saw a large swirl stir the surface of the water off the bow, indicating a large animal moving just below. He looked back at Sergio and pointed to the spot. "*O que e isso?*" he asked. Sergio had seen it also. "*Boto!*" he said, in a way that conveyed a sense of admiration, but the word had no meaning for Taylor, so the identity of the creature would remain the secret of the brown waters for a while. To Taylor's delight, Sergio watched the world with the same intensity as he. His hand on the throttle, body cocked forward, he scanned the waters and trees for movement. A large brown and white river eagle sat perched on a gray snag on an island in the stream, and, as the boat passed, the bird's eyes met the riverman's and Taylor noticed that Sergio was smiling. This surprised him since he noticed that people often become deadened to the beauty in their lives through sheer inattentiveness or by allowing themselves to go numb with monotonous routine. After years of living in the jungle, Sergio still looked at the world with fresh eyes.

Sometime around late morning, Sergio turned away from the main channel and followed a broad tributary to the southwest. "Lagoa Coari," he said to Taylor over the puttering motor. They followed the wide, natural reservoir for a few hours until it narrowed at its source, the Rio Arauá. Here Sergio forked off again onto a nameless little *igarapé* that meandered into the jungle. Unlike the milky brown waters of the Solimoes, the water here was the color of tea, stained black by the steeping vegetation. This was to be their fishing and hunting grounds. Sergio cut the motor and pulled the paddle from the bottom of the dugout. Sitting on a small bench seat, legs crossed and knees slightly raised, he began paddling with strong, controlled strokes.

"*Onde estamos?*" asked Taylor, trying to locate himself on his mental map.

"Shhh," answered Sergio. It was time for silence. Sergio was alternately watching the surface of the water and the movement in the trees. Taylor turned forward and listened to the sound of the jungle. It was nice not to talk, to just listen to the voice of the world. Now and again he heard the far off chatter of parakeets or the high-pitched whistle of a marmoset. Sergio's paddle had a leaf-shaped blade and it broke the water with a liquid "tok," as if the seal on the river's surface tension had been popped. It was musical and methodical, lulling Taylor into a state of quiet meditation. As the little boat maneuvered up the tributary, the water level began to drop and the river developed a distinct channel. On either bank, evenly dispersed trees knitted their limbs together to form a green canopy over the stream. On many of the larger trees, lianas wound their way around the trunks and snaked out onto the limbs before spreading their greedy leaves to gather in the dappled sun. Beneath the trees the forest floor was a duff of brown leaves, dotted sporadically with broad-leafed ferns. The fringe along the shoreline was choked with mats of floating marsh grass.

As the boat slid close to the grass mats near the embankment, the prow brushed up against a submerged limb, making a scraping sound against the underside of the canoe. Just then, ten yards upstream, an enormous creature thrashed its tail, shooting out of the shallows where it had been lying and into the dark brown channel. Startled by the size and force of the animal, Taylor turned to Sergio.

"*Boto?*" he asked, thinking that maybe it was the secretive animal they saw earlier.

"*Pirarucu!*"

Taylor had heard about this legendary creature. It was the largest freshwater fish on the Amazon, reaching up to fifteen feet in some instances. Sergio quickly reached for his net and made swift preparations to stretch it across the small tributary. Using the partially submerged limb he had hit with the canoe as an anchor point, he tied off one end and, with Taylor helping, unrolled the net as he paddled across the stream where he tied off the other end to a tree. The net was designed for big fish. It was about five feet wide with a four inch mesh. Sergio attached an empty plastic bottle near the center of the net to buoy up the top and ensure that the mesh hung straight and touched bottom. If the *pirarucu* got its head through one of the squares, it would get snagged by the gills and would be unable to back out. Paddling quickly, Sergio made his way upstream following the direction of the startled fish. His objective was to overshoot the *pirarucu* and then frighten it back downstream into the waiting net. When he had gone about one hundred yards he guessed that he had passed by his quarry and turned the boat around, facing downstream. Then he handed Taylor the paddle and demonstrated that he wanted him to strike the surface with the broad edge. The sharp slap of the oar set the brown water to humming with dissonant shocks as the current carried the canoe back towards the net. Sergio grabbed the harpoon from the bottom of the boat and tied a line to the detachable point. Standing in the bow, he steadied the weapon at his shoulder.

The boat was now about twenty yards from the net. Suddenly the plastic bottle gave a jerk and plunged violently below the water line. There was a tremendous thrashing in the water and the net strained under the weight of a huge fish. Sergio yelled excitedly at Taylor who scrambled to paddle the canoe towards the churning *pirarucu*. As they drew within ten feet, Taylor could see the armored scales on the broad flank of the fish and its thick, broad tail. Sergio cocked his arm and threw the harpoon, swift and sure. The point struck the fish near the left pectoral fin and it rolled away from the surface and tried to dive. The shaft of the harpoon fell away as Sergio pulled hard on the line attached to the point, now embedded firmly in the fish. The little dugout tipped and wavered throughout the struggle but Sergio used his feet to balance and redistribute the weight. The fish thrashed and roiled, but as it tired, Sergio gave a few great heaves and pulled the *pirarucu's* head out of the water and level with the boat.

"*Mate-o!*" shouted Sergio. Taylor had no idea what the words meant but the urgency of the moment told him that Sergio wanted him to subdue the fish. With the paddle still in his hand he acted on reflex, flipping the blade end for the handle so he could swing it like a club.

"*Mate-o!*" shouted Sergio again, his strength ebbing as the fish fought hard to dive. The taut line was beginning to cut into Sergio's hands. Taylor had to act quickly. Aiming for the spot behind the eyes, he swung the shaft of the paddle at the *pirarucu*, landing a few sharp blows across the back of the head. The fish went rigid with little spasms and then, with one final shudder, it went limp.

It took both men to haul the fish over the side. The six-foot *pirarucu* took up the entire bottom of the canoe and weighed almost seventy pounds. It was a primitive looking creature. The fat blade-shaped body was covered with thick, raspy scales. The head was broad and square, and the huge gaping maw revealed only tiny teeth and a large fleshy tongue—a mouth designed to swallow fish whole. The top and sides were dusky gray but the underside was pastel yellows and pinks.

Sergio paddled the canoe to the shore and gave Taylor a paring knife. Then he went to set up camp, leaving Taylor to gut the fish. He had cleaned trout and steelhead before and figured the process was the same. He ran the knife from the anus to the gills, letting the guts spill out into a slippery jumble of pink organs. The eyes stared blankly into the air. There was no fear or blame in them, only the emptiness that comes with non-being.

Taylor's shirt was covered with blood and he went to rinse it in the river. As he squatted near the canoe he looked over the stilled body. For a moment he was transported to his boyhood and the spring trips he and his father had made to the slaughterhouse. Every year they loaded the fattened lambs into a truck and drove them to Ellensburg where they sold the animals to an assembly-line butchering operation. It always sickened Taylor to see the lambs that he had fed on the bottle walk down the ramp, looking at him with an expression of confusion and terror. He felt a similar sense of guilt now, looking at the rare creature before him. When he had set out that morning, he had seen the trip as an opportunity to merely observe the flora and fauna of the jungle. The hunt and the blood had reminded Taylor that they were in the jungle to kill so the family could eat. Sergio came up beside him and watched him examine the fish.

"*Linda, eh?*"

"Yes, beautiful," agreed Taylor, running his hands down the pink and yellow flank.

"*Muito gostoso tambem!*" smiled Sergio, rubbing his stomach.

It was now early evening and the two men decided to make camp where they were. They tied off the boat and filled the bottom with filets of fish wrapped in broad, insulating leaves. Taylor selected suitable trees for their hammocks and, since they had clear weather, they didn't concern themselves with a roof. The evening was warm and the mosquito netting would keep the bugs away. Sergio made a fire and roasted two steaks cut from the tail while Taylor cleaned up the boat and threw the fish offal to the piranhas. As the light waned, the two sat around the fire and ate their filets. They hadn't eaten anything since they left Guilherme's at dawn and the meat was rich and satisfying. Taylor felt grateful for the food and it brought to mind stories he had heard of Native American hunters who, after the kill, had given thanks to the spirit of the dead animal. It seemed like a custom derived from those who had first-hand knowledge of killing. It was a gory and ugly business, requiring forgiveness. Taylor realized that the killing of the fish was the first time he had actually slaughtered a large animal. At the farm, the work was always performed by professional butchers, allowing him to maintain a distance between himself and the blood. He never had to slit the throats of the lambs or put a bullet in the brains of the steers. Maybe that was a bad thing, as he had never fully appreciated the meaning of death.

He had beaten the helpless animal to death and was now stained with its blood. He thought again of the day's killing—the solidity of the flesh against the shaft of the oar, the sound of breaking bones, the glassy, uncomprehending stare. It made him wonder, what made him different from Bruno? Admittedly, he had felt a rush of adrenaline when he had swung the club. But the blood had repulsed him, whereas with Bruno the shouts of terror and the vision of a helpless victim before him seemed to fuel his viciousness. As Taylor struggled to subdue the fish, he had recognized an instinctive impulse to survive, and he killed out of a sense of necessity, not for enjoyment. The human animal has an enormous capacity for violence, and Bruno had chosen to give expression to that force, to revel in brutality. Taylor began to realize the implications of that fact. Since individuals have it in their power to cause great pain or to promote happiness, whether the world is filled with beauty or ugliness is largely a matter of our own creation.

If acts of brutality and kindness were truly matters of individual choice, it now seemed illogical and even philosophically dangerous to hold Fate accountable for his own misfortune and for human suffering in general. In his more cynical moments, he had seen Bruno as a tool of destiny, acting out a plan ordained by some hostile, external force. But if Taylor persisted in blaming suffering on Fate, that would mean that he would have to excuse every criminal of every crime ever committed. The idea that there is a plan for the universe and that all events, good or bad, have a reason ultimately denies the possibility of holding people accountable for their actions. Instead, Taylor gradually came to believe that the fact that Bruno had robbed him and had beaten him was the consequence of the man's propensity for cruelty combined with a string of random accidents that put them together on the same island at the same moment. Fate had not sent him to Taylor and Guilherme that night. He was not an instrument of a malicious universe. Instead, decided Taylor, he was a malicious free agent acting within a world of ordered indifference where, within limits, one was free to act on the powerful impulses of love or hate. Bruno had chosen hate.

That evening there was a full moon. The white beams filtered down through the leaves and dappled the forest floor in moonshadows. The river glowed blue with the light. The strange energy made Taylor restless and he walked down to the water's edge to gaze at the moonlight on the stream. Sergio had been preparing his nets for the morning by the firelight. His work done, he met Taylor at the river's edge and placed the net in the canoe. He saw that Taylor was still mulling over his role in the kill and guessed that he would benefit from a glimpse at the vibrant life in the nocturnal world of the *igarapé*.

"*Vamos!*" he said. Taylor looked at him, not comprehending.

"*Vamos*," he said again, making paddling gestures with his arms.

"Now? . . . *agora?*" asked Taylor, thinking he had misunderstood.

"*Sim. Agora,*" replied Sergio, climbing into the boat.

Taylor followed, not sure what Sergio had intended, but the idea of a night paddle intrigued him so he was willing to explore. Sergio pushed away from the bank with his paddle and the boat slipped silently into the placid stream. The moonlight shimmered silver on the water and as the canoe cut across the surface it left a dark V in its wake. A few yards behind the boat the ripples dispersed and the blue light settled on the river again, closing up the wake and removing all traces of their passing as they pushed deeper into the jungle. The trees on the banks now stood in dark silhouette and the night was observed in reverent silence. What noise could be heard sounded like church whispers, low and intentionally inconspicuous. Baritone frogs hurrumphed from secret mud holes on the shore and from time to time the fluttering of bats' wings could be heard overhead as they wheeled acrobatically through the sky after invisible insects. Far off a howler monkey called to his troupe with a distinctive guttural rumble that rolled low and droning through the forest.

A few kilometers up the tributary, the stream widened out into a broad marsh which, under the eerie influence of the night, looked like a tree graveyard. There were signs that at one time the area was part of the forest but the course of the river had changed many years ago and had submerged the trunks year-round. The once flourishing giants had died off, leaving only bone-smooth snags to testify to their former glory. Fifty or so of the wooden monuments were interspersed throughout the marsh. Sergio paddled in among the trunks and as they glided past, Taylor reached out and touched the timeworn wood. The trunks were bare and cool like marble. Soon they were surrounded by the ghostly columns and Taylor felt a sense of profound sadness among the dead remains of these centuries-old trees.

"*Morto. Tudo morto. Muito triste,*" whispered Taylor, gesturing to the skeletal trees. He wanted to pay his respects to the departed giants. But he could see Sergio's face by the moonlight and noticed that riverman seemed amazed by the statement and that Taylor had completely missed the point of the graveyard visit.

"*Nao*," replied Sergio, "*a vida continua.*" With this, Sergio produced a small flashlight from his pocket and fixed its beam on the tree. In cracks along the bare trunk of the tree and in every crevice on the limbs some form of life had taken hold. Bromeliads clung to the wood like tufts of spiky hair and a clump of orchids claimed the top of the trunk and bloomed in wild purple profusion. Bulbous orange and white fungi girdled the trunk at the waterline and a dense mat of aquatic plants swathed every inch of the submerged base. Little fish darted in and out of the crooked roots. Sergio then pointed the beam at a hole in a neighboring tree. There, a few black fruit bats took offense at the probing light and took wing, wheeling into the darkness. He flipped off the light and all appeared ghostly and dead again. As they paddled home in silence, Taylor tried to make sense of what he had experienced that day. His impulse was to keep contradictory forces separate in his mind, and thus the partnership of decay and renewal left him perplexed and unsettled. He realized that he could no longer categorize what he saw or experienced as strictly good or bad, beautiful or ugly. He had had the veil of expectations stripped from his eyes and found a world shimmering with chance and ambiguity.

Taylor awoke the next morning before dawn. Sergio was already up making coffee in a battered steel pot. They ate a simple breakfast of hard crackers and stiff guava jelly. By sunrise they were back on *igarapé* headed for home. As they left the smaller tributary to rejoin the broad waters of the Lagoa Coari, Sergio put away the paddle and prepared to start the motor, but something made him stop. He fixed his gaze ahead of the boat to a soft swirl in the water. Taylor wondered if it were another *pirarucu*.

"*Boto rosa!*" whispered Sergio, tapping Taylor's knee and pointing. Taylor looked towards the ripples on the water where suddenly a single pinkish dolphin surfaced, rolled its back and disappeared again.

Taylor caught his breath. "A dolphin!"

"*Sim. Golphinho. Boto rosa,*" replied Sergio, positioning himself for a better look. Taylor had read about these rare river dolphins but never thought he would see one. It surfaced again, seemingly interested in the boat, and came gliding towards them. Rhythmically rolling its back through the water's glassy surface, the *boto* took on the appearance of a pink cloud skitting across a blue sky. Taylor sat transfixed by the vision and would have thought that it was a hallucination had not the animal shown itself to be flesh and blood by taking in a great breath and exhaling, pushing the air out of its lungs with a little spray of mist that lingered above the water as evidence of its passing. Taylor saw the *boto* rise so close to the boat he could have touched it with the harpoon. With that thought a terrible image flashed in his mind and he turned quickly to look at Sergio. Sergio saw the question in his eyes and guessed at his concern. He laughed at the absurdity at the idea of harpooning the dolphin.

"*Nao, nao,*" he shook his head. "*Sagrado. O boto e sagrado para os pescadores.*" Taylor knew enough to translate that the pink dolphin was to be spared since the local fishermen considered it to be a blessing. The fantastic animal made a few circles around the canoe before it dipped below the surface and disappeared. Taylor and Sergio watched the last ripples from its dorsal fin melt away. They sat quietly for a few moments in the magical wake of the unearthly apparition. Sergio caught Taylor's eye and pointed to the fish steaks wrapped in leaves. "*Boa sorte,*" he said, suggesting that the dolphin sightings which had inaugurated and concluded their trip had been responsible for their good luck. Their catch, food to last the family two weeks, stretched from one end of the boat to the other.

"*A vida continua,*" said Taylor. Sergio smiled and started the motor.

"*Vamos.*"

Journal Entry for March 25, 2000

Idea for a painting: Today I was walking along the rise behind Guilherme's house and came upon a massive tree covered in vines. The trunk was ten feet in diameter and it must have lived for centuries, but it was dying under the strangling assault from the other plants. Vines as thick as my leg spiraled around the trunk and climbed into all the highest branches. They spread their leaves to the sun and sprouted their orange trumpet flowers. Other epiphytic plants like orchids wedged themselves between the forking limbs. At some point they will weigh so heavy on their host that the tree will topple over. Then the termites and fungus will have their turn at it. Then in the duff left upon the ground a new tree will take root and send its shoot skyward.

I used to think that the death of a majestic tree like that was a mistake, a divergence from nature's plan. Now I am not so sure. I came to these jungles expecting to see something—lush green forests, rivers teeming with fish, blue skies filled with brilliantly colored birds. And I *have* seen all that. But I have also seen children playing in sewers and murder in another man's eyes. I have had my eyes forcibly opened to a broader vision of reality. Each and every moment can wear, simultaneously, a lovely face and a hideous expression. One must have the courage to see both. The great, green plants of the jungle are engaged in a struggle for life, only in a dimension that moves much more slowly than human strivings. Ugliness in this world exists. It simply is. The trick is to live in such a way that you contribute more to beauty than to brutality.

I am beginning to see what Quinn finds so interesting about investigating the nature of the human soul. We are at once angelic and bestial. One day I would like to do a painting for her in which I describe, through the allegorical characters of the jungle, how, as Guilherme's grandmother puts it, life is a river. So much can happen between the two banks and up and down the current. If I could paint Nature as it is, I would need to paint such a world of incredible paradoxes. Beautiful spiders killing beautiful butterflies. Delicate flowering vines strangling towering trees—the world as a constant balance between life and death. Yet to become too focused on one and not the other is to miss something. I came to the jungle full of my own illusions of what I would see and what it would mean to me. I have let go of my illusions, but I am not disillusioned. I have lost some of my preconceptions and now I see with much greater clarity. The consequence is that I have found reality to be more rewarding than when I was still clinging to the notion that I was making the trip purely for the sake of seeing inspiring vistas.

Maybe that is the way I need to approach my journey. Accept what it gives me and look for the beauty, in whatever form it takes. That may be my first accomplishment on this trip towards becoming an artist. I feel ready now to look, to really perceive the places I'm moving through. At least that way when I sit down to paint, my vision of the truth will come out on the canvas rather than a concept of what I *wanted* truth to be. The best paintings, the kind of paintings I want to create, do not present us with truthful representations of reality; they provide us with representations of truth that are clothed in the familiar images of reality. In order to do that, I need to know more about myself and my subject matter, or I'll run the risk of painting nothing but surfaces. It seems to me, therefore, that before I can begin to paint again, I've got a lot more looking to do.

APRIL

In the spring of his eighteenth year, Taylor discovered that his life of morning chores, calloused hands, and sun-browned neck was the exception and not the rule. That was when he met Gabriella Somerset. Taylor's small, rural school was mostly populated by the children of hop farmers, cattle ranchers, and apple orchardists, but it was beginning to serve an increasing number of suburban families. While some of the other students still worked on the family farm like Taylor, many of these newly arrived families were only tangentially linked to agriculture and the children had a lifestyle that, from Taylor's perspective, seemed mysterious and charmed. These were the sons and daughters of the warehouse owners, the feed store managers, the implement sales dealers, and Farm & Home Loan agents. They lived in freshly stamped out pre-fab homes plopped down side by side along black-topped cul-de-sacs. The roads near the houses were smooth and broad and the neighborhood kids all had skateboards and remote control cars. The most fortunate had above-ground pools skirted by wood decks cluttered with grills and bright lawn furniture; many had two story houses and cars with exotic sounding names Taylor had never heard before like Volvo and Peugeot. Gabriella transferred to Central Valley High for her senior year after her father decided to move the family to "a quiet place in the country."

When Gabriella stepped into the classroom for the first time, she completely disrupted Taylor's conception of himself. Articulate, confident, and well-traveled, she made him acutely aware of how very narrow his horizons had been. He had the most in common with the farm kids, so he spent the majority of his time with a group pejoratively called "the goat-ropers." His friends in this clique—Bill Hennis, Albert Denny, Cort Knudson, and Marla Johnson—wore cowboy boots and denim almost every day, chewed tobacco (Marla included), and belonged to The Future Farmers of America Club. Bill, or "Wild Bill," rode the rodeo circuit and drove a beat-up, yellow Ford pickup. Al was chubby, unkempt, and painfully shy. His father had a pig farm and thus his son had suffered the taunts of the other children who, since grade school, called him "Lard Ass" or "Al the Sow." Cort was the son of a cherry farmer for whom farming seemed to be a genetic birthright. As a teenager, he shared the management and decision-making for the farm with his father and, from Taylor's perspective, possessed a maturity beyond his years. Marla, the sandy-haired daughter of the local Methodist preacher, had no farming background at all, but she found an affinity with the rag-tag group of goat-ropers through her love of horses. An only child, she adopted the farm boys as her surrogate brothers and she avidly attended every state fair and rodeo she could with at least one of them in tow.

Among this little group, Taylor was a reluctant hero. His years of working on the farm equipment had made him a competent mechanic. When the other boys had trouble with their cars, they would bring them in to shop class after hours and Taylor would have the problem diagnosed and repaired quicker than a garage.

At one point, with the use of the school's winch, he helped Bill pull the blown motor out of his truck and install a rebuilt engine. All the other boys and Marla—the one girl who signed up for shop—watched as Taylor lowered the motor into the chassis, straining and heaving it into place on the mounts. Marla stood there with hands on her hips in mock disappointment, shouting "C'mon ya big wimp. You're gonna scratch the paint! I could do better than that ya pussy woman." That always got them going— the preacher's daughter saying "pussy." Cort and Al laughed at her sassiness and joined in her mock insults while Wild Bill, not to be out done by Taylor, tried to lend a hand with the motor, ending up more of a hindrance than a help.

Between Wild Bill and Taylor, there was always a little competition for Marla's attention. Taylor thought of her as one of the boys, but got jealously protective when he perceived that she might be interested in someone else. She was spunky, a little buck-toothed, and flat-chested like a young girl, but she knew more creative swear words than all the boys and she could spit chew juice with deadly accuracy. Wild Bill thought he had a chance to be her boyfriend because she flirted with him at times, but more often in their relationship she pushed him away and treated him like an annoying kid brother. He always tried a little too hard to please her with a matinee cowboy brand of chivalry, but she enjoyed the attention because she knew it made Taylor hover over her. She could never see herself with Bill since he was shorter than her by a half a head. She was sure that if they ever did have to get around to stooping and craning for a kiss, she might laugh out loud and deal a life-lasting blow to his mini-masculine ego. She secretly hoped that Taylor would someday come to see her as a girlfriend, but she did not know how she could transform the punchy, quarrelsome, quasi-sibling relationship she had fostered in their childhood into a more mature version of passion. For Taylor, he depended on his friendships with his goat-roper pals because they were comfortable. It was what he knew.

But he was not wholly defined by his association with the other farm kids. By the time he was a junior, he had become an honor roll student who showed an aptitude for art. By his senior year he was determined to attend college. This put him in all the advanced placement courses and eventually he struck up friendships with Sean Whitehall, the school's SAT champion, and Gabriella Somerset. His growing admiration of Gabriella was particularly concerning to Marla, since the new girl's charm and intelligence seemed to intensify all of her own crude, boyish characteristics. The more time Taylor spent with Gabriella, the more Marla hated her. She began to fantasize about burning her lovely yellow hair into a curling heap of cinders or turning her into the butt of all the locker-room jokes with carefully planted rumors that she had an uncontrollable passion for old coach Harris.

Gabriella's family owned a string of car lots in the Valley— Somerset Autos—and they lived in a large house perched on a bluff that looked out over verdant orchards and snow-capped Mount Adams. The other students called it "The Glass Palace" because it sparkled with a dazzling array of high windows set row upon row along all the jutting and angled contours of the house. Gabriella's father drove a different, shining car every few months or so, and it was rumored that the unnaturally thick clump of auburn hair on top of his head was an expensive toupee. Roman Somerset used his children at every opportunity to advertise his business and his wealth, so he gave each of his three daughters— upon gaining a learner's permit—her own car. Gabriella drove a sea-blue '67 Mustang and had such an extensive wardrobe that she never had to wear the same thing twice in any one month. Despite her good looks and money, she did not concern herself with the social squabbles and popularity contests which are endemic to small, rural schools. Because of all the advantages she enjoyed, she could afford to be kind and generous to everyone, regardless of their rank in the social pecking order. To Taylor, Gabriella's air of worldly sophistication put her in another class entirely from the hair-sprayed cheerleaders and pimply football players. It was as if she had skipped adolescence and had gone directly to adulthood. Her poise and style gave him the impression that, if not for the requirement that she attend school to get her diploma, she would be in college or working in some well-dressed profession.

Taylor sat next to her in his literature class and quickly earned her respect by consistently scoring the highest marks on his tests and essays. He had an advantage over many of the other students in the class in that he was a voracious reader. In his many hours of solitude of the farm, he found opportunities to steal a moment here and there with a good paperback. His history teacher got him started when he gave him the biography of a World War I British flying ace who, after losing both his legs in a crash, had learned to walk again on prosthetics and, against all adversity, realized his dream of flying once again. And from his English teacher he got a tattered copy of *The Lord of the Rings* which he read one summer while helping his father stack the alfalfa cutting. Taylor's job was to prop the leaning tower of hay bales with pine poles after his father had tipped them off the harrow-bed had pulled away. This took but a few minutes for each load and Taylor was left with half hour intervals between runs in which he participated vicariously in the strivings and joys of the characters in his books. In addition, the hours he spent at chores in broad pastures or green orchards gave him ample time to ponder the working of the world and his place in it. At seventeen he possessed a creative sensitivity beyond his years, but his limited exposure to life beyond Yakima and the insular quality of Rockwater condemned him to a naive view of the complex emotions and motives of real people.

The story that helped him strike up a friendship with Gabriella Somerset was "Rappaccini's Daughter" by Nathaniel Hawthorne. For the previous semester, Taylor had spent most of his time in English class with Al and Cort. But he found himself growing increasingly impatient with their disinterest in the stories which he found so compelling and felt more affinity with Gabriella and Sean who sat in the front row and dominated discussion with enthusiastic contributions. Following their lead, he began to be more vocal and revealed himself to be a sharp critic. At the completion of the unit on American Literature, Mrs. Verretti, the English teacher, asked the students to work in groups of three to analyze the symbol of a mysterious purple plant in the story. As the class began to sort itself out into the usual pairings of friends, Gabriella walked directly over to Taylor and asked him, smiling, "would you like to work with Sean and me?" Her hair was pulled away from her face in a broad, white headband and the stream of blond tresses spilled across her shoulders and down over a rich, black, silk blouse. He involuntarily cringed back a little with shock and went completely mute for a full five seconds. Sitting there in his Keep On Truckin' T-shirt and John Deere tractor cap, Taylor imagined that—to anybody watching—he must look like a pitiful, stray puppy which, unfamiliar with kind gestures from strangers, shrinks away in fear from the outstretched hand of a passer-by. When Gabriella repeated the request, he realized she was trying to be friendly and he needed to speak or risk offending her. Operating on reflex, he decided to make the conventional greeting gesture and stood up, extending his hand to Gabriella. "Hi, I'm Taylor," he announced as if meeting her for the first time. To punctuate his awkwardness, he knocked over his chair.

"I know your name," she laughed, shaking his hand anyway. "Do you want to join us over there? It looks like you and your desk are not on speaking terms anymore."

"Yeah," he said looking back at the toppled desk, his foot still entangled in the upturned legs. "I'll be right over." Cort and Al watched him as he picked up his copy of the anthology from the floor and walked as nonchalantly as possible towards Sean and Gabriella at the opposite corner of the room. The expression of disbelief that Cort and Al shot him cried "What are you doing?! You're going to make a fool of yourself in front of those two!" But Taylor pretended he was being dragged away against his will and, shrugging slightly, returned a look he thought would convey that he was helpless to get out of this predicament and they would just have to get on without him. He slid awkwardly into a desk between Sean and Gabriella and cracked his book to no page in particular.

"Well," said Gabriella brightly, "do you need to introduce yourself to Sean too?"

"No, Taylor laughed," grateful for her efforts to dispel his nervousness. "We know each other from Algebra," he explained needlessly. "How are you doing Sean?" he asked cordially, testing out a tone of civility he thought appropriate for the Honor Society set.

"Pretty good. Better, now that you are here. There's a lot riding on this score. We're going to need your help on this project," said Sean bluntly. "And you seem to get this symbolism stuff," he added, making sure there was no mystery in Taylor's mind why he had been invited to sit in the glow of Gabriella's radiance.

"Sean!" protested Gabriella, "You make it sound as if we just wanted Taylor to do the homework for us." She gave him a little slap on the arm that set his lower lip in a pout.

Taylor blushed at the insinuation that he was there simply as a convenient tool. It was as if the doors at the country club had been flung open to him and, for a brief glorious moment he felt like a member, only to discover that he had been admitted merely to act as a caddie. He felt his face getting red and he would have gotten up and walked back to his goat-roper friends, but Gabriella held him there. Laying her fingers—nails polished red and gleaming—on Taylor's hand she explained, "Sean and I were talking, and we decided that it was a shame you didn't work with us more often, since you have such great ideas. We thought that together we might make the strongest team in the class."

"Yeah, that was it," Sean corrected himself, looking back at Gabriella for approval. "You always have a slightly different take on the stories," he admitted to the interloper. "Like a different perspective we need."

Barely hearing Sean, Taylor sat rapt in concentration on the lingering warm spot on the back of his hand where Gabriella had left her touch. "O.K.," he said, already forgetting his wounded pride as he began to imagine himself working many long hours with Gabriella on their project. "I've finished the story already," he said thoughtfully, trying to live up to his new reputation as a lit critic, "and I have some ideas about the symbolism that may help us. Maybe we could meet after school a few times this week." As he formulated the plan, he was wondering if he could find a way to recreate the conditions that had compelled Gabriella to touch him.

That day, they took notes together on the references to the beautiful and dangerous plants in Dr. Rappaccini's garden. What stumped Sean and Gabriella was why Giovanni, a young admirer of Rappaccini's exotically beautiful daughter, could never settle on whether she was an angel or demon. Over the following week, the group met several times to draft a presentation on the project for the rest of the students. Outside of class, Taylor spent all his available time scouring the tale for clues as to the meaning of Giovanni's confusion, perfecting his analysis so that he would be certain to win his new friends' favor and admiration.

As a result of his new focus on academics, he missed his Future Farmers Meeting so he could read book reviews in the library. More damning in the minds of the goat ropers, he was absent from their regular after-school hours in the shop. On Bill's first attempt to fill in for Taylor, he assured Marla he could repair her carburetor, a chore Taylor had promised to do weeks before. He turned out to be a poor replacement and ended up flooding it and leaving it hopelessly out of adjustment. Marla took Taylor's absence as a personal slight. Humiliated at being abandoned, Marla called Bill "a damned faker and an incompetent asshole." Crestfallen, Bill sought out his friend that day at lunch for a confrontation. He waited to meet him on the bleachers where the farm kids were eating their sack lunches. Over the past week, Bill saw the fabric of the whole group falling apart and attributed his own embarrassment in front of Marla to Taylor's refusal to play his established role in his relationship with each of the goat ropers. When he didn't show up after ten minutes, Bill put his untouched peanut butter sandwich back in its wrapper and handed it to Al. "Here. Hold this 'til I get back. I got business to do." He liked the way the cliché sounded. Settling his battered cowboy hat on his head, he marched towards the cafeteria in the way he'd seen Clint Eastwood do so many times before in a showdown. Al waited until Bill had gone beyond the corner before pulling out his friend's sandwich and eating it. Marla caught him stuffing the last morsel in his cheek and punched him hard in his leg. "Owwww!!" he bellowed, looking at her in confusion.

"Why'd you go and eat Bill's lunch ya Lard Ass!" snapped Marla, realizing too late that she had broken the group's unspoken rule to never attack Al with the painful slurs used by the other kids. Cort glared at her. Al stopped chewing mid-bite and looked straight out in front of him. Slowly, he worked the mouthful of sandwich into a wet glob and spit it out on the bleacher seats. Marla turned a hard shoulder on him so she would not have to see the tears well up in his eyes. She felt an anger rise up in her. At first it was directed at herself, for her own cruelty. But the feelings of self-reproach quickly became anger at Taylor, who, perhaps unconsciously, seemed to be comparing her to Gabriella. Now when they got together, she detected in Taylor's expression the faintest involuntary glimmers of repulsion if she cursed and spat as before. His obvious attraction to Gabriella made Marla feel as if the attributes that had once endeared her to him as a boy had lost their appeal to him as a young man. Taylor was moving into adulthood and she could not stand the idea of being left in adolescence.

"I gotta stop hanging out with all you damn hicks!" she hissed at the gloomy boys, leaving them there with spoiled appetites and sour faces.

In the cafeteria, Taylor, Gabriella, and Sean sat at one of the broad tables on orange plastic chairs. Their books spread out in front of them, they chatted earnestly over their notes and compared interpretations of literary symbols between bites of starchy spaghetti. For Taylor, he felt as if he were a rural infiltrator in the heart of the suburban war room. This was where all the preppy matches were made, where the trendy kids decided what jeans were in, and where the most titillating gossip got traded across the table. Already he felt himself the subject of some whispering, but kept his head down and pretended that his first-time-ever appearance in "the caf" had been accomplished without the slightest nervousness on his part.

"So you think we should begin with an overview of the garden?" asked Sean, still skeptical about Taylor's interpretation.

"Yeah," said Taylor convinced of his method. "The garden is like Eden and that makes Giovanni a stand-in for Adam and Beatrice is like Eve. There are enough clues to suggest that the poisonous plant in the center of the garden represents the apple tree from Genesis." Taylor flipped through the pages adeptly, showing the others where he had marked the passages.

"Now that's the part I don't get," said Gabriella, trying to understand. "Why do you think the purple plant represents the apple tree?"

"Well," thought Taylor out loud, "the plant poisons Beatrice and she carries the toxin in her body. When she accidentally touches his hand it leaves a red and burning mark on his skin."

"So?" asked Gabriella, still not convinced. "How is that like the apple from the Eden story?"

"Eve was tainted by sin after eating the apple, and Beatrice is corrupted by the contact with the plant," said Taylor. "Through his contact with her, Giovanni becomes corrupted too. That's why he's so furious with her in the end. He wanted so much for her to be pure and innocent, and in the end she turns out to be flawed to the point of being deadly."

"Oh, I get it," cried Gabriella, laughing at Giovanni's torment over Beatrice, but in a way that made Taylor feel that she was laughing at him too. "When he sees her as a demon, it's because he's kind of turned on and that makes him angry at her for being such a tramp. Just like poor Eve got all the blame for original sin. Typical male hypocrisy," she snorted with disgust.

Taylor failed to see what was hypocritical about Giovanni's attempts to judge Beatrice's virtue and was about to defend the young man's concern for innocence, but he could see she was no longer paying attention. She was looking over his shoulder at someone hovering in the background. Taylor turned and saw Bill standing in the doorway at the far end of the cafeteria, gesturing for him to come and join him. He was frowning uncomfortably. It was clear he did not want to set foot in the foreign territory of the suburbanites as if afraid that he might track manure over the white tile floors of the preppy kids. Excusing himself from the table,

Taylor crossed the lunchroom and followed Bill out into the parking lot.

"What do you want?" he asked, trailing after Bill. "I gotta get back to the books before fifth period."

"You mean you want to get back to your more fashionable friends," said Bill, turning on Taylor with a scowl.

"What do you mean by that?" he asked, knowing this confrontation was inevitable from the moment he joined Gabriella and Sean in English class weeks ago.

"Where were you for the last Future Farmers meeting? We didn't have enough members so we couldn't vote on the Pioneer Day booth idea I proposed. I kinda get the feeling lately that you got more important things to do than be seen with us hicks."

"Don't give me that crap," said Taylor in rising irritation. "I have just decided to put a priority on my studies and the meeting slipped my mind. That's all."

"Since when have you been so concerned about being such a pencil neck? You've always got B's without even trying, leaving plenty of time to hang out. You're gonna graduate for Christ's sake."

"I don't want to just graduate, Bill. I want to do well so I can get into college and maybe get a scholarship." Forced to it by his friend, Taylor expressed for the first time why he felt so attracted to his new friends. They were people for whom Central Valley High was just a stop-over point. In the next year they would be moving on and leaving him behind, and that realization churned his insides up with the fear that if he stood still long enough, he would be absorbed slowly into the soil. Even as he stood there speaking to Bill he felt the dry, ropy roots of the Yakima desert loam pushing up from under the concrete, trailing their greedy tendrils around his ankles, stabbing through his skin and forking through his veins to draw life from his blood.

"I want to get out of this hole. Is that a crime?" asked Taylor. "Kids like us have very few options. If you're a woman, you end up in the warehouse packing apples until some asshole foreman picks you out of the line to be his wife. If you're a man, you'll drive tractors in circles until your mind snaps." Bill tried to walk away, disgusted. Taylor spun him around and forced him to listen. "Or you'll be out bucking hay 'til your back breaks. Now if you're *real* lucky, like Cort your family owns a farm and you can hang around moving irrigation pipe until your folks hand it over to you, but by then you're forty and for each and every day of those forty years you get up and do the same damn thing every day."

Bill looked at Taylor's pained expression and it reminded him of a coyote he had come across in his traps a week earlier. The animal's broken leg was gripped between two unyielding steel teeth. As Bill approached, it looked up at him with the anguish of a wild creature that comprehends that it is powerless to fight the cold, inanimate force that holds it fast; thus it becomes consumed with the panic of flight. Bill was not particularly intuitive about other people's emotions, but judging by Taylor's miserable expression, he had instincts that told him that it was within his power to end his friend's pain. All Taylor wanted, Bill knew, was to be released from his commitments to his old friends, to be free to move on without them. With this realization he felt a sense of betrayal and resentment build up inside and all he could think of was how, a week before, he had put a bullet between the coyote's eyes. Bill took a breath, hardened himself against Taylor's pleading eyes, and squeezed the trigger: "You and I are no longer friends Taylor Moreland," he said with finality. "You can perform your phony smart-kid act for your stuck up friends, but don't bother playing it for me and the gang. You're just not the kind of guy we want to be around anymore."

Taylor was not expecting such a hostile reaction from his friend, and Bill's hurt expression made him feel disloyal and selfish. His mind started working quickly to formulate a response that would set things back the way they were, but it always came down to having to renounce his own dreams. He couldn't tell Bill that he would reject Gabriella and Sean because they filled a void in his life. He couldn't say that he intended to stay around Yakima and continue going to stock auctions and state fairs with the goat ropers for the rest of his life. He couldn't explain to someone who had not seen the ocean the quiet yet persistent yearning one carries around in the heart as a result of seeing those terrifying and comforting waves. So rather than reconcile himself to Bill by apologizing or promising to return to his familiar self, he tried to take his friend with him into the uncharted territory.

"Don't you ever just get curious Bill? Don't you want to know what it would be like to go to college in Seattle or California or somewhere, and meet new people and go to football games and interesting parties?"

"I can go to college right here at Y.V.C.C. if I want, and I think Al and Cort and Marla are pretty damn interesting. But you're not," Bill snapped in rising anger. "You're a two-faced asshole and I don't know why I didn't figure it out before now!" Without giving Taylor a chance to defend himself, Bill threw a windmill punch at his unsuspecting friend that glanced off his chin and sent an instant shot of adrenaline coursing through his body. Flush with anger, Taylor instinctively retaliated with a swift and forceful jab that landed square on Bill's nose. The smaller boy crumpled at the knees and fell to the ground. Before the blow had even landed, Taylor had wished that he could have checked his temper. But it was too late. His friend was now bleeding profusely from the nose and tears of frustration and humiliation washed his red cheeks.

"I'm sorry Bill. Are you all right? Here, let me help you up," offered Taylor, proffering his hand.

"Leave me alone," mumbled Bill through a wad of bloody shirt tails held up to his face. "I don't want to look at your lying face anymore."

"Look, Bill," tried Taylor again, "all I want—"

"That's all you think about isn't it? What *you* want! Well I don't give a shit what you want or think anymore so leave me the hell alone." Bill struggled to his feet and walked away, nursing his busted nose. Taylor began to follow but decided to leave things the way they were. It had been an ugly end to an increasingly strained relationship. Somehow he had believed that he could just drift painlessly away from his farming friends into other social circles and into another life without anyone noticing or getting upset. What he hadn't considered was how much Bill and his other friends had come to depend on him to be what they wanted him to be—a mirror of themselves which, reflecting passive contentment, would re-affirm their belief that there was no need to demand anything more from life than what they already possessed. By expressing longing and dissatisfaction, Taylor had destroyed the myth that the close-knit group had created that their world was sufficient in and of itself, and that they would go on living together in this state of suspended childhood indefinitely.

For the next few days, Taylor gave the goat-ropers plenty of space. He did not eat lunch with them or talk to them between classes or after school, nor did they welcome him back to the group. Bill walked around with a strip of white support tape across his broken nose and dark bruises underlined his defiant eyes. Al and Cort elected Bill their new hero and they trailed after him with dog-like devotion. Of the group, Marla had taken Taylor's transformation the hardest. On the few occasions when he tried to get a word with her alone, she angrily rejected him and seemed on the verge of tears.

Without his regular group of friends, Taylor began spending more and more time with Sean, Gabriella, and the other college-bound students. He joined their after-school study groups and began attending college preparation workshops provided by the counseling office. He was still waiting to hear from the state colleges he applied to, and he was unsure whether or not he would be granted financial aid. The counselor informed him of scholarship money that was still available for a student with high grades and "demonstrated leadership skills." He fit the first criteria but was thin on the second. To ensure his escape from Yakima, he began volunteering for every student government committee possible in order to pad his resume. This pulled him further away from his old friends and into the sphere of Gabriella Somerset.

Despite the fact that Gabriella seemed to enjoy his company, whenever he was alone with her he was reminded of an incident a few years earlier when he had been caught trespassing on a golf course. He was thirteen years old and had scaled the fence and stealthily made his way across the course to fish for crappie in the water hazard. Before he had even rigged his line he was chased off by an indignant greens keeper on a little cart. Thus, he always caught himself looking over his shoulder when he met with Gabriella, half expecting that same keeper to come running in brandishing a golf club and yelling "get your raggedy ass away from her!" But by some stroke of good-fortune, during one particular week he was granted several hours alone with her. Sean left their English study group for a week on a tour of prospective campuses. For a few glorious days, Taylor met privately with Gabriella in the library after school. He would spend hours preparing for their meetings so that he could prove to her that he was not merely some hick who could read well, that he, like her, had a glimpse of the larger world and was destined for brighter things. To his delight, she appeared to look forward to the sessions too. She smiled at him when they spoke and, every once in a while, she would put a hand on his shoulder or touch his arm to get his attention. The thrill he got from such contact would keep him floating for hours.

He began to fantasize about having sex with Gabriella. He let himself believe that she was beginning to feel a fondness for him and that, like him, she was a virgin who was ready to give in to curiosity. At eighteen, the closest Taylor had come to sex was a little groping in a darkened movie theater with a girl named Helen who went to another school. In the past month, he had unconsciously come to associate losing his virginity with part of the quest to leave Yakima and all it represented. With a touch, Gabriella could liberate him from his own conception of himself and—as inexperienced in such matters as he was—Taylor confused this exhilaration for love. At night he would lie in bed for hours and imagine absurdly gushy dialogues in which she would confess a secret longing for him. They would end up naked together, quivering and exploring each other with all the pent up passion of the uninitiated. He would try to imagine the two of them in the act, but at this point his mental images got confused with the romping and panting he had seen in movies and he would break off the vision. The frantic lurching he had seen there offended all his romantic conceptions of sex as an emotional ritual cloaked in darkness and conducted with apologetic modesty.

After a few nights of torment, he decided to confess his desire for Gabriella, half convincing himself that she was awaiting the revelation with great expectation. One afternoon in the library, Taylor had his chance. They had retreated to the stacks at the corner of the room to find some pertinent dates for a history paper. They spread open an encyclopedia on an empty shelf and stood shoulder to shoulder examining the page. Gabriella was reading aloud about a Frenchman named Crèvecouer who chose to see America as his own natural paradise. The vision had a particular appeal to Taylor. The word "paradise" rang like a bell in Taylor's mind. At that moment, as Gabriella stood there with her yellow curls falling across her shoulders, he could almost believe that she was his Eve. He suddenly got the notion to kiss her. He stopped her from her reading, and, looking seriously into her eyes, he said: "Gabriella, don't you think you and I share a special friendship? A closeness?"

"Well, sure, in a way," she smiled, trying to be accommodating.

"From the moment you arrived here, I understood that you were different, and that made me realize that I was different. I just never realized it before. I don't fit in with anyone around here. But when I'm with you, I feel right, and I know I'll get out of here." She looked at him, not comprehending where he was going. "Would it make you happy if we ended up at the same college?"

"Yes. That would be great," she said, politely. For Taylor, this was confirmation enough that she felt something for him, and, trembling with nervousness, he leaned awkwardly towards her face, trying to kiss her quickly on the mouth. But thinking the discussion was over, Gabriella had turned back to her reading. The result was that Taylor—with eyes closed and lips pursed—planted a kiss clumsily on the side of her nose. Surprised but amused, Gabriella leaned away from Taylor and laughed a little out loud.

"What are you doing?" she asked, as if she hadn't got the joke. Stung with embarrassment, Taylor thought he could save face by landing a kiss on her lips this time and tried again. Gabriella dodged him and stepped away. Now she was not laughing.

"Taylor, we need to talk," she said, noticing the longing in his eyes. "We are just friends. Just friends. Don't go and spoil it now," she ended, trying to leave no room for doubt.

"But why just friends?" persisted Taylor, not ready to lose his elaborate myth he had constructed around her. "Is there no way that you could think of me as a boyfriend?" The question came out as a whisper because it felt like a thousand bricks were stacked upon his chest.

"I don't feel that way about you," explained Gabriella patiently. "You really don't know me that well, Taylor." She could see he was shaky. "Come on," she consoled, "let's talk." They sat on the floor amid the ruins of Taylor's romantic dream. "I have a boyfriend," she started matter-of-factly. "He's a biology major at the University of Washington. We're pinned," smiled Gabriella.

"What does that mean?" asked Taylor.

"It means he's in a fraternity and he gave me his pledge pin. I love him, and when I'm done here I'll probably join him in Seattle." She turned up the collar of her shirt and there was a tiny, shining button with Greek letters.

"Oh," mumbled Taylor. He felt angry, as if he had just learned after a long and trusting relationship that his love had cheated on him. The sense of betrayal twisted up his guts and, to lessen the pain, he got the idea to force himself to hate Gabriella. He purposely imagined her romping and panting with an anonymous man just to smash the few remaining fragments of his stupid fantasy. He looked over at her, half expecting her to be suppressing laughter. What he saw was worse. She wore an expression of tender pity, and he was immediately transformed into the scruffy, stray puppy again.

"Taylor, what gave you the idea that we were more than friends?" asked Gabriella.

"I wanted more. I wanted you," he explained, apologizing for even entertaining the idea.

"But we really don't have a lot in common," said Gabriella. "We come from different . . . backgrounds." Taylor heard this and was immediately sobered. Her blouse shimmered. A string of pearls nestled into the curve of her cleavage. He sat cross-legged on the floor, a boy before a woman.

"I'm sorry," he said, realizing how ridiculous he must look. "I think I misunderstood . . . a lot of things." He was still hurting and just wanted to get away. "I'll see you next week in class then?"

"See you there," smiled Gabriella, relieved that he was not going to make a scene. She patted him on the shoulder as he gathered his books and left.

Taylor walked quickly out of the school, wanting to put as much distance between himself and his humiliation as possible. As the numbness from his painful encounter with Gabriella began to wear off, a sense of rejection and self-loathing came over him. He hated himself for his own naiveté and began reviewing in his mind all the preposterous images he had fashioned of himself and Gabriella rolling in fields of flowers or kissing tenderly in a swinging hammock. Now the girl in his romantic fantasies leered at him and mocked him in his mind's eye. He saw her with the fraternity man, a hairy satyr, lewd and laughing. He tortured himself with the image. In it, Gabriella fawned over the rutting beast to intensify Taylor's sense of inadequacy. He wanted to retreat to Rockwater and never look another woman in the eyes again.

Evening had settled over the valley and only a few cars dotted the parking lot. As he neared his battered pick-up truck he noticed that someone was in the cab. It was Marla. She was sitting in the passenger side, arms folded, looking every bit the farmer's wife waiting patiently for her husband to finish up in the feed store.

"Hi Marla," said Taylor tentatively, not sure whether she was willing to speak to him again.

"Done with Gabriella?" she shot back, unable to check herself.

"Why is it your business?" snapped Taylor, still smarting.

"'Cause you're not one of them," asserted Marla, slamming her hand down on his dash to underscore her point." Her frustration surprised him. A single, silent tear rolled down her cheek. It was the first time Taylor had ever seen her cry.

"You're the second person to tell me that today," said Taylor.

Marla turned away so he could not see her tears. "Do you want a ride home?" he asked, climbing in.

"No. Take me anywhere else," she said resolutely. She smeared the tears away with her palms and looked at Taylor to see if he would reject her, but he smiled and placed a hand on her shoulder. He needed her at that moment, and it was obvious she needed him. Sensing her vulnerability, Taylor felt compelled to assume his old role of protector and friend—to joke around or be crude to make her smile again, but as he looked at her now the old playful jocularity was replaced by longing. She took Taylor's hand from her shoulder and pressed it in her own. Marla leaned across the seat and kissed Taylor hard on the mouth. She clasped her hands behind his head and drew him near. His first impulse was to pull away, feeling that a boundary of friendship was being violated which, once transgressed, could never be re-established. But there was an element of desperation in the embrace that Taylor recognized within himself and so he slowly surrendered to it. Her lips were warm and soft, and when she released him he was surprised to discover she did not taste of tobacco, but something that reminded him of sweet apples. His head was spinning with the strange twist of events and his heart raced.

"Where should we go?" he asked.

"To the bend," she said. "It will be quiet there this time of day."

They drove to a secluded turnout on the Yakima River. A little dirt road bent into the undergrowth and ran up onto an embankment overlooking a sweeping bend in the rocky stream. Taylor parked the truck in a sheltering stand of trees and shut off the engine. It was now almost dark. Gray, bare limbs rattled against the pale sky. They sat for a moment in the cab thinking about their kiss, the rushing water the only sound on the air. They knew without speaking why they had come to that secluded spot.

"Will you kiss me?" asked Marla.

"All right." He gave her a little peck on the lips and sat back, nervous. Marla moved in for another, unsatisfied and yearning for more. She held his head with both her hands and kissed until he reciprocated. When she felt sure she would not be rejected, she began to undress herself, discarding her clothes to the floor of the cab. Taylor began to pull off his T-shirt, removing it awkwardly over his head. In the falling darkness they could see each other's bodies in outline and Taylor could hear Marla drawing her breath quickly and anxiously. When naked, they embraced in a cramped tangle on the seat of the truck, exploring each other with shaking hands. Taylor pulled Marla's hair as he tried to position himself above her.

"Ouch!"

"Sorry. Do we need some . . . protection?" asked Taylor, his hands fumbling over her.

"I think we're OK," said Marla. "It's not the risky time." Taylor had a moment's hesitation when he thought about asking: What is the risky time? and, How could she be certain? But she was running her hands over his skin and he tingled with fire and so the question simply burned away and disappeared like a wisp of cinder, spinning away in the flame of their folly.

Ignoring the scratchy upholstery and the steering wheel, they gave themselves over to the blind heat that drove them, clutching at each other, pressing together with their hips. Taylor felt a rush that took his breath away and for a moment he lost himself in a seizure of pleasure. When he came back to himself, he collapsed on Marla's chest, lying still for minutes, not wanting to move. She was sweating a little and her bare chest rose and fell, lifting him and lowering him. He thought how strange it was that he had just lost his virginity to Marla since, if it were daylight, he would be too embarrassed to let her see him nude. But she was warm and she was running her fingers through his hair so he stayed there and pressed his face into her neck. He was grateful for the darkness; he could not imagine what her face looked like or what she what she was feeling at that moment. It was Marla who broke the long silence.

"Are you sorry?" she asked.

"No. Not at all," protested Taylor. A long pause. What does one say? thought Taylor. "That was very nice," he said. It sounded ridiculous, like something one might say after a clerk sacks your groceries. They both laughed.

"Very nice," said Marla, and pulled him close. Her voice had more tenderness in it than he had ever heard before; it was warm with love. Laying there next to her he tried to imagine that he loved her too. He *wanted* to love her because it would invest the moment with magic and meaning. He struggled to come up with the words that would express great affection, to sanctify the act, but no words would come. He searched and searched his heart for the intimacy which, intuitively, he sensed should be present after such physical closeness. A dim realization began to settle over him that what he had hoped would be a moment of love in his life had been a moment of profound dishonesty. He had allowed her to believe that he could love her because it gave him something he needed. Taylor could tell by Marla's soft caresses that she was smiling inside, relieved and elated. Her happiness made him want to suppress his own nagging conscience and join her in her contentment. Marla grew quiet for a moment and then, lifting Taylor's face to her own she kissed him softly and whispered tentatively, "I've always loved you."

Taylor felt a jolt of fear. He began to doubt whether he could trust any of his feelings anymore. Maybe if I just say the words the feeling will come, he thought to himself. He wanted so much to say what Marla wanted to hear, so he forced his tongue to move. Still, the words would not come and he heard himself saying "I've missed you." Marla stiffened involuntarily. There was a long silence and then she pushed him off of her.

"This was a bad idea," she said, reaching jerkily for her clothes. She dressed quickly and Taylor could feel her anger.

"Marla," pleaded Taylor, "I do care for you, too. I've never done this before and I—"

"You think I have?" she snapped back.

"I just didn't know what to expect. The feelings, I mean," blundered Taylor.

"You 'care' for me? What the hell does that mean? You have sex with me and you don't feel anything more for me than you would feel for a dog?" A sharp sob escaped her and she quickly choked it back and gained control. "I want to go home."

"Marla. Marla, just let me explain, I—"

"Now!"

Taylor dressed quickly outside of the cab. Then they drove in silence to Marla's house. Taylor dropped her off at the front gate and tried to kiss her goodnight, but she escaped his embrace and slammed his door. She walked quickly down the path towards her house. Next door stood her father's Church. The lights were on and through the windows Taylor could see the outline of Reverend Johnson near the altar. Taylor had known him for years and had always found him to be sternly pious. He noticed that Marla glanced furtively in his direction and then ducked into the shadows, entering the house through the side door. Taylor felt emotionally bruised. He wanted to console Marla and take her hurt away, but he could not undo what was done. There was nothing to do but drive away.

After that evening, Marla avoided Taylor for over two weeks. On the last day of April, Taylor met her on the bleachers for lunch. She had told him between classes that she wanted to talk to him. Taylor was anxious about their meeting. He wanted to apologize for the way he behaved that night. He had rehearsed what he wanted to say and he had decided that it would be best to be honest with her. He would tell her that he did care deeply for her, but as a friend. In light of what Gabriella had said to him, the irony of this struck him as almost more than coincidence. He missed their friendship, and he wanted to go back to the way things were before when they joked with one another and went to the rodeos together with the boys. Most of all he wanted her to know that if he was not able to love her the way she wanted, it was due to something in him, not because of any defect in her. He was disgusted with himself and unhappy in Yakima and the only way to change that, he would tell her, was to start over somewhere else.

Marla sat on the bleachers looking out over the field. She wore tan cowboy boots, denims, and a woman's western wear blouse. She held a book in her hands.

"Hi," smiled Taylor, sitting beside her. "Thanks for talking to me."

"Why haven't you come to me before now?" she asked accusingly.

"Marla, I tried to get near you every day but you avoid me," protested Taylor

"Well you could try harder. This hasn't been very easy for me."

"Me either," replied Taylor. "But I think we need to talk about it. To talk about us." Marla looked at him expectantly and Taylor tried to remember the words he rehearsed but couldn't remember a thing.

"Look, I've been thinking," he began. "I'm going to college next—"

"I'm late," interrupted Marla, knowing already that she didn't want to hear what he had to say.

"What do you mean?" asked Taylor.

"I'm late for my period. I looked in this book and it says that you can get pregnant any time of the month, not just the middle. I haven't got my period this month." Taylor stared at her, not comprehending. "Taylor, I think you got me pregnant."

For a moment Taylor was stunned and he struggled to deny the truth, protesting to the universe that this was not the way his life was supposed to be. Then slowly the hope drained out of him and he became overwhelmed with a sense of the futility of trying to assert his own will in a world that seemed so bent against him. It felt as if he were out of his body, looking back at himself and Marla sitting on the bleachers. Rural, teenage parents. He saw himself as a stock, tragi-comic character playing out his role in a very cliché—yet relentlessly human—drama. It was as if this scene *had* to happen, as if it was written this way to punish him for thinking he was going to define his own life when in fact some sadistic scriptwriter had predetermined that his fate was to suffer the consequences of his colossal ignorance. Marla had buried her face in her hands, consumed by her crisis.

"Have fun at college," she said bitterly.

"We could both go. You could . . . go with me," he stumbled lamely, trying desperately to cling to some remnant of his dream.

"I'm not going anywhere. I already know what my dad is going to say. I'll be having this baby."

As if compelled by the cruel set of circumstances which he himself had set in motion, Taylor said the words he thought he had to say at that moment of his life.

"Don't worry. I'm not going anywhere. I'll stay with you and the baby." With the words still hovering in the air, an image of a hermit crab lugging a shell flashed into his mind.

MAY

At 8:15 in the morning, May 18th, 1980, Taylor was seated cross-legged on a dusty flatbed trailer, bumping along through the pastures behind his father's rusty green John Deere tractor. The old two-cylinder relic chugged and sputtered down the dirt road towards the waving fields of alfalfa. An hour earlier, Jim had roused Taylor from his bed and, with the yawning eight-year old lending a hand, he made preparations for transporting a new twenty-five horse electric pump to the distant hay fields where he and his son would install this latest costly investment. With Taylor steadying the gleaming pump on the trailer, they drove out about a half mile through the sheep pastures and into the fenced-off alfalfa plots. The tractor came to a stop at the edge of a slow flowing irrigation ditch and father and son unloaded the tools and pump from the flatbed onto a wooden stand near the water that Jim had

constructed the day before. Jim hefted and sweated as he set the pump in place and began securing the electric engine to a sturdy pad using heavy bolts.

"Hand me that nine-sixteenths box end wrench, Taylor," grunted Jim like a surgeon calling orders to an assistant. He handed him a crescent wrench. "Not that one, knucklehead," Jim said, only half-irritated. "The one with the end that looks like a box—closed on all sides—with nine and sixteen written on the shaft."

Taylor rummaged and clanked through the tool box again, eager to please. "This one?" he said, laying the wrench out in both hands for his father's inspection.

"Yeah, that's the one, boy. We'll make a farmer of you yet."

Jim wrestled with and swore at the new implement for over an hour. Taylor watched and tried to be attentive, becoming distracted only a few times. About half way through the project he heard a distant *whumph!* , like some far off sonic boom , that sent little tremors through the ground. He scanned the sky but saw no jet.

"What was that noise? Was that the pump, Dad? Is it on?" he asked excitedly.

"Huh?" said Jim, sprawled out on his back, wrestling with a coupler. "The pump on? No. I didn't hear anything. Now pay attention and hand me that ratchet like I asked for a minute ago."

"What's a radjet?" said Taylor, looking for some airplane-like implement. Jim left his work for a moment and patiently showed his son ten or so of the most important and commonly used tools in the working man's repertoire. Taylor looked on a little confused at the worn and contorted mass of metal before him but tried to make sense of it all by creating images that might help him remember the names of each. "Look Dad," he said, confident he had discovered the mystery behind the name of the crow bar. "It has black, curved toes and a long, skinny, black crow leg!" The father looked at the tool and saw a certain pictorial logic to the way the boy saw things.

"Yeah, you could say that," he said.

Feeling encouraged, Taylor asked about the workings of the pump which interested him far more than the tools. To him, it looked like a heavy, gray bomb that had sprouted pipes out of its nose and tail. The intake pipe leading to the ditch went out over the water on a supporting stand and, at an elbow joint, turned and dropped down into the water. Around the mouth of the pipe, Jim had dredged out a wide, deep hole and had attached a wire mesh fitting to prevent the pump from being choked by floating watercress and algae mats. "Dad, what's that orange thing on the end of the pipe?" asked Taylor.

"That's a filter to keep the weeds out of the pipe. If the intake gets clogged up, the pump will keep running and running without being able to suck up the water," explained Jim, glad to see his boy take an interest.

"Oh," said Taylor, genuinely concerned. He went down to the ditch bank to get a better look at the killer weeds and, with a stick he found near the fence, he fished out bits of floating watercress, grass, and moss while his dad finished installing the pump.

When Jim's work was done he stepped back to survey the equipment and, brimming with pride, he laid his hand on his son's shoulder and ceremoniously explained that they were about to inaugurate a new era of efficiency and productivity for Rockwater Ranch.

"This baby is powerful enough to supply water to over 120 acres at 500 gallons per minute," said Jim, repeating the stats from the turbine's glossy brochure. "Come here, Taylor. You turn it on," he said, indicating two bright buttons, green and red, marked POWER ON and POWER OFF. Taylor stepped forward to a large silver panel on a power pole and reached up to put a finger on the one that looked like a green traffic light.

"This one?" he said, wide-eyed.

"Yeah. Turn it on!" said his father, almost more excited than the young boy. Taylor hit the switch and the impeller whirled into action. In a matter of seconds the pump found its prime and he could hear the water being slurped up out of the submerged water box in the ditch. Then, like a synchronized dance of a hundred little fountains, one sprinkler after another spurted to life until rows and rows of twitching nozzles were shooting water in silver arcs over a sea of green. Everywhere was the smell of rain mingled with dry earth.

"Wow!" exclaimed Taylor, looking up at his father.

"It's gonna be a good cutting this spring," yelled Jim over the hum of the churning pump. The father looked out at the sprinklers and envisioned stacks and stacks of sweet, dry hay he would be harvesting in a few weeks. Smiling to himself he thought, we'll have enough feed to carry us through to next spring and a surplus left over to sell on the market. The son looked over the same fields and saw music in motion—an orchestration of dense, undulating waves of alfalfa and silver bows of dancing water, conducted by his father, he believed, for the sheer sensory spectacle of it all.

After about a half hour of watching the sprinklers spray their showers, father and son loaded up the tools onto the trailer and, with a great belch of smoke from the John Deere, they were soon puttering back towards the barns. About a quarter mile from the house, they noticed an ominous black cloud creeping over the horizon. Jim pulled the accelerator lever down and the tractor picked up the pace.

"Looks like we're in for a big storm," he shouted back to Taylor over his shoulder. "I should've known! The minute I begin to irrigate, a huge rain comes down on us. We might as well leave the pump going for now 'cause the fields are pretty dry. A double drenching won't hurt nothin'. But we'd better make sure the tarps are over the hay to keep the bales dry."

In the direction of Chinook Pass to the west, a huge black bank of clouds was advancing quickly over the Cascade Mountains, blotting out the sun over the little upper valley towns of Naches and Tieton. Taylor watched the phenomenon with wonder, since it was darker and more dynamic than any storm clouds he had ever seen. Huge thunderheads towered over a dense wave of black that fanned out over the valley like liquid night tipped from an ink well. Already they could see great bolts of lightening and peels of distant thunder echoed off the canyon walls. Taylor noticed that even his father looked surprised and there was a sense of urgency in his eyes as he watched the clouds threaten to turn his dry bales into sponges of rotting, rank leaves. Before they could make the barns the boy heard the tap tap tap of rain striking the wooden bed of the trailer. Taylor held out his hand to catch a few cooling drops but felt, instead, faint tingling pricks from a fine shower of black grit and sand. Little flecks of dust collected quickly within the cup of his palm. Amazed, he looked into the sky and realized that a hail of gray ash was streaming down from the sky.

"The volcano!" Taylor yelled. "It's the volcano I heard about in school Dad! Mount Saint Helens blew up!" Suddenly comprehending, Taylor connected the images of exploding mountains and lava flows that Miss Kline had created in science class for the previous two weeks to this experience of dirt raining from the sky. Jim, grasping for a common sense explanation for the hail of ash, was slower in admitting what the boy's agile imagination had intuited. How could that be? he wondered. Mount Saint Helens is on the other side of the state! All the reports he heard on the news predicted doom for the coastal towns, not the central valleys. And yet here was a storm of debris falling on his face and hands, black sand filtering down the back of his collar.

"By God, I think you're right Taylor!" he conceded. With a rush of anxiety, the urgency of their situation gripped him. "Let's get that hay covered and the animals in now! Go tell your mother to close up all the windows!" Running at a full sprint, Taylor flew past the barns and churned up the hill to the house. All along the path he kept his eyes on the smoldering sky thinking great globs of fire might at any time drip through the suspended cinders and cascade down upon the valley below. He burst through the front door, breathless, wiping grit from his eyes.

"Mom! Mom! The volcano blew! The mountain blew up and it's raining dirt outside!" He found his mother already rushing around filling water jugs, gallon jars, empty buckets, and anything she could find at the kitchen sink.

"I know," she said matter-of-factly. The television was on in the dining room. While the reception fuzzed in and out, Taylor peered at the screen and made out a view from a helicopter showing an enormous plume of ash and smoke billowing out of a cavernous crater.

"Where's your father?" she asked without turning, wanting to take stock of all the family.

"He's covering the hay," Taylor replied, fixated on the destructive force of the mountain.

Sara came around the corner, her hands full of empty coffee cans, old milk containers, and an assortment of tiny plastic tea cups from her play set. "I got you more mama!" she said, dumping them on the kitchen counter.

"Go get more, and start filling the bathtub upstairs with cold water. Taylor, you go help your father and tell him that we won't have power for much longer. Can you remember that?"

"Yes." He started to run, but spun on his heels. "Oh, I almost forgot! Dad wants the windows closed." His message delivered, he was ready now for his mother's mission and felt that with this crisis he was suddenly elevated to a position of grave importance. He set into action to discharge his duties with the belief that his mother, sister and father desperately needed him, that the family's fate and well-being depended upon his faithful and effective execution of his responsibilities. He bolted back out the door and ran for the haystacks. His father intercepted him at the barns.

"Taylor! Over here! I've already covered the hay. We need to get the animals in. Go round up the sheep and herd them back to the main barn. I'll get the cattle." Taylor started for the pasture, but his Dad caught him by the arm. "Wear this across your mouth," he said, handing him a red bandanna. Jim folded the fabric into a triangle and tied it around his son's mouth like a stage coach bandit. "Lock the gate behind the sheep when you're done and meet me back at the house. Now run!" he said, sending Taylor off with a thrust on the shoulders.

The sky now was almost completely obscured by clouds. Taylor ran out to the pasture and scanned the field for herd. At this time in the morning, they could usually be found grazing in the far west corner of the fenced-in lot. If they were scattered, it would be a challenge to round them up and then move them to the barns in the fading light. Would the animals be confused and flighty in this bizarre storm? wondered Taylor. But half way out to the grazing area, he was met by the entire flock returning to the barn. As was their habit at the sign of a thundershower or with the onset of night, they were filing in—one after the other in a long line—towards the cover of the barns. Driven by some inbred knowledge of night and storm they trotted off to find the comfort of shelter, a primitive impulse designed for some entirely different purpose now serving—almost accidentally—to protect them against an even more primitive expression of geological impulses. Taylor skirted around the group to bring up the rear and found a few stragglers trailing behind the herd. He hollered and ran at them and soon they fell in line with the flock as they ran for cover. Turning towards the far corner of the pasture, he peered through the sleet of ash and saw indistinct humped forms that could be bushes or could be sheep. With visibility down to about one hundred feet, he could not be entirely sure that there were not more animals near the fence line without running out for a look. Not wanting to miss a single sheep, he jogged towards the fence through the thickening sleet of ash. As he neared the low lying mounds, he realized they were only ash-dusted bushes. He was now at the farthest corner of the pasture where the grazing area was separated from the alfalfa fields by a sturdy wire fence.

Confident that the entire flock was accounted for, he started to follow the herd in, but a faint sound made him stop in his tracks. On the other side of the fence, buried deep in the alfalfa and obscured from view by clouds of dust he heard the muffled pit-pit-pit-pit of the sprinkler lines. He thought of the new pump that he and his father had just installed and saw it plainly in his mind's eye, getting buried under layer after layer of clinging grit. Striving to comprehend the threats posed by this storm of ash, he imagined flurries of falling dirt pouring into the ditch, mixing with the slow flowing stream to form a dough-like sluice which in turn would clog the pump with a silty, sticky mud. He imagined the silver arcs of water gradually slumping down into a choked and blackened trickle, the pump groaning and churning until all the pipes were packed solid with wet ash. "If the intake gets clogged up, the pump will keep running and running without being able to suck up the water," he heard his father say. Thinking that the pump would strain itself to the burning point, he envisioned it over-heating and bursting into flames. He imagined the slouched form of his father hovering over the charred ruin, all his hopes and efforts defeated by the smothering blanket of fine, black grit.

Despite the fact that he could barely see fifty feet in front of himself now, he felt an urgent impulse to go shut off the new pump. He conceived of his errand in comic book proportions, seeing himself as his family's hero, determined to overcome a cataclysmic storm sent by some chaotic evil force bent on destroying Rockwater Ranch. To Taylor, he could almost believe that Hell had burst forth from the gaping volcanic hole in the earth's skin and had loosed itself upon the land, as day was consumed by night and where there should have been a cooling rain there was only a dusting of dried up, clotted cinders. He resolved to save the pump from destruction and bolstered his courage with the image of his smiling mother and approving father congratulating him for his cleverness and selflessness.

He took one last look at the retreating herd. The last straggling ewe dissolved into the flurry and all was still and powdery gray. A tremendous crack of lightening illuminated a bleary cloud and a rumbling wave of thunder sent tremors through the ground. Ignoring a knot of fear in his belly, Taylor turned his back to the house and barns and jogged down the fence line in the direction of the pump. He knew that even if the visibility got worse, he would still be able to find the pump by following the fence separating the pasture and alfalfa field until it intersected the irrigation ditch. From there, he reasoned, he could walk along the ditch and listen for the hum of the motor. Once he found the pump, all he would have to do is hit the red light to shut off the power. "Simple!" he thought.

The darkness descended quicker than he could have imagined. In a matter of minutes, the densest part of the ash plume had moved over the Yakima Valley and Rockwater was completely engulfed in darkness. Within minutes Taylor could barely make out the line of fence posts stretching out ahead of him. The ash was falling harder and faster now and he had to shield his eyes from the sharp flecks of grit. An electrical storm of immense intensity kicked up and successive rounds of thunder boomed over his head. He had to slow his jog to a quick walk and run a hand along the taut fence wire to maintain his bearings. The field he had traversed twice a day from spring to fall while moving sprinkler pipes now became alien and hostile. Grudging stones tripped up his feet and thick stalks of thistles leaned into his path and stabbed at him through his jeans. At a crook in the fence line an unseen log lay across his path and, peering hard into the blackness for traces of the receding fence posts, Taylor missed seeing the obstruction on the ground and struck his shin against the unyielding wood. The boy went down hard and lost his grip on the strand of fencing wire that had been his guide. For a moment he rolled in the dirty grass, rubbing his bruised leg and yelling out a jumble of forbidden words he had heard his dad string together on the occasion of a busted knuckle or cracked head. He definitely felt better for the cursing, although his leg still throbbed. Propping himself up on the log that had tripped him, fear began to set in. Disoriented, he did not know which direction he had come from and, with visibility down to a few feet, he had lost sight of the fence line. His bandanna was now damp from his breath and dirt had started to cake up the patch of cloth that hung over his mouth. Trying hard to fight back tears that started welling in his eyes, Taylor got to his feet and, with arms out like a blind man, groped for the fence. Striking nothing but air, he decided to stop and listen once again for the unmistakable pit-pit-pit of the sprinklers. Standing still in his tracks, he listened intently during an eerie pause in the crashing chorus of thunder. But all he could hear was his own heavy breathing and the steady, dry patter of thousands of grains of ash striking his head and shoulders.

A terrible realization came over him. If the sprinklers had stopped, that meant the pump might be clogged. He may be too late already. Borrowing from images he'd seen on cartoons, he envisioned a fire ball explosion rising from the bomb-like turbine. Spurred on at the prospect that a disaster was looming, he groped around frantically for the fence, walking in a widening circle around the log until, out of the film of dust, a blurry row of posts appeared before him. With one hand tracing a strand of wire, he started to jog now in the direction of the irrigation ditch, stumbling along on his bruised leg with a reinvigorated sense of purpose.

After a few hundred feet, the ground began to slope gently downwards and the grass began to get higher. When Taylor ran into a patch of cattails he knew that he was near the irrigation ditch. A few more steps confirmed this, as he felt the squish of the marshy bank and heard the trickle of water. Now only a few paces from the pump, he climbed the fence and walked along the ditch, knowing he would have to run into the stand that supported the intake pipe. Walking carefully along the edge of the ditch, he listened hard for the hum of the turbine, but picked up not a trace. In a few paces, to his relief, he found the stand. Laying his hand on the round, smooth pipe, he followed it back to the pump and found it was still warm, but for some reason it was not running. He put his nose to the vents and sniffed for signs of smoke but found none. "Just to make sure it is off, I'll push the red stop button," he thought to himself. Feeling his way on hands and knees to the sturdy pine pole, Taylor felt with his hands the large metal breaker box and found, on its face, the two buttons his father had shown him hours before. But the little lights that had burned so brightly in them before had gone cold. This puzzled Taylor and he slumped back to the ground searching for an explanation. He did not know if the pump had already broken down or if his father had stolen his opportunity to be a hero by shutting it down himself. It never occurred to the boy that the power had gone out in the immense electrical storm and that was why the pump now sat idle.

For a flicker of an instant, the sky flashed red with a lurid, dirty light, briefly illuminating the pump and the fields beyond. A few seconds later, a colossal thunder clap rolled through valley and rebounded off the hard basalt cliffs. As the boy sat there in total darkness, ash began to build up on his shoulders, legs, and arms in a fine, clinging layer. The apocalyptic storm became more and more intense, and every crack of lightening seemed to be getting closer and closer. Suddenly Taylor felt incredibly tiny and frail. Tears welled up in his eyes and he fought hard to hold back a convulsive sob that was building in his chest. His throat tightened with fear until he could bear it no longer and he released a long desperate wail. He cried long and hard until all the anxiety he had held so tightly was soaked up by the powdery darkness. When he heard his own moaning he grew ashamed. He scolded himself for betraying both the heroic role he had created for himself and for failing in his one errand.

By degrees, shame turned to anger and Taylor picked himself up and decided to get home so as to avoid the added embarrassment of getting lost and obligating everyone to come looking for him. As he was leaving, he spread his light jacket over the exposed pump to protect it from the sand. "I might as well do something since I came all the way out here," he decided. Up to this point, he had thought only of how to get out to the pump, but never considered how to get home. A half mile out now, he had no consistent track he could follow in this darkness to lead him back. He decided he would follow the irrigation ditch back the direction he had come until it turned a sharp right corner. He knew that at that point he would be near the corral and then getting home would be easy.

Wiping the muddy tears from the corners of his eyes, he gazed into the blackness and made out the faint outlines of the ditch. Walking slowly, sometimes feeling his way with his feet, he tried to keep close to the stream without stumbling in. Intermittent blasts of lightening served as a strobe light, illuminating, for an instant, patches of the path before him. In the blue glow cast by the electric arcs, nothing looked familiar. In one flash the ditch looked straight and narrow, but after walking a few paces in darkness another burst would reveal it to be wide and curving. After a while, he no longer felt certain where he was. Had he passed the bend in the ditch without knowing, or was it still ahead of him? he wondered. Soon, he couldn't even be sure which direction he was heading, and he had to stick his hand in the running water to determine if he was going upstream. After what seemed like a very long time, he even began to imagine that he had crossed over onto the Feldman's property. Fear again taking hold, he turned back in the other direction with the idea of retracing his steps. He was running now, trying desperately to regain his bearings by looking for anything familiar—a rock, a bush, a fencepost, anything that might place him on his own mental map. Suddenly, where he expected solid ground his feet struck at the air, and he found himself lurching forward—hands outstretched to break his fall—into a void. He was falling, falling, falling, into the darkened maw of a gaping grave. In his state of fright, time slowed and Taylor felt himself leave the ashen air and plunge headlong into the rank water of the unseen ditch. Sputtering, he righted himself, planted his feet into the mud, and clutched at the slippery bank. The startled boy hitched himself knee and elbow out of the canal and lay there on the grassy bank, his filthy clothes heavy with water. Grasping for an explanation, for an instant he believed that he had fallen through a hole in the surface of the world and had landed squarely in hell. Exhausted, disoriented, and confused, he remained there for a long time not wanting to move, for every gesture he made seemed to lead him farther and farther from home, away from the errand he had envisioned for himself.

For the first time in his brief life, Taylor considered his own death. He curled up tight in a ball and, with the persistent hail of ash falling on him in the darkness, it seemed to him that he was at the bottom of his own grave and unseen mourners were pouring handfuls of earth over his cold corpse. He was not crying now, but, resolved to whatever came next, he laid there listening to the dry rain and imagined what the world would be like without him. Would his family miss him? What would he miss? What games would he not play and what friends would he never make? Gradually, a sadness came over him as he considered all the trouble he would cause the family by leaving them and getting himself lost and buried. His mother and father would be upset at him, no doubt, for getting them worried. He would never accomplish in life what they had hoped for him. Who would work the farm if he was not there to carry on after his father? His sister would now be the oldest and would have to act like an eldest child. "It's not fair to dump all the responsibilities on her," he thought to himself. The image he had created for himself of the dutiful, heroic son now stood outside of himself and, looking down on the pathetic wet, muddy, huddled boy, jeered and mocked him. "Some son you turned out to be!" it laughed. "Some son you turned out to be."

After Jim had secured the cattle, he returned to the house to get news of the blast. His eyes were sore and weepy from the airborne grit and every crease of fabric on his clothing was loaded with talc-fine dust. He put his hand to his head and found his hair was matted into a stiff dry net. So as not to track piles of dirt into the house, Jim peeled off his over-shirt and jeans on the screened porch and entered the house in his socks and underwear. Inside, Beth and Sara were fixed on a fuzzy image of a smoking mountain on the news. Jim hovered behind his wife's chair and frowned at the television. J.P. had come up to the house from his trailer and Uncle Ed looked nervously from the darkened windows to his sister's anxious face.

"F.E.M.A. officials are asking people to stay indoors until the dangers posed by the falling ash can be assessed," said a serious reporter. "There is some speculation that silicone compounds in the ash may cause damage to the lungs if large quantities are inhaled. Motorists are asked to stay off the streets to avoid interfering with emergency workers. In addition, the fine dust is getting so thick that visibility is limited to a few feet. Due to the powerful electrical storms, some areas in Yakima County have already lost power and it is recommended that people stay indoors to avoid the risk of being struck by lightening."

"Where's Taylor?" asked Beth with alarm.

"He's just putting the sheep in. He'll be right up," responded Jim distractedly, focusing on the cataclysmic images on the television set.

"The mountain has blown clean in half," said Beth, shaking her head in disbelief. "Looks like the fallout all came east on the winds. We're better off than folks in the blast zone, though. Spirit Lake is all but gone. There doesn't seem to be any lava though. It's just all this ash and debris."

"How much ash though, that's the question." Jim tugged at his chin and looked out the window into the clouds pressing in upon the house.

"At this rate, this is going to knock down the June hay cutting," grumbled J.P. "And God knows it won't be good for the equipment. And if the pasture gets covered we'll have to feed hay just at a time when we're trying to stockpile it. Goddammit! this is going to be a pain in the ass."

As the pulverized mountain drizzled down upon his roof, Jim sat calculating his potential losses. Out the window, they could see wisps of fine dirt blow across the pane, little dirty flurries that gathered in the corners and settled on the sill. The darkness was complete, relieved only by the brilliant flashes of lightening. When the hail of ash started a few hours ago, it was only a few bolts and rumbling thunder. Now an electrical storm of enormous proportions was brewing. The charged particles suspended in the air created a vast sea of conductivity and the sky arced and crackled with electricity. They all sat mesmerized at the window. At times the sky would light up red with the fire of sheet lightening. Bolts flicked down to the ground from all corners of the darkened sky, sometimes three or more simultaneously. The resulting thunder was deafening, and the booming aftershocks rattled the panes so violently that Jim began strapping them with huge tape Xs to prevent them from shattering. Concerned now for his son, Jim pressed his face against the window and looked into the sky for any sign of sunlight. At that movement, a thick blue coil of light snaked down from the sky and snapped at the telephone pole in the yard, hitting the transformer and sending a shower of white sparks raining down on the ashy lawn. The strike cut the power to the whole farm and the lights and television went out. Sara screamed and scrambled over to hug her father's legs. They all sat there before the window for a moment, stunned at the ferocity of the strike.

"Where is Taylor?" Beth repeated, now with tension straining her voice. Her husband looked blankly out the window and scratched his head. "What were you thinking sending him out alone anyway? He's only eight years old for God's sake!" Sara saw the fear in her mother's face and started to cry. Stung by his wife's scolding, Jim made hasty preparations to go back out into the storm. Fumbling through the kitchen, he grabbed a flashlight from the coat closet and a bandanna for his face, he headed for the door.

"I'll go check on him. Knowing Taylor he stopped to pet the bummer lambs. I'm sure he's fine," said Jim unconvincingly.

He stepped out onto the porch, put his dusty clothing back on, and walked briskly towards the barns. The gritty airborne sand had an opaque quality which absorbed the beam from the flashlight much like dry clay drinks up water. Jim swung the stubby yellow cone of his light from left to right in the darkness, looking for the tire tracks that would guide him towards the corrals where he last saw Taylor. Every few feet he called out to his son. "Taaaayyllloooor!" He shot his voice forward into the dust-choked air, a feeble punch into a sack of sand, and listened for some response. Out of the clicking hail came one muffled peel after another of tumbling thunder so resounding that Jim ducked his head on reflex at every boom. Feeling the ground shake with each clap, he could almost believe that house-sized boulders would come rolling and rumbling down the gullies of the sky to crush him under their sonorous weight. "Oh Christ!," he thought to himself, shrinking from a boomer, "Taylor's gotta be scared shitless in this storm. What the hell was I doing sending him out to round up the sheep? He can't do the simplest thing without getting distracted, and that's on a good day. And now he's trying to—," another blast of thunder made him wince, "do a man's job in the middle of a goddam disaster!"

Jim checked the sheep corral and found, to his surprise, the animals were grouped in clusters around the hay troughs picking quietly over the remainders of the morning feeding. They kept under the cover of the roof to avoid the ash, waiting out the tempest if this were just any other passing spring storm. All the animals appeared to be in, but the gate stood wide open. At this, Jim's stomach tightened and his pulse jumped in his veins. "Taylor would've closed the gate after them if he had followed them in," thought the worried father. "He knows that much, I'm sure. Where the hell did the little shit go?!" A thin sweat started to bead on his forehead and upper lip. He called out for his son again, as loud as he could now, tension making his voice strain in his throat, squeaky and high. The sheep startled and trotted to the opposite side of the barn, watching the yelling man, ears erect, eyes unblinking and curious. "If he made it this far, it would have been an easy walk to the house," he reasoned. "But he didn't make it this far," Jim argued with himself, "or he would have closed the gate. If I don't find him . . ." For a brief second, Jim pictured the charred body of his son lying on a protruding hillock in the pasture, twisted and smoldering in the ash, thousands of volts of lightening having turned his beloved boy into a cinder. The distraught father violently thrust this image aside and started for the far side of the pasture at a run. "What else could he be doing? Besides rounding up the sheep there was nothing to do out here." He ran through his instructions to Taylor several times and reviewed the events of the morning. The memory of the eager boy handing him a wrench suddenly came to mind. "I wonder if he ? . . ." The idea of Taylor making a trip to the pump in the rain of ash leapt out at him as the obvious possibility. "Shit!" shouted Jim out loud. "Shit shit shit! Why didn't I think of that before?! The little shit has gone out to the pump for some goddamn reason. Why the hell can't he ever just do what I goddamn tell him? I'll give him something to think about when I find him!" resolved Jim, rehearsing a good scolding. But in his heart he clasped the image of the boy tightly to him.

It took Jim a half hour of running to cover the ground which he could walk in fifteen minutes on any other day. Like Taylor had done an hour before, he followed the fence until he reached the ditch. Here he turned and, calling his son's name along the way, he walked the bank in the direction of the pump. As he neared the spot, he could see the power pole outlined against the darkness and the support stand stretched out over the water. As he swung his beam towards the pump, his heart took a terrible shock as he saw what looked like the huddled body of his son lying on the concrete pad. Leaping forward, he bent over the rumpled form and discovered it was only his son's light jacket that had been draped over the turbine. A flicker of elation at finding his son's trail was quickly extinguished by a wave of fear that it would near impossible to follow Taylor since he had left this one discernible landmark in an otherwise featureless sea of grass to go wandering in the dark.

Horrible scenarios of his son electrocuted, suffocated, and drowned crowded into Jim's mind. For a long time, he sat and meditated on these terrors in a conscious act of self-flagellation. He punished himself with the idea that he was responsible for getting his son lost and for whatever danger might befall him. He sat under the steady sleet of cinders, paralyzed by guilt and self-loathing. He imagined what Beth would say when he returned without her son: he—staring at his feet, mumbling ridiculous apologies; she—torn open with his words, wracked with torment, despising him with every pulse of her heart until the day it stopped beating. Then, hating himself even more, he intensified his torment by considering what his little boy must think of him. He imagined Taylor running in an attack of panic in the darkness, calling out for his father, his voice going hoarse from shouting. He worried that the boy might run all the way to the river that bordered the alfalfa fields. His fears growing, he saw him plunge into the water, splash frantically for a moment, and then sink back down into the swirling eddies. Almost worse, he allowed himself to consider what it would be like if, after a day or two, the boy came straggling back to the house, dirty, naked, half starved and shivering. In his mind, he could see the expression on Taylor's face, the hollow eyes that reveal that all traces of trust have been extinguished.

What was most disturbing by far than this parade of horrors was the revelation that Jim had when, in an effort to predict where Taylor might be, he realized that he could not even guess at the intentions and motivations of the boy. In this moment when his son's life might depend on Jim putting himself in his place, he had no insight into the heart and mind of his own son. He had tried, over the years, to integrate the child into his world of plowing the earth, turning a wrench, and counting the hay bales. But always with Taylor his imagination was somewhere else. And it wasn't merely that he was a child with childish fancies; it was that he perceived the world and his place in it differently. Jim talked to his son about all the things he thought were so important—land, family, hard work—and, based on Taylor's responses, he suspected that the two were never really communicating.

A series of tremendous thunder claps brought Jim back from his morass of guilt and reminded him of the urgency of his task. With no sense of what Taylor was thinking or where he would have gone, Jim decided that, in proceeding from here on his search, any direction was as good as another. He looked at his watch. Five hours had passed since the storm had begun. Taylor had been lost for about four. He ran up and down the fields, trying to cover as much territory as he could, but he was never certain of where he was. As he ran along, he poked his beam into the murky air and called out to his son.

After several hours, Jim came within what he guessed was about a quarter mile of the corrals. He looked at his watch. It was now approaching midnight. Just when he was getting ready to rehearse his apology for Beth, he thought he heard a sound, faintly human, between intermittent waves of thunder. Stopping in his tracks he strained his ear. He heard nothing. Then he called out his son's name for the hundredth time, "Taaaaayyyllllooorrrr!!" He waited a moment, straining his ears. Then, out of the powdery air came a muffled but distinct sound of a human voice—his son's voice— that sounded like "heeerrrre!" Jim broke into a run in the direction of the sound, calling out along the way "Taylor! Taylor!" He could clearly hear his son's voice now, calling out of the night. His heart raced as he closed the distance between himself and Taylor. Together, directing each other through the dark and the dust, father and son found each other in the chaotic storm.

The boy was covered with dust and, as he ran erratically towards his father, it looked like a swirl of ash had coalesced out of the surrounding clouds to form a flitting dust devil. The beam of Jim's flashlight illuminated Taylor's grimy face for an instant and Jim saw the joyous relief in his eyes. The boy made a running leap into his father's arms and Jim dropped the beam and clutched at Taylor, holding him fast to his chest. Jim needed to feel the solidity of his son's body to convince himself he was not wrapping his arms around the shadow of his own desires. Taylor felt heavy and real in his arms and all of a sudden the man felt tears welling up in his eyes. He was not prepared for the intense elation that now swept over him at finding the boy unharmed. Embarrassed that Taylor might see him weeping, he choked back his emotion and set Taylor down on his feet. For a moment he held him at arm's length and looked him over. Taylor was wet, muddy, and shivering. Ash covered his hair and face, leaving only his eyes free of dirt, making him look like he had been smeared with mud in preparation for some primitive initiation rite. He was babbling excitedly, going on and on about "thunder like rocks in the sky" and "saving the pump" and "the sky raining dirt." Jim let the bright stream of chatter wash away the images of the little body charred by lightening. Gradually the residues of the visions that had tormented him began to fade and allowed himself to believe that Taylor was safe and that he would be there with him tomorrow and tomorrow after. He wanted to tell him how much he loved him and that he had had a glimpse of what life would be like without him and that it was terrible. He wanted to tell him how proud he was to have a son who would brave a horrendous storm for the sake of his family. He felt he had to express the intensity of his concern, to let him know how the whole family had been thrown into a panic when he did not return. Taking Taylor firmly by both shoulders he gave the boy a little shake to break the stream of chatter for a moment and get his attention:

"Where the hell have you been?!" was all that Jim could think to say. Taylor stopped talking and, stunned by the severity of his father's tone, answered blankly "Dad, that's what I was trying to tell you. I went out to the pump to . . . ."

"Don't you know you worried your mother sick? I've been out here looking for you for hours and hours! What were you thinking?" Taylor looked as if he did not comprehend the question at all. He stood before his father with his mouth agape, his arm outstretched pointing in the direction of the pump.

"No. I uhhh . . . I thought the pump would explode."

"Explode?! Where did you ever get that idea?"

"Well, you said . . ." Tears began to form in Taylor's eyes.

"Never mind what I said. Let's get home before your mother dies of worrying for you." Jim saw his son had started to cry. Taylor stood wiping his tears on the back of his wrist, averting his face from his father. Jim looked at the hurt child and felt a rising frustration at having failed to express to Taylor the depth of his caring. Awkwardly, he put his arm around the shaking boy and tousled his hair with his other hand. "You just got us worried, that's all. Are you OK? You look a little wet."

"I fell in the water," he said feebly motioning to the ditch.

"You look like a muddy muskrat!" said Jim, gruffly nudging Taylor in the shoulder with a closed fist.

"Yeah." Taylor looked himself over for the first time under the beam of the flashlight and laughed a little. "Yeah, . . . a muddy muskrat." He wiped his tears and father and son laughed a little bit together as the ash fell lightly on their shoulders.

"You ready to go?" asked Jim.

"Yes. I think I'm hungry."

Jim took Taylor's hand and, following the ditch, they found their way to the corral. From there they went past the barns and up to the house. When they arrived, Beth was sitting vigilantly at the kitchen window watching for their return. When she saw the beam of the light pushing through the cottony dust, she did not wait for them to get to the door but ran out into the yard to meet them. She swept Taylor up into her arms and hugged him tightly. She cried into his shoulder and he squirmed a little under the barrage of kisses. "I'm OK mom. Dad found me! I knew he would.

I was lost for a while, but I always knew I would get home somehow," said Taylor, trying to reassure his mother. "Don't worry anymore Mom, 'cause I'm OK. See?" Taylor stood in front of her holding his arms out and turning in a slow circle so she could inspect him. He was wet and filthy from head to toe and his jacket was missing. Beth burst into tears again. "Aww Mom," protested Taylor.

The day after, they were not sure what to expect. No one knew whether or not the sun would shine again for days or even weeks. But as morning came, a dirty brown light filtered down through the layers of dust to illuminate the land. Looking into the dense blanket of ash that hung over the valley, Taylor felt a little claustrophobic. After a breakfast of warm milk over cereal ("We have to use it up before it goes bad," said his mother), the whole family went out to survey the aftermath of the strangest storm they had ever experienced. Everywhere the ground was covered with a dense two-inch layer of gray ash. Taylor bent down and scooped up a pile and ran it through his fingers. The bottom layer was black , coarse and gritty. While the top layer was a talc-like powder, the deeper ranges were coarse and abrasive. The stuff clung to everything and as they walked little puffs of dust rose up from every footfall, curling up around the soles of their shoes. Looking around, everything appeared to be either gray or some variation on gray, making the boy wonder for a moment if he had lost his ability to see color.

The transformer, struck by lightening the night before, teetered atop the power pole like a charred marshmallow upon a stick. It would probably be weeks before they could get anybody out there to fix it. Taylor trailed behind his father and his mother took wide-eyed Sara in hand as the family made its way down to the barns. J.P. poked around in the barns and Ed tried to make snowballs with the ash. At first, it seemed that they had gotten through the storm relatively unscathed. The sheep were at the feeders or mingling in groups around the dusty yards. The A-frame roofs on the two larger barns had enabled the ash to slough off, creating little hillocks under the eaves. But the older tack shed and work shop had not fared as well. These sheds had flat roofs and the layers of ash had proved to be too heavy for the old rafters to support and they had caved in under the immense weight of the two-inch layer of ash. Taylor looked at the destruction and then over to his father, stepping back a little in anticipation of the string of curses which he expected would follow. But Jim stood before the wrecked buildings, hands on his hips, shaking his head. He said nothing. This silent brooding was unfamiliar and it unsettled the boy. He almost wished his father would rant and yell at his misfortune.

After the solemn group had surveyed the rest of the buildings and found them intact, Beth and Sara returned to the house to begin what was to be a year-long battle with wave after wave of creeping silt. Jim and Taylor got into the pick-up and drove out through the fields to check on the crops.

"If we can get water on those fields, we should be able to coax the grass through that ash," said Jim, trying to be encouraging as they drove along. "I'm more worried about the alfalfa. We were about to get a great early cutting off those fields. Now . . . who can say. "Jim trailed off, lost in thought. When they arrived at the edge of the field, Jim swung the truck around and drove parallel to the fence line, running slowly in first gear. With one hand on the wheel and his free arm jutting out the window, the man looked out over the fields with set jaw and furrowed brow. Unable to see what his father was seeing, Taylor scrambled to his knees on the passenger seat and looked out of the driver's side window towards the alfalfa. What used to be a luxurious green sea of tall shoots was now a flattened tangled mat of twisted stalks, looking more like battered heaps of kelp washed up on shore after a storm. They drove along in silence surveying acre after acre of flattened crops. That afternoon, instead of turning the animals out to pasture, they opened some of the remaining hay from the last season's harvest and spread it in the feeders.

Over the next few weeks, Jim was able to put a dollar figure on the extent of the damage. The tool shop and tack shed would have to be replaced at several thousand dollars apiece. But this was the least of their worries. The loss of the hay crop was a serious setback. For many nights after the disaster, Taylor could hear the strained voices of his mother and father filter through the walls of his room as he lay in bed. He did not understand all they said, but he knew they were talking about bills and loans and debts, and in the morning they would be serious and subdued over their coffee.

On the morning of what would have been the family's traditional Memorial Day fishing weekend at Beth's cousin's house on the shores of Lake Chelan, Jim sent Taylor out to do his chores as normal. When he had finished, Jim met his son in the hay barns and, sitting across from Taylor on the few remaining bales, he explained that there would be no trip this year.

"We're going to have to make some sacrifices for a while," he explained to Taylor. He looked around at the nearly empty barn and took in the open space with a broad sweep of his arm. "We'll have to fill all this with someone else's hay if we're going to be able to feed all that livestock. It doesn't look like we're going to get a cutting for a while and the grass is just barely poking through that goddamn ash now. If we don't give 'em something to eat they'll be chewing our clothes off!" He tried to force a laugh but it sounded hollow and only made Taylor more worried.

"I have some money I've been saving, Dad," said Taylor earnestly. "All that money I get from helping Mrs. Feldman with her yard is in my room. I saved it." He started to get excited as he imagined solutions to this latest crisis. "I have a lot now. I don't know how much, but I bet it would buy twenty bales, maybe a hundred!"

"Well, that would be a start, but you keep your money for now. I know where to go if I need it." He patted Taylor on the knee. "I don't want you to worry about what's going to happen with the farm, Taylor. Old Saint Helens really dumped on us, but its nothing we can't fix with a little hard work. We may not get to go to the movies as much as we used to and we'll all have to put off buying a few things we might like to get, but before you know it things will be back to normal around here."

"O.K., Dad." Taylor brightened up a little to see his father wasn't defeated.

Jim grew serious and looked into his son's face. "I know we've had a lot of extra hard work lately sweeping up the ash, moving the sprinklers, and carrying the hay out to the corrals. But everything we do here on this farm is for you. You know that don't you?" Taylor looked a little puzzled, so his father continued. "This farm was my father's place before it was mine, and when I'm good and tired of farming, it's going to be yours. Your mother and I have talked about this and we want you to have it. You work very hard with me every day out here and you're a natural with the animals. And, by God, you've got more than three generations of farmers in your blood!" Jim gave Taylor a light punch in the shoulder. "You're a Moreland all right!"

Taylor laughed and looked at his feet. He wasn't quite certain what his father was trying to say, but he knew it was an expression of trust and love. He wanted more than anything at that moment to be worthy of that confidence. "I'll try my best, Dad" he said, looking up with an expression of determination. "I'll help you and we'll have the farm forever," he said. He looked out over the fields and imagined himself as a farmer like his father, standing tall in a sea of green, surveying the land in all directions. It was an image created by his father—his own carefully cultivated dream—handed down now to his son.

SUMMER

JUNE

In spring, when the apple trees are at full blossom, the orchards are a profusion of pink and white crepe petals and the air is honeyed with perfume. Fleshy, nodding pistils thrust their sticky heads into the sun, begging for a caress from a passing bee and, once satisfied with an orange dusting of pollen, curl up to contain the planted seed. With time, under June's summer beams, the seeds swell into tight green orbs, evidence of the consummation of spring's concupiscent desires. So too the passing of season to season inevitably brings to light all our sins and indiscretions, compelling us to recognize our misdeeds and make preparations for their maturity.

By the first week of June, 1989, Marla was still stick thin, but to Taylor it appeared that she had developed the tiniest bulge below her navel. Perhaps it was because he was expecting that his friends would discover their secret, but no one else seemed to notice. Most of the other students were pre-occupied with graduating. During the final days of school, the seniors were excused from classes to participate in commencement rehearsals. Between being measured for gowns and marching down the improvised aisle taped out on the gymnasium floor, there was a lot of time for chatting and milling around. But Taylor often found himself alone. After making a fool of himself with Gabriella, he was too embarrassed to be in her presence. In the nostalgia of those waning days of high school, he found himself longing to re-establish his old childhood ties. He sought out his old friends, but his earlier attempts to escape his farmboy identity had strained the bonds between them and it seemed that they had made a pact to avoid him.

Ever since the day that Taylor had broken Bill's nose, his one-time friend had maintained a hostile distance. They barely spoke afterwards, and Taylor wondered if Bill had suspected that he and Marla had shared a secret intimacy. He had watched them closely the days immediately after they had slept together, scrutinizing Taylor suspiciously when Marla lost her tough composure in his presence. In the final week of school, Taylor made one last attempt to mend the friendship by assuring Bill that he was no longer intending to go to college. He claimed it was because he did not have the money. As a goodwill gesture, Taylor told Bill that he hoped they could try to return things to the way they had been.

"We can't be friends again," said Bill sullenly.

"Are you still pissed off about your damn nose?" cried Taylor, unable to contain his frustration. "I said I was sorry and I'm not going to college. What more do you want?"

"I want you to leave me and Marla alone."

"I don't know if I can do that. Marla may want me around," said Taylor ambiguously.

"Is something going on between you two?" asked Bill, sizing him up like a protective brother. Taylor was caught off guard.

"That's not really your business," said Taylor, trying to sound offended.

"It is, since Marla is my friend and you seem to make her

upset every time you're around her. It didn't used to be that way. Everything was going along fine between all of us until you had to go change things with your big plans and your new girlfriend. Why couldn't you just have left things the same?" Taylor realized that Bill wanted nothing less than a return to the comfort and predictability of his boyhood, but the eggshell innocence that had somehow managed to hold the weighty world at bay throughout their youth had been fractured. In striving towards adulthood, Taylor had inadvertently jostled opened a crack, allowing a little glimmer of sin to shine through—and none of them now could shut their eyes to it. For that, he could not make amends.

Marla made little effort to try to bring Taylor back into the good graces of the group. Her pride was still wounded from a sense that she had been rejected, and, contrary to what Taylor had imagined, his decision to stay in Yakima had only made her more irritable and indignant. "Don't feel like you have to suffer because of me," she would say to Taylor. He tried to show her tenderness, but she knew he was motivated by obligation and not love, and this only drove her further away from him. Her obstinacy surprised him. He had always known her to be head-strong and stubborn, but he assumed that in a moment of crisis she would accept what comfort and assistance he could lend her. But she refused to let him take satisfaction in the sacrifices he was making, and Taylor started to think that she wanted to intensify his suffering.

Giving up on going to college almost crushed him. At times he felt as if he would suffocate. His parents were puzzled at his sudden change of plans, but they accepted his explanation that he wanted to stay near his "new girlfriend" as typical, intemperate teen behavior. He dreaded telling them the full truth. His one consolation was that if he were to claim responsibility for his sins, it would be a demonstration of his moral character to his family and friends, possibly mitigating their inevitable disappointment. But now, effectively shut out of Marla's life, Taylor could not even make amends for his mistakes, and he was left with only failures. Two days before graduation, he managed to find a moment of privacy with her near their lockers.

"We need to talk," he pleaded.

"What about?"

"We need to figure out what we're going to do about this baby," said Taylor.

"What do you mean?" asked Marla.

"Have you told your father yet?" he asked. Marla looked away. "I think we need to start telling people. You're starting to show."

"Well, have you told anyone?" she retorted. Taylor shook his head. "Why not? Are you embarrassed to admit you slept with me? Or is it that you were hoping that I would get an abortion and then you wouldn't have to deal with it?" She started to walk away but he caught her by the arm and turned her to face him. Her cheeks were flushed with anger but her eyes betrayed a longing to be comforted. Taylor pulled her into his arms and she grudgingly submitted. They held each other for the first time since the night they had lain side by side, half-dressed and awkward, on the seat of his truck. He could feel her releasing her pent up anguish in a long sigh. When he looked at her again a spark of hope had returned to her eyes. She stepped away from the influence of his touch to regain her composure before posing the question that had troubled her for the past two months.

"I know you feel that you have to stay for the baby. But do you want to be with me? Can we be together and be happy?" she asked.

"Well the baby's going to need us both and—"

"I didn't ask about the baby," she cut in. "I was asking about me." Taylor looked at her. He thought about a summer's day, years earlier, when they had whittled fishing poles from cottonwood switches and caught minnows from the farm pond. Things had been so easy then.

"I could grow to love you," he said. It was an honest appraisal of his heart. "You have been a part of my life for as long as I can remember, and I don't want to lose that. Everything just happened so fast. I need some time to make the transition from being friends to being . . . something much more." He tried to embrace her again but she backed away, arms folded, fighting back the tears. It was less than she had wanted to hear and it felt like another rejection.

"And if your feelings for me don't change?" she asked.

"They're already changing," he protested. "Once we have a child together everything will be different. I'll take care of you both. I'll have to get a job working at the warehouse or something. And we can fix up the old ranch hand's cabin on the farm and live near my family." As he spoke he worked hard to plant the image of this life in his mind in order to banish forever the last remnants of his desires to leave Rockwater. The result was that the future he had outlined for them sounded more like a regime for penance than the reassuring optimism he had hoped to convey. Marla stood apart from him, considering all he had said. Taylor reached out to her slowly. "Can I touch you?" he asked, gesturing to her stomach. Marla said nothing. He laid a hand gently below her navel. She let it rest there for a moment and then, shuddering involuntarily against a premonition of her own heartache, pushed his hand aside.

"Don't," she said, drawing away. "Please don't."

"But Marla," Taylor protested, "we need to start pulling together."

"Look, you're not the only one with doubts," she said. "I'm not sure I want the little house and the baby with you."

"I didn't say I had doubts. That's what I'm trying to tell you! I think we can make it, but—"

"Well I'm not so sure," replied Marla. She turned her back on him and gathered a few things from her locker. When she turned around, she had hardened herself again and had taken up her old obstinate posture. "I need some time to think about what *I* want out of life. So now it's your turn to wait and wonder for a while." Taylor tried to put a hand on her shoulder but she ducked under his arm and walked quickly back in the direction of the gym.

That was to be the last time he would speak to her for ten years. She missed the remaining graduation practices and sent word in that she was "feeling feverish." On graduation night, she was to be Taylor's partner walking down the aisle but she never showed up. He was paired with Cort at the last minute and the ceremony passed in a blur as he scanned the crowd for any signs of her or her father. For days afterwards, Taylor tried to call but nobody answered. As a last option he drove to her house to see if she was hiding from him there. When he arrived, he found the house darkened and the curtains drawn. Next door, her father's church was open and he could see him moving around inside. Desperate for news of Marla, Taylor went to talk to him.

When Taylor entered the church, Marla's father was at the altar preparing for an evening service. Mr. Johnson was wearing dark slacks and a black shirt, and his hair was sandy brown like his daughter's. He heard Taylor enter and descended slowly to greet him in the center aisle. He was thin-lipped and serious, and Taylor avoided the stare of his pale blue eyes. He said nothing but gestured to Taylor to sit in the front row. The minister remained standing in front of Taylor as if taking a confession, fingers woven together above his belt buckle.

"You've come to ask about Marla?" he guessed.

"Is she all right?" asked Taylor nervously. "We're all worried about her . . . illness."

"Is that what you're calling it?" asked Mr. Johnson, hard and sarcastic.

"She told you?"

"Yes." He stared at Taylor as if he wanted to burn him into nothingness with the beam of his gaze. Taylor shifted uncomfortably, wishing he could oblige the minister and disappear like a wisp of smoke into the air.

"I stopped by to bring her this stuff from graduation." He produced a program and a souvenir cap and tassel. Marla's father reached out and took the proffered memorabilia and stared at them for a while without saying a word. An immense sense of loss and regret seemed to wash over the man, and Taylor immediately wished he hadn't given them to him. The minister looked up from his ruminations, so lost in his own agony that he registered surprise to still see him standing there.

"Marla has terminated the pregnancy," he said with great effort. "I think you should know. We agonized over the decision, but we concluded it was best. For everyone." His cheeks had begun to flame red as he struggled to contain a violent impulse to lash out at the young man before him with all the pent up bitterness and bile of one who's faith has just been obliterated. "And I hope for her sake you will have no more contact with her and you will say nothing more about this for as long as you live." Taylor gave no answer. The threatening demands fueled what little spark of defiance remained in him.

"I came here tonight to talk to her personally," he said. "To find out what she wants."

"What difference does it make now?" He was right of course. Taylor rephrased his objection.

"You never asked me," he said with an edge of accusation.

"What would you have done?" demanded the father.

"I don't know. But I would have liked to have had the chance to decide."

"Having a baby at eighteen was out of the question. It would have ruined her reputation and the reputation of this family. It would have brought shame to this congregation of which she is a part." To hear Mr. Johnson justify the abortion for the sake of saving face came as a great surprise, since neither he nor Marla had even considered the possibility that this professed man of God would permit an abortion, let alone endorse one with such patently self-serving reasons.

Taylor sat contemplating this revelation. In a way the abortion had liberated him and yet, ironically, he felt that he would forever be a prisoner of guilt. Every gesture he had made lately to define himself had been motivated by the wrong inspiration and, in the end, had engendered nothing but grief. He suspected Marla's father had also been acting under misguided impulses but had refused to admit it. For the first time in months, Taylor stopped thinking of his own losses to consider Marla's. To satisfy his conscience, he had to know that terminating the pregnancy was Marla's wish and not strictly her father's.

"Can I talk to Marla?" he asked.

"No. In fact I would have delivered this note to you if you had not shown up today." He produced a letter from his shirt pocket. "Quite frankly, I had figured you would have been here sooner than this," he scolded, trying to put Taylor back on the defensive.

He handed the note to the young man. It was written in Marla's choppy hand and contained only three sentences:

Dear Taylor:

You said that you would give up college for me, but I refuse to be anyone's charity case. We would just end up hating each other. And so I know it is best for me not to have this baby.

Marla

Taylor read it over and over, trying to imagine that she had been forced to write it against her will and that she was waiting for Taylor to come take her away. It wasn't so much because he loved her or wanted the child, but because he wanted a chance to try to set things right, to propel himself into adulthood by taking responsibility for something larger than his own destiny. But he heard her defiant voice in the letter, pushing him away in an effort to protect her heart. She would rather give up on false hopes and bear the disappointment than to cling to her romantic illusions. In this regard she was wiser than Taylor, and he respected her for that. He folded the letter and placed it in his pocket as the solemn minister glared on like an unwilling accomplice to a crime. For Marla's sake, not his own, Taylor wanted to let the man know that he was not a terrible person, that his daughter had been justified in some small way in giving her heart to him.

"When we were about ten years old," he began, "Marla and I used to ride bikes together. She loved to tie toy cars to a string and drag them along behind, peddling as fast as she could until either the car wrecked or she did. Sometimes she would laugh so hard she would cry. She was my friend." By Mr. Johnson's lack of recognition, it was obvious that he did not know Marla as Taylor did. For an instant the man seemed to study Taylor's face as if, through her childhood friend, he might recover truths about his young daughter that he had lost sight of or had neglected. "We grew up together," explained Taylor. "I love her for that." His eyes met the minister's, steady and clear. "Tell her that for me, please." Marla's father nodded. Taylor walked down the aisle and stepped into the glaring June sunlight.

By the summer of 1999, Taylor and Quinn were living together in Cambridge in a tidy two-bedroom flat with hardwood floors. They were both busy with academics and work, but sharing an apartment afforded them much more time together. In the little, comfortable routines of day to day living, each discovered in the other a host of endearing qualities. And yet, while his happiness with Quinn increased daily, he couldn't help feeling like an impostor at school. One June evening, Taylor returned home from a long day at the Boston College of Fine Arts library, hoping to unburden himself to her. But when he found a letter from his mother among a stack of advertisements and bills, he was filled with a sense of dull foreboding. Beth was not a letter writer, so it had to be news of some significance. He sat down to read it, unfolding it slowly as if to let any bad news dissipate. But even after preparing himself, his heart sunk as he read the curtly worded announcement of Sara's engagement.

Dear Taylor:

Your sister is getting married in June. I think it would be important for you to be there. I know you don't have a lot of money, but I hope you won't let that prevent you from participating in such a special event for the family. It would mean a lot to Sara to see you. The rehearsal dinner is set for June 25 and the following day is the wedding. Bring some nice clothes.

Love, Mom

To his dismay, his old friend and rival, Bill Hennis, had been seeing Sara for some time, and Taylor suspected that he was working himself up to propose. But he always hoped that his sister would see the cage that she was walking into and turn on her heels and flee before the door could shut behind her. Now it seemed too late and she was a willing prisoner within the narrow confines of his world.

The last time Taylor had seen Wild Bill was the summer before he left the farm to go to graduate school. Bill had come to the house to pick up Sara for their first date. She was taking classes at the local community college and he became reacquainted with her through a mutual friend. They had deliberately neglected to tell Taylor that they were going out to avoid an awkward scene. So when Bill rolled down the lane to the ranch in his dilapidated truck, Taylor thought he had come to ask for work in the orchards. He watched in bewilderment from the front porch as Sara ran out to meet him in a pretty sun dress, her hair in curls. She hopped in the cab and Bill pulled away without acknowledging Taylor's presence.

In the years after high school, Bill had gone to work for Stellerman's Fruit Company, running the forklift in the warehouse. He worked hard and showed little ambition, qualities that made for a stable employee. He drank with the foremen after work and went fishing with the owner's sons. Through his constant contact with farmers and fieldmen, Bill became pretty well versed in orcharding. He impressed Jim with his knowledge of apple production and—aside from Bill confiding in Sara—neither he nor Taylor ever spoke about their falling out to the parents. They assumed the two were still on good terms. Jim liked the young man's commitment to farming and Beth found him simple and well-mannered.

While Taylor was away at college, Sara had grown into a willowy, soft-spoken young woman. In her early adolescence she had been practical like her mother and single-minded like her father. But as she moved into her teen years, she had lost the ease and confidence of childhood as she became self-conscious about her thin arms and lanky gait. Even after she grew into her body and became slender and athletic, she still felt awkward and gangly. Her goal after high school was to attend the University of Washington. She thought that on her own she might reclaim the self-assurance which had been slowly eroded by the oppressive and numbing expectations which assail a young girl during puberty. But the University of Washington was a huge and often impersonal institution, and she became even more lost and anonymous than she had been in high school. Her freshman year was extremely lonely and while her roommate and the other girls in her dorm were flitting between fraternity parties, she would stay in with her television, thinking of home. When she saw Bill at the farm during her first summer break, she was flattered that he remembered her and his chivalric attentiveness made her feel lovely and charming. Since her high school years had passed in relative obscurity, the conquest of a well-liked local boy gave her the sense that she had redeemed herself in the eyes of a community which, in her mind, had dismissed her long ago as a slight and inconsequential girl.

After the middle of her second year in Seattle, she did not like being far from Bill and dropped out of the University to enroll at Yakima Valley Community College. Beth and Jim didn't argue with her very strenuously because they liked having their youngest back in the nest and Y.V.C.C. was half the cost of the University. She lived at home and Bill came to visit frequently. At the outset, Bill had reservations about getting involved with Sara because he and Taylor had never been reconciled, but her brother came home so rarely now that it seemed like a minor inconvenience. As the relationship developed, he found that Sara's approval validated his life of farm work—a life that Taylor had very explicitly rejected. Both he and Sara gravitated towards the familiar and took pleasure in a life of few surprises. He had his fishing with the boys at the warehouse and she had her embroidery.

With the wedding fast approaching, Taylor wanted to find a way to sound his sister's heart and—if he discovered that her love was deep—to warn her that she would draw little satisfaction from such a shallow man. But he had been out of regular contact with

her so long that he believed he could not assume the role of her
guardian.

When Quinn came home that evening, she found him lost in
thought with the letter wrinkled up in his hand.

"Why so pensive?" she asked

"Looks like I'm inheriting a brother," he replied absently.

"Your parents adopting?" she joked.

"No. Sara's getting married to . . . an acquaintance of mine. I
need to go back to Yakima." It had been a year since his last visit to
his family. In that time he had let communication lapse between
them and the idea of returning now to see Bill gloating at him
across the family dinner table made him feel even more
disconnected. He imagined himself as an outsider in his own home
and felt he needed some support. "Will you come with me?" he
asked Quinn. She knew that relations with his family were strained,
but she had never known exactly why. She was curious to meet his
parents and a visit would help her understand why he had put
such a distance between them.

"I'll need to take time off my summer job," she said. "But I
would love to meet everyone."

"Are you sure you're ready? My family is not like your family."

"How so?" she asked, now wondering what he thought of her
family.

"Your mother makes her living by wielding a pen; mine wears
her hands to blisters on the handle of a hoe. When your father
talks about sheep he's concerned with saving the human soul; when
mine talks about our family's salvation he's always referring to the
spring market for sheep. And my grandfather!" Taylor laughed a
little thinking of the knot-hard old man. "He could curl your
father's hair with the curses he strings together. He takes a perverse
pride in using the Lord's name in vain."

"Well my family is sometimes painfully subdued and cerebral.
A week with yours will be a nice change," she assured him.

"O.K.," smiled Taylor. He was bolstered by the thought that

she would see where he had come from and could better understand the forces that laid claim to him. He reached for the phone book to make flight reservations. "When you arrive, be ready for the inspection from my mother. You will be the first girlfriend I've ever introduced to my family."

"You know, I don't think you've ever mentioned your old flames," mused Quinn.

"There haven't been many. Not much to tell." He flipped through the directory with exaggerated concentration.

"No trail of broken hearts?" she teased.

"I'd rather not say." It sounded defensive, so he tried to make light of it. "You can't compel the accused to give evidence against himself, now, can you?" Quinn was surprised that the question had made him so uncomfortable.

"Taylor, have you ever loved someone more than me?" she asked.

"No," he replied, looking up from his book with concern. "Don't have any doubts about that, Quinn. Improbable as it sounds, you are truly the first great love of my life." She kissed him, secure in the knowledge that he loved her, but she sensed that he was shouldering some heavy burden.

Taylor decided to confide in her the feelings he had been repressing since he had discovered Church's paintings, rather than leave her with the impression that he was dissatisfied with her. "I'm not who I want to be, but I believe I am about to begin that transformation. In the meantime, don't give up on me," he pleaded, taking her hands between his own. "I don't know that I belong in the graduate program anymore, and I'm certain I would make a lousy farmer. That leaves me with nowhere to turn at the moment, except to you." He looked into her eyes for signs that she was willing to wait for him to find some sense of direction.

"Just don't stop living the rest of your life because a few personal goals remain unfinished," she advised him. She said it with a smile, but in her voice was a warning that told him that he could not expect her to stand by indefinitely while he wrestled with the riddle of his existence.

"Something is happening to me." He struggled to explain, not certain himself what he was feeling. "I may need to take some time off from school for a while."

"Why?" asked Quinn, troubled by the announcement.

"I'm no longer certain that I enjoy art. And I don't know how I ever got to the point that I thought I could make it my life's work. My parents will be sure to tell me that I would be better off doing something more productive with my life. They may be right."

It pained Quinn that Taylor lacked the confidence to follow his heart. She had witnessed his enormous capacity for love and creativity and only wanted him to be happy with himself and with her. From her perspective, his sense of obligation to his family was largely self-imposed. She believed that if she could stand before his parents and testify to his artistic abilities and promise as a scholar, she could compel them to support his studies and dispel his concerns that they wanted him to return home. Once liberated from his sense of duty to the farm, she reasoned, he would be free to pursue his academic work with renewed vigor.

"If it's worth anything, I believe you can complete the degree and have the career in art too," encouraged Quinn. Through her consoling, Taylor could feel her gently steering him back into his graduate program. He could see that she was concerned that he might throw away a great opportunity. He feared that in her eyes, dropping out near the final stages would constitute a failure. And he could not bear the idea of her losing faith in him.

"Yes, I think you're right," he lied. "After the trip home, I'll be ready for a new beginning at school."

Taylor and Quinn got a flight to Yakima on the 25th of June, arriving in the afternoon before the rehearsal dinner. Taylor wasn't sure how his family would take to his Ivy League theologian, but she had a winning smile and an appetite for conversation that would get her through the initial suspicion of strangers she would encounter from his family. He just hoped that she didn't act too self-assured around them, since confidence was usually interpreted as arrogance in his family.

His mother, in particular, could be defensive around educated women. But she had reason to be a little resentful. She had experienced hardships and uncertainties from a very early age and had been denied the advantages freely granted to women of her son's generation. For most of her life, she had sacrificed her own aspirations to help care for her family. She had known little of her father who had disappeared quietly in the night shortly after she had turned seven. In response to this betrayal, her mother, Abigail Hargrove, made a steady retreat from the onslaught of little abuses which one suffers over a lifetime. She was a fragile woman who took her husband's absence as a mark of shame, as if it were her fault somehow that she could not keep him at home. The shock of his leaving left her faith in humanity a little damaged, and she never fully recovered. On the rare occasions that she would speak to her children of their missing father, she would say caustically, "He could not have loved you. A good father could hardly wish suffering and loneliness upon his loved ones." This did not prevent two of Beth's siblings from drifting out of her life. Her sister, Jane, married young and moved away to Florida. Rudy, the youngest son, floundered through life without a father to guide him and landed in jail for stealing cars. Eventually he won parole and was never heard from again. As a result of the flight of one member of the family after another, the simple country house on the outskirts of Spokane, Washington never felt like a home to Beth.

It was her affection for Ed, Jr. that kept Beth around the Hargrove household until she was almost twenty years old. Abigail's third child, Ed was severely retarded and needed constant assistance with the simplest of everyday routines. Beth washed him, fed him, and kept him entertained with little games, for her mother was incapable of nurturing anything but her own bitterness. It was this constant care of the retarded boy that made Beth resent her absent father. While she couldn't remember him and thus didn't feel an emotional loss, she could see that Ed could have benefited from the stability of a two-parent household. At one point, her mother decided to put him in a group home in Seattle, but Beth fought the move with a perseverance that wore out Abigail's resolve. To Beth, the idea of placing him in the hands of strangers felt like another act of abandonment and she could not bring herself to do it. She knew that she had won a victory for Ed by keeping him at home, but from that moment on, she realized that she had committed herself to caring for her needy brother for a lifetime. It was a duty she embraced with fierce determination. And despite the many sacrifices she made growing up, she always remained optimistic. Sharp-witted and tough, she carried the Moreland family through some of their most trying of times.

When Jim first met Beth, she was working at a grain elevator in the Palouse. He had dreams of getting out from under the influence of his father and had taken to doing seasonal work to earn his own money. Jim got his father's grudging permission to hire himself out to a large wheat farm near Spokane, upon the condition that he return to Rockwater for the apple harvest. For several months he helped maintain the equipment and, when the grain was ripe, he ran a combine over the gently rolling fields. He earned enough to afford a simple trailer outside of Spokane and a night out for pool and beer once every other weekend. Almost every day during harvest time, Jim would deliver a load to the elevator where Beth worked. He noticed her pretty features and confident smile and began to find any number of pretenses for stopping in at the scale office for a chat. Jim was tan, square-shouldered and modest, and Beth liked his steady reliability. Soon they were meeting for drinks and conversation at the local tavern.

Their courtship was accelerated by their mutual loneliness. For Jim, the brutal solitude of nights spent in front of the television set became too much to bear, and he began staying over at Beth's small apartment. Later they began sleeping together, more out of comfort than passion. Jim liked that she was sensitive and level-headed, and Beth found Jim to be honest and dependable. In this way, each one filled a need for the other that their respective parents had neglected. When Beth discovered that she was pregnant, she suggested to Jim that they get married. She had seen the consequences of an absent father and was determined that the hardships she and her siblings experienced would not be revisited upon her own children. He eagerly accepted her proposal, for her smallest gestures of tenderness—a hand laid lightly on his forearm, a kiss on the cheek, her breath in his ear—were completely novel to him and felt like water to his parched soul. They were married quietly in a courthouse and Jim placated his father with assurances that they would return to the farm as soon as they had stockpiled a small savings for the child.

They would have gone on living in the undulating, treeless plains of the Palouse indefinitely, but towards the end of 1971 J.P. broke his back. When Ida left him, Jim returned with Beth and their infant son to Rockwater to take over full-time care and management of the farm. He assumed the role with some reluctance, but his sense of duty to his father and his determination to keep the land in the family superseded his own desires for independence. They moved into the family house and settled into J.P. and Ida's old room. After J.P.'s wife left him, he closed the door and didn't enter again for years. Much to Jim and Beth's relief, J.P. preferred moving to a converted tenement house on the edge of the property, as he put it, "to avoid constantly tripping over each other." Not long after their arrival, Abigail called Beth to complain about how much more difficult it was to take care of Ed now she was getting up in years. Taking the hint, Beth had him join her on the farm. The move was not accomplished without grumbling resistance from J.P., but the devoted sister was unswerving in her determination. As the years passed, Beth and Jim fell into an easy partnership where she nurtured, he provided, and that security was enough to sustain their mutual affection.

From her earliest days at Rockwater, Beth felt like an intruder around J.P. and he barely acknowledged his daughter-in-law's existence. One day when the old John Deere tractor failed to start, she saw him beat his cane to splinters over the hood until he was red and breathless. From that moment on she worked carefully and persistently to mitigate the more corrosive elements of his influence over her husband and children. As a result, Beth and J.P.

lived in silent struggle where he loudly asserted his authority and she steadfastly subverted it.

As Taylor and Quinn turned down the lane at Rockwater Ranch in a rented car, the memories pressed in upon the young man and he worked hard to draw his breath. Looking at the orchards and pastures, his impressions were layered with the accumulated residues of former days. As he took in the subtle changes, he was simultaneously experiencing the terror of a young boy lost in a hail of ash, the vertigo of a teen hurtling towards adulthood, and the thrill of a young man leaving home.

When they reached the house, Beth heard the car and came out to greet them, wiping the flour off her hands on a dish towel. She hugged Taylor and tousled his hair as if he were still an eight year old. Turning her attention to Quinn, she extended her hand, apologizing for her appearance—"I'm making some last minute pies for the rehearsal dinner"—she explained. Taylor made an awkwardly formal introduction.

"Mother. I would like you to meet Quinn Yarbrough. Quinn, this is my mother."

"Pleased to meet you," replied Beth stiffly, following her son's lead.

Uncle Ed came around the corner to see what had drawn his sister away from the kitchen and, upon seeing Taylor, clapped his hands together and laughed with joy. He gave his nephew a bear hug and latched onto his arm at the elbow, chattering on about a fish he had caught the day before as if Taylor had never left. Beth took her son's other arm and led him into the house, Quinn trailing behind. Inside, J.P. was seated in a reclining chair in the living room watching a baseball game on television. He looked a little older and thinner, but his hands were still thick and powerful and his eyes were as bright and combative as ever. "You remembered where you get your bread buttered huh boy?" barked the old man through a crooked smile. He scrutinized Quinn, gave her a little wave from his chair, and turned back to the game.

"Your father is out moving the wheel line," said Beth. "You may want to help him so he's not late for the dinner. Sara is already at the grange hall with her bridesmaids."

"Couldn't he have skipped it today?" asked Taylor.

"Watering won't wait for weddings," Beth replied.

Taylor put his luggage in his old room and changed into his work boots. He hesitated to leave Quinn alone, but she laughed off his concerns and hurried him out the door. "They've been very hospitable so far," she reassured him. He wasn't sure whether she was being sarcastic or sincere. "And you need to drag your father back here so I can meet him," she added.

Quinn watched Taylor walk out through the fields of alfalfa from the living room window. She barely recognized him in his dusty jeans and baseball cap, but he moved through the fields with an ease born of habit which made her feel very far away from him. Despite her best efforts to maintain her poise, a wave of tension tightened her stomach. She decided to distract herself by keeping busy and joined Beth in the kitchen. She found her mixing up a fruit filling in a ceramic bowl.

"Can I help?" she asked, holding her hands in a knot to prevent Beth from seeing her fidget.

"Sure. Know how to make a crust?" asked Beth without looking up from her work.

"No, but I can find them in the frozen section when I need them," she laughed, trying to make light of her shortcoming. Beth made no reply, but looked up with surprise. "I like experimenting with ethnic cuisine, but I'm not much good at basic fare," Quinn continued, trying to justify her limitations in the kitchen. At this Beth stopped her stirring and studied the young woman's expression, trying to determine if it was an intentional slight. Quinn was smiling at her own joke and she stood off a bit, back arched and chin up in a way that made Beth feel like a bumpkin who had just come in from the barn.

"That won't help me now," said Beth. "Does Taylor like ethnic food?"

"Not too much," replied Quinn, her discomfort rising.

"So do you eat alone?" asked Beth, turning up the oven.

"Only when I cook my really best dishes," replied Quinn, hoping to warm up the older woman, but her dry wit seemed to have the opposite effect. She decided to talk about what they had in common.

"Taylor will try most of my experiments, but when he doesn't like a certain meal, he let's me know. He can be pretty stubborn when he gets his mind fixed on something."

"Well I'm sure he gets some of that from his grandfather, some from me. It can be a good characteristic though. It makes him follow through on his goals."

"Yes. Once he's got a goal," amended Quinn. Beth checked the pie in the oven and closed the door. "And what about you? What are your plans at the moment? Taylor tells me you're a graduate student too?"

"Yes. I'm at the Harvard Divinity School. I'm taking a broad look at theology, but my main interest is the philosophy of the early Unitarians." Quinn heard herself and couldn't help feeling pretentious. "It's really just a study of the different ways people see God," she explained.

"I know what theology is," replied Beth. She went back to her stirring as Quinn looked out the window for an uncomfortable moment. By this time J.P.'s beer had run out and he had walked in on the conversation on his way to the refrigerator. He smelled a little boozy and swayed like a sailor who steps ashore after riding high swells for a day.

"You say you're studying to be a preacher?" J.P. asked skeptically.

"No. A teacher I hope."

"A teacher not a preacher, huh?" J.P. laughed. "Whatta you gonna teach? Preaching? Ha!" He took a big draw on his beer.

"Go watch your game, Dad." said Beth. "We were just trying to get to know each other better." She was visibly irritated by the old man's intrusion.

"You sayin' I can't talk to the gal too? It's a big enough kitchen. I should know. I built it!" he said with antagonism.

"Yes I know. You make a point of reminding me whenever

you're feeling entitled or drunk."

"Drunk?!" he snorted. "Can't a man have a beer in his own house without some woman makin' a fed'ral case out of it?"

"It's *my* house, and yes I can since we have guests, if you hadn't noticed. Now let us get back to work. All this jabbering is going to make us late for the rehearsal dinner."

"I wouldn't know about that. I wasn't invited," growled the old man.

"And do you know why? So you wouldn't make an ass of yourself."

"You told her not to invite me, didn't you!" He pointed a gnarled finger at Beth. Unintimidated, she met his glare with composed force.

"She made her own decision. I only agreed." A little smoke began to filter through the oven door. Embroiled in their conflict, neither of the Morelands seemed to notice that the pie was burning. Quinn, who had been looking for a way to excuse herself from the fray, glimpsed the gray wisps escaping from the stove vents and found the diversion she needed.

"Mrs. Moreland."

"What?" snapped Beth, eyes still riveted on J.P.

"Your pie's burning."

"Shit!" Beth sprung over to the stove and threw open the door. A ball of thick black smoke rolled slowly out the door and fanned out through the room. J.P. howled with laughter as Beth set the charred remains of the pie on the stovetop. She turned on him in anger.

"Is that all you can do? Stand there and watch as your granddaughter's evening goes up in smoke!"

J.P.'s impish grin turned into a hateful glare. He stepped forward with his can in his fist and Quinn started backwards involuntarily, thinking he meant to strike Beth. Instead, he turned the full contents of his can over the blackened pastry. Beer and charred crust washed down the stove and across the floor. The imposing old man looked past Beth and smiled cordially at Quinn.

"Sometimes I act impulsive in a pinch," he said to the

astonished guest. Then he turned to Beth. "I hope I didn't make an ass of myself." Crushing his can into the pie, he stepped through the puddle on the floor, past the two women and out the back door. Beth stood over the mess for a minute gathering her thoughts. Quinn moved to the sink and dampened a towel, offering it to Taylor's mother.

"You didn't need to see that," apologized Beth.

"Taylor warned me that I could expect some outbursts from his grandfather."

"He did?" asked Beth, with a hint of disapproval. "He shouldn't share the family dirt with strangers." Quinn was hurt by Beth's disregard, but she refused to be pushed away.

"No family is without its tensions," observed Quinn. They cleaned the floor without speaking. After a while, Beth broke the awkward silence.

"And what about your family?" asked Beth, trying to turn attention away from the disagreeable encounter. "Where are they from and what line of work does your father do?" She bent over the sink, rinsing a doughy dish towel.

"My parents live in Charleston. My mother is a writer for the newspaper and my father is a Unitarian minister."

"Which one do you take after?"

"Both in some ways. Like my mother, I'm a skeptic, always digging for the truth. Like my father I like to believe there is something beyond this life. That's how I ended up at the Divinity School." Quinn thought that her explanation stood on its own, but Beth looked at her as if she had merely prefaced some more consequential statement.

"So where would you like to teach after all that thinking?"

"I'd like to work at a university or maybe in a non-denominational seminary. Preferably in New England."

"And does Taylor know you want to stay in New England?"

"We've talked about it," replied Quinn, following the implicit question. "I suppose if we come to a point where we need to decide whether to live on the east coast or the west we'll weigh out the reasons for both and determine what's best for both of us."

"Well, Taylor has three hundred and sixty five reasons to come back to Rockwater. He stands to inherit every acre of this place, you know. So get a good feeling for the place while you're here." Beth handed her a sponge and some dish soap. "You may need to think about what it would be like to be a farmer's wife when the time comes to make your decision."

"Taylor may have other options when he completes his program," protested Quinn. "He's a talented artist and art historian."

"Can you make a living at that? You don't see many ads in the paper for art historians. And to make money on your paintings it seems to me that you have to be dead."

"Being an artist is not without its challenges, and Taylor has worked very hard to get where he is now. It's what he loves."

"I know," she conceded with a sigh. "He's always been creative. Ever since he was a boy. We could hardly get him to concentrate on his chores for all his daydreaming. It would have been easier if he had just stayed here. When he gets that degree I think he will have proved something to himself and he'll be ready to come home and get on with life."

"That may not be enough for him," warned Quinn. Beth looked in her eyes to see if she was withholding something.

"Does he tell you what he plans to do after school?"

"He doesn't know himself. I think he needs to feel that he can make a choice and still come back to the farm, whatever he decides."

"Ah, but that's every naive child's dream, isn't it?" said Beth ironically. "To be free from all ties while, at the same time, to be bound by unyielding roots. Truth is, if you cut the roots, the tree withers and dies." She set out the flour for another pie. "Want to learn how to make a crust?" she asked. Quinn nodded.

Taylor found his father out in the alfalfa field, priming the old irrigation pump from a leaky bucket. Jim was tan and wiry like his father and the veins stood out on his forearm as he poured the water into the impeller chamber. Engrossed in his work, he didn't hear his son coming and muttered curses under his breath at the rusting motor.

"Trying to get a few more years out of that relic, huh?" called Taylor.

"Son! How ya doin'?" He grasped Taylor by one hand and clapped the other on his son's shoulder. "You're looking thin, boy," he said, giving him a little shake. "We better work you a little while you're here to put on some muscle. Too much time squinting at books."

"I can still move irrigation pipe if that's what you mean," smiled Taylor.

"You can prove it tomorrow morning in the west pasture."

"You got it."

"For now, help me with the pump," commanded Jim. "Hold the funnel steady while I top her off." He dumped the rest of the water in the spout and closed off the valve. It was the same turbine he and Taylor had installed in 1980.

"Why don't you replace this thing?" asked Taylor, recognizing the pump. "You know they have self-priming pumps now?"

"Yeah, but this one still gets the job done. I've kept it in pretty good shape. See for yourself." He pointed to the power switches on the utility pole. Taylor stepped up and pressed the green button and the pump whirred and wheezed for a full minute without drawing water from the ditch. Finally an air pocket formed in the intake and the impeller spun dry, sucking air.

"Shut it off!" called Jim.

"I thought you said it was working fine," joked Taylor.

"Well, it has been struggling to find a prime lately," he conceded. "But I've always managed to get it going. Fill this and we'll try again." He handed the bucket to his son.

Taylor drew water from the irrigation ditch and gave it to his father. Jim opened the priming chamber and poured water in again, repeating the procedure as before. But the pump refused to draw water, even after several attempts. Taylor began to get concerned about the time and reminded his father that they had a rehearsal dinner in less than an hour.

"We better go in and get cleaned up," said Taylor.

"I think we'd better fix this pump," corrected his father. "There must be something in the impeller that's choked it up. The screen hasn't been cleaned in a while and there's probably weeds in there." He began to rummage through his tool box for a wrench.

"You won't have time," objected Taylor. "It can wait until tomorrow. I'll get up early and we'll fix it together."

"I've got to get spray on those apples tomorrow. Things are gonna dry up around here if this pump goes down."

"Yeah, but not overnight. I'll work on the pump and you run the sprayer." Taylor turned and began walking towards the house thinking it was settled.

"What do you know about the insides of an electric motor?" challenged Jim. "You haven't turned a wrench in about five years. I'll have to do it or it won't get done."

"Well, I'll run the spray rig then," offered Taylor. "Come on. You don't want to miss Sara's dinner."

"But this is just the rehearsal," countered Jim. "I'll make the wedding. That's what counts."

"Dad," protested Taylor, "leave it until tomorr—"

"You can't just up and leave a farm!" barked Jim. "You seem to have forgotten that. You have to make sacrifices sometimes or things fall apart. I'll make it if I can make it, but right now one hundred acres of alfalfa take priority over a dinner." He stood his ground and Taylor realized that he was also standing on a deeply held principle that commitment to his land was a commitment to his family. The older man waited for his son to see the rationale behind such logic and join him in his labors.

"I'll help you tomorrow," said Taylor. "I'd better go to the dinner. What should I tell Sara and Bill?"

"Tell them I'm a farmer and this sort of thing happens. They'll understand."

That evening the dinner passed without incident. No one seemed concerned with Jim and J.P.'s absence, although Taylor thought his mother looked conspicuously uncomfortable sitting next to the empty chair that had been set for his father. Bill and Taylor managed to have a cordial—if not superficial—conversation and Sara was genuinely thrilled to see her brother present.

The following day, Sara and Bill were married at a little country chapel in Selah, a suburb of Yakima. The ceremony was well attended, composed of friends from their high school days and relatives from Bill's side of the family. The reception was held at the ranch. Following the wedding, friends and well-wishers climbed into their cars and dusty trucks to make a rag-tag motorcade back to the farm. Beth and Mrs. Hennis had worked hard to transform the patio and yard into a festive environment. Mrs. Hennis had filled a stainless steel watering trough with ice and beer, and Beth strung paper bells and streamers between the rain gutter and the fruit trees in the yard. Several picnic tables covered with sheets served as the buffet table, and a trio from the local Grange played country music on a fiddle and two guitars.

While Quinn tried to get better acquainted with Jim, Taylor circulated through the crowd, carrying trays of cheese and crackers to keep himself occupied. The years had not diminished his feelings of estrangement, and he felt self-conscious and out of place around his old acquaintances. Al was there, heavier and balding, but with the same animal complacency and masticating jowls. He saw some of his old teachers—a few still working at the high school—and some familiar faces from Sara's class. At the church, he had scanned the crowd for Marla, but she was not to be seen. He felt relieved that she was not there, but he wondered if Bill had decided not to invite her on account of his presence. But just when he felt he would be spared the awkwardness of seeing her again, she arrived with Cort and two freckled children. Taylor watched as Marla and Cort moved through the greeting line, pulling the children in tow. Al sidled up to Taylor and plucked a few sandwiches off the tray. "They're married," he said between bites. "Going on seven years now." Taylor excused himself before Marla had seen him and went back inside the house to load up with some cheese and crackers.

When he returned to the party, she was standing near an apple tree at the edge of the lawn. Her children ran off to play with the Morelands' dog, giving Taylor an opportunity to speak to her in private. He wound his way through the crowd and stood before her. She recognized him immediately and greeted him with an enthusiastic hug.

"I was not sure if I would see you tonight," said Taylor, stepping back and taking her hand in his. She smelled of sun and rose hips.

"Do you wish you hadn't?" she asked playfully.

"I thought at first I didn't want to," admitted Taylor. "But now that you're here it feels good. We left a lot of things unsaid between us."

"It's too late for some things now," she replied, glancing over at Cort and the children. Cort's daughter tugged at his hand as he talked to the father of the groom. His son scrambled between his legs. Taylor realized he would only have a minute or so in which to address the questions which had been nagging him for ten years.

"Are you happy?" asked Taylor, surprised to feel a pang of jealousy.

"Yes. Very," she smiled.

"Why didn't you let me know that you and Cort were married?"

"'Cause I was afraid you'd come to the wedding and break his nose like you broke Bill's" she replied, revealing some of her old jocularity. "Got anything planned today?" she asked holding up her fists.

"Oh, just a tug of war with Bill over the bride when they try to drive off for the honeymoon."

"You two still feuding?"

"Not feuding exactly," replied Taylor. "More like ignoring each other."

"So what have you been doing with your life since high school?" she asked.

"I just kept avoiding the world by continuously enrolling in school," he laughed. "Now I'm doing graduate work at a fine arts program in Boston."

"A city boy now. I bet you don't miss the ranch. You always

wanted to get out of this town."

"Yes, I suppose you're right. But not towards the end," he amended. "At the time I was prepared to stay . . . with you."

"For all the wrong reasons," added Marla. "You would have been miserable."

"Yes. I wanted to believe otherwise. But at some point I may want to come back to Yakima." He looked around at the fertile orchards, the sun setting over the white capped Cascades. "Living here seems to agree with you. Are you working?"

"Ha! You definitely don't have kids of your own do you? Being a mom takes up most of my time and helping Cort out in the orchards takes the rest. We live on his family's farm. Cort pretty much runs the orchards and warehouse for his dad. We built a little place on the acreage across the road from his parents. It's been handy to send the kids over to Grandma and Grandpa when I need a break." Marla looked over towards Cort and her children. Cort caught her eye and smiled. He saw Taylor and gave a friendly wave. Taylor knew he had but just a moment more in which to confront his old ghosts.

"Do you ever wonder what life may have been like if you had . . . made different choices? If I had acted more responsibly?"

"I was a just a girl then and you were still a boy." She became very serious for a moment. She could see that he was looking for absolution. "I made a decision and moved on. It doesn't matter what I think my life may or may not have been like, since I only have the life I've made."

"I think I was very selfish then."

"No more than I was. I wanted you to come and take me out of my life, away from my father."

"I always wondered if you blamed me," he said, feeling his throat tighten with years of pent up anguish.

"Blamed you for what?" she asked, genuinely confused.

"For creating a crisis in your life and walking away at the most trying time."

"My father didn't give you much choice."

"He gave me a note. It looked like your handwriting." He

searched her eyes for confirmation.

"It took me half a day to write that. Dad suggested it was in my best interest to make the whole thing just go away." Marla shook her head and laughed ironically. "But he was thinking about himself too. It all worked out the way he wanted. No one ever found out and he's still preaching at the same old church."

"And for you?" asked Taylor. "Did things work out the way you wanted?"

"Yes, eventually," she responded. "I had time to grow up a little. I went to Y.V.C.C. for a while. Then Cort and I met up again on the rodeo circuit and we've been together ever since. He's a good man and a good father." They looked at him playing with the kids, one dangling from each arm. "What about you?" she turned to him. "Your life seems to be going just the way you had dreamed. You left home, went to college, and now you're studying art in Boston."

"School can get tiring, but I like the life I've created there," he answered honestly. "But then every time I come home I feel I should be here," he sighed and cast a glance at his father.

"But you never belonged here, Taylor," she laughed, pointing out the irony. "Even when we were kids. You were always restless. You used to go on and on about the first time you saw the ocean. You'd get all worked up talking about it and you'd torture yourself thinking about another look. I've still never seen the ocean!"

"Why not? You used to tell me that you'd dip your toe in the Pacific one day."

"I just stopped wanting," she replied with contentment. "It makes life a lot easier, Taylor. Maybe you should give it a try." There was no bitterness. No spite. Her life had gone on very much as she had desired and in keeping with needs very different than his own. She smiled at him and he finally felt released.

"I would like you to meet someone," said Taylor. He left Marla for a moment to pull Quinn away from a gathering of the Ladies' Grange. He brought them together and Quinn extended her hand. "Marla is an old friend of mine," explained Taylor.

"You went to high school together?" guessed Quinn.

"More than that," replied Marla. "We grew up together." Taylor heard the echo of his own words and looked to see if it had been coincidental. It wasn't. Her eyes met his and bore an expression that told him "Thank you." He smiled his appreciation. She balled up her fist and playfully socked him in the shoulder. Soon they were joined by Cort and the children. The three old friends took turns trying to embarrass each other in front of Quinn with exaggeratedly comic episodes from their youth. The laughter was a refreshing tonic for Taylor.

Encouraged by the sympathetic reception from Marla and Cort, he decided to try to initiate a more open and friendly relationship with Bill. Eventually he saw an opportunity to get a free moment with the bride and groom. Sara was dressed in a simple but elegant white satin dress and Bill wore a rented tux with the cummerbund belted on upside-down. He was reveling in the attention, puffing on a cigar, while Sara clung to his elbow and smiled and chatted with bubbling enthusiasm. Taylor drew Quinn towards the couple and, after a few of Bill's buddies from the warehouse moved on, he stepped up and congratulated his sister and her new husband. Bill was glowing from his celebrity status and, feeling secure now in his claim on Sara, treated Taylor with an exaggerated magnanimity.

"Welcome to the family," said Taylor, offering his hand. Bill laughed unnaturally loud and shook Taylor's hand vigorously, much like a champion on a podium might do to the runner up on the step below.

"Sara's a great gal. I aim to make her very happy," said Bill.

"You already have," smiled Sara.

"How did you two meet?" asked Quinn.

"A friend from school knew that Bill was lonely and so was I, so she proposed a date," Sara explained. "But we would have met sooner or later. It was fate. Bill works for the warehouse that buys Dad's fruit."

"Look like a good crop this year?" asked Taylor.

"It's O.K.," replied Bill "but he's gonna need to spray for aphids pretty quick," he said, furrowing his brow with authoritative concern. "I'll be back from the honeymoon by next Saturday and I'll help him then."

"Dad counts on you a lot," said Sara, squeezing her husband's arm.

"Well there's a lot to do around here for one man," said Bill seriously. Sara then addressed Taylor, seeing an opportunity to sing her husband's praises.

"Last year when the sheep got foot rot," she began, "Bill came over for two weeks straight, after work and on weekends, to help with trimming the hooves. Almost half the herd was infected."

"Dad never mentioned that to me," said Taylor.

"There wasn't much point with you being on the other side of the continent," explained Sara.

"Together we were able to get the animals treated," said Bill. "He would never ask for help. I think he would have tried to do it on his own if Sara hadn't told me. He would have worked himself to death."

"Yeah, he can be pretty stubborn," laughed Taylor, shaking his head.

"No, I wouldn't call him stubborn. I call it determination," corrected Bill. "He's a proud man." Bill happened to see Jim crossing over to the beer trough and waved him over. Jim joined the foursome and threw an affectionate arm around Bill's shoulder.

"Here's a beer for my number one son in law." The two men clacked their cans together and drank.

"Tell Taylor and Quint—" began Bill.

"Quinn," corrected Taylor.

"—Quinn about the work we did on the sheep last spring." He nudged Taylor's father in the shoulder.

"Now that was a damn mess!" remembered Jim. "We had a run of wet weather and the sheep came down with foot rot. We had about two weeks of turning up every animal and trimming all their hooves."

"Some of them were in bad shape," added Bill. "I remember a few of your prize ewes got to the point that they had to kneel down on their front knees in order to eat."

"I ran the whole herd through a foot bath," Jim explained to Taylor. "I couldn't have done it without Bill. He helped me at picking time too." He turned to Bill. "You've been a big help around here."

"Any time! I'll be just around the corner when you need me. Sara and I plan on living in the trailer at my folk's place until we can build."

"Well I know a few things about carpentry when the time comes," said Jim.

The two became engrossed in a discussion of floor plans and Taylor turned his attention to Sara. She detached herself from Bill and then she and Taylor settled themselves in plastic chairs on the patio while Quinn went to refill her drink.

"How long can you stay?" asked Sara.

"We leave in two days."

"We're going to miss you," she said, looking at her father. Taylor looked at his hands and said nothing. "Dad talks about you all the time. Every year he thinks you're going to come home and when you don't he gets more and more disappointed. It's been hard on him running the place on his own."

"Well, I have a few more things I have to do for myself," replied Taylor defensively.

"And when you're done with school and done drifting around you'll return and run the farm?" Her voice betrayed an edge of resentment and frustration.

"Maybe. I can't see that far," said Taylor, refusing to acknowledge her implicit criticism.

"Well, we can't wait forever," she complained, her frustration bubbling over. "Bill and I have to make some decisions about our future, too. He wants to build a home for us and I want it to be here. There's a nice spot near the apple orchard, and we'd be close to Mom and Dad and Bill's family too."

"Are you looking for my permission?" asked Taylor, his anger rising. "I think that's really up to Dad."

"Don't you even care what happens at Rockwater anymore?" she asked accusingly.

"Yes," he answered sharply, "but lately I feel like just a spectator and not a participant."

"Well that's your doing and no one else's. The ranch is still yours if you want it. While you're out looking for your destiny, Dad tries to find a way to believe that all his efforts are going to be appreciated by someone who gives a damn. Bill has given him that feeling. Now don't begrudge Dad of that." Taylor looked away, subdued and smoldering. Sara stood up indignantly, screwed her frown into a smile, and returned to her husband and father to talk about their house plans.

On their last day at the farm, Taylor took Quinn through the barns to see the spring lambs. Born in February and March, they were now sturdy animals, bounding with energy. The couple watched them race around the hay feeders in groups of ten or twenty. Sometimes they would veer off course into the dozing ewes and the whole sprinting herd would leap over the backs of their sleeping mothers. One lamb, smaller than all the rest, caught sight of Quinn and Taylor and broke off from the race and ran right up to them like a bounding puppy.

"What's it doing?" asked Quinn in surprise as it tapped Taylor's shin with a hoof.

"It's a bummer lamb," he said, bending over and scratching its ears.

"That's a mean thing to call it!" she said, stroking its head.

"That's what we call orphaned lambs," he explained. "Do you want to hold it?" He hoisted the lamb up into his arms. It prodded at his neck and chin with its nose, insisting on being fed.

"Oh, it's so cute," cooed Quinn.

The lamb was just a month old, born unusually late in the season, and still had a long, fuzzy tail. Its back and legs were downed with a tightly curled fleece, and the feet and face were covered with smooth, black hair.

"They're smarter than people give them credit for," said Taylor, handing the wriggling lamb to Quinn. She cradled the animal in one arm and scratched its neck and ears with her free hand. The lamb leaned into the caresses and closed its eyes, indulging in the pleasure.

"You must have loved living here," she observed.

"I used to give all the orphans names." He smiled at the memory of the lambs crowding around him as he bottle fed them, one at a time. "At the peak of lambing season I could have twenty or more. They would follow me around the barns or through the fields as I did my chores. I spent most of my time alone, but I was never lonely." The lamb became restless and started to squirm.

"What do you miss the most?" asked Quinn, settling the animal to the ground.

"The work. The feeling of accomplishment when you could actually see and hold the products of your labors. There is a sense of certainty in this life—in a healthy lamb, in ripening fruit, in the smell of freshly mown hay."

"Are you considering coming back to stay?" asked Quinn. Taylor looked over the herd before him and out past the barns to the orchards beyond. Part of him wanted to claim the ranch as his own, but merely for the nostalgia of it. What he really wanted was his family's acceptance and approval. If anything, this visit had made that seem more unlikely than ever. He faced Quinn and saw by her changed expression that she was anxious that the pull of the farm might have a greater claim on his life than she. An anecdote came to mind that expressed how he was feeling.

"In 1980, just before St. Helens blew, Dad and I installed an irrigation pump. It finally broke down this weekend. I promised Dad I would help him fix it, but we never had time."

"That's not your fault," she consoled.

"I know. But even if I had to fix a pump I couldn't do it. I don't know how to mix the sprays, I've forgotten how to maintain the swather, and I never could manage all the details of the crop cycles." He laughed a little at his own ineptitude. Quinn laughed with him, her relief bringing a smile to her face. Taylor looked at her and thought of their life together—the uncertainties he faced, the constant pressures they endured from a lack of money and a lack of time, their erratic stumbling towards something neither could define—and he was happy. Amidst the chaotic din of the world, and in spite of it, they loved each other. "I think I'm ready to go home," he said, folding her hand into his.

On June 30th, 2000, the phone rang in their apartment. She rolled over in bed and let the answering machine pick up. When she heard Taylor's voice through the speaker, she threw back the covers and dashed for the phone.

"Hello! Hello!? Taylor, is that you?" she cried.

"Quinn? Can you hear me?" replied Taylor through heavy static.

"Yes! Where are you? Are you OK?" asked Quinn in rapid fire.

"I'm in Coari, Brazil. I stopped over here to get some supplies before continuing on to Ecuador."

"Why haven't you called lately? I've been worrying night and day," she scolded. "I haven't heard from you since I got a post card from Manaus. Are you really OK?" she pressed, sensing something was left unsaid.

"I got a little . . . sick," he said evasively.

"Sick? So sick that you couldn't write or call?"

"Well, I got robbed too, but I wasn't hurt . . . too badly—"

"Robbed? Hurt?! Taylor just tell me what happened," demanded Quinn, losing patience with Taylor's stalling.

"Don't worry," he reassured her. "I'm all right now. I got some sort of stomach flu outside of Manaus and then I got robbed on the river, but I have a friend here who has helped me out. I have a little money left and I am moving again."

"Taylor, stop this journey and come home now. Please." Taylor could hear the desperation in her voice.

"I can't," he explained. "I lost my passport and plane tickets. It would be easier to make it to the U.S. embassy in Quito than to backtrack all the way to Manaus. She could tell it would be futile to try to convince him to give up the journey.

"Can I wire you some money?" she asked.

"Yes. I could really use a little more to get me through. When

I get to a town that has a bank or cambio I will contact you. Can you call my family and let them know I'm all right?"

"I would be lying," said Quinn. "It doesn't sound to me like that's the case at all."

"Quinn, please."

"OK," she conceded. "I miss you. If you can find some way to come home soon, please tell me you will try." A chime rang in on the line to indicate the calling card was expiring.

"I'll be home after I've made it to Cotopaxi," he promised. "Write me a note in care of the Quito embassy."

"I love you," whispered Quinn, trying to keep her voice from betraying her anxiety and reservations.

"I love you too," said Taylor, but Quinn did not hear him. The line had already gone dead.

JULY

July 10, 1857

   Early in the morning, Quipo appeared, the Indian guide
who had visited Sangai. A picturesque man was Quipo and
the success of my trip depended upon his services.
Unfortunately, he spoke only his native tongue so that my
bad Spanish was of no avail. I learned this morning that we
could proceed on horses no farther than Ysapan,—the
remainder of the journey must be accomplished afoot . . . .
During the first part of the ride I noticed several huts perched
on the steep slopes of the mountains with a few rich green
patches of cultivated soil adjoining them . . . Rocks began to
crop out of the fields and as we progressed, the peaks became
more craggy and wild. An extraordinary stillness struck me

which was heightened by the rapid movements of the clouds about the mountains tops,—we are very near them now.

Frederic Edwin Church

On the morning of July 10, 2000, the rain filtered down upon the jungle in a fine spray. Taylor awoke to the sound of Ana Paula making coffee in the kitchen. Outside, on the decking, he heard Sergio and Guilherme talking in a low musical cadence that blended with the sound of the water lapping up around the stilts. He slipped out of his hammock and rechecked his gear: a back pack, a tent and sleeping bag, a few changes of clothing, a pocket knife, toiletries, and a few hundred dollars tucked into a plastic bag and secured in the sole of his shoe. Guilherme had given him an additional fifty reais to get him by until he could change the dollars and loaned him his boat and outboard. "Keep the money. Return the boat," he said.

During his stay with Guilherme, Taylor poured over Church's journals with fascination and began to grow impatient to move on. By the end of June he had fully recovered from his wounds and felt strong and healthy again. It was impossible for Guilherme himself to act as Taylor's guide since his leg was not strong and he had lost his depth perception. But he discussed Taylor's dilemma with Sergio and, out of a sense of loyalty to his new friend, Sergio agreed to take him as far as the Peruvian border.

The plan worked out by the two Brazilians was for Sergio to accompany Taylor as far as Tabatinga, several days distant on the Solimoes—depending on weather and the temperamental motor. There, Taylor intended to make his way to Iquitos where he could line up another river guide to take him up the Rio Napo to Misahualli within approximately sixty miles of Cotopaxi. Proceeding from here by boat, bus, and finally on foot, Taylor intended to walk the final leg of the journey to Cotopaxi, just as Church had done over a century before. After he had had his fill of the exotic vistas of the equatorial Andes, he planned to go on to Quito where he could replace his passport at the embassy and get some money before flying home. He had minor reservations about crossing borders without documents, but with the nearest U.S. embassy in Brazil almost as far as Quito—but in the other direction—, it made more sense to him to sort out his bureaucratic problems after the trip. The idea of getting to Cotopaxi and Church's beloved Andes drove him to act with the stubborn single-mindedness of his father.

After a light breakfast of bread and cheese, he kissed Ana Paula and the children good-bye and met Sergio at the boat. He was adjusting the gear in the center of the canoe for proper ballast. Guilherme was inspecting the carburetor. Both men worked with a degree of seriousness, and it struck Taylor at that moment that this important event in the course of his journey had become as significant or more so in the lives of these friends. For a split second, this realization inspired a twinge of guilt. He had not meant to disrupt their lives or burden them by his presence. He looked again at Guilherme's crooked leg and expected that grotesque emblem of his forever altered life to intensify his self-reproach. Instead it was replaced by a profound feeling of love and appreciation. These two men were helping him because they had come to genuinely like and respect him. It had always been difficult for Taylor to accept other people's kindness because he never felt worthy of the effort. But seeing his friends now, straining at their preparations, he realized that they were reaping a very tangible reward for their investment in him. He knew what they were feeling. He himself had made a point of extending kindness and generosity to the people he cherished because, in truth, the only times he ever felt he could know his own moral character was when he had seen it reflected in the eyes of another. By refusing to accept charity at various times in his life, he had deprived many of the people closest to him—Quinn included—of the satisfaction of demonstrating, through caring for him, their capacity to love. Too often, he realized, he had lived under the assumption that any emotional indebtedness to another meant only his own impoverishment and he had avoided situations which imposed any great emotional obligation upon him. Now, seeing Guilherme and Sergio busying themselves over the preparations, he was grateful for the way his life had become entangled with the lives of these people. He realized that he could not get by without depending on them and that it would be impossible in his lifetime to repay their kindness. Once he had accepted this fact, he was able to watch their work with a feeling of reverence instead of berating himself for imposing on their lives.

Taylor stepped forward and placed his hand on Guilherme's shoulder.

"Thanks for all your help. I don't know where I would be now without you," he said.

"I do. In the bellies of a hundred vultures!" smiled Guilherme, clapping a hand on Taylor's back. "Now don't run this boat through dense grass, because if the prop gets tangled in weeds the motor will stall out," advised the guide. He was merely inventing things to say, since he knew that Taylor had become a competent boatman.

"All right," said Taylor.

"And let Sergio do the guiding because you don't know upstream from down."

"O.K., Guilherme," he nodded, listening respectfully. Sergio continued bustling over the gear, trying to distract himself while Taylor and Guilherme parted. "I'll write," said Taylor with effort.

"Don't bother. The mail never works here and, besides, we will see each other again."

"How do you know?"

"Didn't I tell you? The rivers around here run in circles." Guilherme laughed loud like he did the first time they met first. Taylor didn't understand his friend's riddle, but made an effort to make his prediction sound plausible, even though in his heart he doubted whether he would ever find himself on this stretch of the Rio Solimoes again in his lifetime.

"I'll try to find a way to come back," he promised, "even if it takes me a while. You'll still be here?"

"That I can't guarantee. Depends on the currents. But I hope to be here or pretty close."

Taylor extended his hand. Guilherme smiled and shook his head at his friend's formality. Stepping past the hand, he embraced him. Ana Paula watched from the doorway; her eyes hovered anxiously over her husband. Guilherme released Taylor and held him at arm's length to look at him one last time. His good eye welled up a little and his empty socket streamed a tear. He forced a smile for his friend and laughed at himself.

"Everything about that damn eye stopped working except the plumbing, and that seems to work double time now." Sergio started the motor. "You better go before I raise the water a couple of meters," said Guilherme brusquely.

"Take care of yourself," said Taylor, and stepped into the waiting boat. As they motored away, Ana Paula stepped out to the deck and the children too. The whole family waved until they could see Taylor no longer.

Over the next few weeks, the two men made good progress up the river. Each day they motored along for around eight hours before turning in to some cove or village for the evening. Sometimes they accepted the good will of strangers and strung their hammocks in the cramped quarters of a floating house, on other days they would make a camp and sleep under an impromptu thatched roof. Their pace was slow enough that Taylor had plenty of time to write in his journal. When it was Sergio's shift at the outboard there was little else to do. In the afternoons, Taylor pulled out Church's manuscripts and, under the cooling shade of the high jungle canopy, read about the young man's impressions of the landscape.

As Taylor read over Church's journals from his travels through the jungle, he began to see patterns in the observations that suggested that the artist was collecting a storehouse of sensory detail and emotional impressions that would later serve as a catalyst for painting. Church's approach was to jot down the date followed by commentary on his experiences at that particular point in his travels, progressing in chronological order. The artist recorded the types of plants and animals he encountered, the weather he experienced, and the scenes he witnessed, all with a flare of a dramatist envisioning a potential plot.

As the weeks passed, Taylor's daily contact with the astounding beauty of the jungle coupled with the epic visions of Church moved him to think of painting again. He made a few aborted attempts to articulate an idea for a full scale composition, but found that all his sketches ended up feeling affected and forced. Looking back at Church's process for guidance, he noted that rather than outlining plans for fully articulated paintings, the young artist chose to write down constellations of themes or images. Thus, his writings took shape as a series of phrases and anecdotes which formed a pallet of colors necessary to create his grand romantic visions. After a week of reading Church's entries, Taylor decided to test the method out for himself.

Journal Entry, July 12, 2000

On Seeing and Perceiving: Sergio is trying to teach me how to throw his fishing harpoon. He can hit a moving *macaco d'agua* or "monkey fish" (named for its ability to leap out of the water and snatch its prey from the leaves and branches of overhanging trees and bushes) while standing in the rocking canoe. The shaft is made of heavy teak and it feels like iron in my hands. It is worn smooth and Sergio tells me that it has been passed down in his family from father to son so long that he cannot say how old it is. The shaft narrows to the diameter of a pool cue at the point and Sergio affixes a detachable barb tied to a nylon cord. He makes his marksmanship look easy. When he throws the spear, the line flows out freely behind like a jet trail. He usually hits his fish just behind the gill slits. When I throw, on the other hand, the shaft wobbles erratically and the line drags along like an anchor chain. My harpoon usually enters the water at an angle throwing up a tremendous splash. I often pull in weeds while Sergio smiles and shakes his head.

This evening, Sergio asked me to go out and catch some fish for dinner. It wasn't until I was twenty minutes out that I realized that he had packed the harpoon for me and not the fishing line. Probably on purpose. I've become pretty adept with managing the boat, and I maneuvered it parallel to the fringe of floating grass that lined the shore. I watched for fish but could not make out anything through the surface glare. I was never sure how Sergio was following his target. Watching the surface, I could quickly pick up the ripples of a moving fish and determine its speed and direction. But I could not actually see the shape or judge the depth of the body below. Switching to a deeper focus, I could pick out the dark form under the surface and determine the depth. But because of the way that deep water bends light, I could not be certain of its exact location. I found myself switching back to the surface detail to give me the fixed reference points necessary to calculate the true position of the fish, only to lose it in the glare. This made me slow and clumsy, and I would see a swirl on the top and throw the spear at a fish below that had already moved.

After following a few flitting forms for a while, I finally gave up on forcing the eye to adhere to details and looked with a broad, encompassing gaze. It was then, all of a sudden, that I found that I was perceiving the world through both kinds of sight. Taking in shimmer and shadow, movement and stasis all at once, I recognized a bass-like fish in a straight line across my bow. I saw the green form glide through the water, a wedge-shaped ripple curling up in its wake. Taken together, I judged the fish to be four inches below the surface and two inches behind where it appeared to be. Cocking my arm, I lined up the shaft parallel to my shoulder line as I had seen Sergio do so many times before and rested the tip between index finger and thumb, launching the harpoon with a swift, steady throw. The spear hit the fish in the middle of the body, just below the dorsal fin. It shot off with a wild thrashing, but the barb held firm. I was so excited that I pulled in hand over hand, almost wrenching the tip out of the fish. When I got it along side the boat, I could see that it was a fourteen inch *Tucunare'* or tiger fish. When I got back to camp, Sergio had a fire ready and I presented my fish, grinning and holding it up for inspection as if it were a prize catch. Sergio congratulated me by handing me some roasting prongs he had whittled.

Journal Entry for July 13, 2000

On Movement: Today I was witness to the most amazing kinetic sculpture I have ever seen. I was walking through the jungle near camp in search of Brazil nuts when I saw a spark of flame-orange dancing down the trunk of a tree. At first I thought the tree was on fire. When I came closer, I saw that it was in fact a trail of leaf cutter ants carrying blossoms to some distant hive. They marched along in single file down the trunk, each one bearing aloft a jagged sail of orange snipped from the flowers in the upper canopy. The petals billowed full and heeled over with the light breeze, giving the bright procession the appearance of hundreds of little sailboats gliding along under their fluorescent sheets. As the line of ants flitted along the trunk, the flame of their sails alternately winked and flared through shade and sun, creating a cheery regatta of sparkling luminarios, blown across the surface of an arboreal sea.

Journal Entry for July 14, 2000

On Color: Nature here in the Amazon spares no expense in painting its flora and fauna. I am going to have to entirely change my pallet if I am going to accurately represent the pigments and hues of the jungle. The tiger fish, aptly named for its brilliant yellow and black stripes, is sunflower gold—richer in the spine and merging into a cream ochre towards the underbelly. I caught one on a line yesterday and tried to do a quick study in color in my notebook just to lock the impression in my mind. But as I painted I found myself constantly adding more and more earth tones to my yellows. Then I realized that with every minute that the fish spent out of water it became duller and duller. By the time I had finished, the twitching gills lay still and I had a rather drab looking coffee-colored fish in my notebook. I was reminded of one of my favorite poems by Robert Frost, "Nothing Gold Can Stay,"

> Nature's first green is gold,
> Her hardest hue to hold.
> Her early leaf's a flower;
> But only so an hour.
> Then leaf subsides to leaf.
> So Eden sank to grief,
> So dawn goes down to day.
> Nothing gold can stay.

Perhaps because color draws its flush and glow from life, it is transitory and, therefore, inspires both exhilaration and longing. Every living being is every second closer to the grave; springtime green must give way to autumnal orange. We tend to want to hold on to color, to dress ourselves in prisms and bathe our eyes in luster, because it allows us the pleasant self-deception that we can hold our colors and cheat mortality.

It is not surprising then that the indigenous people of the Amazon believe that the most brilliant of creatures in the jungle— the radiant blue morph butterflies—are immortal. I have run after them through the shadowy forests on a few occasions, following the flash of their azure fire like a madman chasing wood sprites. The locals say they are the spirits of children who, as compensation for their premature passing, are dipped in the glowing sheen of immortality and returned to this temporal world to enjoy an eternity of play. They are phantasmagoric, beautiful, and illusive.

Green is a color more fitting mortality. It is life—fertile and fetid. I never appreciated the possible variations of green until I had lived in the jungle. The shadows under the canopy are a cool green, almost merging to black. It's the wet, herbal, compost green that Church used to hold down the background like an earthen foundation. When plying the waters in the canoe, I am often drawn by this color to gaze into the undergrowth with a probing eye. With its endless depths, the Shadow Greens compel the viewer to stare and speculate at the secrets contained within. It is a green that soaks up the eye, making it difficult to look away. When I gaze long enough and allow myself to be pulled in, I start to smell the color. It has a scent, like damp moss or a darkened well. Using the Shadow Greens in a composition creates a sense of rootedness and solidity.

Then, where the sun sifts through the canopy to the leaves in the under foliage, the green whispers playful invitations. It is soft and pliable, faintly humming with the muted glow of refracted light. This Leaf Green inspires the most nostalgic sentiments in me, and I have seen Church and other romantics use it with great effect in hidden groves and pastoral meadows. It is the purest of greens; it is the spring bud, the tree frog, the lacewing, the lily. Dotting the leaves under the canopy with Leaf Green says to the viewer "come in quietly. Sit. Breathe in the breath of the forest. You will be as a leaf lit by the sun upon the water." It is a powerful color when used sparingly. But when overused, it loses all efficacy and becomes trite and laughably unconvincing in its exuberance.

The last hue of green prevalent in the jungle is Canopy Green. This green is blindingly brilliant and close to white or silver in tonal qualities. It is the green of high noon equatorial sun striking broad flat leaves in the highest trees. It is loud, brash, and reverberating green that tricks the eye into seeing no green at all. It sometimes looks yellow or blue or metallic for all its shimmering, but this is only because it soaks up the colors of the surrounding air. From the center of the river, this green looks like a protective gloss over the trees and vines that fixes the eye on surfaces and frustrates the penetrating gaze. But the artist who knows how to use this green over the Shadow Greens and the Leaf Greens can create the most convincing illusions of depth and three-dimensionally. In this way, Church was able to paint groves and meadows that placed the viewer in rounded space and one is perspectivally enfolded in the scene.

On Light:

When we needed fish, we usually set out at dawn or at dusk. When the sun was high, we worked twice as hard and brought in half the catch. In this way, fishing is a lot like painting: it is better at dawn or at dusk when the light is not direct. The colors all become muted in the intense tropical sun and it is difficult to see all the subtle hues within the spectrum. Everything blazes with an aggregate white light.

The works of all those artists who have mastered light are done in half light or less. Church, too, had a facility for painting with an indirect light, which may be more properly termed illumination. This sort of refracted light absorbs the pigments of the objects it touches, staining the very air with the myriad essences of many colors. I have known artists to make treks all over the world, targeting specific seasons and certain hours of the day just to experience a powerfully luminous moment.

By the third or fourth day on the river, I started to recognize phenomena of light which are unique to water. When the wind raises little ripples on the surface of the water, under the bright sunlight the surface becomes a field of glinting diamonds that stab at the eye. It is possible to watch for a while, and then, in reaction to the scintillating shimmer, the eye closes to a slit and all the distinct points of light begin to blur together into one electric blue-white light, like a welder's arc, and one can almost believe the world has been consumed by a purifying flame. I can actually hear the light in these moments. It tinkles like icicles on pine leaves, clinking together in the breeze. When light feels like this, I can hold the fleeting image but for a short while before the trance is broken.

Then, when I come back to myself and open my eyes to the immediate
world, everything looks washed out and flat—a steel gray. Afterwards,
I always feel that I know what it would be like not to exist—I would
be the diamond glint on the water merging into blue-white
nothingness, shimmering, without form, whole.

Last night, I was witness to a spectacle of light that I had never
encountered before. Sergio and I had gone night fishing, netting what
looked to me like little freshwater shrimp in shallow pools near the
river's edge. The sky was clear but the humidity was palpable and the
heat hung heavy in the air. When I inhaled, it felt as if I had taken in
a great lungfull of steam. I almost expected my breath to come gurgling
out when I exhaled. For most of the evening I waded along with a dip
net, stooping over and peering into the water. But when our basket
was full of shrimp and we made our way back to the boat I was
confronted with a startling image. While fishing, the moon had been
at my back; now, as I turned to face the beams of the full moon head
on, I found myself looking straight into a lunar rainbow! The moon
shone white in the black and saturated sky and all around it there
shimmered a distinct halo of yellow, green, blue and faintest purple.
I was speechless at the spectacle and even Sergio stared open-mouthed.
The circular rainbow hung there like a promise of regeneration over
the flooded forests. Sergio stood still for minute and rested the net in
the boat so we could take in the vision. He looked back at me, white
teeth gleaming in the dark.

"*Lindo, eh?*" he whispered.

"*Lindo,*" said I, breathless.

On the afternoon of July 27, Taylor and Sergio arrived at the
Brazilian border town of Tabatinga, on the "Triple Frontier," where
Brazil, Columbia, and Peru share a common border. They motored
up to a decaying dock near the edge of town and tied off. Tabatinga,
Brazil became Leticia, Columbia somewhere in the middle an
unmarked dirt alley which snaked its way across town. Colombians,

Peruvians, and Brazilians moved freely across the three borders and paid little attention to the imaginary lines drawn on maps. All that they knew is that they were bound together by their common heritage as Amazonians and that international diplomacy meant sharing your gas can with a neighbor when his outboard ran dry or giving a friend some eggs when his hen stops laying. There were some guard posts manned by customs officials for the odd tourist boats here and there and the larger commercial ships, but Taylor discovered he could cross the border into Peru without having to worry about being detained for not having documentation.

He and Sergio decided to stay a day or two while Taylor lined up another boat. They went to a small hotel on the outskirts of town and enjoyed a shower and a cooked meal. Afterwards, on advice from the hotel keeper, Taylor went back down to the port where tour boats from up river stopped over in Brazil before returning to Iquitos in Peru. In discussions with a few fishermen near the docks Taylor was disappointed to learn that there were no tour boats scheduled to arrive for days. However, one man pointed to an ill-kept freight packet and noted that the skipper had just arrived from Iquitos the night before and could be found getting good and drunk at a nearby tavern. Taylor found the owner of the boat where he had been told and in the predicted state of inebriation. With some encouragement from a few more beers, Taylor was able to convince the man, who delivered ice up and down the river, to take him with him on his return visit to Iquitos in the morning.

That evening, Taylor treated Sergio to a steak dinner and the two friends laughed at Taylor's naiveté when he was newly arrived in the Amazon. Sergio imitated his inept harpoon throwing technique with a straw and a pile of rice, flinging the plastic tube like a propeller into the plate and saying "shit! shit!" Taylor laughed until he cried to see himself impersonated, and Sergio ended the game by complimenting his friend on his hard won proficiency with the spear. They said their good-byes that night, since Taylor would wake with the dawn and leave while his friend slumbered. He shook Sergio's hand after the meal and explained in his best Portuguese that he did not have a brother back home, but that if he had been granted to right to choose someone for that role, Sergio would be the man. His friend received the compliment warmly and said that he was "*muito orgulhoso*" or very proud to have earned Taylor's high esteem. As with Guilherme, Taylor found that parting with Sergio was difficult and, knowing that in all likelihood he would never see this gentle and patient friend again, he told him that in the months and years to come, he would certainly feel *saudade*—a melancholy longing—for his company. That evening he mourned his loss a little and went to bed with a heavy heart.

The next morning Taylor met his new guide, Javier, at the dock as agreed and they sped off up the river. The man was hung over and sullen and seemed to take it out on his motor. He ran the engine at top torque and the brawny boat plowed a brown wake through the river. They made good time to Iquitos, arriving in about twelve hours. Once there, Taylor checked into the possibility of getting money wired to him, but none of the cambios would accept his word that he was who he claimed to be without giving them some identification. So he tried to convert some of his dollars into sols but the exchange houses wanted to deal only in the new bills with watermarks. Taylor had only the older U.S. currency and it was badly mangled. He converted his few remaining reais and tried to call Quinn and, once again, got only her answering machine. Fearing he would run low on money with repeated attempts to reach Boston, he decided to try his luck calling home. He expected to hear his mother or father's voice answer the phone, but it was a younger man's voice. Taylor apologized for the wrong number and said he was trying to reach the Morelands.

"This is the Moreland's place," replied the voice, now sounding more familiar.

"Who is this?" asked Taylor.

"Bill Hennis. Who is calling?"

"Taylor."

"Oh," replied Bill unenthusiastically.

"Are my parents around?" asked Taylor.

"No," replied Bill. "Mom's in town and Dad's in the field." Taylor grew irritated at the presumptuous usurper.

"Then what are you doing in the house?" asked Taylor.

"Sara and I are living here now. Your father just couldn't manage on his own anymore."

"What do you mean, couldn't manage? He's as strong as a mule and about twice as stubborn."

"What would you know about it?" replied Bill accusingly. "You've been gone since you were eighteen. He is not a young man anymore. He gets tired."

"Don't get too comfortable there Bill," snapped Taylor

"Why? You planning on coming home soon? Need your old room back?" taunted Bill caustically. Taylor said nothing. "I thought not," said Bill.

"Look, just tell my folks that I am O.K. and I will call again from Quito. I'll need a little money."

"Didn't they cut off your allowance when you went to college?" jabbed Bill.

"Just give them the message." Taylor hung up furious, but felt that he had no recourse against Bill's intrusion into his family. He wanted him off the farm. But by his long absence he was beginning to feel he had lost any right to assert his will in family matters, and Bill knew this.

After a few more failed attempts to contact Quinn, he decided to cut his losses and went to the docks to try to line up transportation to Misahualli, Ecuador on the Rio Napo. He bargained with a riverman for a reduced fare on a boat transporting portable generators and settled in for the ride. After an uncomfortable yet uneventful trip crouching near the engine compartment, he arrived in Misahualli and walked to a secluded stand of trees at the outskirts of town where he strung a hammock. In the morning he went to change his dollars for Ecuadorian sucres and discovered that over the prior months, Ecuador had slipped into an economic crisis. There were talks of converting to the dollar, but few people had enough of the inflated sucres or dollars to break his hundred dollar notes. After being frustrated at the few shops in town, he asked a clerk at a hotel that catered to tourists where he could change his old bills. The man was skeptical, but suggested he try to swap with another tourist. He knew of no other Americans in town, but suggested that Taylor walk several miles down a lane to the north of town where, following a scribbled map on a napkin, he would find a Pension run by a Swiss man. There he might be able to give him smaller bills or change his hundreds for a pile of sucres. Hungry and completely out of useful currency, he set out around dusk for the lodge.

At the margin of town, the roads had no markers and the main track often splintered into animal trails or private lanes, making it necessary to explore and backtrack. Taylor began to rely more and more on his compass and the advice of local farmers. Several hours into nightfall, he rounded a bend in the road and saw lights twinkling through the jungle foliage up ahead. The lights appeared to come from a grouping of three or four houses perched upon a little hillock near a tributary to the Rio Napo. Tired, hungry and foot-sore, he quickened his pace towards the lights, not knowing exactly what he would find.

As he turned down a well-tended cobblestone lane, he could see that the place was not a cluster of houses, but a little hotel. A hand carved sign designated the place as Pension del Oriente. Through a dense shroud of trees, Taylor could make out a main lodge and several smaller cabins flanking either side. A line of torches made of oil soaked rags on bamboo staffs lit the path leading up to the lodge. Abstract sculptures carved of wood and stone lined the path and at the base of an enormous tree sat a Buddhist temple illuminated by a constellation of candles. Walking up the path, the tired traveler felt as if he were stepping into a tranquil oasis of luxury and cultivation. Curious to meet the proprietor, he quickened his pace for the door. Nearing the porch, he startled a large German shepherd from its sleep. The dog bolted to its feet and lunged forward, ears flattened and teeth bared. Taylor stumbled backwards and barely had time to swing his pack off to place between himself and the attacking animal. The dog hit the pack at a full run and pushed Taylor back up against a tree. The shepherd mauled the straps and tried to get his jaws around Taylor's hand. Trying to alert the inn-keepers, he yelled for help while he staved off the attack. His cries worked, for the lights went on in the lodge and a woman in a long skirt came running to his aid carrying a broom. As Taylor' attention turned to his rescuer, the dog leapt at his leg and bit through his jeans down about the calf. Taylor winced, but held his ground, just as the woman came to chase the dog off. The shepherd retreated, but hovered at a distance, growling and eyeing his victim for another opportunity to advance.

The woman guided the shaken stranger inside and went to get him some salve for his wounds. Taylor was left in a large, rustic lodge, with high open ceilings borne up by heavy, rough-hewn rafters. The furnishings were simple but fashioned with great attention to quality and durability by the hands of artisans. Handmade chairs of black, oiled wood sat solidly around a massive dining table planed from a single block of teak. In the center of the table was a red mahogany bowl filled to overflowing with an exotic bounty of jungle fruits. The floor reminded Taylor of the Manaus Opera House—parquet with wooden tiling of alternating blond and walnut squares.

The woman who had rescued him returned with a slim man with dark, brown, inquisitive eyes and a wild shock of white hair. He appeared to be in his forties but possessed an air of youthful vigor that made it difficult to determine his age. He looked surprised to see Taylor, but he was gracious and bowed a little in a gesture of servile decorum.

"How can I help you," he asked, seeming to have guessed with one look that English was the most likely candidate for a language.

"Well, saving me from that dog was a good start!" he said good-humouredly.

"But you didn't come out of your way here to confront our dog. You must have stopped by for something else, yes?" The man had a German accent and smiled politely as he spoke.

"Yes. I was passing through on my way to Cotopaxi and someone in Misahualli mentioned that you might have an American here who could trade dollars for sucres."

"Passing through to Cotopaxi?" he asked incredulously. "You must have more to say than that," prodded the man encouragingly. Taylor laughed a little at how absurd his explanation sounded. The man looked at his watch. "It is quite late. You really should stay tonight and exchange your dollars with my guest in the morning."

"Oh." Taylor looked at his watch. It was near midnight. "That sounds nice, but—," Taylor hesitated, looking around at the rustic luxury. "I don't have a lot of money," he replied, "but thank you anyway."

"As you like," bowed the host. Taylor was about to go back to the jungle and sling a hammock when an athletic looking man came in asking for towels.

"Hello Donald!" said the white-haired man. He called to Taylor. "This is the American tourist I mentioned."

Taylor introduced himself and explained his dilemma to his countryman. After looking over the notes Donald agreed to the exchange, but said his currency was with his wife who was sleeping.

"I could come back tomorrow if you would prefer," offered Taylor.

"Come back from where? We're in the middle of the jungle," Donald laughed. Taylor detected a southern accent.

"I have camping gear." Taylor shouldered his pack and made ready to go.

"Nonsense. You'll be drained of your blood by mosquitoes," countered the American.

"I have a camping budget," clarified Taylor with a smile.

"Then you'll stay tonight as my guest," Donald persisted.

"No, really. I couldn't impose," he protested, embarrassed by the generosity. But Donald was set on the idea and without listening to the objections turned to the host, who Taylor would later learn was named Marcel, and ordered him to make ready one of the cabins.

"You'll offend me if you refuse," said Donald, closing the subject. In a matter of minutes Taylor went from planning on sleeping in the jungle, exposed to rain and biting insects, to checking into a luxury jungle lodge.

In the light of the morning, he had a better look around his cabana and was even more impressed by the artistry with which the inn had been constructed. A small but comfortable bed occupied the center of the room and a gauzy canopy hung down from ceiling, draping all in a soft light. The floors were made of huge, gray, slate tiles and a brightly colored handmade blanket was folded neatly at the foot of the bed. A lamp made from bamboo sat on a small table near the bed and a bouquet of red ginger and white orchids filled a vase near the window. As he pushed back the wide windows and the exterior wooden shutters, he was greeted with the view of an expansive, densely wooded jungle. Within a few hundred yards, a small stream snaked and curled its way through the forest on its way to join the wider Napo River down below. In the trees nearest to the cabin, flowering orchids and spiky bromeliads clung to the moist black branches. Palmettos and banana plants crowded around the lodge and large black and green hummingbirds darted from flower to flower. Everything was a profusion of bright blooms and luxuriant growth.

After a breakfast of fresh-squeezed orange juice and papaya, Taylor strolled around the grounds, enjoying the attention to detail. Marcel, an eccentric Swiss expatriate, had built the main lodge using the rich, red wood of the Brazil tree. The beams which framed the walls and ceilings looked like ancient rail road ties. They were heavy and gnarled and the joints were all snugly fit, tongue and groove. Overlapping red tiles formed the roof and the walls were a pale yellow stucco. The window and door casements were also made of the red beams and the doors were of a softer rose wood, stained and varnished. Large, double windows ran the length of the main hall, and they remained open throughout the day to admit the light and a cooling breeze.

The pension was set up to handle up to around twelve tourists at a time and it catered to an exclusive species of traveler that was willing to pay exorbitant prices to have their luxury accommodations and gourmet cuisine in the most exotic of areas. Marcel had been traveling in the region around Iquitos fifteen years earlier when he met the woman who would become his wife, Teresa Salvador del Maldonado, daughter of a prominent Peruvian importer. With the help of Teresa's father, he built the inn and began bringing in a list of celebrities and wealthy travelers who wanted to see the jungle in its primitive beauty but without being subject to the privations of the wilderness. The business had done remarkably well, and adorning the walls were photographs of Marcel and Teresa flanked by rock stars and politicians. Taylor filled his day wandering through the exuberant gardens and dozing in his cabana. Later that evening, he met the other guests and his host in the main hall. Donald came down to dinner in white linen pants and a breezy white linen tunic. He was tan with piercing blue eyes, and he swept his thick brown hair back from his forehead with a light scented oil.

Donald Vasio fit the elite profile of Marcel's clientele. A thirty-five year old heir to a tobacco fortune, he would never have to work a day in his life if he so chose. He was a man with a prodigious appetite for aesthetic pleasures and, as a matter of principle, indulged himself without moderation. When he became interested in opera, he spent the summer months in Verona, Italy, watching every show in the Opera Festival. For a while he flirted with the idea of being a vintner and toured Burgundy, Madeira, Sonoma and all the finest wine growing regions in the world, amassing a huge private collection of vintages which he stored in a temperature controlled cellar in his home in Raleigh, North Carolina. His artistic tastes were similarly refined, and he had a wild enthusiasm for the Pre-Raphaelite painters for their doughy women with fleshy forms, plush robes, and porcelain complexions. He owned a small painting of a nude shepherdess from the workshop of Millais—all that he could get his hands on with his small fortune—which he suspended on the ceiling above his bed so that it was the last thing he closed his eyes upon in the night and the first thing that greeted him in the morning.

His family had made its money off the bent backs of so many impoverished blacks—sharing peerage with the Dukes in that blighted nobility of the South. He was well educated, taking a degree from Emory University in literature. From time to time he dabbled in a white-collar career to keep himself entertained, and he had been an importer of cigars. Toying with the idea of becoming a chef, he bought a fashionable restaurant in Raleigh when all the new money was clamoring for overpriced cuisine to validate their membership in the suburban class. His parents felt he should be in a position of executive leisure and took a rather dim view of his bourgeois, bohemian hobbies. But they tolerated his whims because it was much easier for them to make excuses for him to acquaintances at golf club mixers than his drug addicted brother. Despite his life of privilege, Donald was very warm and outgoing. He was gregarious and good-natured, for the world was his plaything and he had not yet exhausted its ability to amuse him.

Accompanying Donald was a stunning olive-skinned woman of regal carriage. Wearing an orange skirt with a purple silk blouse, she appeared to Taylor to be a human bird of paradise. He learned over the course of the evening that she went by the name Taj and she was the daughter of a British diplomat and an Indian Brahmin. She had met Donald during a performance of *Madame Butterfly* in the Roman coliseum of Verona three years earlier. They had been traveling the world together ever since.

Taj shared Donald's appreciation of an aesthetic life, but unlike Donald, who possessed an almost childlike excitement at discovering pleasures, she was rarely moved by a lovely scene because she *expected* the world to be beautiful. Consequently, when she saw ugliness or pain she took offense, as if a pot-bellied, famished child or a trash-choked stream were disagreeable anomalies which threatened to ruin her enjoyment of life. At these moments, her brow would cloud and the corners of her mouth hang down and an affect of utter disdain would settle upon her countenance, transforming her beauty, ironically, into sour irritability. What's more, she herself was not unaware of this ugly transformation, and it exasperated her to the point that she would try to stamp a smile upon her face to hide her displeasure with the world, resulting in an even more ridiculous grimace. In her vanity, she had become accustomed to assiduously avoiding situations which exposed her to suffering, asymmetry, discord, or imbalance. When things were going well, that's when she was the loveliest. Thus, in the pleasant and lush environment of the jungle lodge with the candlelight glowing and the rich wood shining, she was the most radiant being Taylor had ever seen.

"So you must tell us about your pilgrimage this evening Mr. Moreland," said Marcel to Taylor as they all sat down to dine together.

"Well, I don't know if you could call me a pilgrim, but I—"

"Are you searching for something?" pressed Marcel.

"Yes, in a way."

"And is this something vital to your sense of self and happiness?" the host continued.

"Yes."

"It is settled then. You are indeed a pilgrim like the rest of us!"

Donald raised his right hand as if swearing an oath. "That description fits me. Donald Vasio: pleasure pilgrim."

"And I thought I was alone in my quest," smiled Taylor.

"On the contrary," said the exotic flower to Taylor's right. "I think most people are drawn to beauty." She smiled and swept her indigo-black hair into a shining arc down one shoulder. "I hope to see the loveliest places in the world, and I don't think that I'll find anywhere more sublime than this." Marcel smiled at her praise and lifted his wine glass in thanks.

"I suppose we are kindred spirits then," replied Taylor, "because I'm trying to discover how the masters capture something as intangible as beauty."

Teresa came in from the kitchen and set the table with slivered mangoes with mint sprigs, smoked pirarucu, and caviar. Donald ordered three bottles of Chilean cabernet as the rounded notes of John Coltrane floated up and resounded off the high tiled ceiling.

"What do you want to know?" asked Donald. "I have dedicated my life to the pursuit of The Beautiful. The trick is to just immerse yourself in the things that give you pleasure," he said, raising his hands to indicate the glowing room. He filled all of their glasses to the rim with the garnet-red wine. "In fact, I see no reason to ever leave here! What do you say to that Marcel? How would you like a permanent boarder?"

"Wait until you've lived through a few rainy seasons before

you commit," cautioned the host.

"What do you say, Taylor? Stay here for a while. We'll have great fun together. Taj is not one for trekking—you know, with the mosquitoes and all—and I could use someone to go fishing with me."

"It sounds tempting, but I need to move on fairly soon."

"Oh yes. You mentioned something of Cotopaxi," remembered Marcel.

"I'm on my way to Cotopaxi, Ecuador where I plan to see some of the vistas painted by Frederic Church," explained Taylor.

"Church? The Hudson River School painter?" asked Donald.

"Yes, you know of him?" asked Taylor with surprise.

"Donald is an art snob," explained Taj. "His family has a long history of patronage."

"I can't say I know all his works, but I am familiar with the most famous of his South American landscapes. He was a big fan of volcanoes if I remember," continued Donald.

"Yes! That's him. There aren't many people who know about his work. I've been going over his journals for months now, and I'm beginning to feel as if I understand what he was trying to accomplish with his romantic visions. It's not reality he was after, not exactly, but rather a real depiction of the *experience* of reality."

"So you are a traveling art historian then?" speculated Marcel.

"Not primarily, although that is part of my background. I'd like to consider myself an artist," he apologized.

"Well then why don't you?" laughed Donald. "Better yet, don't consider yourself one, be one!" Taylor laughed uncomfortably as all eyes watched him. "What sort of work do you like to do?" Donald asked, emptying his glass. "Oils? I bet you're a watercolorist," he prodded.

"I like all mediums, but primarily oil." Taylor felt like retreating a little under the questioning, but Taj now pressed him.

"What type of paintings have you done so far? Landscapes? Portraits?" she asked.

"That's the problem," Taylor replied sheepishly, feeling as if he had been caught in a lie. "I haven't done much at all recently.

That is one of the reasons I am on this trip. I hope to generate some ideas for my work."

"Ah! So it is a real pilgrimage!" beamed Marcel.

"What more do you need for inspiration than this place?" asked Donald. "Come on, stay here and paint the lodge, the flowers, or Taj. She'll pose nude," he cajoled.

"Donald!" cried Taj in mock protest.

"It's a lovely place," agreed Taylor. "It really is. It's not that I lack vistas. It's more that I have to overcome some of my own reservations about my ability and my selection of themes and subject matter," he explained, beginning to feel a little more comfortable with these strangers who showed so much interest in his art. "It's odd. I want so much to create beautiful paintings, but when I get half way through I begin to look back on what I have done and I am overcome with disappointment. Nothing ever seems to live up to my preconceived notions of what I set out to accomplish. I haven't been able to complete a painting for so long because of so many looming doubts and nagging frustrations," confessed Taylor, the wine loosening his tongue.

"Then why torment yourself with painting if it doesn't bring you enjoyment?" asked Taj.

"It's not all torture. I've been working on a journal during this trip and that has been going quite well. I have some notes that should be very helpful when I get back in the studio."

"It seems like it would be easier for you to be an art critic or maybe even Church's biographer," observed Donald, filling the glasses. The notion had occurred to Taylor also and for a moment he imagined himself going over documents and letters, arranging the pieces of another man's life, acting as an interpreter of another artist's work. He felt his anxiety lifting as he dropped the expectations of himself.

Teresa disappeared into the kitchen and returned with the main course—roasted pork tenderloin in ginger and guava, sweet potatoes in butter and piles of fresh breads. The pork was served in a heavy pewter tray and garnished with sword-like heliconia blossoms of red and orange. The sweet potatoes came wrapped in banana leaves and as Teresa pulled the crease apart with a fork a buttery stream of steam wafted into the air. Donald ordered two bottles of oaky merlot and the plates were soon piled with the rich feast. Between bites of food, Donald returned to Taylor's struggle to paint.

"Taylor, Why the need to paint at all? For my own selfish reasons I appreciate that there have been great artists in the world. They have contributed enormously to my enjoyment of life. But the old cliché that one must suffer for art seems true and most artists have made great sacrifices in life. That's not for me. Maybe it's not for you either. Art will still happen, whether you dash a bunch of paint on your canvasses or not. Even if you were to become famous, you'll end up a corpse. If your day to day existence is marked by pain, what's the point? Why not leave the creating and the suffering to others and take pleasure in introducing people to the works of Church and other masters?"

Taylor could not come up with a reasoned response for why he continued to push himself to create when he seemed incapable of sustained artistic effort. The effects of the wine combined with thoughts of drawing what pleasures could be had from life seduced Taylor with visions of ease and indolence. Soon the dinner conversation turned away from the subject of art and for the rest of the evening Donald regaled all with his stories of smuggling Cuban cigars into the United States under Dominican labels. He would never let anyone's glass slip below half full, and, by the end of the night, Taylor found that he was quite drunk. He excused himself unsteadily around two in the morning and wobbled off to his cabin.

The following day, he awoke late, head throbbing, and tried to formulate an answer to Donald's question: why continue to press himself as he did to become a painter? What good would it do for him and what had it gained for him thus far in his life? The answer he kept coming up with was that when he had only dabbled in painting he had found it to be a pleasant pastime, but from the moment he began graduate school and had committed himself to a life of art he had suffered the greatest anxieties. Graduate school had left him close to penniless. Even if he were to finish with the degree, his employment prospects were extremely slim. His long hours at trying to perfect his skills had pulled him away from Quinn and had yet to yield a representation of his talents. To continue to pursue painting as a career condemned him to almost certain poverty, and he could not expect Quinn to burden her life by continuously having to compensate for his selfish indulgence in art. A commitment to living life as an artist would also prevent him from participating in the running of his family's farm and would further alienate him from his father and mother.

Once again in his life, he began to think that it would be so much easier to drop his vain imaginings and go back to Rockwater. Ultimately, he decided, he had become a victim of his own romantic conceptions of life in which he pictured himself as a unique and talented soul and the universe as a benevolent force which was always witnessing his striving with the design of reaching down at any moment in an act of divine intervention to elevate his star to the constellation of master painters. This brooding deflated his enthusiasm for continuing on his journey, and he asked to stay on for a few days at a rate he could afford. Marcel agreed, saying that Donald had already insisted on paying his whole tab, whatever it turned out to be.

Later that afternoon, Taylor met Donald for some fishing. They went winding their way into the forest on the back of the great, green Rio Napo, looking for whatever quarry they could find. They pulled in a number of toothy brown piranha and spotted what looked like a large pirarucu. When they moved closer to investigate, it turned out to be a river dolphin.

"I'd like to get a better look at that!" exclaimed Donald as the animals darted away in a swirl of water. "Move in. Move in!"

"They're beautiful creatures," admired Taylor, "unique in all the world, but very shy." Rather than paddling closer, Taylor maneuvered the boat away so as not to disturb the animal. Donald watched the sleek dolphin greedily and he shot a glance over his shoulder at Taylor that expressed his irritation at having been denied a chase.

Later that evening they met for dinner again in the lodge. The meal was as sumptuous as before. Piranha soup, fried plantains, rich chocolate mousse with fresh mango. Donald ordered bottle after bottle of wine and as the evening wore on, everyone began to feel the affects of the drink. Fragments from a continuing disagreement between Taj and Donald began to rupture the friendly conversation. Taj, who was the least inebriated of all, was beginning to grow impatient with her drunken husband's hilarity. Donald was describing how he could tell just by looking at the pubic area in a nude portrait if the male artist had slept with his female model. His explanation was laced with slurred profanities and punctuated with riotous laughter.

"You don't have to scream, Donald," scolded his wife. "We're all within arm's distance." She had left half her plate to get cold because she had been becoming more and more outraged with his antics.

"Maybe you're just sitting too close!" he joked, unrepentant. To bait her he ordered port for everyone for an after dinner drink. She turned to her host to continue the attack circuitously.

"We need to change our cabin," she stated.

"Certainly," replied Marcel. "Is there something wrong with yours?"

"There are bugs in our room," she complained.

"Don't mind her Marcel. Our room is fine," Donald waved a rubbery hand in the air to dismiss her as if she were the bug.

"It is not fine!" Taj snapped. "There was a huge spider on the windowsill when I woke up this morning. And I have mosquito bites!"

"She's complaining about mosquitoes in the jungle," sneered Donald to Taylor. He turned drunkenly to Marcel. "Listen, do you have any spray? We could spray the place. Spray the whole jungle while you're at it." Taj had set her jaw and an angry furrow was working its way from her brow to the bridge of her nose. She looked haggard and twisted.

"There is no reason why I have to live with bugs just because we are in the jungle. Someone can take care of them. What's the point in paying these high prices?" She turned to Taylor in the hopes of soliciting an ally. "If you have the money, why would you sleep with vermin and blood suckers?"

"Funny. That's what my parents said to me before I married you," slurred Donald nastily. The furrow that started between Taj's brow was now a series of ugly, cavernous faults that traversed her forehead, intersecting at all manner of bizarre angles. Sensing the veneer of her pretty marriage had shattered, she forced herself to show her teeth in what was meant to be a smile. But the effect it produced was like broken tiles in a gutter. She shot a glance at the other diners to see if they had witnessed the humiliation. They had.

"Ha! ha!" she tried to laugh. "Donald is known for his one-liners at dinner parties. He'll do anything for a laugh in the moment. It's the moment with Donald that matters. He doesn't think much ahead if he's enjoying himself." She got up and, exerting a great effort to smile graciously to all, walked over to Donald who was now slumped over his plate. "Come on dear, you've been witty enough for one night." She tugged at his arm, trying to coax him out of his chair.

"Get off me bitch!" moaned the drunken husband, jerking his arm out of her hand with such exaggeration that he toppled a string of wine glasses, spilling the dregs on his sleeves and into Taylor's lap.

"Donald, you're making an ugly scene," hissed Taj through a grimace. "Don't you dare make me look bad," she whispered hot in his ear. But Donald was oblivious, sunken already into a Bacchanalian slumber.

"Good night," said Taj with pathetic dignity, turned on her heel and walked quickly out of the hall. Taylor and his hosts looked at their plates in the prolonged and uncomfortable silence that followed while Donald snored in his plate, a dollop of caviar matted in his hair.

The next day Taylor awoke near noon with a headache again. It occurred to him that he had been drunk two nights in a row—something that hadn't happened since college. All he wanted to do was to drink glass after glass of water and purify himself. He had become disgusted with Donald's hedonistic wallowing and Taj's foolish vanity. Walking to the kitchen, he met Donald who seemed to have suffered no ill affects at all. He was carrying a fishing pole and a rifle.

"Let's go see what we can get!" he insisted.

"You go ahead. I think I'll rest here a while."

"Come on," pushed Donald.

"No, really, I would prefer not to," he replied, tiring of the man's constant demands to be entertained.

"What do I have to do to get you out of doors, stop paying your tab?" he laughed, but Taylor heard the bullying reminder that he was indebted to him. Smoldering at the other man's shameless manipulation, he went back to his room and got his fishing gear, all the while tempering his anger with the notion that this outing cleared his debt and that he would leave the inn the moment they returned.

They went out on the Rio Napo in a small canoe, Taylor paddling, Donald alternately scanning the water and the canopy. He pointed the gun into the trees, looking through the scope for birds, monkeys, or anything moving.

"You won't find anything to shoot worth a bullet here," advised Taylor.

"Are you some sort of expert?" challenged Donald. Taylor sensed he was perhaps embarrassed from the night before and was now punishing him on the off chance that he had passed judgment. Taylor let the challenge drop. Donald continued his vain search for a target for an hour. No quarry bigger than a parakeet presented itself and so, sullen that the jungle had failed to provide a diversion, Donald set the gun in the bow.

Arriving at the bend in the river where they had pulled in so many piranha two days before, Taylor laid aside the oar, threw in the light anchor, and rigged his line. He began fishing but his companion appeared bored and restless.

"I thought you wanted to go fishing."

"I did, but I'm tired of the piranha. There are thousands of them. They're common. I want something a little different this time. Something . . . unique," said Donald, watching the ripple on the surface of the water. Taylor guessed at his intention and felt a knot of apprehension form in his stomach.

"You don't mean the *boto*?"

"The what?"

"The dolphin. You can't kill those," insisted Taylor.

"Why not?" asked Donald, still staring at the water. He picked up the rifle and was fingering the stock.

"Well, for one thing I am certain they are protected," he answered , his tension rising. Donald held the gun now in his lap.

"And who is going to bust me out here," he snorted.

"To kill one is bad luck" threw out Taylor. His voice betrayed a twinge of desperation. The other man smiled to hear it.

"Does it bother you to kill a fish, Mr. fisherman?" asked Donald, gesturing towards the pole with his rifle.

"Look, what's the point? Why kill a dolphin?"

"For the teeth," said the hedonist flatly, looking back at the water.

"The teeth?"

"Think about it," said Donald. "How many people do you know that can say that they have teeth from an Amazon river dolphin?" He stared hard towards the center of the river where they had seen the dolphin before. Taylor watched the gun and was about to appeal to Donald's sense of morality.

At that moment, a ripple broke the surface within a few feet of the canoe. Taylor saw Donald swing the barrel towards the spot just as the distinctive pink hump of a *boto* rolled out of the little wake. Aiming from the hip, he took a shot at the slow-moving animal. Simultaneous to the discharge, Taylor had leapt to his feet and grabbed at the barrel to wrench it away from Donald, but the blast rocked the boat, sending him into the water. As he went under, the canoe drifted off and instinctively he thrashed his arms and kicked his legs to propel himself to the surface. Gulping air, Taylor felt the weight of the water tugging at his clothes and he grasped all about for something to buoy him up. His hand struck something solid in the water—like wet suede stretched taut over muscle. It was the dolphin. Fearing that Donald would get off another shot, he kicked hard to thrust himself between the animal and the boat. But the body of the dolphin bobbed lifeless beneath his sheltering hands and a gaping hole in the head streamed a steady trail of blood. Taylor gasped in horror and thrashed away from the body. He felt a despair at the hardness of the world that leadened his heart. His soaked clothes pulling him down, his head went under and a stream of red blood and green river rushed into his gaping mouth. For a moment he could see the green foil membrane between sky and water close like fused glass over his upturned face. He was a boy again in a black and cinder-choked stream, sinking to oblivion. In an eternal moment he was ready to succumb to the ugliness, to let the indifferent meanness of the universe snub him out. But an image of Quinn smiling at him over a table set with flowers came to mind, and he decided it was worth bearing all of it—all the viciousness of humanity and the disappointments of his own failings—to have flickering moments of bliss here and there in one's life. Kicking violently, he burst to the surface and took in a great lung of air.

In the canoe, Donald was half standing, half crouching as he whooped and celebrated over the kill.

"I got it! I got it!" shouted the hunter, standing awkwardly to look at his prize from the wobbling canoe. Taylor's panic turned to rage as Donald became an emblem of orgiastic gluttony. He lashed out towards the boat, covering the short distance in a few strokes. Grabbing the side of the canoe, he jerked at it violently, toppling Donald into the water. Then, in one fluid motion, he heaved himself over the side and kicked off on the flailing man, pushing him away from the boat. Sputtering and pawing like a frightened mutt, Donald lurched through the water, inadvertently colliding with the bleeding corpse.

"Help! Help! Get it away from me!" He struck at the dead animal in terror. "I can barely swim!" he cried.

"Here. Hang on to this," replied Taylor, throwing the rifle into the water before the struggling man. A little flurry of fins cut through the river towards the red stain which now drifted on the current.

"The piranhas!" cried Donald. "You've got to help me!"

"They won't eat too much of you before you make it to the shore," shouted Taylor as he paddled away.

"You bastard! You . . ." Donald choked on his venom, struggling to find the right slur that might sting Taylor and turn the boat around. "You ungrateful bastard!" was all he could think to say. Taylor regarded him with the indifference that the river shows for a drowning ant. Swimming in a cloud of blood, the man was gripped by terror and began wildly flailing his way towards a large fallen tree near the edge of the flooded stream. Taylor dug his oar into the water and slipped quickly back down the river in the direction of the lodge. As he rounded a bend he looked back and saw Donald hitching his leg up on the log, slapping futilely at the nipping piranhas as he pulled himself out of the water.

An hour later, Taylor was back in his room packing his gear. By sundown he was many miles from Pension del Oriente, bouncing down a graveled road in the back of a truck bound for Puerto Napo. He had left a map under Marcel's door as he slept, explaining to him where he could find his guest. Attached was a brief note.

Marcel:

    I thank you for your hospitality. I doubt, however, that Donald will be willing to pay for my charges after my actions today. He killed a boto, so I left him to the piranhas. Let the river do with him what it will. When (if) he returns, I suggest you turn him out. As you may know, he has brought misfortune upon himself. I will send you money within the year for my bill.

                         Taylor Moreland

AUGUST

The end of summer is always accompanied by an unsettling sense of regret. As the days begin to grow shorter and the sun draws a lower arc across the sky, every minute lost becomes a reminder of unfulfilled dreams and unrealized potential. When we recognize that the slow slide into fall is on the horizon, a sense of urgency sets in. For those driven by the most ardent passions, the waning season gives rise to erratic and impulsive acts meant to compensate for all the opportunities foolishly squandered. In this way, the human heart mirrors the workings of the cosmos, as summers seldom give way gracefully to their falls. As the season of the sun senses its diminution, it will rage against its passing with tantrums of heat that exceed even the most intense days of the solstice—a final demonstration of potency to forestall its own decline. As if bent upon scorching all of the growth which its warmth had so carefully nurtured before, the sun flares with explosive surges which threaten to parch all within reach of its beams. Yet for all its anguish, the fading sun suffers only a fraction of the torment which the lover feels when a shadow falls across the inflamed heart.

On Saturday, August 7, 1999, Quinn and Taylor were sharing breakfast together in their Cambridge apartment. On the side facing the street, two French windows opened up onto a narrow balcony, and the couple scooted a small table right to the edge so they could sit outside in the dappling sun. Quinn set the table with a cluster of red geraniums and Taylor brought them fresh fruit and coffee. It was their weekend ritual: a leisurely morning together with time to talk and hold hands. Their balcony overlooked an elm-lined residential street, and they loved to listen to the chittering sparrows and watch the people come and go. Sometimes they would see the same quick-stepping lady walking her poodle or their friend the Chinese grocer on his way to open the store. It was sacred time, and they looked forward to those precious hours throughout the week. But on this morning Taylor was fidgeting before the meal was over, distracted with excited energy. He pushed his half-finished food aside and took both her hands in his.

"I need to know if you are free tomorrow morning for a date," he said, brimming with anticipation.

"Well, I was going to work on a paper," she hesitated, puzzled by his intensity.

"A special date," Taylor emphasized, pretending to twist her arm.

"OK, OK," she laughed, pulling her hand free. "I'll make time."

"Great!" He was beaming. "See you later," he hopped up from the table and kissed her forehead. "I have some reservations to make." With that, he headed for the door, gave her a wave, and was gone. She went to the computer and began working on her essay, but his bubbling enthusiasm started her guessing as to the source. He had been in unusually good spirits of late, and she wondered if he had reconciled himself with his graduate studies as he approached his final year.

The following morning, she was awakened by Taylor clattering around in the kitchen. She got up to see what he was doing and through the cracked door saw that he had set a tray for breakfast in bed. She hopped back under the covers and pretended to be asleep. In a minute, he pushed the door ajar with his foot, making a grand entrance with coffee, toast, preserves, and a cluster of daisies in a little blue glass vase.

"Time to get going sleepy head," he sang.

"What's the occasion?" asked Quinn, sitting up and rubbing her eyes. He pushed back the curtains to admit the light. It was a brilliant Sunday morning.

"We're going canoeing," he announced. He left the room for a moment and returned carrying a loaded picnic basket and a white cotton blanket.

"I reserved a boat out at Concord and borrowed a car," he continued with excitement. "Let's get an early start so we'll have more time on the river." While he prepared the car, she quickly finished her breakfast and they were soon underway. In about an hour, they arrived at the river and hired their canoe. They began a few miles upstream from the Old North Bridge, Taylor paddling, Quinn poised in the bow, her face tipped up to the warming morning sun. In her sky-blue sun dress, her hair pulled back with a white barrette, she had the appearance of a forget-me-not blossom gliding across the surface of the water. For a while they drifted along on the meandering stream through pastures and woodlands. Taylor maneuvered the canoe along the winding channel as the August sun hummed in the clear sky overhead. Wading herons watched the two lovers indifferently from the shore, and from time to time an indignant snapping turtle, its carapace covered in clinging moss, waved its stubby fore-fins to steer itself out of the course of the drifting boat. Taking their time, they floated down to the bridge where Taylor stopped for a picnic. He tied up the boat near the shore and together they spread a blanket under an enormous elm not far from Emerson's home, Old Manse.

"I wouldn't be surprised if Emerson didn't paddle the same route we followed today," said Taylor, uncorking a bottle of wine. "Maybe he even picnicked under this tree."

"Maybe," said Quinn, waiting for Taylor to develop the thought.

"Somehow, in between being cooped up in that house and bantering with Thoreau, he found time to think about love," continued Taylor.

"Love? How so?" asked Quinn to humor him.

"Listen to this," exclaimed Taylor, happy she had taken his bait. He produced a volume of the poet-philosopher's essays from the basket.

"Oh, how convenient!" laughed Quinn. "Did you plan that?"

"Of course. I know you like him, so I've been doing some reading."

"Hey! That's my book!"

"Very observant! You'll get it back. Now listen." He began to read:

> By conversation with that which is in itself excellent, magnanimous, lowly, and just, the lover comes to a warmer love of these nobilities, and a quicker apprehension of them. Then he passes from loving them in one to loving them in all, and so is the one beautiful soul only the door though which he enters to the society of all true and pure souls. In the particular society of his mate he attains a clearer sight of any spot, any taint which her beauty has contracted from this world—

"'Taint'?" interrupted Quinn in mock offense. "Exactly just what are you trying to tell me, Taylor?"

"Wait. You'll see," he assured her. "He's romantic, but it's an idealism informed by reality. That's what really caught my attention." He continued:

> . . . he attains a clearer sight of any spot, . . . and is able to point it out, and this with mutual joy that they are now able, without offense, to indicate blemishes and hindrances in each other, and give to each all help and comfort in curing

the same. And, beholding in many souls the traits of the divine beauty, and separating in each soul that which is divine from the taint which it has contracted in the world, the lower ascends to the highest beauty to the love and knowledge of the Divinity, by steps on this ladder of created souls.

"Do you like it?" asked Taylor, as if his hopes hinged upon her approval. "It talks of a love beyond shallow infatuation or blind selfishness. It reminds me of us. I mean, the way we help each other, always towards a greater happiness, a greater love."

"Yes of course Taylor," she assured him. "It's lovely. Why is it so important that I like it?"

"I thought it might be nice to include in our wedding vows," he smiled, searching her eyes for an answer. She was caught by surprise and sat speechless for a moment. Taylor thought she did not understand. "That is, of course, if you agree to marry me." He reached into his pocket and produced a velvet ring case. On bent knee before her, he opened the case, revealing a sparkling white solitaire. A spontaneous expression of joy escaped Quinn's lips, laughter mixed with tears of happiness.

"Is that a yes?" asked Taylor.

"Yes! Yes . . . I wasn't expecting this, that's all. But yes!" She took his face in her hands and kissed him long and tender—crying, smiling, laughing. They embraced with a fervent possessiveness, each wanting to feel the solidity of the other, to know what it meant to have another and to give oneself to another.

"When?" asked Quinn, holding Taylor before her.

"As soon as possible . . . but," Taylor struggled to preserve the glow, a conflict lingering in his heart, corrupting his almost-perfect happiness.

"But what?" asked Quinn, not comprehending.

"I need to do something first."

"What is it?"

"I'm going to take a leave of absence from my studies."

"I still don't understand, Taylor. Why can't we get married

before or even during your leave?"

"I'm going to South America."

"South America?" repeated Quinn incredulously.

"Ecuador. I need to get—"

"Is this about Church?" sighed Quinn, unable to mask her disappointment.

"It's not about Church. I'm going to try to start painting, to find the will to create again. Then the moment I get back we'll get married." She shook her head in disbelief and looked away.

"I promise," said Taylor, catching her hands up in his. She knew she could turn him from his plans with a single word, but she would never have him entirely if she did.

"OK, Taylor, but not a moment more." He breathed a great sigh of relief and pressed his face into her neck. Quinn stroked his hair and consoled herself with the knowledge that he loved her. In the corner of her mind she held out the hope that he would abandon the trip or that if he went, he would quickly tire of the hardships and return early. For the moment, the joy of committing her life and love to Taylor diminished all other concerns.

The following weekend they were headed for Charleston to visit Quinn's family. It was Taylor's idea. He insisted on meeting her parents and winning their approval. They left in the morning, driving I-95 in the frantic stream of traffic through Massachusetts, Connecticut, and New York. On the second day, the pace slowed down and gradually the landscape was transformed from strip malls and gas stations to rolling farmland. Along the roadside, Kudzu vines climbed up into the trees and threatened to pull down old telephone poles, abandoned barns, or anything stationary in their path. Here and there, patches of honeysuckle bloomed in the fields, and they rolled down the windows to take in the sweet perfume.

They arrived in the afternoon as towering thunderheads piled up over the Sand Hills. The Yarbroughs lived in a stately two-story brick home on a residential street not far from the Battery. As the travelers pulled into the driveway, Gail and Franklin were busy in the garden. Quinn's mother wore a long sleeved, floral patterned shirt and a tennis visor. Her hands were protected by green cotton gloves, and she carried a pair of clippers. Franklin was a little portly and wore suspenders to hold up his khaki slacks. His thinning gray hair poked out below the rim of a wide straw hat. He trailed behind Gail, raking her clippings into untidy little heaps. From time to time, he pulled a white kerchief from his shirt pocket to wipe the sweat from his brow. They laid aside their work when their daughter came up the path, luggage in hand.

"Your scholarship run out?" joked Franklin, looking at her suitcases.

"No. Just home for a good meal," replied Quinn. She gave her father a great hug.

"Well then, you've come to the wrong place," said her mother. "You know I can't cook." Gail stepped up to offer her cheek. Quinn kissed her mother and then pulled Taylor into the little circle.

"I make a pretty good parmesan chicken," he announced.

"Well, well," enthused Gail, looking from Taylor to Quinn. "You really have found yourself a liberated man."

"Taylor Moreland," said Taylor, extending his hand to one parent and then the other.

"Yes, we know," said Gail. "Considering you are about to become part of the family, we thought we would have met you before now." She said it with a smile, but he felt the intended rebuke. Quinn noticed it too and she scooped up her bags and scooted Taylor inside to spare him any discomfort at being left alone with them. She put her luggage in her room and set Taylor up in a guest room on the first floor.

"We're not staying together?" he asked, feeling a bit abandoned.

"Not yet. I don't know how my parents will react. I'm in uncharted waters here," she explained. It seemed silly to maintain the pretense of abstinence considering they were living together, but he accepted the arrangement, willing to do what was necessary to make her parents comfortable. He recognized that it was important to her that they sanction their union, and, out of a sense of pride, he too wanted their approval.

That evening, hoping to win a little good will, he offered to make them dinner. With Quinn's help, he prepared his chicken recipe, mashed potatoes, and buttered beans. Gail and Franklin treated the meal as a formal affair and set the table with the family silver and china. The feeling of being scrutinized combined with the unfamiliar kitchen made Taylor slow and inefficient. When he finally got the meal on the table, the beans were cold and the chicken was tough. He apologized profusely; everyone protested that it was fine. Franklin made an effort to alleviate his embarrassment, offering up humorous anecdotes about his own experience of catching the curtains on fire while lighting a flaming Christmas pudding.

To shift the focus, Quinn turned the conversation to the wedding. Shortly after Taylor had proposed she had called her parents with the news. They were reserved in their enthusiasm, having never met Taylor before, but supportive in the end. Now, with their future son in law at their table, the two parents were eager to know more about him.

"So, Quinn tells me that you are headed for South America?" asked Franklin.

"That's right," confirmed Taylor. "As soon as possible, which means this December."

"Have you set a date for the wedding?" asked Gail.

"Well, tentatively, yes," replied Taylor. "Probably next summer."

"Still want to give yourself time to back out, eh?" teased Franklin.

"No," laughed Taylor. "I am very excited about marrying Quinn, but I . . . I have some work to do towards the studio component of my program that I can only do in South America," he explained ambiguously.

"Well I suppose that we had better start interrogating you now," concluded Gail, putting on an expression of suspicious mistrust, "because the next chance we'll get to talk to you may be in the reception line after the wedding."

"Mom!" protested Quinn.

"No, she's right," conceded Taylor. "I should have made a more concerted effort before now to introduce myself. But I am looking forward to getting better acquainted this week."

"As are we," smiled Gail. "In fact, what are you doing tomorrow?"

"Going to the art museum," cut in Quinn preemptively. Taylor looked at her blankly, missing her attempt to extricate him from her mother's coalescing plans.

"I was hoping they might help me trim the roses," said her father.

"Taylor doesn't look so excited about either of those two options," observed Gail. "Why don't you come with me?" she proposed. "I have my own weekend routines. Birding near the Ashley River. Sound good?" Quinn shot him a look that said "better to come with me," but he could see no polite way around it.

"Sure," he said. "But I don't have any binoculars."

"Can you do any calls?" joked Gail.

"As an ex-farm boy I can do a pretty good rooster if I'm hard pressed," he laughed.

"You're hired!"

"It should be fun," he said. "I'm looking forward to it."

"Then it's settled," smiled Franklin. "Quinn can help me in the garden."

The next morning, Gail and Taylor drove the family station wagon out to Drayton Place on the Ashley. Arriving just after sunrise, they wound up a secluded gravel lane, past massive live oaks hung with Spanish moss. The place was closed, but a guard let them in. "She's a friend of mine who works part-time security at the newspaper," explained Gail. They parked at the water's edge in view of an ostentatious ante-bellum house with manicured gardens.

"What's this?" asked Taylor.

"Plantation turned tourist trap," replied Gail, stepping out of the car. "I hate what it stands for, but it has provided a great haven for wildlife."

They walked down to the estuary and settled some lawn chairs on a deck over the dark waters. The river was wide, slow, and muddy. Along the flood plane grew swaths of tall yellow grass, intersected by winding, narrow channels. On the far bank lie clumps of stately oaks. Little crabs scuttled in and out of muddy holes in the embankments, and from out of the slime came the faint "plock, plock, plock" of filtering shellfish. Quietly they watched the inhabitants of the little stretch of river go through their routines of life. Following Gail's extended finger or a silent nudge of her chin, Taylor was introduced to a number of local birds.

"There's an egret!" she would whisper; or "That's the call of a male kingfisher."

Taylor watched and learned. She was birdlike herself—with piercing eyes, a sharp nose, and a jerky intensity. She barely spoke for the first few hours, but she was quite communicative, pointing out wildlife and making eye contact with Taylor to make sure he had seen a school of fish, an unusual seabird, or a retreating alligator.

Around noon they returned to Drayton and put the folding chairs away in the car. Gail produced a cooler with drinks and sandwiches and they sat in the garden under a blooming magnolia tree as they ate.

"This sort of wetland is in trouble all across the state," she said between bites of the lunch. I did a series of reports exposing a number of politicians and corporate farms who had teamed up to undermine existing environmental regulations. I don't think it's that people don't care about nature. I think that they just begin to take things for granted, assuming that beauty will always be there. But it isn't a given. You have to be vigilant, you know?"

Taylor heard in her words the timbre of his own sentiments and he nodded on agreement. Even though she was predisposed to be critical of him—no doubt for the sake of her daughter—he found himself liking her for her uncensored and unapologetic insights.

"I think sometimes people feel that they are entitled to good fortune in their lives. That's when they're in greatest danger of losing it." She studied him closely to see if he understood her. The subject had now clearly shifted to Quinn.

"I think you're right," agreed Taylor. He felt a need to justify himself to her. "I don't know how much Quinn has told you about us, but we love each other very much. I think we each fill a need for the other. When I return, we want to set the wedding plans in motion as soon as possible."

"Is that what Quinn wants?" she asked.

"No," replied Taylor, feeling she would respect his honesty. "But I think we will both be better off if I know what role, if any, art is going to play in my life." Gail was quiet for a moment, thinking. Her eyes scanned the horizon, focusing on nothing.

"So Quinn is your second love," she observed, presenting the idea to Taylor for confirmation. It was more blunt than he would have expected, even from her.

"Well . . . no," he protested. "I love her. I love your daughter, really love her. I never said my art was more important."

"You didn't have to," observed the shrewd reporter. "You say so with your life." He looked at her with a twinge of shame. Then she said something which surprised him even more.

"Realize that I am not judging you," she smiled with sincerity. "We are all defined by our passions. Just be prepared for the consequences of placing ideas before people. I have had to remind Quinn of that fact, over and over again throughout her life." It was criticism not motivated by rancor, but clearly intended to bring them together. He nodded in agreement and she responded with an encouraging smile. Satisfied that they had established a point of common understanding, she turned to watch the birds flit over the gardens. For the remainder of the trip Gail and Taylor got along quite well, and later in the evening Quinn was pleased to overhear her father say that Taylor "seemed like a genuinely sensitive young man." It was as close to a blessing as she could have hoped for.

Roughly one year later, Quinn returned to visit her parents, this time without Taylor. They were sensitive to the fact that she missed him and did not press her to justify his continued absence. After their first day together they knew that something more was troubling her. In casual conversations it came out that she was a bit embarrassed that her fiancé, after assuring her parents that he

loved her intensely and was anxious to marry, had not returned
and—worse—she could not even tell them with certainty where
he was or when he would come back. But that would have been
bearable, perhaps, if she had her work to distract her. Even that, it
seemed to her worried parents, failed to lift her spirits. She slept
late most mornings and spent a great deal of time alone in thought.
On her last weekend with her parents, her father sought to place
himself by her side for the day, just to give her the opportunity to
lean on him for support if she needed.

"Want to go to church with me today?" he asked over breakfast.

"You mean to hear your sermon?"

"No. I'm taking the day off," he explained. She looked up, not
understanding. "A friend of mine, Tyrel Wilson, is getting baptized.
I got someone to take my early service for me so I could go."

"Is Tyrel a baby?" she asked.

"No, a golfing friend. He's Baptist," explained her father.

"Oh. Well, . . ." she hesitated, "I've got a good book I'm
reading." She tried to sound upbeat.

"It's not your everyday service," he prodded.

"O.K.," relented Quinn. "It will be a nice chance to spend
time together."

Franklin drove her an hour outside of Charleston to the Calvary
Baptist Church. It was a small cinder block chapel off a county
road, tucked in among the soughing pines. On arrival, Franklin
led Quinn inside and they took up a pew near the front. It was a
simple church, cozy and welcoming. The brick walls were painted
in a soft peach and the windows consisted of alternating panes of
tinted glass. The squares of color transformed the slanting sunlight
into a soft quilting of elongated patches along the length of the
hall. The congregation was racially mixed, but predominantly
black. The older ladies wore dignified Sunday hats and white gloves,
while the men all wore suits and ties. Children skipped along the
aisles, their mothers keeping the fun in check with watchful eyes.
As father and daughter settled in for the service, the people around
welcomed them with a smile or with a warm clasp of the hand.

Soon the church was filled to capacity, and girls in teal dresses walked up and down the rows handing out folding fans—one side printed with a representation of the crucifixion and on the other, ironically, an ad for a funeral home. It was a warm morning and soon the place was aflutter with vigorous fanning. After a few minutes, the preacher—a black man with soft white hair—took his place at the altar and a quiet settled over the congregation. Quinn was half expecting a welcoming prayer when, without a word, the preacher raised his arms and a great burst of music rose up from the back of the church. Turning around in her seat, she saw around twenty choir singers, men and women and youths, all dressed in teal satin robes. Hands raised, voices lifted, they filled the small church with such a joyous sound that it amazed Quinn that they were not a hundred singers strong. The procession streamed down the aisles on either side of the pews until the small congregation was entirely surrounded by the singing, swaying, clapping, praying choir. They sang until the room shook. They sang with big voices. Voices that lifted up from the stomach and burst from the chest, soaring up to the rafters! They sang everyone out of their seats until mothers, children, old men, and the women in their staid hats—all, all were clapping and singing along. They sang out with light and exuberance. And Quinn—hoisted to her feet, humming along, swaying and smiling—felt a rush of emotion she had never experienced before, making her face flush, her chest tighten, and the hair on her arms stand up on end. To her amazement, she found warm tears rolling down her cheek, rolling uncontrollably so she had to catch them on the back of her hands. With the tears she felt self-conscious and turned away from her father, looking to see if he had noticed. What she saw astonished her even more. He was weeping himself!—singing and clapping, caught up in the moment.

When the music stopped, Quinn stood there breathless for an endless moment. She would have stood there indefinitely in rapture had her father not tugged her hand to settle her in her seat. Then the preacher stood before them with his dignified white hair and pressed cream suit. He welcomed the guests, even mentioning Quinn and her father by name, and announced the happy circumstances of their gathering: a baptism for Mr. Wilson. The service continued with a sermon drawn from the Gospel of John, the preacher pacing back and forth, underscoring the necessity of coming into one's spiritual life through the exercise of free will. His voice rose and fell with intensity as he dramatized scenes from the life of the Baptist. But it was not purely didactic; it was a dialogue. Along the way, he would pause and address the congregation with questions: "Do you know what I mean?" he would ask, or "Have you felt that?" And spontaneous voices from the pews would respond "Yes! God a' mercy above!" and "Amen!"

At the end of the sermon, two men from the congregation went up to the altar and removed the lectern. Then they rolled back a carpet revealing a trap door in the floor. As they lifted the door, Quinn could see a small tiled pool built into the raised platform of the altar. Mr. Wilson was led forward, wrapped in a long white robe, his hands pressed together in prayer. The preacher had stepped out and had changed into a similar costume and now stood knee deep in the Baptismal font.

"Are you ready to give yourself to God?" asked the preacher.

"I am," replied Wilson. The preacher motioned to the initiate to take his place beside him in the water. He recited baptismal liturgy while the church organist played "Amazing Grace" softly in the background. Quinn felt someone take her hand—a smiling woman next to her in the pew. She looked around and saw everyone in the church had clasped hands. She took up her father's in her own and they exchanged a smile. People began to sway and hum along with the music as the preacher continued with the baptism. At the end of the ceremony, the preacher submerged Wilson in the water three times, supporting him with an arm behind the small of the back and tipping him like a dance partner. When done, he presented him to the assembled friends and neighbors as "Brother Wilson." Everyone clapped and cheered, and people streamed to the front of the church to kiss and embrace the man. Again, Quinn found herself tearful. It was an emotion that had no easily identifiable "cause," but it was akin to gratitude one feels at being loved. It made her recall a time when she had slipped from the climbing bars at a park and skinned her knee. A woman—a complete stranger—had swept her up in her arms, washed the wound and dressed it, all the while soothing her with "There, there. I know how it is. You'll be all right." Quinn left the church that day with a profound appreciation for the human capacity for compassion.

Following the service, Franklin took Quinn for a walk along the Battery. She was quiet and reflective. In the heat of the day, they found a bench under the shade of a huge spreading oak and sat down in view of the harbor.

"You liked it," said Franklin, knowing she was still reviewing the morning's experiences. She nodded. "And that surprises you," he intuited. She looked at him, feeling exposed.

"How do you know?"

"I know my own daughter" he said, patting her on the knee. "You never did go in for the emotional stuff."

"Before today, it always made me suspicious," she admitted. "Passion has a way of distorting people's judgment . . . of getting in the way of truth. But now I think . . ."

"What?"

"But now I don't know," she confesssed. Her father said nothing, letting her sort through her thoughts. She became brooding and pensive. "I wish you'd never taken me there."

"You don't mean that," Franklin guessed.

"No. Not really. But before today I was certain that all I needed I could get from my books and from a few moments of solitude here and there." He chuckled in a way that suggested amusement at her unselfconscious naiveté.

"What are you laughing at?" she said, mildly irritated. "I thought that you approved of the path I've taken." He turned to her, concerned.

"My dear, if you are pursuing theology because of me, you are doing so for all the wrong reasons."

"Well, I'm not. Not for you entirely," she amended. "But at least in part." He considered the revelation, thinking of her years of hard work and self-sacrifice.

"What do you hope to find for all your searching?"

"Proof, I guess. Proof that the universe is not indifferent. Some sort of evidence to indicate that what we do and who we are more than accidents of time and matter. So I've always thought that a rational, academic approach to religion was the most promising. And already I've learned so much from looking at what some of the greatest minds have said on the matter."

"There are other approaches to truth. Think of what you experienced today."

She began to feel a little defensive, wanting to justify her choices to her father and to win his approval. After all of her carefully laid plans, she could not bring herself to admit that she was unsatisfied at Harvard. "I don't know what to make of what I felt today. I don't know if it comes from outside of me or inside. With all that . . . emotion, I don't know what to trust. I'd rather not change my path now."

"What do you make of Taylor's radical change of direction?" he asked.

"What has that got to do with it?"

"Do you condemn him?" he asked.

"No! Of course not!" protested Quinn. "He is trying to figure out what makes his life meaningful."

"Then why can't you grant yourself that same liberty?" he asked. "Why not entertain the possibility that there are different definitions of spirituality?"

"It's not the same," she objected.

"Why not?"

"Finding meaning in art is subjective and shifting. After all, art is artificial—man made. It's really whatever Taylor makes of it. Taking a different approach towards art is not like altering one's notion of God. The religions of the world all seem to be dealing with permanence, with immutable laws. They all seem to promote the same virtues and condemn the same vices. But it takes a certain degree of distance and objectivity to distill all those ideas down to their essences. I guess that's why theology suits me." She said it with conviction, but with the intent of shoring up a shaken resolve.

"It sounds like you thought this out quite thoroughly," he

said, laying the issue back in her hands. "As long as you are happy, I'm happy," he said patting her hand. After a moment he added thoughtfully, "I wonder what changes Taylor will experience as the result of his journey." She looked at him, puzzled, unable to read his intent. "I like him," he said with genuine approval. "I hope you two don't drift apart. Because, if you're anxious to marry soon after his return, I'd like to do the ceremony." The announcement surprised her, and she was overcome with gratitude. But in her heart she did not believe that she would see him any time soon.

"We'll be fine," she said, trying to reassure him. She did not want him to think less of Taylor for worrying her. "He's bound to be making his way back by now. He'll be back soon. Very soon." It was a comforting thought. And yet, as she approached the point in their relationship when she needed him the most, he was—by his own choice—conspicuously absent. In the space in her heart reserved for loving him, she detected the inklings of a new, troubling emotion. For the first time, Quinn felt a shadow of resentment.

The following week, Beth decided to call Quinn to check in for news of Taylor. It was, by coincidence, the anniversary of his marriage proposal. While Beth was reluctant to admit it, she knew that her son would call Quinn before he would contact his family. For her, the call felt like a concession of sorts in which—if she wanted to be closer to Taylor—she must accept that she needed to be more intimate with this woman who would eventually become her daughter-in-law. When she had met Quinn at Sara's wedding, it seemed to her that the young Harvard student viewed her as a provincial farm wife. She was friendly but reserved, well-mannered but uncomfortable. She had enjoyed the privileges of wealth and education that had never been even a remote possibility for Beth. This had the effect of heightening her sensitivity to her own lack of culture and led her to imagine that Quinn felt a certain pity for her insular life. As a result, Beth had made little attempt to mask her resentment during her visit. However, after a few months had passed, Beth began to realize that Quinn may be the only person with whom Taylor had been completely open and intimate. Despite her attempts to understand the reasons her son had given for his unexpected departure from school, she found it difficult to find a point of empathy with him. His enigmatic brooding and his restless dissatisfaction were a source of great frustration. Just when he was reaching the age when he should have been settling down, it seemed to Beth and Jim that he had thrown his life into confusion and, in doing so, disrupted the lives of all those closest to him.

While there remained a distance between herself and Quinn, she knew that, at the very least, they shared a sense of anxiety over Taylor's trip. In their few conversations since her son's departure, she recognized that this normally composed and independent woman was troubled by his leaving, more for the potential transformations that Taylor would experience than by his absence from her life. It was enough to make her like Quinn a little.

Quinn picked up the phone on the first ring. She had stayed home from work in the hope that Taylor would remember their special day.

"Taylor?" she answered.

"No. But close. It's his mom." Quinn tried to greet her warmly; her disappointment was clear. "Do you have any word from Taylor this week?" asked Beth. "He seems to call you more than he calls us."

"Nothing since last month," sighed Quinn.

"How are we going to get the money to him if he doesn't call?" complained Beth. It was stiflingly hot in Boston too, and, a continent apart, each woman could sense the other's emotional fatigue.

"I guess we just have to keep on waiting," speculated Quinn. "He is usually better at communicating than this."

"Really?" replied Beth, genuinely surprised. "He's always been a solitary person, even when he was a boy. Does he talk to you about what goes on in that head of his?"

"Well, yes, actually," replied Quinn apologetically. "That's why it is so strange to me that he hasn't been in better contact. I was hoping that it was just a bad habit of his—that he doesn't write or call when he travels."

"That's the way he's been dealing with us since he moved to

Boston," replied Beth, feeling slighted.

"I don't think he means to be uncommunicative with you," observed Quinn. "I think it's just the distance and the cost that prevent him from more regular contact. At least that's what I prefer to believe about this stretch of silence. It's better than imagining that he's forgotten me."

"Well, when he comes back from this trip, I hope he is a little more conscientious about others' feelings," concluded Beth. "To keep everyone in the dark about his whereabouts and his intentions is just plain inconsiderate. I love my boy, but he can be a little selfish sometimes," she fumed.

"I'm afraid I have to agree on that point."

"What if he is hurt or something? We would never know!" Quinn thought of Taylor's last call and the distressing news that he had been robbed.

"Maybe we'd better try to find him rather than wait only to have our worst fears confirmed."

"I agree," said Beth. "Where do you think he is?"

"I remember that he kept a set of maps with his whole route marked out." Quinn walked into the spare room they had converted into a study. With the phone wedged under her chin, she searched through his papers.

"Here's his books on Church," she said, unpiling the stacks on his desk. "And here are his maps." She leafed through them looking for a clue.

"Any notes?" asked the concerned mother. "Any addresses or phone numbers?"

"Nothing." Quinn moved to a pile of his personal journals on the shelf. She tipped them open to see if he had drawn out his route and dislodged a yellowed, folded letter. "Here's something," she said hopefully. She opened it and gave it a quick glance to determine if it were relevant. It was a brief letter. Three sentences. The signature read "Marla." Quinn paused for a moment, debating whether or not to read it.

"Quinn? You there?"

"Yes." She put down the letter without reading it and left the study.

"Find anything?"

"Nothing that will help me," she replied, distracted. "Listen, I'm expecting that Taylor will call today. It is exactly one year since he proposed to me. I'm just certain that he'll call," she continued, propping up her flagging hopes. There was a silence on Beth's end that said she did not share Quinn's optimism. "He's a romantic. As soon as I hear anything, I will call." After hanging up, Quinn spent several fretful hours trying to forget the letter. She wondered why he had bothered to save it. Her imagination began to torment her, and she thought that perhaps Taylor had loved this other woman with an intimacy or a passion which she herself was unable to inspire. By nightfall, when he had failed to call, she became angry with him and turned her disappointment into justification for reading the note. She entered the study and, with trembling hand, read the letter.

She could not have guessed at its content. The revelation hurt her. It was not the fact that he had gotten a girlfriend pregnant. The ancient letter suggested that at the time he was but a boy. And the fact that he had been a party to an abortion—willing or unwilling, she could not exactly tell—did not greatly trouble her either. She had always been sympathetic to arguments on both sides of the polemic debate. What disturbed her the most was that the long-secreted letter suggested that Taylor had been withholding details about his life and his feelings. For the first time since he left, she felt as if the light of his love had dropped beyond the curve of the earth and she could no longer feel its warmth.

Over the following week, she went through her daily routine mechanically, replaying in her mind a million interactions with Taylor in search of clues that he did in fact love her and trust her with his whole heart. For every ten memories that seemed to confirm his affections, she would find one nagging concern that would grow and loom large in her imagination, pushing out all the other reassurances. The possibility that Taylor had not been entirely honest with her hurt like a canker and she poked and prodded at it against her own will. The sting was constant.

Following a week of this self-torment, she felt raw. After work at the museum one afternoon, she simply did not feel like returning to their empty apartment. The day was still oppressively hot and the haze of Boston hung brown upon her shoulders. All she could think of was escaping the heat of the city. Rather than getting off at her subway stop, she remained on the T and rode it all the way out to the end of the line. At Alewife station she caught a bus for Concord. She was halfway there when it occurred to her why she was making the trip. It was where she had agreed to be Taylor's wife, where she had promised to wait for him. But he had been gone since December, and the vacuum of his absence had been filled now with loneliness and reservations. She needed to be reminded of the reasons she loved him, and she needed him to answer for all the frustration and anxiety he had caused her. She was going back now to walk in the glow of some of her brightest memories so that they might exorcise the doubts which had crept into her heart.

In Concord, Quinn went to the great elm tree between the river and Old Manse, the place where the two lovers had picnicked. The river was low and turgid. Slow eddies curled around little leaves, brushing them up against the trailing blue flowers along the channel. It was not enough to wash away her pain. For her, the letter had crystallized the central dilemma in Taylor's life; the relationship with Marla was merely emblematic. His life had been marked by one abortive effort after another. The farm, his painting, graduate school—all abandoned at some point along the way. Nothing ever coming to fruition. And her? What was to become of her? She could not bear the idea—after all the emotional energy she had put into Taylor—of their love dimming to cold embers, like an untended fire. Already, after a year of waiting, of receiving only a hurried call and some recordings on the answering machine, she sensed her passion being thinned by anxiety, her anticipation diluted with tedium. She could not understand how Taylor had failed to recognize his own tendency to leave the threads of his life hanging at loose ends. Over the course of his trip, would he come to see her love as just one more tie to cut, one more unwanted obligation? she wondered.

Looking over the Concord, she thought how little the scene had changed and yet how immensely different the river was today than the one that flowed within the banks the year before. She went to the center of the Old North Bridge to gaze into the water and see if the river could tell her anything. In her hand she held a leaf she had plucked from the ancient elm. She turned it over in her hands and examined the delicate veins, the rich green mantle, the tiny imperfections, and dropped it from the bridge to settle upon the currents. The steady stream caught her little burden and carried along on its course through the shade-dappled meadow. She watched it until it turned a bend and she could see it no longer. She decided to tell him he was in danger of losing her. Perhaps with an ultimatum she could shake him into realizing that their love was in jeopardy and bring him home. Perhaps then they could begin anew. That evening, using the only address she had for him, she wrote to tell him that her feelings had changed.

Dear Taylor:

Time seems to have passed so tediously without you. In the early days following your departure, I could console myself by going to the places that we loved so much and I would find you there. I could feel your presence in my room, or across from me at our window table at Green's Cafe, or on the footpath along the Charles River. But those images are losing their power to comfort me lately. Taylor, I went back to Concord to try to restore my will to wait for you. I saw us in my memory—I was hopeful and you were reassuring. But that feels like a distant lifetime ago, and I see no reason to hope you will be returning soon. In fact, I have reasons to believe you will disappoint me. Taylor, why did you never tell me about what happened between you and Marla? I found her letter to you by mistake while trying to discover some clues about where to find you. I hope that you know me well enough to realize that I don't blame you. But from your evasiveness I can't be certain of that. I am no longer certain that I know you completely. However, the time and distance between us has allowed me to understand at least one thing about you. There is a deep seated sense of repulsion that drives you away from your home and your past.

Your decision to leave me and go to South America has made me wonder if you number me among the forces that you are trying to escape. Since you were not fully open, you leave me no option but to guess at the truth. The conclusion that I keep returning to lately is that you do not fully trust me. You don't trust that I will be able to love you when confronted with the fact that you made a stupid mistake in your youth. More significantly, it seems that you do not find me sympathetic or understanding enough to deserve your confidence.

This has been a time of transition for you, I know. I have tried to support you along the way, but I can't continue to do that if you refuse me insight into your heart. For now, the strain of having to reconcile myself to loving the memory of you has become almost too painful. I am finding it difficult even to conjure your image. If you were to show up at our apartment tomorrow and I were to marry you at a moment's notice, I don't believe I would know just who it was I was marrying. I think it is best for now to postpone our engagement.

My life has been on hold since you left, and now I feel that I must go on searching for my own answers. I must go on looking for meaning in my faith while you look to your aesthetics. I have no way of knowing if or when you might get this letter. But should you read it, and if you still love me, come home to me. Give up this personal quest for absolution or validation or whatever it is you seek and come home before it is too late for us. Come home and we'll start again. I don't think you will be disappointed in giving up your journey. As our love is renewed, I will be willing to talk about marriage again . . . if you decide it is still what you want. For, if you search your heart and you think of our time together, you may discover that, with our love, you had all you needed for a perfect understanding of Beauty.

With love in my heart,
Quinn.

Quinn wept for Taylor and for herself when she posted her letter. Her hand hesitated for a moment before pushing it across the counter to the clerk.

"Is this the right APO for the embassy in Quito?" she asked.

"Yes."

"Is the postage correct?"

"Yes."

She retrieved the letter a minute, turned it over in her hands. And then a wave of fear washed over her so she hastily thrust the letter into the out-going mail bin and slammed the lid. Solitude and despair threatened to undermine her resolve, but she fought hard to steel herself against second-guessing her decision. At a bench overlooking the Charles River, she sat down to compose herself. She allowed herself to cry for five minutes, then dried her tears and walked into the library. Finding a silent corner, she sat down, opened her books, and filled the shell of her heart with an endless stream of words.

FALL

SEPTEMBER

By the second week of September, the apple orchards of
Rockwater Ranch hung heavy with fruit. The straining limbs, laden
with their reddened orbs, bowed in gothic arches towards the
ground. To shore up the branches against breaking, Jim had wedged
weather-grayed timbers at the zenith of the arcs, giving the entire
orchard the appearance of an arboreal cathedral. The trunks formed
sturdy columns down the nave, the line of props became a colonnade
along the aisles, with the blue sky resting softly on the curves of
vaulting limbs. The fruits—tart Winesaps, sweet Romes, and
dappled Macintosh—swayed glossy among the bright, green leaves.
And hanging upon the air was the essence of apples! It wafted in
among the boughs and, mingling with the shafts of light which
streamed through the chinks between the leaves, splashed down
upon the earth and pooled up rich and thick within the hollows

and the shades. To walk the rows and breathe the air had always filled Jim Moreland with satisfaction and with dread. He could never put it in words for himself, but he sensed in the colors and the fragrance the elemental transience of life. He wanted to hold everything he could see, but every year the season would peak and pass all within a matter of days.

The 2000 harvest promised to be a good one, but it would require a massive picking effort to get all the fruit off before it got too ripe. The trick was to get the apples to the warehouse with just the right combination of color, firmness, and sweetness. The longer the apples were left on the trees, the sweeter and softer they became. Then they would be labeled as low grade juicers valued at only a few dollars a ton, since the fruit would bruise easily and deteriorate quickly into a mushy consistency. Jim worried that a good portion of his crop would be left hanging on the trees because of a shortage of labor in the valley. Spurred on by right wing political posturing of a number of vociferous state and local politicians, immigration agents had been raiding the valley's farms, looking for illegal aliens. The crackdown had ugly racists overtones, and many of the migrant workers, both legal and illegal, were too frightened to respond to advertisements of high wages which—in any other year—would have filled the orchards. The great irony in all this was that the pressure to remove the workers had come from a large segment of the rural voters, the very farmers who depended on the Hispanic pickers for their livelihoods.

Jim had hung plywood HELP WANTED signs at the end of the driveway and had attracted only a few pickers. He had lined up a few teenagers from the high school and the Blancos, a Mexican family who returned each year to work his orchards—not enough by far. Two days before the picking was to begin, Jim confessed his fears to his wife over their morning coffee.

"I don't think we're going to get the apples off in time," he said, staring out the window.

"Why don't you call Bill and Sara? They would be willing to help," Beth offered encouragingly. Contrary to what she had intended, her suggestions only heightened Jim's anxiety as he found that every option failed to offer him any relief.

"Bill's job in the warehouse keeps him busy all day hauling apples and Sara's got her college." He began pacing the kitchen floor.

"She would be willing to miss some classes. And there's Dad and Ed. They can—"

"Hmmph! They can what?" grumbled Jim, his frustration rising. "A cripple and a—"

"Jim!" Beth was surprised to hear him disparage his own family. She sensed his ill mood stemmed from being overwhelmed. "You're going to have to ask everyone to contribute, no matter how little that may be. Everyone is willing to help you if you just ask."

"That so?" countered Jim sarcastically. "What about Taylor? Huh? You think I can just pick up the phone and give him a call in Ecuador or Peru or wherever the hell he is? Maybe he'll just pop on over for a week to help out the ol' man." He stared at her as if she could explain why his son had chosen to live like an exile, continually drifting and disconnected when in fact he had land he could call his own and a lineage with roots as stable and stubborn as those of the apple trees.

"He never was much of a farm boy, Jim," offered Beth, resting her face in her hands. She released a long sigh that expressed both her sympathy for her husband and her fatigue at trying to defend her son. "But he cares what happens to us and the farm. He cares about you, Jim." He was standing against the sink, his face etched with sorrow and confusion. Suddenly he looked old to Beth. Old and bone tired from years of hard work. She noticed as if for the first time that her leather-tough husband had gray hairs. She ran her eyes over his face and realized that deep lines framed his mouth and sharp creases had formed around his eyes and across his forehead. A shudder of anxiety washed over her as she thought about the strain that the successive harvests would put upon her husband if his fate were to work the farm alone to the end of his years. She looked at her own hands, red from work and dabbled brown with a few age spots and realized that mingled with her fears was a palpable residue of anger. She thought of how so many of Jim's plans and expectations hinged upon Taylor's returning one day to Rockwater. As that day now seemed increasingly unlikely, she could not suppress her feelings of resentment and disappointment brought on by her son's seeming disregard for his family's needs. This year, as with the previous nine years, the harvest would go on without him.

On the first week of picking, Jim set up the Blanco family and the two teenagers with ladders, picking bags, and bins. They worked quickly and efficiently, but finished their working day at five in the evening. He, Sara, and Beth picked along side them and continued on until the last autumnal twilight melted away in the sky. J.P. could still run the tractor, so he hauled full bins to the barn, replacing them with empties. Even with the Morelands working every hour of daylight, a significant portion of the apples were at risk of going soft on the trees.

Growing desperate for more help, Jim asked Bill to join the pickers after his working day was done, but his son-in-law was training for a new job at the warehouse. After several years of running forklifts and packing apples, Bill was being considered for a recently vacated position of grade inspector or "field man." To assess his acumen for the work, the outgoing field man was taking him on training runs to the growers. Bill was a natural for the job, since he was familiar with grading criteria and he knew every dirt driveway and barking dog in the county. For Bill, the opportunity to work as a field man was a long-cherished dream, since it meant he would escape the drudgery of packing apples. If he were to get the position, his new duties would entail driving from farm to farm, checking pesticide records and monitoring fruit maturation. The tools for the job were paper and pen, so the position carried higher prestige in the warehouse than the sweat labor. Throughout his training, he was competent and eager to please, inspiring his supervisor to appoint him the position, quite unexpectedly, before his instruction was completed.

By some strange twist of fate, on the day Bill was given his new title, he was assigned to the Moreland's orchards. For his first inspection, he was accompanied by his supervisor, Dale Crawford, a slick, dispirited man with a hook for a hand which he had lost it in the packing machinery. (The white collar job he held was offered by Stellerman's Warehouse as compensation for the unfortunate amputation.) Taking bitter consolation in the authority of his position, Dale derived a sense of power in pressing down the grade on the produce from his farmers. He had a reputation of writing parsimonious contracts with the growers which he maintained with vigilance.

While Bill was new in his role, Dale's job was to shadow the young field man and pass judgment on his grading. The normal procedure was to inspect a few bins in the load and give the whole shipment a quality score based on that representative sampling. Dale had already been out to inspect the first half of the Moreland's crop that had been sent to the warehouse and grudgingly gave them Grade A Fancy—a rating that brought a good price. Since that time, a week had passed and it was routine to re-check the fruit. When he arrived with Bill, Ed was dumping blemished or damaged fruit in a bin set aside to make juice for the family. Dale caught sight of the retarded man pouring his bucket into a bin and steered Bill over to it for an inspection, ignoring several other bins in the vicinity containing high grade fruit.

"What would you give these, Bill?" he asked, holding up a bruised Winesap.

"Obviously, that's a cull," replied Bill, encouraged by the ease of his first quiz. Ed reached into the bin and handed Dale another with a limb-rub, grinning broadly.

"And this one?"

"Another cull," answered Bill, "but I think Jim wanted to set this bin aside for—"

"It's not your job to think what the farmer wanted the bin to look like. You are supposed to be objective," scolded Dale.

"Yes, but this bin contains all culls because they have been sorted for—"

"Exactly," interrupted Dale. "And it is not the job of the farmer to sort the fruit. That is the job of the warehouse. By going through the fruit this way the farmer is intentionally trying to mislead the field man. Don't you see?" he said, laying the hook on Bill's shoulder. "This only shows that the shipment you have here has a high proportion of juicers," said Dale, shaking his head.

"Don't we need to sample the other bins?" replied Bill, trying to avoid revealing his suspicion of Dale's intentions.

"Of course, by all means," said the older man irritably. He turned Bill loose and looked at him disapprovingly. "Go ahead. But don't let your personal friendships with these farmers bias your opinion. This is a business Mr. Hennis." Dale folded his arms and stood back to watch Bill go from bin to bin. The younger man felt himself scrutinized with every step.

"They look pretty good on the whole, Grade A, with the obvious inclusion of the odd cull here and there that we discovered."

"What is the proportion of culls here, Bill?" Dale asked condescendingly. "What do you see over there?" He pointed to Ed who was going through the other bins, removing the culls and placing them in his bucket. "What kind of field man calls a grade by looking at the top of a bin that's been tampered with? You've got to dig a little. See the big picture." Bill twisted his hands into knots and thought hard about his options at the warehouse. He needed this job. He wouldn't go anywhere driving a forklift all his life. He thought about his chances of inheriting Rockwater. He had made it perfectly clear that he and Sara wanted the ranch and, to his great frustration, Jim had remained tight-lipped about it, preferring to hold on to it until Taylor came around. That could be a very, very long time.

"I think we have a high ratio of culls to packing apples," said Bill, trying to make it sound like his decision.

"If that's your call, I will back you," said Dale patronizingly. "You still need a little guidance, but you could make a fine inspector." He put the hook around Bill's shoulder and steered him back to the truck where Bill wrote up the grade sheet. They found Jim up at the end of the orchard, moving bins for the pickers with the tractor. Sara saw Bill get out of the truck from atop her picking ladder and, surprised to see him away from the warehouse, came down to visit with him. Jim, who had pulled up on the tractor shut off the engine and addressed the men.

"How do they look?"

"O.K.," croaked Bill unnaturally.

"With some exceptions," corrected Dale.

"What are you doing here, Bill?" asked Sara, a half-filled picking bag slung low on her stomach. "I thought you were running the forklift today."

"He left the warehouse 'cause he knows I pay my pickers better," joked Jim, launching a little barb at Dale.

"I'm going to be a field man," announced Bill. Sara looked back and forth between her husband and the oily man at his side for confirmation.

"That's right," chimed Dale. "He has a sharp eye. Makes calculated decisions."

"You got it? Honey, that's great!" Sara swung the bag to her hip and threw a sideways arm around Bill who received the embrace stiffly.

"So what's your call, Bill?" asked Jim expectantly. "How'd they look?"

"I'm sorry, Dad," began Bill, "but there were too many juicers mixed up in this last group of bins." Jim stared at him in disbelief for a moment. Then he looked at Dale, standing smug and arrogant at Bill's shoulder.

"What the hell are you talking about," rumbled Jim, stepping down off the tractor.

"Dad!" broke in Sara. "He's just doing his job."

"If he had done his goddam job, I'd have a ticket for Grade A Fancy's now!"

"There were some good bins but you had a lot of culls," whined Bill, taking a step back from his father-in-law who had gone taut with anger.

"A lot of culls?" Jim repeated, insulted.

"Yes, Uncle Ed was filling bins with culls," protested Bill, leaning back a little away from Jim who loomed over him like a storm.

"Filling bins?! He couldn't have found enough culls to fill *one* bin! And it was for our own press. Bill, you knew that! How could you betray your family like that?"

"I didn't know that. I've been busy all week running the forklift or driving all over the valley grading with Dale. This is the first look I've had at your apples." He paused, gathering his courage. "And I have to say," he shot a glance over his shoulder at Dale, "honestly, they are not the best in the valley." Jim snorted in disgust at Bill's unconvincing act. "I gotta tell you that Dad—"

"Stop calling me that, snapped Jim."

"Let him talk," interjected Sara. "Maybe he's right . . . about some of them." Sara's conflicted attempt to lend Bill support only exacerbated Jim's fury. He looked between Bill and Dale and then ripped the grade sheets in half.

"That's what I think of your skills as an inspector," said Jim, looking past Bill, meeting Dale's unblinking, contemptuous gaze.

"Seems like you don't have much of a choice," threatened Dale. "Try to sell your fruit somewhere else and we'll sue." He folded his arms and smiled in victory, waiting for Jim to reconcile himself to the humiliation. Jim was unyielding. "Despite your unprofessional behavior, we'll still take that fruit. As a favor to your family," he patted Bill on the back with the hook. "But they get a cull rating." The stubborn farmer thrust the shredded forms at the man defiantly.

"I'd rather let them rot!" Dale looked at his ripped forms and his face glowed red with angry indignation. Reaching out with his claw, he snapped them up with a metallic bite and stormed back to the truck. Bill followed reluctantly, and the two men drove away in a cloud of dust.

Later that evening, Jim calculated that the bins that had been sold would not cover the expenses incurred in irrigating and spraying the orchards. Even if he relented and sold the remainder of the apples for juicers, they would bring such a low price that he would barely break even. Almost ten acres were left unpicked, the apples hanging on the trees. The shipment that had been downgraded by Bill and Dale amounted to almost thirty bins, each wooden crate weighing around half a ton. Unless he could get those apples re-graded, there was little point in continuing the harvest. The bins sat stacked three high in the barnyard, stretching the length of the barn in a solid wall of ripening resentment.

Jim was determined not to exhibit any anxiety or grief over the loss because, from his perspective, it would only signify a victory for Dale Crawford and Stellerman's Warehouse. As the apples slowly went to ruin, he shrugged off the loss as inconsequential. To show that he made it through the ordeal unscathed, he insisted on having the family's traditional end-of-harvest party. Every year, the Morelands invited all the orchardists from the neighboring farms for a cider making party and a barbecue. "Since we stopped picking, we'll just have more time to prepare for the party," he joked. But everyone in the family knew that the strain from the lost income and the humiliation of watching his efforts go to waste laid heavy on his mind. Only J.P. remained unsympathetic to his pain and openly criticized him for his handling of the situation. As a result, Jim took to avoiding his father whenever possible.

On the night of the party, the old man started drinking early in the afternoon and, as the evening wore on, grew increasingly embittered over the loss of the apples. He sat in his chair and mumbled vituperative curses at his own misfortune to have been burdened with a brainless boy, a disrespectful daughter-in-law, and weak and selfish grandchildren. He blamed his son for running the farm into the red; he blamed him for making it necessary to take out operating loans; he blamed him for what he imagined was the first step towards bankruptcy and the eventual loss of the farm. By dinner time, he was staggering drunk and offensively aggressive. He found Jim at the cider press pouring apples into the grinder. A pile of sweet smelling pulp collected in the press basket.

"What are you gonna do, boy? Press the entire ten acres?" sneered J.P. Jim tried to ignore him, which only intensified the old man's irritation.

"Maybe you could make a bunch of hooch. That'd suit me fine."

"You don't need anymore of that Dad."

"You lecturing to me on what I need? Seems to me like you're the one needing the advice considering the way you've fucked up my farm." The few neighbors helping with the bottling had seen flashes of J.P.'s belligerence and, knowing how it pained and embarrassed Jim, busied themselves over the press and tried to pretend not to notice.

"That's enough Dad," said Jim firmly.

"Well here's some advice for you for next season," continued the toughened old man. "Don't have a retard manage your picking operation!" he shouted. The women with the pies, the farmers with their beers, the boys and girls at play, they all stopped to look at the brittle stick of a man. He was now the center of attention. "Instead, get you're son to do it. Oh, that's right," he added sarcastically, "you don't have a son. He decided he was too good for hickville and took off." Jim saw the shocked and offended faces of his friends and neighbors and he burned with humiliation. He turned his back on his father to walk in the direction of the house which only goaded J.P. to spew more venom. "Here's some more advice," he sneered, hobbling after his son on his gnarled cane. "Don't let your daughter screw the field man unless you get something out of it!" He laughed perversely at his obscenity and began to dance a little jig.

"Enough J.P.! Enough!" roared Jim, spinning on his heels to confront the drunkard. "You're an embarrassment to the entire family!

"Me?!" he scoffed. "This place will go to ruin because of you." He pointed a bony finger in his son's face in accusation.

"It's my farm and I will run it the way I see fit." Jim stood his ground before his father. J.P., unused to being challenged, became enraged and puffed up his chest like a fighting bantam.

"I scraped this farm together out of rocks and thistles," he cried, punctuating each word with a jab of his finger, "and at the rate you're going, it'll be scrubland or hardpan again before long."

"So what if it is? So what if I let it go to weed or sell it?" The old man started back as if stung by the words. His rage now boiled at his son's heretical disregard for his land, his heritage, and he burst forth with an explosion of curses. Jim withstood the tirade without flinching. Astounded at his son's unshakable resolve, he threw a wobbly punch towards his chin. The younger man caught his father's fist in the air with his broad hand and, gripping it with a force that surprised J.P., pressed down with a steady determination until the old man crumpled upon one knee. Jim loomed over him.

"Don't you *ever* sell this farm!" raged the twisted figure.

"That's my decision now since you handed it over to me twenty five goddam years ago."

"It's not your farm yet, boy," spat back the drunken man, refusing to yield. "I ain't dead." Jim cast J.P.'s fist aside in contempt and began to walk away. The shaken father, desperate with anger upon being dismissed, barked after him. "Now what are you going to do about my apples!"

"*Your* apples?!" Jim spun around and would have struck his father had not several of the men stepped in to hold him back. "What am I going to do with *your* apples?!" shouted Jim, struggling to contain the anger which his father had nurtured since his childhood. The rage snaked up from within him, finding a crack in the layers of hardened resentment, threatening to explode in an eruption of chaotic violence directed at anything within reach. Struggling to contain his fury, Jim left the crumpled form of his father there on the front lawn and strode deliberately towards the barn.

"Jim!" Beth rushed to follow her husband as the guests parted to let them pass.

He walked straight for the barnyard with fiery determination. As Beth looked on with terror and foreboding, her husband climbed up onto the seat of the large Case tractor and fired up the huge diesel with a furious roar. With a wild flash in his eyes, he drove erratically towards the wall of rotting fruit. Dropping the front forks to the ground he plowed into a stack of three bins and raised them precariously high. Then, revving the engine, he rumbled between the hay loft and the tack shed, stopping in front of his father's trailer. An anxious knot of neighbors had now come down from the house and stood in the barnyard. Dumbfounded, family and friends watched as Jim raised the loader arms to the level of the eaves and dumped the groaning crates through the roof of J.P.'s house. Beth cried out in horror and disbelief and made a run at the tractor to try and climb up into the cab but Jim swung the loader around, forcing her to scramble out of the way as he went back for another load.

Back at the wall of fruit, Jim slammed into the stack as he lifted the forks. From the force of the collision, the topmost bin in his load sat a-kilter on the other two, threatening to fall. Bill ran out in front of the tractor to try to warn him, but Jim was oblivious to everything except his rage for destruction. Raising the loader again, he raced towards the old man's house in a swirl of dust and diesel smoke. No one doubted the seriousness of his intentions and the string of onlookers were forced to stand back and let him work his vengeance. He glared straight ahead, stone faced, as he prepared to dump another load on the trailer.

Half of the roof still hung intact and Jim aimed his heavy load at the central beam to bring the whole flimsy structure down. Throwing the smoking tractor into low gear, he lurched closer to the house. The loader was raised as high as it could go and the forks tilted backwards on a dangerously sharp incline. Just as he was preparing to drop the bins down upon the house, the front tire dropped in a little ditch in the yard and the erratic jolt sent the highest bin skidding backwards off the stack. Slowly, heavily, it toppled with its ton of apples onto the cab. Jim was crushed between the massive crate and the steering wheel, his raging heart bursting in his chest. Beth and Sara screamed and ran towards the tractor. Neighbors scattered in confusion, some running for the house, others calling out for help. A few of the men scrambled to board the still-rolling diesel and shut it down before it could do any more damage. J.P., who had hobbled down to the barnyard with the intention of trying to take another swing at Jim with his cane, arrived just in time to see his son get crushed—the red blood trickling down upon the red, round hillocks of spilled apples.

In the chaos that followed, Beth and Sara were dragged away from the horrible scene by a crowd of neighbors. Mr. Feldman called an ambulance and it took four firemen and an hour of gruesome labor to extract Jim from the crushed cab. Bill stayed on through the night to explain the events of the evening to the local Sheriff. By two in the morning, Rockwater was deserted except for J.P.

Alone and embittered, the Moreland patriarch surveyed the destruction set in motion by his own hatred. For a moment his understanding became very distorted, or very clear—he wasn't sure which—for he could not be certain whether he had become crippled and then hardened his heart or whether his heart had atrophied first and his body had shriveled and twisted around it. In the darkness, he picked through the ruins of his house, taking stock of the sum total of his life. Finding his hard bed amid the rubble and the pulp, he lie awake in the darkness upon a sickly sheen of juice, looking at the night sky through his shattered roof. At the first light of dawn, the withered and broken man took a rifle from his splintered gun rack, walked to the very center of his ranch and shot himself in the bowels. He died slowly, bleeding to death among the frost-tipped stems of alfalfa. He wanted it that way. He laid there on a little rise in the browning fall field, looking at a world tilted on its side—soil and grass, thistles and mole hills— letting his life's blood drain into the earth. All of it, everything encompassed within the bleary gaze of his fading eyes, belonged to him. In his dying breath he realized with great astonishment that in truth he had never taken any joy from Rockwater. He had had loathed the land and had spent his entire life in a futile struggle to subdue it—sowing his anger and reaping only sorrow.

At the moment that J.P. Moreland died, Taylor was having dinner with a shepherding family in the rolling, green hills southwest of Cotopaxi. Earlier that morning, he had been walking past their stone and mud house when he smelled the scent of freshly baked bread. Calling to the woman over the little rickety pole and wire fence which ringed their house, he offered to buy a loaf or two. She was happy to give him the food, but rather than money, she asked for help with a troublesome lamb. The animal had got a length of loose barbed wire tangled around its hind leg, but, even hobbled, it was too agile for the woman to catch. Taylor cornered the lamb in the corral and deftly caught it as it tried to spring past him. Then turning it up on its rump, its back braced against his knees, he quickly untwisted the wire from the leg and released the lamb. The woman was impressed to see that the stranger had some skill with livestock and thanked him warmly. Taylor was running low on supplies, so he asked if there were more chores he could do in trade for bread, cheese, and dried corn and beans. The woman agreed and Taylor spent the day repairing a tumbled stone wall on the pig sty. When the husband and an uncle returned from the fields at lunch to find another helping hand, they were all too willing to put him to work hoeing weeds. Later, as the sun set over the close-cropped pastures and garden plots, he helped the daughter round up the sheep and cattle and herded them back to a corral near the house. It felt good to work hard on the land. At the end of the day his clothes smelled of earth and his hands were sore. It reminded him of so many days spent working at the ranch and he was surprised to find himself feeling a little sentimental for home.

His host family helped to ease his sense of loneliness. They were very welcoming, and they offered him the couch to sleep on and said there was work for as long as he wanted. The husband and wife, a grandfather, an uncle and two children—a girl and a young boy—all shared close quarters in the small house. One small room off the kitchen housed the couple, another larger room was occupied by the men and children, a blanket stretched down the center serving as a makeshift wall. They were hard working and poor in the way of money, but they had an abundance of everything they needed and lived a comfortable life. Members of their clan, the Otavalos, had been working the family plot for as far back as the living could recall the lives of the departed. The current stewards of the land had a few sheep, some pigs and chickens, and a cow. In clearings made on the wooded hillsides, they grew vegetables and corn.

That evening, crowded around a small, sturdy table set with hot beans and corn, Taylor tried to explain to his hosts in his rudimentary Spanish how he had arrived in their fields that morning. With the combination of maps, pointing and pantomime he made himself understood. After hitching a ride from the Pension Oriente to Puerto Napo, Taylor was able to get a bus to Tena, an agricultural town on the eastern slopes of the Andes. He was able to cover many miles by following rough-hewn dirt roads and footpaths that wound their way into the sharply rising foothills. Most of the time he traveled on foot, following an outdated but adequate topographical map he had purchased from a tour guide in Misahualli. On many occasions he found himself relying on the good will of farmers and herdsmen who directed him up cobblestone switch-backs and muddy livestock trails.

The transition from the flat and often flooded jungles of the Amazon Basin to the green mantled hills of the equatorial Andes was dramatic. It was as if the world had been abruptly tilted on its side and everything was pulled towards the sky, including the jungle. Even with the gain of altitude, the dense trees, delicate ferns, and clinging vines swathed the hills and valleys in green, creeping up the sides of even the steepest inclines. He followed the Chulupas River valley for a few days and then began his ascent into the foothills. The rain forest of the Solimoes with its high canopy gave way to a different kind of tropical growth, and the trees became lower to the ground. The limbs were covered with mosses, bromeliads, and orchids which spread their tendrils to the damp, warm air. In places where the terrain leveled off—in river valleys or on the high shoulders of hills—Taylor came across a few homesteaders who had shaved patches in the tropical forests in order to cultivate crops or pasture their animals. It was in one of these high, green valleys, hemmed in by Andean foothills, that the Otavalos had made their home. Based on a few landmarks on his map, Taylor and the Otavalo men estimated that he was now within twenty miles, or three days of rigorous hiking, of Cotopaxi.

While Taylor was anxious to move on, his continuing nostalgia for family made him linger. He fell into the routine of rising early, taking care of the livestock, and then heading off with the men to the fields with an ease that came with familiarity. By the end of several days, he began to enjoy swinging the hoe and the rhythmic pick and sift, pick and sift of the blade as it struck and turned the soil. The cadence of his stroke and step accompanied by the regular sound of his breathing had a pleasant, meditative quality. He even fancied he could see himself settling into a life of farming. The open air and sunshine, the tangible rewards of one's labors, and the predictability of the seasons all held a certain appeal for the young man.

In the evenings when the dinner plates had been cleared away, Taylor went to work in his sketch books, drawing figures of bent backs over hoes, stone walls around cultivated fields, lambs bedded down with the ewes, and cups and pots along a shelf. At first the children crowded around and the adults looked discretely over his shoulder to see what he was up to, but eventually they got used to his scribbling and left him in peace. Taylor's favorite subject was the house, and he made several studies in watercolor of the solid, squat, mud and stone structure and the surrounding fields backed by steep, green hills. He painted it from every angle and in a variety of damp earth tones, finally settling on a frontal view with the house at foreground left with the stick-and-wire corrals to one side and the cultivated fields on the other. In the far distance he added the blue and brown slopes of the Andes, their peaks continuously hidden by a stubborn layer of mist. He spent several days on this sketch with the hopes of turning it into a larger oil upon his return. In the end, it turned out to be a pastoral image, awash in romantic sentiment for living close to the land.

Looking at the glowing impressions in his sketch book, Taylor almost convinced himself that he could go back to the ranch and claim his inheritance. But the young man realized that he had selected only the details that he wanted to see. He knew from experience that farming was a lonely life. The hard work wore a body down much in the way that the beating of ten million rain drops over a thousand winters erodes and etches the surface of a stone. He knew from experience that Nature was a stern employer. There was little room for diverging from the dictates of the seasons. When it was time to plant, one needed to get the seeds in the soil or face hunger and privation later. When it was time to harvest, the farmer had to work long hours to get the crop in or suffer the disappointment of seeing one's labors go to waste. And while the fields may lay fallow and rest at times, the farmer never did. There was always some pressing work to do and another indispensable chore looming on the horizon. With its solitude, repetition, and uncompromising natural mandates, it was a life which left little room for the production of art.

Several times during the course of his stay with the Otavalos, he thought of how his father had taken such pride in the quality of his produce or the health of his livestock, and the notion came over him that perhaps he had misjudged him. Gradually, he began to suspect that it was not his father who had been unconscious of the beauty in the world, but he himself. One day while tilling the soil, he looked back over the dark rows which he had curved around the gray boulders. He took pleasure in the line and form, as if he had been granted creative liberties on a great earthen canvas of soil and stone. Considering how Senor Otavalo had curved his rows of potatoes around a lone flowering tree in the field, Taylor recognized that farming could provide a kind of aesthetics for those with a different poetic sentiment. If one was awake to the possibilities of life, every act—even the most routine—could be infused with beauty. Looking at the regular and geometric patterns cut in the soil and a few terraces carved into the hillsides, he was reminded of the Japanese Zen gardens with their even sand rows and their pensive rocks. But if Taylor were to present this idea to his Ecuadorian host, the farmer would never call what he had done "art," nor would he find it a practical use of time to discuss the reasons for his actions. He simply lived. And Taylor respected that. Unlike the Otavalos or his father who took immediate satisfaction from what they accomplished with their own hands, Taylor's happiest moments were found in contemplation and representation of the world. The farmer's art was distinctly unconscious and Taylor's was necessarily self-conscious. One was the act of living and the other the interpretation of the act. Of the two, he thought that perhaps the former was a truer aesthetic. But intuitively he understood that only through the reflections of the artists could the invisible art of living be made visible. Looking over the clean, stark symmetry of the fields and the play of light and shadow over the undulating rows, he resolved to try to reacquaint himself with his father as soon as he returned home.

That evening, over a dinner of potatoes and lamb stew, he announced his intention to move on. When Taylor asked for directions to the volcano, his host father looked confused. He explained that he was in the very shadow of the great Cotopaxi, that on a clear day the mountain hung on the horizon like *"una gran onda helada de agua blanca"*—a frozen wave of white water. Taylor's goal, the sublime peak which had haunted his imagination for so long, had been there all the time, obscured by clouds. Thrilled at the prospect of reaching the mountain, he packed his provisions that night, intent on leaving with the rising sun. Before he went to bed, he said his good-byes to the Otavalos. To the children he gave some piranha teeth which he had saved from his fishing trips with Sergio. To the husband and wife he gave the small watercolor sketch of their farm which he had worked on over the course of his stay. The woman gave him a warm hug and the farmer, wanting to reciprocate, went to his room and came out with a present wrapped in a hand-embroidered handkerchief. It was a small carving of a stone ram with semi-circular horns curling against the neck.

"Mis antepasados lo han hecho esto!" explained the man with excitement. He made a hoeing motion and pointed to the family fields to indicate where he had found the relic, carved by his ancestors. Then he grew very proud and stood squared-shouldered before his guest. Placing the gift in Taylor's palm and closing his hand around the heirloom he proclaimed: *"Ahora usted es un Otavalo,"* formally initiating him into the family. The woman, too, stepped up and wrapped her hands around her husband's and Taylor's and smiled at him. A spring of gratitude and affection suddenly welled up from within Taylor's heart and, unexpectedly, he felt tears roll down his cheeks. Filled with a sense of belonging and release, he cried and laughed while everyone in his newly

adopted family crowded round to pat and embrace him. That night, lying on his couch in the dark, Taylor realized with crystal clarity that it was time to complete his journey and return home.

OCTOBER

Quinn arrived in Quito on a clear afternoon in early October, 2000, as the sun was climbing high over the snowy domes of Cayambe, Ruminahui, and Cotopaxi. Weighted down with the burden of having to relate to Taylor the tragic deaths of the Moreland men, she dragged her feet through the airport and collected her bags. She carried with her a letter from Taylor's mother. In Beth's typical matter-of-fact tone, she explained to her son that his father had died in an accident and his grandfather had shot himself. She asked, considering the circumstances, that Taylor cut short his travels and come home as soon as possible to help put the family's affairs in order. Included in the envelope were $2,000 and a copy of his birth certificate which his mother added to help him secure his passport. Quinn had promised Beth that she would try to find her son and bring him home. Beth had made it almost impossible to refuse. She had called the week prior and, exhausted and numb with grief, asked if Taylor had managed to call on the anniversary of his proposal. When Quinn revealed that she had not come across any further clues regarding his whereabouts, Beth became even more despondent.

"It's too late for Taylor to do much about anything," she sighed. "But his family needs him now. Sara's a wreck and Bill's gotta stay here to help me run the farm. And I can't go running off to find my son. There are lawyers to deal with and all sorts of arrangements to be made. J.P. left no will; neither did Jim. Could you fly to Quito and try to locate Taylor? Tell him what's happened?" asked Beth, her voice strained and thin.

"Of course," assured Quinn. She had not confided her decision to postpone the wedding to his family and wanted to avoid the unpleasant complications it would raise now. "But I can't be certain I'll find him. Lately I'm not really confident that I can guess what he's planning or doing," replied Quinn, thinking of her letter to Taylor.

"But you know more than any of us what areas he's visited and what sights might appeal to him," admitted Beth. "If you find out nothing in two weeks, leave a message with the embassy and return to Boston. At the very least he should have a letter waiting for him at the embassy. He should know the situation before he comes walking in the door expecting a full house."

"You're right," agreed Quinn. "I'll do all that I can to help you through this."

As she hauled her luggage through the airport, the effects of going from sea-level to 9,000 feet made her light-headed and sapped her energy. Tired and anxious, she questioned whether she was on an errand for Beth or on her own mission of penance for betraying her heart. Even though more than a month had passed since she mailed her letter, she had never fully reconciled herself to her decision to call off the engagement. She grieved for him to think of the pain he would suffer at his father's passing. And the sad set of circumstances which now pulled her back into his world rekindled her most tender sentiments. She wanted to be the one to give him the news. She wanted to be there to comfort and console him, for—despite the frustrations he had caused her—she loved him still.

She had booked a hotel in the old town where it would be a quick cab ride to the embassy in neighboring El Belen. Her plan was to wait for Taylor to come pick up his documents, make contact, and deliver the news about his father. In between checking to see if he had stopped by the embassy, she intended to work on her studies, since she had left school in the middle of the term when many of her most important assignments were due. Weary from many tedious hours in planes, she had hoped to make a quick trip into town, check in and rest. But from the moment she stepped out of the airport she became disoriented and nervous. She had never been out of the country before, and almost immediately she was beset by three men offering taxis and two girls selling chiclettes, all rolling out their sales pitches in Spanish. She hugged her bags and walked in the other direction, smiling apologetically and saying "I don't speak Spanish." Hearing this, the small throng that followed her switched to English and re-doubled their efforts. Quinn ended up buying gum from both girls and accepting a ride from the most insistent of the taxi drivers at double what her guidebook suggested she pay.

In the cab on the way to the town center, Quinn held out little hope that she would find Taylor. She was fairly certain, based on the information he had left on her answering machine, that he was now in Ecuador. But he could be anywhere in the bustling city or within the wild and untracked terrain around Cotopaxi. In all probability, she would leave when the two weeks were up without speaking to him. This prompted her to imagine Taylor arriving at the embassy at the end of his journey only to learn through an impersonal letter that both his father and grandfather had died. Her own letter would be waiting for him there also, denying him the solace he may have derived from the constancy of her love. She knew that she needed to redefine the nature of their relationship, but at the same time she didn't want to give him the impression that she was prepared to abandon him. Not after all that had happened. She started to think that her letter had been cruel and cowardly. Now she wanted it back in her hands so she could rip it to shreds.

The fragments of Ecuadorian life that Quinn viewed through her cab window made her realize that her perspective of the world—and of humanity in general—had been rather restricted. Up to that moment, she had always considered herself worldly because she had amassed such a storehouse of knowledge about other cultures and customs through her research into comparative religion. But she had never experienced life outside the narrow confines of school and work. Creeping through the heavy mid-day traffic, she saw Quichua women with babies slung on their backs in bright blankets; she heard the Latin rhythms of salsa and merengue seeping out of street-side bars and markets; she smelled the scent of roasting meat and noticed a man selling guinea pigs on skewers from a roadside barbeque. All familiar reference points were gone and thus everything she experienced needed interpreting. It was exhilarating for Quinn, but she also discovered that being a stranger in a strange place was a bit frightening and lonely. She began to marvel at the risks and inconveniences which Taylor must have assumed in making his journey.

After a jarring and noisy ride, she arrived in the historic district, El Centro, and asked the driver to drop her off at Hostal Nunes where she had a reservation. It was a two-storied colonial hotel within view of Quito's prominent hilltop statue of the Virgin. The Spanish architecture, red tile roofs, narrow alleys, and peeling whitewashed walls gave the place an air of quaint decay. The desk clerk was the fourteen year-old daughter of the manager who knew enough English from popular music and movies to communicate the basics. She showed Quinn to a cramped bedroom with a shared toilet in the hallway. The room was clean and a large shuttered window looked out onto a view of the busy little plaza and the steepled Spanish church across the way. Quinn threw the window open to admit the cool breeze and plopped down on the bed for a rest. The thin air made her head throb and her throat dry. She lay awake on the bed listening to the noises of the street and when she finally dozed off, she fell into a fitful sleep marred by anxious dreams.

In the morning, Quinn went immediately to the U.S. embassy, a large, white, blocky structure surrounded by a cyclone fence. After waiting a short time in line, she was greeted by an abrupt consulate officer who was trying to manage several people's cases at once.

"Has Taylor Moreland been in to pick up a new visa?" asked Quinn. "He was robbed, and the last time I talked to him on the phone he said he intended to get his documents here in October."

"And your name is?" asked the consulate clerk.

"Quinn Yarbrough. His . . . fiancé, girlfriend, err family friend," bumbled Quinn. The clerk looked at her suspiciously. "Look, I sent him some mail here," she continued. "If possible, could you check to see if he has picked that up? If not, I'd like to have the letter back." The woman behind the counter raised her eyebrows. "I sent it to him," Quinn assured her. "My name will be on the return address. I . . . I want to hand deliver it," she lied.

"Wait here please." The clerk went back into the recesses of the office, leaving Quinn in the lobby for several minutes. When she returned, she was officious and bureaucratic.

"I am not allowed to give you other people's mail," she replied flatly.

"Then it is still here?" probed Quinn.

"I can't tell you that either." The people in line behind her shuffled impatiently.

"Is there any way that you can help me get in touch with him? It's urgent. His father has died and I am trying to deliver the news to him," Quinn explained, hoping to enlist her as an ally. The clerk looked in Quinn's eyes and could see that her plea was sincere and softened a little in light of the tragic circumstances.

"Leave a message here with me containing information about how to reach you and I will give it to him if he shows up for his passport," offered the clerk. Quinn left with the small consolation that if he arrived at the embassy, at least he would know she was in Quito. But her mind kept returning to the suffering he would go through if he were to open her letter. During the cab ride back to her hotel, she felt powerless to do anything. Now, she could only wait for Taylor and be there to help him mend the holes in his life as she could.

On the morning of October 2, Taylor awoke to gray skies and began to doubt whether his dream of seeing Cotopaxi would ever be realized. Since leaving the Otavalos three days earlier, a dense, clinging drizzle filtered down from the sky, dampening his spirits and totally obscuring the mountain. His going had been much slower than he anticipated. He had been hiking up and down densely forested mountain valleys on his approach to Cotopaxi, but he had yet to get a glimpse of the towering, white dome. He considered staying in his tent all day and began flipping through Church's journals. Feeling his own journey was coming to an end, he parted the pages towards the later sections of the 1853 visit and his eyes paused over an encouraging entry. "After a disagreeable journey across an elevated plain with a cold piercing wind and sprinkling of rain," wrote Church, "we finally come to the edge of an eminence which overlooked the valley of Chota." Taylor knew the area from his maps. It lay to the north of Quito. He concluded that here Church must have been making his crossing from Columbia into Ecuador along the Andean plateau. The painter described the vision that greeted him as he reached the outlook. "A view of unparalleled magnificence presented itself that I must pronounce it one of the great wonders of Nature. I made a couple of feeble sketches this evening in recollection of the scene. My ideal of the Cordilleras is realized." Taylor was approximately the same distance from Cotopaxi as Church had been when he made the entry, but on a southwest approach instead of the painter's northern approach. The thought of finally having his efforts rewarded reinvigorated the tired traveler and he quickly broke camp and set off in the direction of the volcano.

By late morning, an opening appeared in the sky over the Andes through which Taylor saw a patch of brilliant blue and what looked like a bright white snow field. Thrilled at the prospect of seeing the mountain, even for the briefest moment, he doubled his pace up a footpath made by local herdsmen. When the trail dipped back down into a ravine, he decided to leave the path and continue on up the steadily rising hill where he could see the opening in the clouds. Off the trail the hillsides were clothed in a dense weave of tall ferns, broadleaf anthurium, and vine-entangled trees; but he pressed through in a great rush, ignoring his scratches and scrapes. At the top of the hill, the slope inclined steeply towards the sky and Taylor had to use rocky outcroppings and roots as handholds as he scrambled on all fours towards the light. Just when he began to get concerned that he was going to get hopelessly lost, he saw a glimmer of blue sky near the crest of the hill that suggested he was near the top. Straining until his thighs ached and his breath came hard and fast, he dragged himself over a few fallen trees and crawled hands and knees up a mossy embankment and made the ridge.

Taylor looked out over the valley expecting to see only cloud forests and a low lying fog, but there before him loomed Cotopaxi, a monumental conical dome, crystalline light yet ponderously weighty above a range of rocky foothills. The scene filled him with a sensation that he had never experienced before—an exhilarating awe tinged with terror. From where Taylor stood on his ridge, a band of lush jungle ran from the valley below him to some sharply rising foothills in the distance. The far slopes became increasingly bare and the trees thinner in the higher elevations, and he could make out earthen brown and red ridges running up to the snow line. At the base of the glacier, great fields of scree flanked the mountain, fanning down the slopes in wide brown swaths until they spilled over the edges of sheer rock bluffs. A band of mist hovered between this rocky fringe at the base of the dome and the blue-white glaciers above, giving the impression that the cone of Cotopaxi was floating upon the clouds.

Beautiful was not an adequate word to describe what he was seeing. It was too small and delicate; it was a word that passed judgment on the world. At that moment, what he experienced was more akin to being judged himself. Standing there on the high shoulder of the world under the wide, blue sky, the gaze of the universe was upon him. The view of Cotopaxi—with its brooding red mantel, massive stone ramparts, and shimmering peak—made him feel like an insignificant being looking up from his plodding little life to catch a privileged glimpse of the stunning grandeur of existence. What's more, his recognition of his insignificance in the face of the infinite interplay of time and matter did not strike him as something to be lamented; it strained his heart to overfilling with gratitude for life, for death, and for the flicker of a spark in between that would add his light to a cosmic fire that knew no beginning and had no end. Involuntarily, a peal of joyous laughter burst from his chest and he threw his arms wide to embrace the sky. No, it was not beautiful; it was sublime!

Long he looked, transfixed upon the weightless brilliance of the summit. Then, wanting to commit the experience to memory, he ran his eyes over every aspect of the scene. It was a satisfying moment—the culmination of months of travels and hardships. He thought about the string of events that brought him to this moment: a chance look at Church's paintings of the Andes, a break from his life of academics, a trip to Manaus, a robbery on the river, the generous assistance of so many kind people, and day after day of strenuous travel in boats, on buses and on foot. When he had started the journey, he did not fully believe that the experience would change anything for him. It had seemed more like a risk that he was willing to take, since the other alternative paths that presented themselves seemed so futile and meaningless. But standing before the great mountain, every fiber of his being still humming with exhilaration, Taylor knew that he had made the right decision.

Excited at the prospect of actually walking upon the icy flanks of the great mountain, Taylor back-tracked to the trail. He traversed the valley he had seen from the ridge and began a steep climb towards the volcano. After gaining several thousand feet in elevation, the temperatures dropped and the tropical vegetation gave way to a narrow fringe of "*paramo*"—a high-altitude grassland dotted by dwarf trees, clumps of sharp grass, and strange orange tufted thistles. The air was now quite chilly, and he had to stop and put on layers of shirts and pull socks over his hands for gloves. By early evening, Taylor arrived at a high plateau at the base of the sharply rising volcano. Finding a sheltered depression between two large rock formations, Taylor made camp for the evening. His plan was to spend the night in the ravine and then, with the sunrise, he would walk up to the climbers' lodge, or *refugio*, at over 13,000 feet. From there, he would pick one of the routes that led up to the glaciers and climb Cotopaxi as far as his limited gear would allow.

The next morning was brilliantly clear and crisp. Throwing on several layers of shirts, he topped them off with a light polar fleece, the only long-sleeved item to have survived the trip. Then he pulled his pants over his shorts, and doubled his socks with his tennis shoes. He looked a bit puffy and awkward, but he was satisfied that it would keep him warm as long as he kept moving. Taylor filled a small day-pack with a light lunch and water and set off to climb as high as he dared. He skirted around the base of the mountain until he met up with the winding dirt road leading up to the *refugio*. He took the steep road to the lodge and, from there, followed a rocky switch-back trail up to the snow line. Deciding to push the limits of his flimsy shoes, he continued on up the glacier at a steady pace, sometimes kicking footholds into the snow, until he was standing high above the world—the blue foothills and green valleys stretching away as far as the horizon. Along the jagged spine of the Andes he could see other mammoth volcanic domes of Cayambe, Ruinahui, and Chimbarazo jutting high above the sawtooth mountains, all dusted with white. When the winds began to pierce his clothes and his head reeled from the thin air, he turned around to make his descent. Skiing the slopes with his tennis shoes, he zipped down the mountain in a quarter of the time it took him to climb up. He passed a few teams of climbers coming up a parallel trail, roped together and fully rigged with ice axes, crampons, and below-zero gear. They looked at him with amazement and disapproval as he skittered by in his thin clothes and sneakers.

Over the course of the following few days, he hiked around to the west flank of Cotopaxi in order to be able to study the soft evening light on the face of the dome. Each day Taylor would walk for several hours along the high, wind-swept *paramo*, stopping at various vistas to sketch and record his impressions in his notebooks. He sketched the mountain again and again from multiple viewpoints until he knew every rock formation and every snowfield on the peak. When he found a site suitable for camping he settled in for a few days of doing watercolor studies. His daily routine revolved around painting the volcano. He awoke with the first rays of dawn and watched as the rising sun slowly compressed the wide fan of a shadow cast by the mountain until it was only a compact triangular wedge along the western flank. Then from mid-day to dusk as the sun arced wide over the summit and dropped down towards the Pacific, Taylor tried to record the shifting qualities of sunset red and orange on the white snow and ruddy brown stone.

On one day, the mountain released a small plume of steam from the crater at the summit. The little white cloud wafted out gentle and wispy, like a trail from a cottage chimney. It gave the mountain the appearance of a slumbering white giant. But Taylor was reminded of his experience twenty years earlier when Mount St. Helens had erupted with explosive violence. The contrast between the tranquil feather of steam from Cotopaxi and the black fury of Saint Helens was a paradox which, in an instant, solidified all the abstract and unformulated observations he had been making on his pilgrimage. Life was at once lovely and terrible. The white dome appeared solid and immovable, but at its core was an explosive force which could, in an instant, transform stone into dust, day into night. All was flux. And in that maxim, both the transcendent and transitory were confirmed. There was only one certain and permanent law of existence: everything changes. At first the concept shook him to the core, because there seemed to be nothing to hold on to any longer. But as soon as Taylor recognized and embraced the frail and fleeting nature of life, he was lifted by an unspeakable ecstasy because suddenly every single gesture he made and every dream he had nurtured became precious *because* life was transitory.

Mortality was the great blessing of the universe. Impermanence and uncertainty made Beauty possible. When he looked at the soaring Cotopaxi, he recognized that he could not take its existence for granted. So many unknown and unpredictable variables of matter and time came together to create the scene and to place him in it. And his appreciation for Beauty was intensified in knowing that eventually—perhaps in one minute, perhaps in one millennium—Cotopaxi would be leveled. But the loss would merely be material. He had not come all this way just to see Cotopaxi. He had come for an aesthetic experience that was not inherent in the object itself, but that was above and beyond it. For Taylor, this was the greatest paradox. Everything he had witnessed and experienced on his journey compelled him to reject the notion of a permanent, ordered, and meaningful universe; and yet, once he applied this principle of indeterminacy to his life, it was the one transcendent truth which imbued everything with meaning. Considering the smoking white dome, Taylor thought of the Gods on Mount Olympus—embodiments of immortality and permanence standing on the shifting and quaking foundations of the material world. It was appropriately ironic that the Greeks thought to put them there, since without the existence of pain there is no joy, without longing there can be no gratification, without things transitory we cannot even conceive of the transcendent.

Filled with a new sense of urgency and exhilaration, the work of painting consumed Taylor. He knew he had to find some way to explain his journey and the revelation he had experienced to Quinn, his family, and anyone who would listen. Quinn, in particular, would understand. He did not know how or why, but his sense that meaning came from Indeterminacy resonated with what she had said about faith. For days he did nothing but sketch and paint in his notebooks. He lost track of time and began to live only by the changing phenomena of light. Over what he could only guess was about week, he painted dozens of studies of the mountain and filled every page of his journal with notes and sketches. His intent was to use the best of the drafts in pencil and watercolor to create full-scale landscapes in oil when he got back to a studio.

Near the end of October, running low on food, Taylor prepared himself to leave Cotopaxi and make his way to Quito to begin his journey home. On his last day, he went through his studies of the mountain and felt a great satisfaction at having generated enough material to keep him busy for months. His only regret was that he would have to wait until he got home to see the final fruits of his labors. He was no longer tormented by the feelings of guilt and inadequacy which had prevented him for so long from even attempting to paint. He reviewed his works with an unmitigated and uncompromised sense of accomplishment and pride. For the first time in years he wanted to share his art with his family, and he smiled to think how they would react. He imagined himself returning to the ranch and laying out all his works before his mother and father for their approval. If at that point, with words or with a look in their eyes, they were to tell him "you are truly an artist my son," then all of his efforts would be justified.

On her second day in Ecuador, Quinn checked again at the U.S. embassy for any word from Taylor. Hearing no news, she returned to El Centro and walked from one colonial plaza to another hoping to find a quiet cafe where she could get some work done for her courses. What she found instead was streets packed with jostling crowds, vendors hocking their wares, and blaring car horns. Passing through a crowded street market, she came across La Plaza de la Independencia with its green trees, monument, and park benches and thought she would sit in the shade and work on an essay that was due in her theology class upon her return to Boston. But as she entered the square she was intercepted by a young man claiming to be a guide. He had been sitting at the base of a statue watching the people stream past and made out Quinn to be a gringa. He quickly trotted up to her side as she went past and began a high pressure sales pitch. She tried to decline politely, but when that only made him more aggressive she decided to lose him by quickening her step and ignoring him. This only inspired hostility, and he began to hurl insults at her in both Spanish and English. When she showed signs of being rattled by the barrage of insults, he tried to grab her arm and she jerked it away, pressing into the crowded street opposite to the Cathedral. Two blocks later she looked back to see the man trying to push past the clumps of wandering pedestrians to catch up to her. Up ahead on Calle Cuenca she saw a large church off a cobblestoned plaza—the church of San Francisco. Making for the entrance, she hovered near the doorway without the man's notice and watched him from the steps as he looked around the street in frustration and gave up the chase.

Quinn decided to take refuge in the church for a while, maybe gather her thoughts with some quiet meditation. But when she pushed open the heavy door and stepped inside she was greeted with a vision that stopped her breath in her chest. The altar, ceilings, and walls blazed with gold, reflecting a thousand glowing candles. Some sort of service was in progress and a small cluster of worshipers knelt in the first few rows. Gaping at the opulence of the gilding, she slipped quietly into the back pew to look around. Everywhere she looked she saw gold. Gold on the altar, gold on the cupola, gold on the friezes, gold on the pillars, gold adorning the frames of painting and the halos of saints and the raiment of the Virgin. And everywhere there was sacred art. Every little corner and crevice of the church that could be carved, painted, and gilt had been embellished by the hands of artisans. She gazed in wonder, straining her eyes to take it all in until she felt as if she were floating above herself. She drifted up above the nave, winding her way through the ornate chapels in the transepts to hover high within the lofty dome—a field of royal blue set with winking splinters of golden stars.

The lush extravagance that surrounded her ran contrary to all her prior experiences of churches in New England, where interiors and exteriors alike are relatively spare in detail and stark in lines. She had become accustomed to churches made of plain and humble stone. Here, rather than to provide the intellect a space for contemplation, the intent seemed to be to use the senses to lift the worshipper heavenward upon flights of emotional ecstasy, inspired through art. Whereas she had come to think that the mind alone could wrestle with comprehending divinity, the extravagant surroundings encouraged the spirit to enfold itself in the sensual mantel of heaven in order to experience the divine.

Quinn sat there in her pew for the length of the service, absorbed in the images, without hearing a single word. When the congregation was dismissed, they filed past her down the aisle, bringing her back from her reverie. She lingered on a little in the golden glow until the kindly priest coaxed her out the door at the mid-day closing hours. She stood there on the steps feeling at once exhausted from her intense concentration and invigorated by the storm of impressions that whirled through her imagination. The crowds had thinned a little and she made her way through the streets to her hotel. She forgot to eat that day, consumed so completely by the desire to make sense of the feelings inspired by the gilded chapel. She tried to go back to her studies, but instead found herself wanting to recapture the experience. Giving in to the impulse, she pulled out her journal and wrote about every detail she could remember—the Moorish patterns on the ceiling, an angel with a flaming sword, an altar decorated with notes and photos of loved ones in need of miracles, a cross rubbed smooth by the hands of the penitent. She wanted to hold on to the images, sensing that they were essential evidence she needed to solve the central mystery of her life: what made her existence, human existence, meaningful? After searching her heart for a way to reconcile these new emotions with her concept of spirituality, she kept thinking that she would give anything to share the moment with Taylor. She sensed that the vision of God and humanity expressed so exuberantly in the Church of San Francisco corresponded with the way Taylor saw things, but she could not explain for herself how. At three in the morning, dizzy from fatigue and hunger, Quinn fell asleep in a chair, her journal and a pile of papers spread out on the small table before her.

Over the following days, she resolved to visit every church she could while waiting for Taylor. She started out early each morning with her pen and notebook in hand and systematically visited one church after another until she had seen every corner of every holy site in El Centro. She started with the Cathedral and finished in the afternoon touring San Augustin. The next day she visited La Compania and the Monastery at San Francisco and the attached museum. On the following day she finished out her tour at Santo Domingo and San Diego. In each sacred place, she encountered the same soaring spaces, celestial light, and exquisite art. It was as if all of it was orchestrated to appeal almost exclusively to excite the passions. She realized that she had become so determined to obtain intellectual control over the idea of God, that she had forgotten that faith was not a concept, but an experience. The architecture, art, and music were merely catalysts that had the potential to lead one to a spiritual ecstasy.

She had seen plenty of sacred art before, but it was only now—seen in such profusion and variety, and at this particular time in her life—that she began to perceive the collective implications of the art. Quinn found it astonishing that in order to facilitate the contemplation of the divine, religion had relied so heavily on a vocabulary drawn from worldly experience. The glow cast from the gilded altars and stained glass windows was not merely wistful escapism. When she looked carefully at all the images of saints and angel and demons, it was unmistakably a version of *this* world: mothers nursing their babies, soldiers slaying one another, the down-trodden begging for alms. Very few of the holy images depicted God. And when a church displayed the likeness of God for the benefit of the faithful, he was invariably human. He had to be. For the only point of reference for the divine is necessarily through the mortal. In all the sacred art she witnessed, Quinn noted that human qualities, noble and base, were exaggerated to heroic or villainous proportions.

Over the altar at La Compania, she had seen a small portrait of Mary that had helped her find a focus for her thoughts. The Virgin was draped in royal blue, her hands folded before her. Suspended above her hands was a human heart pierced by several daggers, plunged to the hilt. The most compelling attribute of the portrait were her eyes. It was not the face of a deity, for they were the eyes of a woman, and they revealed immeasurable suffering paired with an indomitable dignity. Quinn had seen the look before throughout her life, on the subway, in the streets, in her father's congregation, and on the news. The churches and the scriptures told the history of real people—a complex and familiar narrative of love and sin, selfishness and altruism. And the view of life endorsed over and over again was irrepressible faith in the face of suffering.

Quinn was shaken with a revelation. All the art, all the icons, even the chapels and churches—it was all a grand and beautiful metaphor, she decided. Religion itself was a figurative language in which the abstract moral codes for human interaction were communicated through symbol, allegory, and imagery. And if God was the master metaphor, then religion was, after all, the practice of Art. Through her academic work, she had given herself the illusion that she was stripping away metaphors and that, if she peeled away enough layers, she would arrive at a notion of God that actually corresponded with the Deity. And yet, looking at the statues and the paintings, she recognized that she would always be dealing with a *representation* of truth and not Truth itself. The elaborately ornate churches, with their indulgence of human passions would never reveal to her the face of God. But, in a small but significant way, the impressions created by the metaphors had succeeded in communicating a *feeling* which resonated deeply with her sense of the beauty of Creation.

That evening, footsore and brimming with ideas, she tried again to make sense of what was happening to her. She found a cafe with a window overlooking a bustling Plaza Santa Domingo and she sat down for a coffee. As she watched the people come and go she was reminded of her times with Taylor at Green's Cafe. She wanted so much at that moment to share her thoughts with someone who cared that she had seen a cherub that made her laugh or that she had stood in the kaleidoscope beams cast by a stained glass window and positioned a red patch over her heart. Around her the warm chatter of people and the cozy clink of silverware made her painfully lonely, and she began to sense, ironically, that she was now closer to Taylor than she had ever been. She had always understood that for Taylor, art was a spiritual experience; and now she had come to see her own approach to religion as distinctly aesthetic. She was burning to talk to him. She realized that the letter no longer reflected the way she felt. If he opened it, she knew it would be difficult to undo the damage. To prevent this from happening, she decided to leave a post card at the embassy written in bold letters saying simply, "Don't read my letter. Please talk to me first. I'll explain. Quinn."

While she sat in the cafe writing her note, Taylor stepped out of a bus at the Terminal Terrestre four blocks away and started walking in the direction of New Town. A dusty pack on his back and two well worn journals under his arms, he strolled through the historic district on his way to the U.S. embassy. He would have preferred to find a place to set down his burden and get a good warm shower, but his worries about how he would get documents, money, and plane tickets compelled him to try to do his business first. The clerk who greeted him at the consulate was not the woman Quinn had talked to, so when Taylor received his mother's note without postmarks, she could not explain how it got there. Then he saw Quinn's letter and his heart leapt with joy. He began to tear the envelope, but the letter from his mother inspired an overpowering sense of concern. She only wrote to him about matters of great significance, so he was curious to know the circumstances which prompted her to get hold of him. He sat down in the waiting area and opened his mother's letter. As Taylor read the news of his father's death and of J.P.'s suicide, all the joy he had accumulated through his travels drained away and his whole being went numb with sorrow. All the guilt that he had felt for leaving Rockwater which he had only recently managed to disarm came rushing back to sting him, and he began to berate himself for not having been there. And now, just when he felt he could ask for his parents' blessing to leave Rockwater for good, his father had died.

Taylor showed the letter to the clerk and asked them to expedite the passport. She looked over the documents his mother had enclosed, made a few calls to verify his identity, and soon they were printing up a new passport. While he was waiting for his documents, Taylor paced the room and ran through a hundred scenarios of how, if he had just given up graduate school and gone home, the tragedy would have been averted. Distraught and sickened with sadness, Taylor thought of the letter from Quinn and opened it in the hopes of finding comfort and reassurance in her love. The sense of loss that came over him was even greater than the first, since this loss was not the result of an accident, but was due to his own shortcomings. Choked with sadness, he stepped out of the building and sat on the curb, weeping silently for all the pain he ever experienced—all the loneliness, all the doubts, all his failures and his fears. The rarefied light which had illuminated his spirit since his time at Cotopaxi was now almost totally obscured by a cloud of grief which loomed over him, casting a pall over all of his thoughts. What good was it, he wondered, to have gained some personal insight, if those insights were accomplished only by neglecting the people who meant the most in the world to him? With this tempest raging in his mind, he concluded bitterly that it had been a selfish journey after all.

At the cafe, Quinn finished her note to Taylor. Intent on attaching it to her letter, she wandered back towards the embassy. She hoped in her heart that she would never have to explain to Taylor why she had tried to call off the engagement. As she approached the main avenue outside the embassy, she saw a young man who looked like Taylor walking quickly down the sidewalk towards a taxi. Her heart raced for a moment but she doubted her eyes. He was thin and unshaven and his clothes were worn and faded. But the long strides and square posture were Taylor's. She changed her course to intercept him just to be certain. When the man hailed the car, Quinn heard his voice and she knew it was Taylor. She was still fifty yards away and he was setting his pack in the trunk of the car. She began running towards Taylor, calling his name: "Taylor! Wait! Taylor!" He appeared to hear and paused a moment, looking over the heads of the crowded square, but seeing nothing he opened the passenger door and stepped in. Quinn dodged and jostled her way past the crowds but saw to her dismay that the car was already edging into traffic. For a split second, she thought that he had seen her but was purposefully avoiding her, perhaps because of her letter. Fearing she would lose him forever, she stepped out into the lane and waved wildly at the taxi. Perturbed, the driver began blowing his horn and Taylor looked forward to see the source of the commotion. He saw what appeared to be a young woman trying to hail his cab, but the face was obscured by a grimy tinted window. The driver made an evasive move and quickly darted down the highway. Taylor slouched back into his seat and stared out the window as a gray drizzle began to fall over Quito. In an hour he was settled into a plane bound for Seattle, alone and tormented with regret.

NOVEMBER

The shadow of despair which settled over Taylor called to mind emotions he had not experienced since the cataclysmic eruption of St. Helens. His grief was intensified by his recollection that the fall had always been his father's favorite time of year. It was a preference he shared. In the orchards, the cold snap in the air seemed to spark embers of red and gold among the brittle leaves, adorning the trees with flecks of fire. The cottonwoods, quaking aspen, and birch along the river dotted the valley with splashes of orange and gold. He remembered how every autumn, just for a few days, thousands of tiny little spiders would hatch in the tall orchard grass and each would throw up a long thread of silk to the breeze. Then when a little gust would blow, a veil of little silk filaments would float up upon the air, hoisting aloft their tiny parachutists upon the brisk currents. When the sun set on such days, the whole valley took on a gauzy glow as the soft rays of the evening were filtered through the silken streamers. By early November, the harvests were in. He recalled the feeling of satisfaction he derived from seeing the storerooms stacked to the rafters with sacks of grain and the barns filled with sweet, green alfalfa. In the house, the cupboards always strained to overflowing with the bounty of the land. From the gardens there were butternut squash, sweet corn, snap beans and carrots. Taylor remembered that his mother's kitchen always smelled of cinnamon and nutmeg, and the shelves in the cellar were lined with canning jars filled with cherries, apricots, plums, and pears. And there were always pies: honey rhubarb, apple and blackberry, pumpkin spice, and blueberry peach cobbler.

What place did death have in the season of bounty? wondered Taylor. It seemed a great injustice. For as long as he could remember, his father had tilled and sowed and tended, only to have death deny him the chance to reap the benefits of his labors. It seemed too cruel an irony for a disinterested universe. In a benevolent world, autumn should have been the season in which all the efforts and sacrifices made throughout the year were rewarded with tangible returns. With the deaths of the Moreland men, winter had reached its icy fingers into the golden twilight of the sun's last frontier and had blighted the harvest.

When Taylor arrived at the ranch and drove the long dirt lane leading up to the house, it appeared to him at first that the farm had been abandoned. A third of the orchard was littered with rotting apples and some of the limbs had snapped under the weight of the unpicked fruit. The weeds grew high around the trees and the pastures were dried out and dotted with thistles. A few stray sheep had pushed through a gap in the fence and were craning their necks to pluck the leaves off the fruit trees. They looked up at the car for a moment with blank, unconcerned eyes and then went back to grazing. Something about their indifference made Taylor angry. He stopped the car and chased the animals back through the hole in the fence.

As the car pulled up to the house, Beth looked out the window for a moment and went back to her work sorting laundry. Taylor lugged the bags in the front door and set them in the entryway. No one came to greet him. The house was much as Taylor remembered, with every piece of furniture and picture where it had been since he was a boy. But sounds now seemed to echo hard and hollow off the walls, and the air smelled stale.

"I'm home," announced Taylor, his voice ringing empty in his own ears. Beth came down the hall with a basket of clothes in her arms.

"You're a bit late," she said in a voice pressed flat by fatigue.

"Well, I hit traffic coming over the mountains," he began in explanation, "and—"

"That's not what I meant," interrupted his mother. She went back to folding clothes, leaving him standing in his coat, bags in hand, in the entryway.

Taylor carried the luggage upstairs to his old bedroom. It was much as he left it so many years earlier—a small bed, a bureau cluttered with a few trophies and some fishing tackle, art posters and a photo of the Future Farmers Club with himself in the middle, Marla, Bill, Cort and Al on either side. His parents had turned the room into a temporary storage space and the floor was crowded with old boxes and a broken T.V. set. He sat down on the bed and looked out the window over the pastures and alfalfa fields towards the Yakima River. He began to wonder if he belonged there, if he had a right to his home any longer. A sense of claustrophobia came over him, as if the wall of the house were closing in on him in an effort to expel him. He had to get out for a walk.

He changed into his work clothes and went down to the barns to check on the animals. At the edge of the field, he could see Bill and Sara in the corral spreading bales of hay in the troughs for the livestock. In between Bill's work at the warehouse and Sara's classes at the community college, they had been trying to maintain the ranch. The animals were getting fed, but the manure was beginning to pile up and the equipment showed the wear from not being serviced. The old John Deere that he and his father had used to haul the pump to the back fields sat idle near the tool shed, water pooled up in the seat, weeds growing to the axle.

At any moment Taylor expected to see his father come around the corner of the shed carrying a wrench. A few times he thought he heard his whistling echoing through the barns. But the yard lay silent except for the clucking of a few chickens and the bleating of the sheep. A heavy cloud settled over Taylor. His sorrow drained his ability to take pleasure in anything and he felt sullen and resentful. Memories of his father fueled his grief. Everywhere he looked he saw something that triggered an image of the man: the tack shed they rebuilt together after the ash storm, the pens where he had nurtured countless ewes and their lambs, and the hay loft where he promised to give the farm to Taylor. He realized how desperately he would miss his father.

For his grandfather Taylor felt only pity. J.P. had always exhibited an edge of contempt for his grandchildren, and the only memories Taylor could conjure now were of a cruel and bitter old man. He remembered feeling anger and humiliation on behalf of his father after a repair that Jim had made on a mower axle had failed. His grandfather kicked at the broken shaft with his boot and cackled "You dumb ass! I knew you'd fuck it up!" As Taylor wandered through the barn, a darker image—long repressed— came back to haunt him. He found himself standing before one of the livestock pens where he had seen the old man brutally beat a ram. When it was still a lamb, Taylor had tamed the animal and, as a game, had butted him with his head. As the lamb gained weight, the sport became more dangerous. One day, while J.P. was spreading hay in the troughs, the ram leveled the old man with a solid butt of its head. Furious, the hobbled man somehow managed to secure a rope around the animal's head and thrashed the frightened beast with his heavy cane until it was dead. Afterwards J.P. made Taylor haul the carcass off to a pit. "This is your doing, boy," he snarled, still panting from the exertion. "Now you see what happens when you get all nice and soft with em'! Huh?!" Recalling only painful memories of the old man, Taylor could not mourn his passing.

His mother's letter had been vague on specifics about the deaths. To help himself try to understand what happened, Taylor wanted more details about what caused the fight between the two men and how it could have ended in an accidental death and a suicide. He knew his mother was in no mood to talk, so he went out to the corral to get answers from his sister. He found them feeding the cows in the pasture. While Sara drove a tractor pulling a flatbed trailer loaded with hay, Bill worked to pitch bales off the side to the hungry cattle trotting after them. As they spread the last bale in the pasture and turned for the barnyard, Taylor opened the gate and let them in. Sara smiled sadly and waved as she drove past. Bill hailed him with a hay hook. When Sara went to welcome her brother, she was happy and relieved to have him home, but seeing him made her think of her father and she started to cry before she could get any words out. Taylor hugged her and let fall a few silent tears into her shoulder.

"It was more fun coming home for your wedding," he said when he regained his composure.

"Oh, I don't know," laughed Sara, wiping her eyes. "We didn't part on very good terms. I meant to say I was sorry for heaping so much guilt on you. I had no right."

"No need to apologize. Much of what you said was true. For the past few years I haven't been there for Dad, or the whole family for that matter. But I'm home now." Taylor saw Bill look away awkwardly. "I'll stay for as long as I'm needed or until I make amends. Mom in particular seems to feel betrayed." Bill's head jerked up at the comment and he wore a guilty face.

"Betrayed?" he repeated. "Did she say something about the apples?"

"No," replied Taylor. "But now that you mention it, I couldn't help but notice a large part of the crop was on the ground." Bill snorted a little under his breath.

"Bill, it's not your fault," broke in Sara. With a look, she urged her husband to keep silent.

"What do you mean?" asked Taylor. "What happened?"

"Nothing," replied Sara, trying to close the matter. But Bill wanted to vindicate himself.

"I was just doing my job," he said, sinking a hook into a bale. "That's what happened. I was in charge of grading the apples and I gave them a cull rate. That's what they were." Taylor stared at him in disbelief. Bill grew uncomfortable under his gaze. "Or at least that's what they looked like at the time," he amended. "I wasn't the only field man to say so. Dale Crawford backed me up," he added defensively.

"Dale Crawford?!" repeated Taylor incredulously. "That crooked bastard—"

"Taylor! Please," pleaded Sara. "What's done is done. It was all a big misunderstanding. Uncle Ed's cider apples got mixed in with the sample bins and it made the shipment look bad."

"What I don't understand in all of this is how Dad got himself killed," cried Taylor throwing up his hands. Sara turned away from his rising frustration and began to cry. Her husband stepped up and comforted her.

"Your dad and J.P. had it out about the apples," continued Bill. "Dad refused to sell. You know how he can be sometimes. The loaded bins are still sitting out back. Twenty or more." Bill walked Taylor behind the hay loft to the lot where they prepared the apples for shipment. There sat a wall of crates stacked three high; a black sticky sheen ran out of the seams in the wood and collected in a rank lake of syrup on the ground.

"I'll give your dad this much," said Bill, "he was one tough son of a bitch. He didn't appreciate it much when J.P. started cutting into him about losing part of the crop. The old man said some pretty awful things about your dad and . . . just about everybody. It was enough to make your dad take his anger out on the old man's house." He laughed a little and pointed towards J.P.'s trailer.

Taylor left the bin lot and walked back through the barnyard and down the little lane that led to his grandfather's place. Rounding the corner, he saw the trailer in ruins. The roof gaped open to the sky, a few spindly beams jutting out like fractured ribs. The door was off its hinges and Taylor could see mounds of blackening apples covering the furniture and floor. The pulp had fermented, and a sickening, yeasty ooze crept out the door and down the steps. A few yards away stood the large white and orange Case tractor, the splintered boards of a fruit bin hanging off the cab. The whole scene spoke of such a violent outburst—an eruption of bile and resentment—that it astonished Taylor to think that his father was capable of so much rage. He went up to the loader and climbed up on the forks where the bins hand been piled, peering tentatively over the engine cover at the seat where his father had died. It was crumpled a little and leaning to one side. Some of the spongy foam stuffing in the back support poked out and Taylor noticed it was stained brown, though by blood or apples or earth he did not know—probably all three he thought to himself. The elements of Rockwater had flowed thick through his father's veins.

Later that evening, Bill told him the entire story. He had dropped his old hostility towards Taylor and seemed to want his approval. His act of betrayal and the tragic chain of events he had set in motion had shaken him to the core. More than anything, he needed forgiveness. He turned now to his one-time friend in the hopes that the son might be willing to give him the family's blessing. They shared a bottle of whiskey and talked about the family and their high school days until the late hours of the morning. For Taylor, the weight of so many years of accumulated mistrust fell away, and it felt as if it were he who was being forgiven. Bill, too, seemed liberated from his old grudge, and by the end of the night, warmed by the drink and feeling it was time to begin a reconciliation, he confided something momentous to Taylor.

"Sara's a month along now. We're going to have a baby."

"My little sister? A mother!" Bill nodded his head in confirmation and, grinning wide, raised his glass for a toast.

"To Papa Bill!" said Taylor, raising his own.

"To Uncle Taylor," he replied. "But don't breathe a word. Sara wants to tell your mother when there are less distractions. Now's not the right time, you know?" They clinked glasses and drained the cups. Taylor was happy for the expecting couple, but when he went to sleep that night he felt painfully alone, with little to show for his life.

The next day dawned bright and crisp, and he awoke with an urgent desire to call Quinn and reconcile with her. He lifted the phone several times, but, thinking of her letter, he could not bring himself to do it. What would he tell her? He wasn't ready to return to Boston. And he could not bring himself to ask her to wait for him any longer. Needing time alone to resolve what he would say, he set off for the river where he could sit and consider some way to win back her faith. Cutting through the fields where he used to watch the sheep, he headed for a fringe of trees that spread out along the length of the flood plain. The river, like the farm, was not quite as he remembered. While it still smelled of cottonwoods and wet stone, it did not look the same. There were new twists and torrents, and it was obvious the course had changed several times, pushing around rocks and logs, carving out holes and moving sandbars. Taylor felt a sadness well up in him watching the current roll past, steady and relentless. Nothing stays the same, he lamented. The life he and Quinn had created a year ago was gone. He had let it slip away, in part through neglect, and now he wanted to recapture it. Yet he knew in his heart that they could not go back to where they were before his journey. He had hurt Quinn, and she wanted to move on. And as for himself? He thought how odd it was that he was the exception to nature's rule, that he alone had remained in stasis while everything around him was shifting. For all his efforts, it appeared that he was right back where he had started and yet he was no closer to becoming an artist.

He sat on an embankment at the edge of the stream for a long while, sinking slowly into self-pity. He would have stayed there until nightfall unless a curious phenomenon had not caught his eye. He had been throwing little sticks into the water to pass the time, watching the current carry them out of sight. But a few of the pieces had been swept back into the near bank before him. At the edge of the swiftly moving river, the current reversed directions and flowed back upstream, carrying the stick to where the river poured into a swirling pool. Then the stick would become caught up on the current and make its circular route again. Every time the journey was different, but there was a certain order and predictability about it that comforted Taylor—change and permanence all in the same motion. When he finally got up to go, he knew that he had not yet come full circle himself, and that he must continue his pilgrimage to its end.

That afternoon he called Quinn, not knowing exactly what he was going to say, but hoping that they could find a reason to trust one another again. She was unmistakably happy to hear from him, and this lifted his spirits.

"I'm sorry about the letter," she said. She could feel him waiting for something from her. "I went through some difficult times while you were away, Taylor." She gathered her thoughts, struggling to find a way to justify her words. "For a while I thought you didn't believe in me. In us. When I wrote those words, you felt so far away from me."

"Do you still feel the same?" he asked.

"Only in some ways," she said, searching her heart. "I want to make things work between us, but I need a little help from you. Will you come home now? I miss you." Taylor considered her proposal for a moment. It was what he had wanted to hear. She was willing to begin anew, and, while he knew that he had strained the bonds that tied them, she still loved him. But he found his loyalties divided.

"I have to stay here," he answered. Quinn's heart sank. For a tense moment, neither could think of anything more to say. Taylor took a deep breath and struggled to hold on to her.

"In my mind, the grand culmination of my trip was going to be showing my paintings—maybe just one great painting—to my father," he explained. "And now . . . ," his voice was choked off by emotion. "And now I think I need to stay for mom and Sara, . . . and for myself," he added. "I've got a lot of work to do to get Rockwater back in shape."

"So, when will you be home?" she asked haltingly, trying to comprehend the implications of this latest revelation.

"I don't know. But when I do return it will be with an unburdened heart."

"Part of what I said in the letter was true, Taylor," she said, shaken. "I can't wait forever."

"I know."

(Quinn shuddered involuntarily.)

"The apartment is so cold."

"I'm sorry, my love."

"I love you," she whispered.

"I love you too," said Taylor.

Quinn hung up the phone and sat silently gazing out the window at the gray sky. Her eyes welled with tears as the breeze pulled the leaves off the trees and sent them swirling through the air.

For the following two weeks, the Morelands set aside their grieving for a while to put the farm in order. Taylor ran the disk through the orchard rows, turning the fallen apples into the soil. Bill mowed the thistles in the pastures and Sara put a blade behind the John Deere and scraped the barns clean. Uncle Ed took over the routine of taking the sheep to graze in the alfalfa stubble, and everyone shared in the chores of feeding the animals and cleaning out stalls. Taylor in particular worked long hours. But the hard labor was a tonic for him and it brought back a flood of feelings and sensations long forgotten. In the mornings he pulled on his old denim jacket, faded and tattered, but still smelling of hay and earth. His work shoes had long since disappeared so he took to wearing his father's battered leather boots. They felt good on his feet and he noticed that when he wore them he had the same solid, determined step as his father. Together the family had the farm looking close to the way Jim would have wanted by the end of two weeks.

All that was left to do was to deal with the rotting bins and the ruined trailer. Since the accident, everyone had avoided walking near the crushed shack and held their noses when passing by the bin lot. At the end of a particularly strenuous day's labors, Taylor walked by the rotting piles and was unable to ignore the stench any longer. He decided it was time to bury the last reminders of death at Rockwater. While Sara and Bill were at the evening chores, he announced his intention to his mother as she prepared dinner.

"I'm going to clear out the bin lot and the trailer site today," he said, reading her face for a reaction. She said nothing but stiffened a little. "Is that O.K. with you?" he probed.

"Do what you want. You always did anyway. Besides, it's just a pile of shit now anyway," she snapped. Taylor started to go out but, unable to bear her coldness any longer, turned back and pressed her more forcefully to air her grievances against him.

"Look, Mom, I'm sorry," he started in frustration. "What more can I say or do now?"

"Nothing!" she exploded, turning to face him. "Do nothing! That's what you've done in the past and that's what you can do now. When we needed you around here for years you stayed as far away as you could get, and now that you're here there's nothing you can do that will bring my husband back."

"But every time I asked, you said that you could manage—"

"I told you what you wanted to hear because I thought you needed a little time to grow up. But you never did! You're still a boy playing at daydreams and drawing." She was shouting at him as tears streamed down her cheeks. It was the first time he had ever seen her cry, and he realized with a great stabbing pain to his heart that she had loved Jim with the slow, steady force of tree wrapping its roots around a stone. And now that he was gone she swayed precariously, buffeted by an overwhelming fear of solitude. In her anguish, she turned her anger on her son. "I thought you'd come back after you realized that painting is not a life. It's a hobby, Taylor! A worthless, idle game!"

"I'm sorry Mom," he stammered. "But I had to find out exactly what and who I am. And I think we both know that I don't belong here." She would not look at him and hid her face in her sleeve. He waited for a while and then tried to lay a hand on her shoulder, but she jerked away. Turning, he walked to the door.

"Don't go this time," she said as he reached the door.

"What?" said Taylor, not comprehending.

"You asked what you can do and I'm telling you. Don't go.

Stay here at Rockwater and claim your inheritance. It's all settled with the lawyers. The place is yours if you want it." Taylor stood speechless before the open door. "I can't run it by myself," said his mother, almost as a plea.

"But you have Sara and Bill, and Ed can help, too." Taylor felt the words fall empty to the floor.

"Go," said Beth through set jaws. She stared hard at him and wiped the last tear from her cheek.

"Mom, don't think I don't want the farm. I love this place," he protested. "I just need time to—"

"Go!" she shouted. "Go clean that rotting pile of stink and then just go!"

Taylor stepped quickly out of the house, leaving the door ajar. He strode resolutely down to the barn, his father's boots thumping heavily on the ground. Anger and self-justification contended violently for his heart as images of volcanoes, his mother's tears, the shattered trailer, Guilherme's twisted leg, and bloody water mixed together in a confused montage of rage and suffering. He found the Case tractor as his father had left it and, thrusting away the splintered bin and apple pulp, he climbed up into the cab. The battery cranked slowly at first but then caught and fired as a huge cloud of black smoke blew into the air. Revving the engine, he raised the front forks and drove into the bin lot.

Sara and Bill heard the roaring of the engine and came running. As they reached the lot, Taylor lowered the forks, picked up a stack of three crates and drove his heavy load back out into the barnyard. He had a look of wild intensity which frightened Sara.

"What are you doing?" she screamed as he drove by.

"Finishing the job!"

Turning down the little lane that led to the trailer, he raised the bins high and sent them crashing down upon the house. Then throwing the smoking machine into reverse, he backed all the way into the bin lot and scooped up another stack. Fearing her brother would be crushed in the same manner as her father, Sara tried to run to him and calm him down but Bill held her fast. They both watched as Taylor systematically buried J.P.'s house with the emblem of his father's wasted labors. By the time he dropped his last load on the pile, the crumpled trailer was entirely covered with broken bins and pulp. A lurid sun sank on the horizon and the small mountain of debris cast a long shadow over the farm.

Taylor parked the tractor and marched to the tool shed. When he came out he was carrying a can of diesel and a torch. He went to the pile and flung the fuel over the mound in great splashes.

"You're gonna need more than that!" shouted Bill. He ran to the shed, poured a bucket for himself, and came to Taylor's aid. Sara too filled jugs and buckets with diesel and soon all three were pitching fuel upon the stinking heap. For Taylor, something in the act snapped the chains of duty and guilt which had bound him to the ranch. He discovered that he felt free of gravity and began laughing. It was infectious and all three broke into peels of laughter as they expended the last of the fuel preparing the pyre. All stepped back to survey their work and a stillness settled over them. The sun had set on the wreckage and in the falling darkness the pile of debris loomed dark and defiant before them. Taylor lit a match and touched it to his torch. Holding it aloft, he prepared to throw it on the pile.

"Wait!" cried his mother from somewhere in the shadows. Taylor stayed his hand and she stepped out of the darkness and into the circle cast by the torch. Her eyes were clear and her countenance bore a look of sad resolve. Taylor handed her the flame. Gripping the wooden staff in both hands, she reeled back, hesitated for a split second, and hurled the torch onto the mound. It burst into flame, sending a shock wave of hot air into their faces. They all stepped back as the fire quickly enveloped the debris. In a matter of minutes the flames leapt high into the air, spewing rolling waves of black smoke into to night. Hot embers shot up upon the billows, glowing coal red against the darkening skies. As the night wore on, the somber group watched the fire consume the last remnants of the trailer until only a mound of orange and gray cinders remained. They went to bed that night exhausted and blackened by soot, but purged of regrets and blame.

The next day, Taylor cleared out space for a studio in a large room off the barn. He set up an easel and bought oils, canvases, brushes and pallets. In the corner was a cast-iron stove, and large windows on the south side admitted ample natural light. He began sketching out several plans for the piece, annotating the drawings with notes about the symbolic significance of the various elements. After pages and pages of drafts, he came up with a plan which reflected his experiences and his appreciation of the paradoxical nature of life. He began painting every hour that he could. In the mornings after the chores were done, he slipped away to his studio, working until the light began to fade. Then he would break for a few hours to tend to all the needs of the livestock before returning to paint. Sometimes he would work until the early morning, forgetting to eat or sleep. But his art consumed him, and he painted as if he were painting for his life. There was an urgency to his work which he couldn't explain. He believed in his heart that he could paint, but he needed others to know it too. He wanted to create a work of art which would earn him the right to call himself an artist.

Drawing from his notebooks, he settled on painting a view of Cotopaxi from the west, looking out from a high and distant vista. He was working on a way to capture both the ephemeral feeling of the mountain while still retaining a true sense of realism in his depiction of the geography and the flora. What he decided upon was a sweeping landscape—six feet across and just as high—of the mountain with the lush green valley of the Amazon River Basin in the foreground. What kept returning to his mind was the emotional exhilaration he experienced during his first view of Cotopaxi. His objective was not to be too literal, but to create a sort of allegory for his entire trip. When he was satisfied with his design, he worked for days on the final painting, spending every free moment in the studio in a state of intense effort. For long stretches of time he would completely lose himself in the euphoria of creating—becoming his work, desiring nothing. During these sacred moments, he experienced complete and unselfconscious happiness.

On the eve of Thanksgiving, Taylor completed his painting.

He walked up to the house—dabbled in paint, his clothes disheveled—to look for his mother. He found her preparing the pies for the holiday meal and asked her to come to the barn.

"Why?" she asked. "Can't it wait?"

"I have something to show you," he smiled.

"Let me guess," she said looking him up and down with exaggerated scrutiny, "a painting."

"Yes, a painting."

"It can wait until tomorrow" she said, turning back to her pie filling. Then Taylor saw something in her face which caught him by surprise. She was frightened. He knew then that she did not want to see what he could do because if it were good, really good, she might be compelled to admit that he had indeed become an artist. At that moment she would lose him to the world. Suddenly feeling very tired, Taylor sat down and allowed his mother to hold on to her image of him, if just for a while.

"All right mom," he smiled. "You can have a look tomorrow." He saw her tension dissipate.

"Here," she said, thrusting a bowl at him. "Make yourself useful and peel some of these apples for me." He reached for them with painted hands and she pulled back the fruit. "No, no. Wash the color off you first," she scolded. Taylor complied and they sat side by side at the kitchen table making their pie.

Thanksgiving was subdued without Jim and J.P. The family tried to recreate the festive mood of other holidays, but everything felt forced and hollow. Uncle Ed exasperated Beth's feelings of loneliness by repeatedly asking "Where's Jim? Where's Grandpa?" The football games on T.V. provided a little relief because they allowed everyone to pretend to be spending time together without really having to talk to one another. By dinner, the evening was threatening to turn into another wake when Sara decided to make her announcement.

"Mom, we have some good news for you," she smiled over the table.

"What's that honey?" her mother asked, incapable of anticipating any good fortune at the moment.

"I'm going to have a baby," she said looking at Bill. Beth sat silent for a minute, her fork hovering above her plate as the realization slowly dawned on her that a new life was coming into her world. Then she laughed for joy and threw up her hands.

"I'm going to be a grandmother!" she cried and ran around the table to hug Sara. Mother and daughter embraced each other as Uncle Ed clapped his hands in delight and broke into a spontaneous chorus of happy birthday. Bill beamed from his chair. When the glow had cooled, Beth slipped into a new anxiety and began pacing the floor.

"You'll have to quit school and your part-time work to stay home to take care of the baby. And you'll need help, you know. Having a baby is a lot of hard work. You're going to need me."

"I'll be all right," said Sara, trying to reassure her.

"And Bill, are you getting a raise with the work as a field man?"

"Well I haven't got it for certain. They're just trying me out this season," he said. Beth stopped her pacing to sit in a chair and look out the window.

"Why don't Bill and Sara take over the farm?" suggested Taylor. Everyone stared at him, struck dumb. "Bill could quit his job in the spring when the lambs start coming. By early summer you'd get your first check from the wool and that would easily get you through until the hay cuttings. You'd make more here than at the warehouse."

"But Rockwater has been willed to you," protested Sara. "It's already done. The papers are signed."

"Sign some new ones," he replied. "It's no secret that I'm not much of a farmer." Beth frowned and began to clear away the dishes. Taylor stopped her from going to the kitchen and took the plates from her hands. "Mom, I love this land, but I can't give my life to it. I'm going to paint. That's what I love most in life." She looked back at her daughter and Bill, then at Taylor.

"That's between the three of you now. I put it in your hands as your father wanted. If your final act here is to scorn all his hopes and dreams, then go ahead. But I'll have none of it." She set her napkin down on the table and walked stiffly out of the room.

Taylor left for Boston the next day. He rolled up the canvas in a shipping tube and packed all his gear. Bill agreed to drive him to the airport so the two of them could set in motion all the steps necessary to transfer the farm to Sara. By the spring, Rockwater would be theirs and the young couple would have to work hard to accomplish what Jim had done all those years on his own. But Bill bubbled with enthusiasm at the idea. "It's what I've always wanted," he told Taylor when they discussed the plan the night before. Sara had talked excitedly about planting a more extensive garden with room for more flowers and speculated that she might make a little money on the side with her embroidery. After the baby was born, she didn't plan on returning to the dental hygienist program. "The idea of working in people's mouth's all day never really turned me on," she laughed. "I was only doing it for the money."

As Taylor was loading the car, he looked around for his mother, but she was nowhere to be seen.

"She's not coming out," said Sara when she saw him peering in the windows.

"Will you tell her I love her?" he asked. "Tell her I won't stay away so long this time." Sara nodded and wrapped her arm around his shoulder. Uncle Ed came outside and gave Taylor a big bear hug.

"Happy birthday!" he cried.

"Oh my God! He's right!" exclaimed Sara. "It is your birthday today. Happy birthday Taylor." She embraced him too. "Why didn't you remind us?" she asked, knuckling him in the shoulder in rebuke.

"I completely forgot," he replied, amazed. "I guess I had more important things to think of."

"Let's celebrate! Can't you delay for just a while?" pressed his sister.

"It's time that I go," said Taylor. Bill placed the last of his things in the trunk and Sara noticed of the large cardboard tube.

"What's in there?"

"My painting."

"Can we see it?" asked Sara.

"I'd like that," said Taylor. He removed it carefully from its canister and unfurled it over the hood of the car. Bill and Sara stepped close and looked long with genuine amazement. It was Bill who eventually broke the spell.

"We're gonna miss Taylor's plane," he reminded them.

Taylor packed up the painting and hugged Sara good-bye. They drove away and Sara walked quietly back to the house. Inside she found her mother standing at the living room window looking out towards the river.

"He's gone?"

"Yes. We got a look at his painting," said Sara.

"Was it . . . ," Beth's voice trailed off, tears welling up in her eyes. "Was it beautiful?" she whispered tentatively.

"It was . . ." Sara paused to find just the right word. "It was sublime."

The afternoon of November 30th dragged on tediously for Quinn. She had been at school all day trying to complete an essay that was now long overdue as a result of her trip to Ecuador. In a secluded corner of the library, she took a break from her studies. Her attention was focused on a letter of application to the coordinator for the school's outreach programs. Ever since her return, she found herself wanting to become more integrated in the day to day existence of the people she called neighbors and friends. But her excitement for her new interests was diminished by the emptiness of her personal life. She missed Taylor more than she was willing to admit. To lessen the pain, she tried to tell herself that if he never came back into her life she would be spared a great deal of suffering.

At five in the afternoon, unable to shake her sadness, she decided to make her way home for dinner. The thought of sitting alone in the fading light of her empty apartment made her shiver and she pulled her collar tight around her chin. Exiting the building, her progress was impeded by a clump of students in the foyer who had gathered around one of the large bulletin boards used for posting flyers. Not in the mood for announcements about night clubs or parties, she tried to edge her way past the little cluster, but out of the corner of her eye she saw a flash of brilliant color that compelled her to stop and take notice. It was a painting, tacked to the pressboard. Maneuvering to the front of the crowd, she saw a huge canvas, luminous and bold. At first she thought some villain had gone to the American Romantics wing of the museum and cut some revered work out of its frame. But as she looked closer, she realized that the style was uniquely its own.

As the people around her chatted excitedly about the use of light and the fine brush strokes, she became absorbed with the story unfolding on the canvas. The artist had created a sweeping panorama of a volcano which devoted equal space to foreground, middle ground and background. Leading the eye into the painting was a river, brown and wide, its banks crowded with a dense matting of tropical palms, lianas, and orchids. The stream wound its way through the lush jungles lit by brilliant sunlight. Then it took a sharp bend into a dark chaos of drowned trees and flooded swampland. There, harbored in the limbs of a spectral tree, sat a crouching, black vulture. The bird presided over a swath of fallen trees and rank mud into which an unsuspecting white lamb had wandered. The struggling animal was buried up to its belly in the thick slime and the oily, black bird trained its greedy eye on the sheep. Then the line of the winding river pulled the eye towards the lower left frame where it emerged from the dark mire into an oasis of green touched by sun. Perched on a slim margin of bank along the river sat a thatched hut on stilts. The place was light and airy. Near the house, children and a dog played in a fertile garden. A woman could be seen sifting manioc flour over an open flame. Two men fished from a boat in the placid stream, one with a harpoon, the other at the paddle.

Then the river cut back across the canvas towards the middle right. There it passed a small rise where a clearing had been made for a temple. But the temple grounds had long since been desecrated, and two broken statues—their heads and limbs hacked away—stood over the ruins of a pyramidal altar. Huge blocks had fallen away from the shrine and all the trees had been razed, leaving only stumps dotting a blighted and withered land. Where the wasteland met the river, the corpse of a pink dolphin could be seen upturned at the water's edge. Then the river then curved into the undergrowth and was lost. But the course continued in the form of a trail which turned away from the riverbank to lead the viewer's gaze back towards the center of the middle third of the canvas. This middle zone was dominated by exuberant green growth that spoke of life and vitality. On the upper fringe of the jungle, the forest gave way to undulating foothills. At the base of the mountains was a pastoral valley crisscrossed here and there with carefully maintained stone walls. Grazing sheep dotted the lush pastures and farmers worked their row crops, the sun glowing warm on their bent backs.

The upper third of the canvas was dominated by the soaring white cone of a volcano. The mountain itself was luminous and bright, standing lofty yet indifferent to the happenings of the world around it. The south face of the mountain was marked by shimmering ice fields and rock buttresses. It was nearing sunset and a subtle alpine glow warmed the snow fields with a rosy light. By contrast, the northern quarter of the dome was captured in the act of erupting, a huge dark plume bursting out of a wide, black fissure. Billows of ash and debris rolled out of the mountain, drifting away towards the horizon and casting a shadow over the valleys below. But the violence of the eruption did not obscure the sun. In the upper left hand quadrant of the background, a radiant light poured down from the sky in celestial shafts.

For Quinn the painting told the story of a yearning for the idyllic that had been tempered by profound suffering. But the luminous quality of the light spoke of great optimism in spite of the pain. It infused the frame with a spiritual glow which resonated with her own sense of wonder for the world. For its recognition of harmony and order, the painting was in essence Romantic; but the artist possessed a willingness to look directly into the brutality of life and admit that chaos was a powerful force in shaping the world. As she looked at the vista, she had the sensation she was listening to carefully orchestrated music—not a lofty and pompous symphony, but a chamber orchestra playing a full and graceful composition, at once both intimate and grand.

As she devoured the last images with her eyes, her head raced as she sought confirmation for what her heart knew. Stepping past the onlookers, she scanned the lower quadrant for a signature and saw that in the far right hand corner, dwarfed by the epic size of the piece, was a tiny card. Coming closer she discovered that someone with a careful and confident hand had inscribed the envelope with a single word: "Quinn."

Astonished, she grabbed the letter and opened it with trembling hands.

Dearest Quinn:

I have given up my search for the beautiful. I do not think that it exists in a pure and unadulterated state. It is the distorted fabrication of those timid spirits who close their eyes to anything that does not conform to their expectations of the world. Instead, I have come to believe that there is only the Sublime—an eternal state of flux in which the exquisite and the terrible exist in a necessary paradox. If my journey has taught me anything, it is this: one can't know anything with full certainty. But the aesthetic and moral ambiguity of this world does not cause me to despair; it compels me to live each moment with intensity. One must live through the ugliness in order to bear witness to all that is noble in the world. My experiences have given me a profound faith in the possibility that if we act with compassion we can create beauty amid the brutality, and if we look with an eye attuned to the wonders of this life, we can see the Divine in the commonplace. In light of this, I have decided to continue my pilgrimage, but with the objective of discovering what *is,* rather than yearning for what should be. If you believe that our paths lie in the same direction, my heart would spill over with joy if you would join me.

Love, Taylor

With the last line, Quinn folded the card and tucked it into her jacket, the chambers of her soul still resounding with his music. Then she carefully untacked the painting from the bulletin board, to the groans and raised eyebrows of the other students, and prepared to make her way home. As she pushed through the crowd, she saw Taylor waiting for her next to an old elm tree. He was smiling expectantly, radiating light and contentment. She walked over to him, the canvas under her arm. Without exchanging a word, they kissed and joined hands. Side by side, they walked the footpath out to the street. The curious group of onlookers watched them go. As the couple turned the corner, their forms became lost in the white glare of the slanting November sun—two pilgrims of the sublime stepping fearlessly into a tempest of shadows and light.